TRA   Tran, Van Dinh,
1923-

Blue dragon, white
tiger

TRA   Tran, Van Dinh,
1923-

Blue dragon, white
tiger

JUL 27   Z 4681

SEP 21   Z 360

DATE   BORROWER'S NAME   JAN 18   7 678

Blue Dragon
White Tiger

BLUE
DRAGON

WHITE
TIGER

A Tet Story

by

Tran Van Dinh

TriAm Press, Inc.
Philadelphia
1983

For information address   TriAm Press, Inc.
5015 McKean Avenue
Philadelphia, PA 19144

PRINTED IN THE UNITED STATES OF AMERICA

ISBN 0-914075-00-4

The *Thanh Long*, Blue Dragon,
designates the eastern quadrant of the
Uranosphere, the *Bach Ho*, White Tiger, its western
section. The Blue Dragon represents spring
and tenderness, the White Tiger, winter and force.
All beings and all things on earth
are affected by the constant struggle
between the Blue Dragon and the White Tiger.

A traditional Vietnamese belief

The first month of the year is for eating *Tet* at home,
The second month is for gambling
And the third month is for going to the festivals.

From a old Vietnamese folk song

The minds of the Vietnamese in Saigon
and the other cities were preoccupied
with the approaching *Tet* holiday,
and our efforts to change this state
of mind were only partially effective.

General W. C. Westmoreland, Commander
U.S. Military Assistance Command, Vietnam
Report on the War in Vietnam, 1968

Contents

Preface

While I was growing up in Hue, the old imperial city of central Vietnam, it was customary in my family to have a reunion on the second day of Tet, the Vietnamese lunar New Year, during which my father would review all our *Tu Vi* horoscopes. *Tu Vi* is the major constellation in the galaxy.

During the Tet of the Year of the Dog, the year of the first full cycle of my life, one cycle being 12 years, my father was particularly concerned about my future. When he had carefully read all my horoscope's stars, balancing their effects on one another, he concluded that by the end of my second cycle I would have begun to "eat" most of my Tets overseas in "strange and cold lands." My mother was saddened by that prediction. That same evening, she spent several hours alone with me. She told me about legends and symbols relating to Tet, most of which I already knew by heart. She described for me, in detail, how to cook certain dishes and to make certain special Tet cakes. She made me solemnly promise that wherever I might be, I would eat Tet in truly Vietnamese fashion. "That way," she said, "you will always remain Vietnamese."

This novel is humbly dedicated, with all my respect, love, and admiration, to my parents. In the "Kingdom of the Everlasting Peace of Lord Buddha the Compassionate," they can rest assured that their still wandering son, still in a "strange and cold land," continues to eat Tet in truly Vietnamese fashion and is still, therefore, very much Vietnamese.

.   .   .

Most of the characters in this novel are real people. They have suffered, though some of them have found happiness; some have died, but they all have known me. Obviously, I have changed their names and rearranged their situations, but I have not modified their essential positions in the drama. If I hurt or seem to misrepresent anyone who, by experience or imagination, identifies herself or himself with a particular character in this book, it is not due to any malice on my part, but to the limitations imposed on me by language.

This story, as the subtitle indicates, is a Tet story. For the Vietnamese, Tet, a mobile festival corresponding to the new moon and placed halfway between the winter solstice and the spring equinox, is much more than just a New Year holiday. It represents a yearly truce in the constant struggle between the Blue Dragon and the White Tiger. It is the moment of the manifestation of the soul of Vietnam itself. It embodies in its ceremonial as well as its essence the whole concept of man and his place in the Cosmos, his relations with the dead and with the spirits. It is an annual burst of latent and indigenous Vietnamese romanticism—a romanticism that has been nurtured in a rugged and beautiful land over centuries of painful conquest and bloody battles. Only against the background of Tet can the incidents and characters in this story be understood.

It is a tragic irony of the encounter between America and Vietnam that Tet, a celebration of life and a period of prolonged joy for us, was introduced brutally to the public in this country by way of the daring Viet Cong attacks during the last days of January, 1968, the Tet of the Year of the Monkey, one whole cycle ago. That unexpected "Tet Offensive," which startled so many Americans, brought a cruel, unseen war from the distant rice fields of Vietnam into the United States Embassy in Saigon and, indirectly, into the heart of America itself.

Some of you may be curious to know if I myself am reflected in the main character. In answer, let me quote from the famed Eighteenth-century Chinese novel, *The Dream of the Red Chamber*.

> *When seeming is taken for being,*
> *being becomes seeming;*
> *When nothing is taken for something,*
> *something becomes nothing.*

To me, fiction is texturized by the *Ying* of imagination and the *Yang* of experience. In every *Ying* there is a seed of the *Yang*, and in every *Yang* there is a germ of the *Ying*. But please do not try to decipher the mind of an "inscrutable Oriental." Read the story and forget about the author, who, after the publication of his novel, may already have disappeared or been transformed into a white butterfly.

Tran Van Dinh
Washington, D.C.
Tet of the Year of the Monkey 1980

I

Indivisible Water, Unmovable Mountains 4666 Year of the Ram 1967

*Away from woodland, birds miss trees
and long for roots
Away from fellow men, people
drift in many places
Water and mountains are parts of heaven
No one can divide water,
no one can move mountains.*

A Vietnamese folk song

April 4, 1967
Saigon

Dear Elder Brother Minh,

I have not written you since I phoned you from Paris, a year ago today, to wish you happy birthday. It was difficult to write because all overseas mail was censored. I am able to write you now, again on your birthday, because a friend of mine, Mr. Frederick S. Adams, the special assistant to the American ambassador, is going home for a consultation and agreed to see that you get this letter.

First, let me congratulate you on this important moment in your life when you have reached four full *tuan*, forty years, of your existence. I am sure you have ahead of you at least six happier *tuan* to fulfill all your dreams. But this letter is really to give you news of our family. Last month, I went to Hue to celebrate Father's seventy-fifth birthday. He is in good health, although he bitterly complains that he now has to eat the tasteless imported American rice. He misses the perfumed "imperial rice" he has eaten since he was born. There is nothing we can do about this. Phu Loc, the area where this rice grows, is now unsafe. It is Viet Cong–controlled.

As he does at all family reunions—but especially during Tet—he asked about you constantly. This last time he told me that he wishes very much to see you before he dies. For the first time, he talked about his death. You know well that of all his children, you are the one he loves most. The early death of your mother, who occupied such a special place in his heart, can only enhance his affections for you. He has never quite understood why you have remained in the U.S. for the last four years. He was told that you are opposing U.S. policy in our country, and he was made aware of the circumstances of your resignation from the foreign service. He approves of your political position but suspects that you are in prison and that we conspire to keep the truth from him. Even when I showed him an article bearing your name in a U.S. magazine, he did not quite believe it.

The decision to return is yours, but I take the liberty to suggest that you consider it seriously. To watch Father's suffering and longing for you is very painful to all of your relatives and friends, even though deep in our hearts we understand the position you have taken concerning this cruel war and admire your integrity. It was a great pride and comfort to me recently when during a chance meeting in the street, writer Long Van— perhaps you know that he is the author of the best seller, *Stagnant Water*—told me that a "poet of your brother Minh's honesty and vision cannot be wrong on any political or moral conclusion he comes to."

Incidentally, Long Van is now in some kind of trouble. The government has forbidden the tenth printing of his book. The Minister of Information's wife, who is barely literate, read it and told her husband—he's not very bright either—that the novel was an oblique criticism of the war and the government. Likewise, your publisher has been denied permission for the fifth printing of your last novel, *A Flower Grows in the Pentagon*. You probably were informed that your book has already sold more than 100,000 copies. Reprinting has been refused because an army intelligence officer reported that he saw a copy of your work on the dead body of a North Vietnamese soldier.

Back to your possible return. The moment, I think, is opportune. I know you are still persona non grata with the government, and you know that no one can assure you one hundred percent safety. But there is now a very good chance to convince the government to leave you alone. I have been made a lieutenant colonel and am also being named deputy director of military intelligence. Your former classmate and close friend, Lieutenant General Vu Binh, is now the commander of the Saigon military zone and is very much trusted by the President. Our uncle will soon be Rector of Hue University and I have no doubt that he will welcome you on his faculty. At any rate, please think about all of these facts, and if you want to get an inside view of the present situation at home, you can ask Mr. Adams. You probably guess by his title—special assistant to the ambassador—that he is a C.I.A. station chief; but he is a liberal, reasonable man. It was he himself who showed me your most recent article in the New Direction and told me that he agrees with some of your critical points. He has said that he would like to meet you. I think the C.I.A. likes to check out the politics of all overseas Vietnamese. It would probably help if you did see him. He can be reached in New York at (212) 344-8879.

Whenever you make the decision to return, just let me know directly or indirectly that you agree with the substance of this letter. It would be a happy moment for all in our family, especially for father, if you could eat Tet with us in the coming Year of the Monkey.

I wish you good health.

Your affectionate younger brother,
Tran Van An

P.S. Your recent poem, *Golden Thread*, published in the Tet issue of the Literary Magazine, has received much praise. In the March issue the editor printed ten appreciative communications from readers, one of whom was your own cousin Mong Lien, Uncle Thanh's daughter. Poor thing, she did not realize that the poet who signed *Co Tung*, Lone Pine Tree, was you, her own relative. Judging by the poem, you must be in love with someone whose "cascade of golden hair brought an avalanche of desires and a tumultuous river of dreams."
Congratulations.

.   .   .

Minh spread a checkered napkin on the soft grass. From an old Air Vietnam travel bag he took out a bottle of Chateauneuf du Pape, their favorite wine, half a loaf of bread, three glasses, and a big piece of cheese. Like most Asians, he had never liked cheese before, but Jennifer had made him an addict. The cheese before him today was a peppered Wisconsin, sent to him by a colleague from the Midwest. It tasted like *chao*, a kind of fermented bean curd his mother used to make on Tet to offer to the Buddhist monks.

Looking around, Minh hoped that he would not be disturbed by a passing student, then realized he didn't have to worry. This Tuesday fell on a special college holiday: Thomas Paine's birthday. The campus was deserted.

Uncharacteristically, Jennifer arrived on time. She planted a kiss on his cheek.

"Great, I didn't expect a picnic."

"Well, it's the least I can do for a very special friend on a very special day."

She pointed at the three glasses. "Is someone joining us?"

"Of course not." He pulled a white tea rose from his bag, poured red wine into one of the glasses, put the rose in, lifted the glass with both hands, and offered it to Jennifer. His movements flowed together steadily.

"Minh, you're adorable! Thank you very much."

"When we finish our meeting the rose will have become red, and you can take it home. Take a drunk rose home and your night will be filled with multicolored dreams. Taoist discovery—over two thousand years ago."

Jennifer smiled, and touched his hand. "I'll dream about you. Now, what's on your mind?"

"I received a letter from my brother."

"What did he say? He wants you to come home?"

"How did you know?"

"I just guessed."

"And you guessed right. Do you want all the details? Shall I translate it for you?"

"Yes, of course, please."

She listened attentively, her hand fondling the back of his neck as he lay sprawled on his side, his elbow on the grass, resting his head on his hand. When he finished the P.S. she pressed his other hand against her lips.

"What do you think I should do?" Minh asked.

"I can't advise you on this, Minh. It's your family, your future, and your decision, though I'll support whatever you do and wish you well. But do you have to make a decision right away? Think it over. Perhaps it would help if you met the C.I.A. man first. What's his name?"

"Adams. I'll call him tomorrow for dinner on Thursday. Can you join us?"

"Yes. My last exam is Thursday morning. I need to unwind and New York City is the only place in the world where I feel totally relaxed. Last time I was there I discovered a fantastic restaurant, and I want to show it to you. Besides, I'm curious to meet a real live C.I.A. man."

"Where's the restaurant?"

"I don't want to tell you now."

"But I have to tell Adams where he can meet us."

"Tell him to go to 69 East 69th Street."

"Are you sure that's the real address?" Minh said with mock suspicion.

"Have I ever tried to fool you?"

"No."

"Then have confidence in me! I tell you what: why don't I pick you up at your apartment on Thursday at four and we'll drive to New York? We'll be there easily before seven."

.   .   .

Jennifer's driving style changed the moment they emerged from the Lincoln Tunnel and entered New York City. Her monotonous sixty-mile-per-hour, middle-lane, disciplined cruising gave way to a bold racing and squeezing that required conscious planning and occasional calculated risks to beat the yellow-to-red lights. Her New York style of driving, he thought, reflected the pattern of her life since he'd known her. He was certain that she could not, would not, be satisfied with the secure life of an upper-middle-class physician in some affluent suburb. She would put her medical education to some other use. She would be bold, seize every opportunity that came her way to politicize and humanize those with whom she came in contact at every step. She might meet with failures and disappointment, but someday she would have the whole world in her grasp. Though he had never told her so, Minh dreamed that her world would include him.

"I love your driving, Jennifer," he said, caressing her hand as it pressed firmly on the gear shift.

"That's the only way to get anywhere in New York City, especially at this time of day."

"Now I can see how much of a New Yorker you are at heart."

"Is that a compliment or a reprimand?"

"Very much a compliment. Have you lived here before?"

"No, I came here often with my mother when I was very young, but I haven't driven in the city for over two years. Do you like New York, Minh?"

"I lived here for four months in 1958 when I was on a short assignment at the United Nations."

"Oh yes, I remember you telling me about that."

"I loved every minute of my stay. To me, New York City is America—dynamic, maybe brutal, but always aspiring towards the higher, the better, the impossible. One thing I'm sure of is that New York will always be a turbulent, ungovernable city. It will never be tamed or settled or grow stagnant. It will have no past, no history, because it will be changing all the time. Perhaps, someday, New York City will collapse under its own ambitions, its own dreams and excesses, but until then it will never stop creating, hoping, trying." Minh paused for a second. "It's a lot like you, Jennifer."

She glanced at him, put her hand on his cheek and pulled it back quickly. Their car was suddenly flanked on either side by two gigantic trucks, and, at the front and rear ends, by taxis, all appearing as if from nowhere. It was as if Jennifer's little blue Vega had been miraculously lifted from the ground and dropped back into the midst of a protective covey of admiring vehicles. It was like a brief duel between the Blue Dragon and the White Tiger, he thought, with the Blue Dragon scoring a temporary victory.

"It's amazing how you've maneuvered this little car into this position."

Jennifer smiled at him. "It's not as amazing as how we've maneuvered ourselves into our present situation. How alike we are, though that makes no sense, how we travel along together as if we've known each other for a long time, how someday we ..." Her voice was melancholy, but the sadness in her face disappeared as she smiled. Her youth made her vulnerable.

Jennifer concentrated on her driving. "Here we are!" she cried triumphantly as she turned sharply onto East 69th Street. Glimpsing a car pulling out of a parking place halfway down the street, Jennifer accelerated, stopping just short of the rear bumper of a white Cadillac that was waiting to take the place. The driver of the Cadillac had no choice, now that the Vega blocked the departing car's exit, but to pull up and let it out. Within seconds Jennifer was majestically parked in her unfairly conquered territory.

"A superb guerilla tactic," Minh commented as they left the car and started to walk.

"Yes," Jennifer answered. "In the Vietnamese guerilla lexicon, it's called 'waiting for the tiger to leave its den, and while it occupies the mountain, driving the lion out,' right?"

"Right. I'm pleased to see you practice what you learned in my seminar. Perfect harmony of theory and practice. Chairman Mao would have you decorated with the Order of the October Revolution."

"What time is it?" she asked.

"A quarter of seven."

"What time did you ask your friend to come?"

"He's not my friend," Minh protested. "He is, as I told you, a C.I.A. man."

"O.K., what time will the spy come out from the dark to see the light with us?"

"Seven."

Halfway down the second block Jennifer stopped. With a proud smile, she announced, "Here is my famous Thursday restaurant."

"What a coincidence. Today is Thursday."

"I didn't plan that part. Come on in."

A short corridor opened up into a long, wide room that looked at first glance like a Spanish garden: trees, real trees, almost touched the ceiling, forming unexpected nooks where candle-lit tables were artistically arranged. A young waitress greeted them.

"Are you open yet?" Jennifer asked.

"Not until seven, but you can take a seat."

Jennifer pulled Minh's arms around her waist. She was wearing a short lavender skirt and a white turtleneck sweater that flattered her. The combination made her look taller. They stood for a moment in a light embrace.

"Let me show you something," she said, turning. At the end of the room, she pointed to a door leading to a kind of arcade. Above it a brightly lit sign read, CHEESE AND WINE.

"Here," Jennifer said, "you can drink as much wine and eat as much cheese as you like for only five dollars."

Minh was more attracted by an adjoining room called the SPECIAL FOOD ROOM.

"It looks like an opium den decorated for Tet in the days when the Hue aristocrats came to the Imperial Landing Pavilion to celebrate the Welcoming of Spring."

"Do you like this place?" Jennifer asked in a pleased tone. "If you don't, don't tell me. You see, your favorite Chateau Louis XIV isn't the only candlelit restaurant in New York, as you once claimed."

"The claim isn't mine. It was in the New York Clarion."

Minh looked more closely about him. The restaurant reminded him of the "Cavern of Light and Longevity" that he had read about in a Taoist fairy tale book when he was very young. More precisely, it looked exactly like part of the Grotto of Everlasting Spring on a mountain in North Vietnam where a post-Tet week-long fair is held every year. When Minh was eleven, during the Tet of the Year of the Dragon, his father had gone to Hanoi to participate in a reunion of all living Doctors of State of the Imperial Exams, and had taken his wife and Minh with him. After the reunion they had gone to the grotto for a festival in honor of the Goddess of the Western Sea. His father's friends had thrown a special party to welcome him as the new president of the Twenty-Eight Constellations Club, an exclusive gathering of the most prominent philosophers and intellectuals in the nation. These great men were the last heritors of a glorious age, now tarnished by the humiliating French conquest.

Minh remembered his own pride as he was admitted, though for only one night, as an honorary member of the club. He was even prouder that his mother was the center of admiration among the most prestigious elite of the land.

After dinner, which was brought by small boats gliding in and out of the grotto, they played the "poetic game." A poem, with a word cut out of it, was hidden in a piece of red paper and rolled up inside an ivory stick and everyone attempted to guess the missing word. His mother won nearly every game.

Finally, all the guests separated into small sampans, some alone, some in the company of their wives or their minor wives. Minh's mother insisted that he should remain with her and his father. He obeyed with great reluctance, thinking that after such a night his father must feel more deeply in love with his mother than ever and that they should be left alone to be "immersed in clouds and rains." He'd heard this phrase once and knew that it meant to make love. But if they did, he did not know it. He slept very soundly that night, a night that had opened his young life to the wonders of a Vietnamese civilization and culture critically threatened by foreign domination.

Jennifer's voice broke his reverie.

"Minh, someone's coming in our direction. Is it the C.I.A.?"

"Maybe." Minh stood up and approached the stranger.

"Are you Professor Tran Van Minh?" the man in a dark suit asked.

"Yes, Mr. Adams. How are you?"

"Very well, thanks, and I'm glad to meet you, finally."

"Please join us."

They returned to the table.

"Mr. Adams, Miss Jennifer Sloane."

"Very glad to meet you, Miss Sloane."

"Hi, Mr. Adams." Jennifer greeted him casually. Minh was relieved that she hadn't said, "How are you, Mr. C.I.A.?"

Frederick Adams was about fifty and looked like a small-town banker or a dean at a junior college somewhere in the Midwest. He had sharp, almost piercing eyes in an otherwise unremarkable face; his expression was cold—almost hard.

"I'm glad you could come on such short notice," Minh said. "The phone number I had for you is the Center for the Study of Peace and Freedom, isn't it? Are you affiliated with it? Is it a government-sponsored organization?"

"Not quite." Adams answered briskly and changed the subject. "Professor Minh, how do you like America?"

"I love the American people and I love teaching." He glanced at Jennifer but repressed the desire to touch her face.

"I'm glad to hear that. As I told you over the phone, I would like to invite you to have dinner with me at the Harvard Club."

"Yes. I hope you like this place." Minh waved a hand in the air.

"It's nice ... Your brother An probably told you that he and I are good friends."

"He did. And how is he?"

"Oh, he's well. He's in a very responsible position now—deputy director of military intelligence. He's still very much a playboy, but he also works very hard."

"Does he have the confidence of the President?"

"I don't know. But I do know that his boss, the director, is the President's wife's nephew."

"How is the situation in Vietnam now? I've been away, as you know, for several years, and I'm eager for any information you can give me."

"Yes, that's what your brother asked me to do." Adams turned to Jennifer. "Miss Sloane, do you mind if we talk politics?"

"Not at all," Jennifer's voice was sharp.

"Miss Sloane is a student of politics herself, and she would be interested in anything you say," Minh interjected. How had so many American males ever gotten the idea that women should not be interested in politics, he wondered. He would never dare ask such a question of a Vietnamese woman—or of any woman, for that matter.

Adams ordered a dry martini while Jennifer chose Chateauneuf du Pape for Minh and herself.

"Professor Minh, I have read a number of your articles, and I agree with some of your points. I'm fully aware that the Saigon government is corrupt and unrepresentative, that the Vietnamese want peace, that they respect Ho Chi Minh as their George Washington, and that perhaps the U.S. should never have been in Vietnam at all; but it's too late, and even irrelevant, to talk about that. The stakes are very high, the alternative unpleasant and intolerable. For the Vietnamese, the alternative is communism, for the U.S. and the free world, it's the weakening of the world's fragile balance of power."

Jennifer stared at Minh. Her lower lip moved forward, a sign that she was about to explode and call the whole thing "crap." He reached for her hand under the table, trying to calm her. She remained silent.

"I don't necessarily agree with your views," Minh replied, "but what I would like to know about is the situation in my country."

"Oh, the present situation is encouraging. There are still difficulties ahead, but there is light at the end of the tunnel. The New Life strategic hamlets program is progressing well, and the Phoenix Operation, which as you know aims at destroying the Viet Cong infrastructure, is doing equally well, though not in all the areas we had expected."

Jennifer couldn't control her silence any longer.

"Mr. Adams, as I understand it, the 'Viet Cong infrastructure' is a bureaucratic euphemism for the Vietnamese peasants who support the National Liberation Front, who are defending their land as they have been doing for the last two thousand years. Why don't you just admit that the Phoenix Operation is conducted to kill Vietnamese civilians?"

"Miss Sloane, I know how you feel, how our youth, my own children in fact, feel about this tragic war. But it's unfair for you to attribute such inhumane objectives to our government. We are providing the Vietnamese with the necessary strength to build a free, democratic nation. Things are much more complicated than you think. Perhaps when you're a little older, you'll see the problems better."

Minh realized that the conversation was getting heated. He was not in the least surprised at Adams's position, but his main concern was to salvage the evening for Jennifer and himself. He suggested that they order dinner. They ate in strained silence and with little appetite.

"Mr. Adams, do you believe that the war will be over soon?" Minh asked. His question was like a bomb exploding the quiet.

"I hope so. Some optimists among our military think that Hanoi will negotiate within months, perhaps before Tet of this year. The Rolling Thunder operation has crippled the North Vietnamese economy and pulverized their industrial centers. Captured documents show that there is deep dissatisfaction among the people in the North against their government." He paused to order a bottle of beer.

"Incidentally," he said, his voice rising, "I was in Hue during Tet last year. It was incredible. I've been in Latin America, Mexico, and I've seen many fiestas, but nothing can compare with Vietnamese Tet. It was just as a Vietnamese writer I read once described it: 'the once-a-year display of Vietnamese culture, civilization, history in song, music, light, food, laughter, and love.'" Adams did not know that the writer he quoted was Minh, who had written the article two years ago for the Saigon Courier under his pen name. Jennifer had read the article. She smiled, feeling a little less hostile to Adams.

"Miss Sloane," he turned to Jennifer, "if you ever visit Vietnam, go during Tet, which usually falls between the end of January and the middle of February. Not only is it a beautiful time of year—there are flowering peach branches everywhere, in every home—but you will experience the real Vietnamese national psyche, and see the true Vietnamese people. It made me realize how romantic they all are."

"Thanks for the suggestion. I hope to be able to visit Vietnam sometime, but not before the war is over."

The restaurant was now filled to capacity. Some couples were dancing. Adams looked at his watch.

"I'm afraid I have to leave in a few minutes to catch the last train to Washington. We have an interagency briefing with the President early tomorrow, and I certainly can't miss that."

"When are you returning to Saigon?"

"In about a week. Would you like to send a message to your brother?"

"Please tell him that I'm happy and I'll get in touch with him soon. I hope you enjoyed the dinner."

Minh escorted Adams to the door. More than ever he was convinced that bureaucrats like Adams who still believed in such outdated abstractions as "the free world," "communism vs. democracy," were going to destroy his people. More than ever, he was determined to go home, before it was too late, to prevent it from happening. He had to help stop this war—for the Vietnamese people, for Jennifer, for all the Americans he had met and liked or disliked, for humankind. He felt relieved, happy that his decision was final; still, he could not bring himself to tell Jennifer.

"Let's enjoy the rest of the evening. I'm sorry," Minh said as he returned to the table. Jennifer had ordered another bottle of Chateauneuf du Pape.

"Don't say that. I'm amazed you were so polite to that man. Imagine! Still talking about balance of power and nation-building."

"He went to an Ivy League school, Jennifer, not to an innovative, radical school like Thomas Paine College."

"Or the London School of Economics, like you," she added, laughing and hugging him.

"Besides," Minh said, "he understood a little about Tet. He even quoted me. We should forgive him."

"Tell me about Tet, Minh, about the peach branches."

Minh smiled. "We decorate our homes with flowering peach boughs to keep bad spirits away while we celebrate the holiday. When I was very young my mother told me that the peach tree was discovered by the Vietnamese thousands of years before in the mountains of Soc Son near the Chinese border. It was an enormous tree then, big enough to harbor the benevolent gods *Tra*, Tea, and *Uat Luy*, Angry Fortress. The devils were afraid of them, she told me, and they were also afraid of the tree they lived in. So that's why the branches keep away evil. Once my mother took me to see a peach tree that was suppose to change into a phoenix every ten cycles—that's a hundred and twenty years. I was so impressed I wrote my first poem that night, 'Phoenix Feathers and Peach Petals.' It made my mother cry."

"That's lovely," Jennifer said. "It makes me want to see Vietnam all the more."

It was midnight when they left the Thursday Restaurant. New York City was alive, and the fresh, cool air resounded with laughter and loud conversation.

"Jennifer, we now have three choices: we can drive home, go someplace in the Village for coffee . . ." He paused.

"What's the third choice?"

"There's a hotel that recently advertised in the college newspaper that a student accompanied by a faculty member can get a twenty-five percent discount."

"Let's take the third choice—discount or no discount." She stopped in the middle of the street and kissed him sensuously.

·　　　·　　　·

Minh awoke at nine o'clock the next morning. Jennifer was still sleeping beside him. He stared at the ceiling; then, as he turned to look at her, a paragraph from Dag Hammarskjöld's *Markings* came with sudden clarity to his mind;

As she lies stretched out on the riverbank—beyond all human naked-
ness in the inaccessible solitude of death, her firm breasts are lifted to the sunlight—a heroic torso of marble—blond stone in the soft grass.

The connection frightened him. He moved away watching her in-
tently. She could, perhaps, transform herself into a white fox—as in a story he had read when he was in high school—but die? No. He reached for her face but did not touch it. She was breathing softly. He detected a few fading freckles on her left eyelid and thought about the contradictions in her life: a twenty-six-year-old body, a forty-year-old mind, a fifteen-year-old face. The contradiction was fully expressed in the ironic contour of her lips—sensual-
ity, innocence, and intelligence.

It was her intelligence that had first attracted him to her. She had been in his class on the politics of national liberation, and she was the only one of his students who not only understood the structure of the course, and its components, but could link them together, grasp the "unity of the opposites." Once he had quoted to the class T. E. Lawrence's description of guerilla war—"the algebraic element of things, the biological element of life, and the psychological element of ideas"—only to be greeted by an embarrassing, blank, prolonged silence from his students. Frustrated by their obvious lack of poetic perception, he had looked at Jennifer. She smiled, and he knew that she had understood and shared his moment of anxiety. Then his eyes had fallen to her white blouse, tracing the outline of her high breasts. A surge of desire had overtaken him, followed by a sense of calm and well-being. He had reached his "intellectual satori" through the sensual, un-Buddhist path. That night they had had dinner together for the first time.

Minh tiptoed to the window, opened the heavy red curtains slightly, and looked out.

"Minh, where are you? What time is it?"

"Nine."

"Already?"

Without answering, Minh took a yellow daffodil from the dresser and laid it, gently, on her hair spread across the pillow. Then he turned and went quickly to the bathroom. The cold shower dispelled all his fears about death, about the possibility of losing Jennifer, about seeing her drowned in some distant and unknown river.

For the first time they had breakfast together, and in bed. The comfort of a bourgeois way of life reassured him, though he was a little amused that he'd thought of it consciously as bourgeois. The fresh sweet-
ness of the honeydew melon cleared his throat and mind.

"Jennifer, I've decided to return to Vietnam as soon as I can."

"I'm not surprised, Minh—I sensed it in the last few days. And I'll support your decision, but it's going to be hard to continue my life without you. I've begun to realize in the last few weeks how much I love you."

"Thank you Jennifer," he said softly, fondling her hair, "thank you."

"But you must be careful. You need a safe line of communication with your brother. Am I right? Do you have one?"

Minh thought for a moment. "Yes, I think I have. When I was in Thailand—that was almost ten years ago—I was very close to a Thai officer who is now deputy Chief of Staff of the Royal Thai Army. He wrote me a very warm letter last month. As you know, there are lots of contacts between Thailand and South Vietnam since Thailand has sent troops there to fight with the Americans. My Thai friend could act as a liaison between my brother and me."

"That sounds like an excellent idea. What's his name?"

"He has a very long name, like all Thais: Chamras Panyakupta. His friends call him Chamni. He's a major general and a former graduate of West Point."

"Can you call him now?"

"What time is it?"

"Ten."

"Then it's ten p.m. Thai time. I don't have his phone number, but I'm sure they can find it. He's a big shot. Do you think it's safe to call from the hotel?"

"The safest place you could find. It would be hard for the F.B.I. to bug all the hotel telephones. Besides, we registered after midnight, and I doubt anyone knows we're here. The F.B.I. may be smart, but they're not that smart; and you *are* a very important person, but not *that* important," she teased him. "They know you're a harmless person in love with an American girl who is not subversive. Place the call and see what happens."

This was one of those rare occasions when Minh was anxious to hear the phone ring. It did, about ten minutes after he had placed his call.

"Professor Tran Van Minh?" a woman's voice asked.

"Yes."

"One moment please. General Chamras will be with you shortly."

"Hello, friend until death." The General's voice was brisk and cheerful.

"Hello, Chamni, my dear friend. I'm surprised you're still at your office. You must be working too hard. Don't strive to become a field marshal while you're still in your late forties. No girl wants to sleep with a field marshal of the Royal Thai Army."

"You know I never work hard. I'm *mai pen rai*, the never-mind, type. But tonight there's an alert, a precautionary measure against a possible *coup d'état* by some elements of the Air Force. But I don't think anything will happen. As a matter of fact, I'm going home in about ten minutes. And where are you?"

"In New York City for a visit."

Jennifer smiled.

"Ah yes, good, good. What can I do for you?"

"Chamni, I want you to serve as liaison between me and my brother in Saigon for some urgent family business. I know it's preposterous for me to ask the deputy Chief of Staff of the Royal Thai Army for such a personal, petty favor."

"Stop it. We have been good friends for many years, and friends must help each other in all matters, big, small, official, or private. Who is your brother?"

"The deputy director of military intelligence of the ARVN, Lieutenant Colonel Tran Van An."

"Ah yes, he was here yesterday."

"What did you say?"

"Lieutenant Colonel An and several high-ranking officers of the ARVN visited me here yesterday to discuss a plan for an exchange of military information concerning our joint military operations in Laos and Cambodia. He doesn't look like you. I should have asked him. But then, there are too many Vietnamese with the Tran family name."

"He doesn't look like me because we have different mothers."

"I see. But how can I help you?"

"Can you call my brother and ask him to call me through your communication system? He has my number."

"Of course. The U.S. just put in a most sophisticated satellite communication system between Thailand, Vietnam and continental America. Have you noticed how clear this line is?"

"Yes, I have. Clearer than between New York and Washington, D.C."

"Do you wish to contact your brother now?"

"No, not right away. But if possible, tomorrow. Please let him know that I have his letter and I agree with his suggestions. Also ask him to call me a week from today."

"That's easy. With American know-how and Thai friendship, you will get what you want. If you contact me in the future ask for the overseas line and then number TPO 007. That's the direct military line to my desk. We call it the warm line—it's somewhere between hot and cold. If I'm not in, my officers will reach me wherever I am, even in Massachusetts. By the way, my son is going to M.I.T. this fall and my daughter to Vassar in the spring. I'm sure you remember them. You spoiled them when you were here. I'll ask them to look Uncle Minh up, and I hope you will help them."

"No problem. I'll do anything I can. But I'm glad you warned me that your daughter will be here. Otherwise I might have run into her on the street and flirted with her."

"The same old romantic Minh, but as always I trust you. When are you going home? Are you tied down by some American woman?"

"I don't think so," Minh said unconvincingly, staring at Jennifer.

"What did he say?" Jennifer whispered.

Minh cupped his hand over the phone. "I'll tell you later."

"I didn't hear what you just said," Chamni responded. "If you go home—and I think you should, because your government needs good people like you—you must pass through Bangkok and spend a few days with me. We'll relive our good old days." He paused. "I have a confession to make."

"Yes?"

"Do you remember that woman who drove with us one day to Chantaburi to eat the first jack fruit of the season? You should remember. After all, you were the one who talked about how her pretty eyes could 'drown you in the valley.' I still don't understand exactly what you meant— nobody did. But she was flattered."

Minh burst out laughing. "Chamni, you've been down to the valley and now you are trying to climb to the top of the mountain."

"What do you mean?"

"Forget it. It's too long a discussion and not a decent topic for conversation over the telephone."

Jennifer pinched Minh's arm.

"Anyway, she is now my minor wife, and we had a daughter last year. We named her Moonlight over the Mountain."

"Beautiful name. Congratulations. Chamni, I could talk with you for hours, but I'm afraid I'll have to stop now. The *coup d'état* may have already started and nobody can get you on the phone. I don't want Thailand to be lost to the Royal Thai Air Force. I promise, whenever I go back to Vietnam, I will stop on the way and see you."

"Keep in touch. I'll do everything I can to help you."

"Thank you very much. I appreciate all you've done and will be doing for me."

"Don't mention it. Goodbye, and see you soon—in Bangkok."

"What did he say that you promised to tell me later?" Jennifer asked after Minh had filled her in on the details of the conversation.

"He asked if I was tied down by some American woman."

"You are not. You are loved, and love, as you often say, is a liberating, creative force. What made you tell him about the valley and the mountain?"

"He has a *mia noi*, a minor wife. Most wealthy Thai have one *mia luang*, or principal wife, and several *mia noi*."

"Did he understand what you were saying?"

"I don't think so. But the telephone is hardly the place for explanations of references to sexual techniques, don't you agree?"

She kissed him. "I'm going to get dressed, it's almost noon." She headed for the bathroom.

Minh pulled back the covers. On the sheet lay a few curls of hair, soft and blonde. He gathered them together and wove them into a small ring. He stood for a moment, holding it in his palm. Smiling, he kissed the ring and hid it in his wallet behind the picture of his mother.

·   ·   ·

They both looked radiant as they emerged from the hotel and walked hand in hand to the corner of 33rd Street and 8th Avenue. Jennifer's car, in a no-parking zone, hadn't been towed away as she had suspected it might be. There wasn't even a ticket on the window.

Minh decided not to drive back with her. He thought that any attempt to artificially prolong this supreme but fleeting moment of happiness could only lead to frustration. A friend of his once said, "After an excellent dinner, you go to bed. You don't roam around town looking for a place to eat your dessert." Strongly influenced by the Buddhist concept of the impermanence of all things, Minh believed that holding on to permanence could only lead one to a dark pit. Of course, one could go from the mountain to the valley. In the valley, one sees the blue sky above, the grass and the trees beyond; but in a pit, there is nothing but darkness.

His mind wandered to a time when he had asked his class what was "the most dangerous part of the Declaration of Independence," a document he greatly admired. Caught by surprise, the class was silent. "It's the pursuit of happiness," he told them. "Happiness can never be pursued; it must be realized effortlessly." The class fell into a deeper silence, but it was, he thought, the silence of understanding. Minh believed that there were situations and moments when nonaction and noncontinuation were more natural than anything anyone could say or do.

He leaned over the trunk of the car. "Jennifer, I think I had better not drive back with you. I want to drop in and see a lawyer friend of mine. He only lives two blocks from here. I need his advice on a few things."

"Okay. But I'm not going back right now, anyway. I'm going to Columbia to attend an organizational meeting for an antiwar demonstration that's going to be held here in the next ten days or so."

"Be careful my love."

"You sound like an American father. There's no such thing as being careful, only being safe."

"Be safe, then."

Indivisible Water, Unmovable Mountains

For the first time since they had begun seeing each other, Minh did not make provision for their next meeting. He knew that it was their last meeting on American soil, and she knew it too, he mused, though her pride and her idealism would prevent her from saying so. But he thought she wept as she turned away.

II

A Land Where Honor Is Betrayed

A thousand years of Chinese reign,
A hundred years of French domain,
Twenty years of American intervention.
The heritage of our Motherland,
People untrue to their race.
The heritage of our Motherland,
A land where honor is betrayed.

The Heritage of our Motherland
A popular song in Saigon, 1967
by Trinh Cong Son

Minh moved to a rear seat to have a better look at his country 20,000 feet below. He saw large forests of dark reddish-brown vegetation stretched along several canals, with here and there huge craters, some filled with water, some almost dry, that resembled spots of drying blood on an old face disfigured by smallpox scars. He knew these were the effects of defoliation and bombings.

The pilot's voice came over the loudspeaker: "Gentlemen, please fasten your seat belts. We will be landing at Tan Son Nhut Airport in approximately twenty minutes." Minh went back to his own seat. He didn't want to see his mutilated country any longer. It upset him, and he wanted to look happy when he arrived. He pulled out his wallet and took out Jennifer's picture, but as he looked at her face, her smile, he was pierced with regret. He put the photo away.

The plane was a military DC3; the flight had been arranged for him by Chamni in Bangkok. The only other passengers were two American Green Berets.

Chamni had outdone himself, Minh reflected. Not only had he made all the arrangements for the flight home, but he had arranged parties in Bangkok, meetings with old friends, a trip to the beach. He certainly meant well, Minh thought, and he's certainly still my *phuong tai*, friend until death—but he's changed. Bangkok has changed.

There were soldiers everywhere in the Thai capital now, including Americans on "R and R," rest and recreation, from Vietnam. "You know what a friend of mine calls R and R?" Chamni has asked him. "Room and rush. The Americans come here, find a room, rush to the massage parlors, pick up a girl, rush back to the room, fuck her, and rush her back to the massage parlor. Crazy people," he laughed, "but they contribute a lot to the booming Thai economy." He had stopped, as if he regretted his words, then went on. "Do you know how the U.S. command in Saigon selects soldiers for R and R? By body count."

Later that first night in Bangkok there had been a stag party at the home of another old friend, Ching Heng, grown immensely fat and rich in his war-related business. A "companion" had been provided for Minh—Thailand's best-known actress—but she had been as relieved as he when he had taken her home early without availing himself of the favors she had been paid to provide. Two days in Bangkok had been more than enough.

The gleaming DC3 was surrounded by Vietnamese and American military police as soon as it touched ground. The pilot's voice, tinged with annoyance, came over the loudspeaker: "Please remain seated until the authorities have inspected the plane."

"I'm trapped," Minh thought, sure that he was about to be arrested as a neutralist. Jennifer's face flashed into his mind: her ironic mouth, her shining hair, her legs, the way she embraced him, the times they had spent together in New York, the conversations they had had, all these memories came to his mind like torrential rain on a hot afternoon.

The rear door of the plane opened. Two M.P.s, one American, one Vietnamese, approached him.

"Professor Tran Van Minh, please follow us," tne American M.P. commanded in a terse voice. "No others may leave."

Minh was sure now that he was being arrested and on his way to execution. He wondered why they didn't handcuff him. The execution, he speculated, would take place tomorrow morning at Ben Thanh central market, the same place they shot the young mechanic Nguyen Van Troi, who had attempted to assassinate Secretary McNamara when he visited Saigon. He would have several hours left to think of Jennifer, or perhaps, if he was allowed, to write her a poem.

Minh looked around. The airfield was a gigantic garrison: rows and rows of all types of planes, some camouflaged, some about to depart, with soldiers and pilots everywhere. It was hot, but he forced both heat and terror out of his mind. Suddenly he heard a familiar voice calling his name.

"*Anh*, Brother, Minh, I'm coming." A wave of relief flooded Minh as he recognized An running toward him, his sword dangling on his waist, one hand holding his army cap. The two M.P.s stood at attention and saluted.

"You may go now," An told them before turning to embrace Minh. "You must have thought some trouble was waiting for you. I'm sorry. It's a long story. I'll tell you about it later." He hugged Minh again and looked him over. "You look very healthy, very well indeed."

Minh laughed with relief and pleasure. "Oh, An, it is good to see you! Not only did I think that something was wrong, but I thought I was being arrested for execution as a neutralist."

"I wouldn't let anyone do that to you. Do you have anything suspicious in your luggage, like Playboy magazine?"

Minh laughed. "Nothing suspect. I do read Playboy, but I didn't bring any copies with me. Why do you ask?"

"Well, the military police will search the plane and all luggage; but I've asked them not to confiscate anything of yours without first reporting it to my office."

"Why are they searching the plane?"

"It's routine. Planes originating in Laos and making stops in Thailand en route to Saigon often carry opium. In fact our intelligence agents in Bangkok signaled that a suspect—a Green Beret captain—might be on your plane. Did you speak with him?"

"No, I didn't."

"He is suspected by both Thai agents and our own of having been contacted by an international smuggler a few weeks ago in Bangkok. That's all we know, and we take no chances."

"But this plane is the C.I.A.'s," Minh remarked.

"That makes no difference whatsoever—on the contrary . . ." An's voice trailed off. "I would have been here immediately, but I was delayed by the President's departure. He's going to Hue. And after he left, the chief of staff wanted to discuss some urgent matters with me. That's why I couldn't meet you sooner. I'm sorry."

"Don't be, An. It's nothing. You know, I read a lot about this business of opium and heroin smuggling in the American press, but I didn't know that U.S. military personnel were involved or implicated in it."

"The American press always reports what is wrong with us, never what's wrong with their own people."

An beamed again at his half-brother as they walked across the airfield. "I'm really very happy that you're home. I haven't told anyone in the family exactly when you'll arrive in Hue. I want it to be a happy surprise for father."

"I can't wait to see him," Minh replied. "And I'm so glad to see *you*. You look wonderful. It's been such a long time. But tell me, why did you insist that I be here this morning?"

"Because we had you scheduled for an audience with the President late this afternoon. But now the whole plan is upset. There were incidents—demonstrations by the Buddhists—in Hue a few days ago, and the President decided at the last minute to go there to get a first-hand report from the I Corps commander. He won't be back this afternoon, so we'll have to make another appointment for you. Of course, you'll have to stay in Saigon longer than I planned, but so much the better. You'll have time to become acclimated and familiarize yourself with the political situation in the capital. You can also see a few of your friends."

"I'll leave everything to you, but the sooner I get to Hue the better. I've already spent too much time in Bangkok."

"What do you mean? Didn't you enjoy seeing Chamni?"

"Oh, yes, and it was good to renew our friendship. But Bangkok's depressing—corrupt, noisy, dirty, and up to its neck in our war. I had no idea how involved Thailand is. Of course I knew there were American bases, and American soldiers everywhere, but did you know the Thais had troops in Laos?"

An only smiled.

They stopped outside an iron gate on which hung a huge sign that read: AUTHORIZED UNIFORMED PERSONNEL ONLY.

"What about me?" Minh asked. "I'm neither authorized nor in uniform."

"Don't worry. The guards know me. They're expecting us."

They were allowed to pass without question. One of the officers on duty, an Air Force lieutenant, ran after them and handed An a brown envelope marked "Top Secret." An put it in his pocket and thanked the officer.

"And now," he turned to Minh, "if you don't mind, we'll drive to Saigon in my uncomfortable military jeep. I couldn't get an air-conditioned car from the office. My boss's wife and children are using it for a trip to Nha Trang Beach."

"It's quite all right. It's hot, but not as hot as Bangkok. It's quite bearable."

"Good. You'll have an air-conditioned room, so you won't have to suffer from the heat too long."

They drove along a wide concrete road that cut into the main boulevard leading to the city. On the left side, a huge glass building occupied almost the entire side of the street.

"What is that big building? An insurance company?"

"No, it's the U.S. Military Assistance Command—Vietnam, referred to as 'Pentagon East' by newspapermen."

Minh could see that Saigon, to an even greater extent than Bangkok, had been transformed by the war into a huge barrack. Military vehicles of all sizes dominated the streets. Shacks and small thatched houses were sandwiched between tall brick and concrete buildings with rows and rows of tin-roofed cabins mushrooming on all sides, even under bridges.

"Who lives in these tin-roofed places?" Minh asked.

"Refugees."

"From where?"

"From the Viet Cong. The official explanation is that they left the Viet Cong-controlled areas because they hate communism, but in most cases they left to escape the intensive bombing of the countryside around Saigon."

The center of Saigon swarmed with bicycles and Japanese Honda motorcycles. Minh used to enjoy the noise of the streets, so full of life and activity; but now the clamor was irritating. The jeep had practically to push its way through the crowds and the swarming vehicles. At the intersection of Nguyen Hue and Tran Hung Dao Boulevards a policeman had to stop the flow of people and cars to let them pass.

"Here we are," An said, as they pulled up in front of a modern-looking six-story building next to the U.S. Information Agency's Lincoln Library. "This building is owned by the vice-president's mother-in-law. The army has rented two floors, one for the Army senior officers club and the other a sort of hotel for visiting high-ranking officers from the provinces or, sometimes, American brass."

The uniformed valet who operated the elevator—although it was automatic—recognized An and greeted him politely.

"Please take us to the sixth floor, Mr. Sa."

"Sure, Colonel. By the way, Miss Tan Diep was looking for you not long ago. She asked me to tell you that she'll be late for dinner tonight, but she will certainly come."

"Thank you."

The elevator door opened into a large, tastefully furnished lobby. A captain behind the registration desk greeted An with a firm handshake.

"This is my brother, Minh. He just arrived from the U.S. Do you have a room for him?" An asked.

"Of course. We'll give him the best. Room number six. He'll have a color TV and all the luxuries he needs."

Room number six looked exactly like an executive suite in any large American hotel. Two big vases of gladiolas stood on the desk, envelopes dangling from their necks. One card was signed, "The Colonel, Manager of the Senior Army Officers Club"; the other was General Vu Binh's gold-lettered business card. The note on it read, "Welcome home, my dear classmate. With affection and admiration. I'll see you tonight."

Minh sank into an overstuffed leather chair and motioned An into the one next to him.

"An, I must confess I'm impressed by the arrangements you've made for me. You either have a lot of power or you have a lot of powerful friends."

"Neither. As a matter of fact, I know that I'm not fully trusted by the President. He trusts no one but his relatives, and besides, he knows that I'm your brother. And I have no powerful friends, either. General Vu Binh is actually a friend of yours. My only assets are that I'm clean and honest and the American officers who deal with me often tell the President that I'm a very capable officer."

"You know," Minh interrupted, "during the late President Diem's regime, if you were liked by the Americans, you were in trouble."

"I know. But the present President is no Diem. He cannot and will not resist American pressures." He paused and then added quickly, "Which, of course, are stronger now than anytime before. But I must say he is very skillful in dealing with the Americans, and with the regional military commanders, too. He knows how to play the generals off one another to remain in power. He closes his eyes to their commercial activities and lets them operate fairly independently of Saigon, on two conditions: that they keep their wrongdoings out of the American press and keep the casualties very low."

"What do you think of the reports in the American press about corruption in high places, among the generals?"

"Fairly accurate, except that their reports represent only one one-hundredth of what actually takes place."

"I see." Minh shrugged his shoulders. "By the way, General Vu Binh said in his note that he would see me tonight. Has something been planned?"

"Yes, he's giving a dinner in your honor tonight at seven. He's invited about a dozen senior officers, all from Hue, and their wives or girlfriends. Your companion will be Tan Diep. She's the number one songstress and beauty in Saigon now. She speaks English—self-taught."

"Is it essential that I attend? I don't need another party like the one I just went to in Bangkok."

"I'm afraid it is, Minh. These are all influential people, and they're your friends. But let me tell you the rest of our plan. The day after tomorrow you'll give a lecture at the Staff and Command College. It can be a straight lecture about American foreign policy, or you can just open with a few remarks and let the students ask questions. There are sixty of them, majors and up. You must be careful not to be too outspoken. There might be some students there who work for the President's Office of Strategic Intelligence and report directly to him. In fact, I'm sure there'll be two or three among the group. This is your only official duty besides the audience with the President, which I think will take place within the next three or four days, if not sooner.

"After that, we'll go to Hue. During your free time here, do as you wish; but you'd better let me know in advance where you're going so I can alert my agents—in case trouble arises. Saigon today is not like the Saigon you left. It's full of gangsters. You know what I mean. Cowboys, pimps, informers, pushers, you name it."

An stood. "Well, I'll let you rest. It's going to be a long evening. If you're hungry or need anything, just call the desk. If you want to call long distance, you should wait and do it from my office. Otherwise, you'll have to make an application for permission at the post office."

"Thanks, An." Minh put a hand on his shoulder. "I think I'll take a nap."

Minh turned on the Sony TV. "I Love Lucy," with Vietnamese subtitles, was on. He turned it off and went to bed.

When he woke he thought for a moment he was still in the States. His surroundings were at least as comfortable; there were the same TV programs, the same pastel Kleenex-like toilet paper. He took Jennifer's picture from his wallet, kissed it, and put it on the bedside desk. He resisted the temptation to call or write her: he had decided before he left that he wouldn't communicate with her until he knew what his life in Vietnam would be like.

·   ·   ·

General Vu Binh, dressed in a dark brown civilian suit, took both of Minh's hands in his. "Well, well, I'm very glad to see you." He turned to An, who was also in civilian clothes.

"Don't you think he looks younger than when he left Saigon seven years ago?"

"I think so."

"I'm glad to see you, too, Binh," Minh said, "and I'm very grateful for all you've done for me. Frankly, I didn't expect such a V.I.P. reception. I don't deserve it."

"Don't be modest, my dear Minh. You deserve everything. You are bright, handsome, a good poet, a good writer, a professor in America, you are in love and are loved—or at least that's what I guess from reading your recent poem, *Golden Thread*. But above all, you're my classmate and friend—and we both come from Hue."

"Thank you, Binh. You look happy too, and ten years younger than your age."

"Yes, I'm happy. Ask your brother. I get along with everyone and I have no ambitions. I do my duty, obey my superiors, and leave the intrigues to politicians and other smarter generals. Correct, Colonel An?"

"Yes, sir."

"Have you told your brother about the guests at tonight's dinner—especially Brigadier Quang?"

"What about him?" Minh asked.

"Quang is the deputy chief of staff for external affairs. I don't think you know him. He's about your brother's age, but he was recently promoted to brigadier because he married a distant cousin of the President's wife. He was the only one out of ten officers who raised some doubt about your loyalty when we met to decide on inviting you back. He said that you were associated with communist organizations in America. But we challenged him to have the information confirmed by the American Embassy, and the Embassy, fortunately for all of us who defended you, said that you had no connection with any subversive organizations, although you disagreed with the war. In fact the Embassy felt that you've been away too long and aren't aware of the realities at home—which gave us one more reason to invite you back. Despite all this, when you meet him tonight, try to be as pleasant as possible, and more so to his wife."

"No, his wife won't come," An interrupted. "Brigadier Quang's secretary called a few hours ago to say that he'll bring a girlfriend instead."

"So much the better," Binh said with obvious delight. "Do you know who she is?"

"Yes. Pink Orchid is her name. She's the most sought-after girl at the New York Bar in Tu Do Street. At the moment she's the mistress of an American Air Force general who keeps her in an apartment near the Peace Cinema. But she is also under suspicion by the special police as a leader of the Viet Cong Organization of Artists and Entertainers for Liberation. They say her main duty is to collect U.S. dollars for the Viet Cong overseas operations—and they also say they can't touch her because of her important connections."

"You're a good officer, Colonel An. Keep a complete dossier on her. It might be useful in the future."

"I will, sir."

"Now, dear Minh," Vu Binh continued, "except for Brigadier Quang, all the men invited are either your friends or your admirers. I'm sure you'll enjoy the dinner and what we've arranged for you afterwards. Tan Diep will be your companion for dinner and she'll stay the night with you. Everything is arranged."

"Thank you, but I think I'll pass that up," Minh objected. He was a little annoyed that his friends in Bangkok and now in Saigon thought that coming from America he should be sex-starved, and he was disgusted by the depravity that allowed them so easily to provide a remedy.

"You surprise me, Minh," Vu Binh retorted. "A poet like you refusing to spend the night with the most beautiful flower in town? Of course, I know she doesn't have blond hair and long legs—the willow legs you wrote about in your poem—but she's very beautiful. You'll change your mind when you see her. As one of our proverbs says: 'Go bathe in your home lake. Limpid or polluted, it is still an accustomed lake.'" He roared with laughter.

Minh grinned. "I'm very tired, Binh. A long voyage, so many things on my mind. I'll be impotent and I don't want to disappoint a beautiful compatriot."

Vu Binh laughed again. "I don't believe it! If you're tired, ask her to give you a massage. She also carries a special medicine for such occasions. She'll sing you to sleep and you can make love to her in the morning. She's yours for twenty-four hours if you wish." He looked at his gold watch. "But now let's go downstairs for dinner. It's already past seven. Our guests have probably arrived."

Ten couples were already assembled in the bar. Binh took a glass of scotch and soda, gave one to Minh, and in a solemn voice announced,

"Ladies and gentlemen, may I have your attention, please. We must all empty our glasses to welcome home a talented son of the 'Land of the River of Perfume.'"

"Welcome home, Professor Minh," the audience shouted, applauding.

"Thank you all," Minh responded in a low voice.

"Now," Vu Binh continued, "I want to introduce everyone to our friend."

Brigadier Quang was the first to come forward. Minh shook his hand firmly. Quang was short, about five feet, with gleaming black hair plastered down with lotion. He wore a pink sharkskin suit and pointed-toe shoes; his body reeked of cheap French perfume, *Soir de Paris*. He looks like a pimp, Minh thought.

"I'm glad to know you, Brigadier Quang. Is your wife here? Can I pay my respects to her?"

"My wife isn't here. She's busy," Quang answered coldly. "I've heard a lot about you, and I'm glad to see you've come back to use your talents to help us fight the communists until victory." His "eel" eyes moved quickly but stared straight into Minh's.

"I'm afraid, sir," Minh said, "that you've overestimated me. I don't think I can be of any use in the fight against the communists, in which our army has already done so well. What I hope is to be able to go back to our hometown and teach."

"Yes. Well, we'll meet again, I hope." Quang retreated to the bar, pulling his mistress, whom he had not introduced, behind him.

A youthful-looking tall man, who was waiting for Quang to leave, moved forward and shook hands with Minh. Vu Binh introduced them. "This is Brigadier Song, my chief of staff. A very good soldier when he wants to fight. In his spare time, he writes poetry and novels."

"Oh? Have you been published?"

"Yes, but I'm nothing compared to you. I've admired you for a long time. I read *A Flower Grows in the Pentagon* three times."

"Thank you."

"May I introduce you to my girlfriend?" Song asked. He pushed a petite girl forward gently. She smiled broadly. Wearing very heavy mascara and a Thai silk miniskirt, she was the only Western-dressed woman in the room.

"Sir, can you tell me about the latest fashions and movies in America?"

"I'm afraid not, Miss," Minh replied. I know nothing about women's fashions and I was too busy to see many movies."

"She was in Japan recently to have her nose corrected," Song blurted.

"I see." Minh looked at her nose. It was disproportionately high against her moon face and flat bones. Minh thought that Song's tactlessness would cause her some embarrassment, but she seemed very proud.

"If I had more money," she said, "or if Brigadier Song loved me more, I would also have my eyes broadened like Sophia Loren's."

She grinned coquettishly. Controlling an urge to express his disapproval, Minh turned to his brother and asked, "When is dinner? I'm starved."

"Didn't you eat lunch?"

"No, I slept until six."

"OK. We'll have dinner soon."

As the guests were eating the third course, a typical Hue dish of shrimps cooked in honey and fish sauce, a young woman dressed in a black satin *ao dai* decorated with small gold peach flowers made her entrance into the room. She walked slowly and confidently up to Vu Binh, sitting on Minh's right. Binh stood up, wiped his mouth and announced, "My friends, I don't think I have to introduce Miss Tan Diep, who is kind enough to join us in honor of our friend, Minh."

"I'm sorry to be late," she said in a sharp, clear voice, "but I hope to make it up by granting any request Professor Minh, or any of you, wishes to make." Everyone at the table applauded. Minh pulled back the empty chair next to his and invited her to sit down.

"I've already eaten," she said, "but I'll keep you company. I can help you pick up your food. Having lived too long in America, you might have forgotten how to use your chopsticks."

"Thank you," Minh said, using a northern accent to impress her.

"But I thought you were from Hue."

"Yes. I was born there, but I spent several years in Hanoi during my schooling."

"Your northern accent is perfect," she complimented him.

"Thank you," Minh responded, adding, "and you are very beautiful."

"I'm not as beautiful as the American girls," she raised her voice to be heard by General Vu Binh. "Right, General?"

"Wrong. You are the most beautiful girl in the world."

When coffee was served, Vu Binh stood and made another announcement. "Now that Miss Tan Diep has promised to grant any request we should make, I suggest that she sing for our guest of honor."

"With pleasure." She moved slowly toward the piano, which stood on a small platform in the corner of the room. A life-sized portrait of the President stared down at her. She sat down, played a few notes, and stood. "The latest and most beautiful song is *Golden Thread*, written by the poet Co Tung and put to music by composer Thanh Thien."

An and Vu Binh looked at Minh with obvious satisfaction. Minh was surprised, not only that his poem had been set to music by his friend Thanh Thien, whom he hadn't seen in years, but that only Vu Binh and An seemed to know that he was Co Tung. Saigon was known as a city without secrets.

Tan Diep was still speaking. "I choose this song not only because it's the latest and most beautiful, but also because it's about the love of a poet for a young blonde woman. Perhaps our guest, just coming from America, is also in love with a young blonde."

She looked teasingly at Minh, who blushed and whispered inaudibly, "No, not true."

Tan Diep's limpid voice seemed to flow:

The cascade of golden hair
brought an avalanche of desires
a tumultuous river of dreams
Dreams of golden hair
Dreams of jade black hair—
Mingling—caressing—fondling
The lovers speak-silent
And wait
And wait

For the golden moon to rise
And for the time for going
Into Eternity

Each note, each word, brought to Minh the poignant, nostalgic memory of Jennifer. He touched his face, imagining he was caressing hers. He wished he could go to his room to look at her picture.

The song ended; the room was still. As Tan Diep bowed to the audience, Minh saw tears on her aristocratic face. He thought that he, too, was crying, but when he touched his lashes, they were dry.

Sadness seemed to have seized the audience too, these men and women whose business it was to make war and to profit from it. Yet the Vietnamese, Minh reflected, were of all peoples the most romantic: it was both their strength and their weakness.

Minh stood up when Tan Diep returned. "Thank you," he said softly, "for the most beautiful singing I've heard in a long time."

"Thank you for your compliment."

Minh was tempted to tell her all about the song, its author, and Jennifer. Her singing made him feel close to her; yet he hesitated. Suddenly, the room exploded into long-delayed applause, and gaiety returned.

Minh looked at his watch. It was 10:30. He whispered to Vu Binh that he wanted to go to bed. He wasn't tired, but after that song there was nothing left for him to enjoy. Vu Binh stood up.

"Our guest of honor has made a long trip in the last few days—he has experienced many sleepless nights on planes, changes of climate, differences in time zones. He must be exhausted, and I guess he wishes to retire."

The guests started moving out, each waiting his turn to shake hands with Minh. Finally only Vu Binh, Minh, An, and Tan Diep were left behind in the spacious, well-lit room, with its decorations of flags and army insignias.

"May I invite Tan Diep—all three of you—to my room for a nightcap?" Minh asked.

"Thank you," Vu Binh smiled knowingly, "but Colonel An and I have a long day tomorrow. We have to go, but we'll escort you to your room."

.   .   .

Tan Diep was silent as the door closed behind them. Minh watched her as she paced the floor, then walked slowly to the window and looked down into the street.

"Do you mind if I raise these thick curtains? The moon is full tonight. We may see it if the sky is clear."

"Please."

Minh raised his head at the sound of distant thunder. "Is it raining outside?"

"No. It's bombing."

"At night?"

"Yes. Maybe there are mortar shells, too. I really don't know. But you must realize that we're at war in our country. You're no longer in peaceful America. Wake up to the sad realities of your homeland! The war stops only for a few days during the Christmas and Tet truces. This Tet, I'll go to Hue to eat Tet the Vietnamese aristocratic way."

Minh was pleased to know she was concerned about the war, although her remarks showed more bitterness than political awareness.

"Would you like something to drink? I don't know what I have here, but I'll find out." Minh went to the kitchen and returned with a bottle of Johnnie Walker Red. "Do you like your Scotch straight or with soda?"

"I can drink anything in *my* profession, you know." She laughed nervously, quickly. "Did General Vu Binh tell you anything about me?"

"Nothing, except that you're the most beautiful woman in town and the most talented songstress."

"That's not all. I also sleep with whomever pays me well." Her voice was harsh.

"I don't know if I can afford to pay you well, but I'll say right now that I will not make love to you tonight."

"But you must! General Vu Binh has already paid me. He'll be angry and I'll have all kinds of trouble."

"Of course I won't tell him," Minh said hastily, regretting his thoughtless words. "I'll tell him that you are 'all storm and rain' in bed. Please, finish your drink. We can talk."

"What is there to talk about? I am, to be honest, a prostitute, and you're a big shot, an important customer. My duty is to satisfy your desires. I must say, however, that this is the first time I've been in this special room number six with a Vietnamese. Last month, I spent the night here with a foreign dignitary who promised to send me a diamond from Hong Kong. I haven't received it yet. A man's promise . . . "

"You may not believe it," Minh said, "but I respect women—of all professions. I'm sure you know that Thuy Kieu was also a prostitute, yet for centuries our whole nation celebrated her and remembered her as the woman with 'rosy cheeks and pale face,' while emperors and generals fell into oblivion. Besides, we are compatriots and we should treat each other like brother and sister of the same family."

"Brothers and sisters don't sleep together, and we don't have a genius like Nguyen Du to write verses for the modern Thuy Kieu," she retorted sarcastically.

Her cynicism distressed him. He decided the moment had come to tell her about himself.

"Tan Diep, I'd like to tell you something. You sing very well and with deep feeling. I was moved tonight by the way you presented that song. You may not know it, I guess very few do, but I am Co Tung. You expressed my feelings in your song better than I did with my words."

Tan Diep's face changed visibly: her hard and cynical mask became vulnerable, fragile; her black eyes were moist.

"Co Tung! Then you can't be like those brutal, vulgar friends of yours—except maybe your brother An, who's a rather nice playboy." She pulled her chair closer to his and took his hands. "You're very handsome. You have very soft skin, too, you know?"

"Thank you. Tell me something about yourself."

"There's really nothing interesting about my life. I'm the oldest daughter in a family of five, a refugee from the North, twenty-three years old, not officially married, no children—except two ghosts."

"What do you mean, 'ghosts?'"

"I've had two abortions. Aborted children become ghosts to pursue you and punish you for the rest of your life."

"I don't believe in that, but I can imagine the agony you must have been through. Is your father in the army, too?"

"No. He's with the department of education, but with the galloping cost of living the last two years, his monthly salary is barely enough to feed the family for ten days. I had to give up school to work, first in a bar, and later in a restaurant. That's where I began my singing career—thanks to the encouragement of the composer Thanh Thien. I was his minor wife for a while, but he was so poor himself that he couldn't support me. Once he gave a party and had to sell his bicycle to buy wine for his friends. I asked him how he planned to survive in the future and he said, 'I don't even know how I survived until today.'" She shook her head slowly. "Artists and writers are a sad, destitute lot in our country now. Only the armed forces officers prosper, and you know how they do it."

"Thanh Thien is a friend of mine. Where does he live now?"

"The same place—off Nguyen Cong Tru Street. A few weeks ago he rented his house to a noncommissioned Thai officer and now he lives in a shanty behind his own house."

"Can I visit him sometime tomorrow?"

"I'm afraid not. He left this morning for a concert in Dalat and will be there for two weeks."

Tan Diep unbuttoned her *ao dai*. From her bra, she pulled a tiny package wrapped in red flowered paper.

"What is that?" Minh asked.

"A new drug called Heavenly Ectasy, made of cocaine, heroin, and a Mexican liquor. It's very expensive but terrific. Your soul and body seem to dissolve into nothingness, and then after a few minutes you want both sex and food. The dignitary I told you about acted like a crazy baby after he sniffed it. He ordered a large beefsteak and ate it quickly. Then he put on his uniform and insisted I urinate on it while sitting on his bald head. Can you imagine?"

Minh laughed. "Where do you buy this stuff?"

"You can't buy it. This was given to me by General Vu Binh for special occasions to entertain his honored guests. He says it's very difficult to make, and that either the police or the army prepare it in a secret laboratory in the western highlands. They export it to America and make millions from it. Why don't you try it? It will change your mind about your virginity, or your loyalty to your American girlfriend. Or have you had it in America already?"

"No. I never heard of it. I've never taken any drugs."

"It's entirely up to you, but you're missing something wonderful." She paused and lit a cigarette. "You know, I think I love you, and that's not something I say to everybody, certainly not to any stranger. I want to make love with you—with or without Heavenly Ectasy. Why don't you take your clothes off and lie on the bed? It's such a comfortable bed. We live on this horrible earth such a short time. Why waste any of it?"

Unable to refuse her a second time, Minh removed his shirt and lay down in his trousers. Tan Diep went into the bathroom. When she reappeared completely nude, Minh saw to his shock that she had no pubic hair. He turned away from her, feigning sleepiness.

"You must be very tired," she said.

"Yes, I am. I'm sorry. Why don't you turn off the lights?" Minh had never treated a woman so before, but the thought of making love to a *bach bang* terrified him.

He lay in the dark, remembering the time he had visited a "house of pleasure" in Hue. He was nineteen. The woman he had slept with there had had no pubic hair, either. He remembered what his mother had told him when he had confessed the experience to her.

"Have you ever seen a mountain without trees or a valley without grass?" she had asked. "It's unnatural. Pubic hair is sacred to the lover." A woman with no pubic hair, a *bach bang* white plate, is condemned by Heaven, she had explained, laid bare to the attacks of the White Tiger. Contact with such a woman could only bring calamity. She made a very hot bath for him to purge his body and soul of the inauspicious elements. Later, during his travels in America and Africa, he had seen many mountains without trees and valleys without grass, but he still believed in the validity of his mother's advice.

Minh pretended to snore, but his eyes were wide open in the dark for hours. The distant thunder, the reflections of the flares dropping on the battlefields around Saigon, became tranquilizers for his distraught nerves. He didn't know when he really fell asleep.

When he woke at eight, Tan Diep was gone. He was relieved and happy, and he felt very hungry for a bowl of hot beef *pho*. Remembering that the Kim Phuong Restaurant used to make the best in Saigon, he dressed quickly and went out into the street.

. . .

"Please sit at any table, sir."

"Thank you. How come the place is deserted? The last time I was here, seven years ago, it took me half an hour to get a table."

"It's still pretty crowded between seven and nine. But even then, it's not the same as seven years ago. Then a bowl of *pho* cost twenty piasters at most, now it costs ten times more. Besides, fewer people eat *pho* at breakfast now. Rich people eat an American-style breakfast: cereal, fruit, and orange juice. But good Vietnamese need something more solid in our stomachs before we start the day." The waitress laughed good-naturedly. "What can I serve you, sir?"

"A bowl of *pho*, of course, with a large cartilage, one or two drops of seasoning and some large thread rice noodles and bean sprouts, please."

"Very well, sir."

Minh picked up a newspaper that had been left on the next table. The lead article began: "The President, at a meeting in Hue yesterday evening with officials and representatives of the people, affirmed that the recent disturbances in the former imperial capital were instigated by communists and students." Another news item announced the coming visit of Defense Secretary McNamara and Chairman of the Joint Chiefs of Staff Wheeler, for an on-the-spot review of the war.

The waitress brought his bowl of noodles and beef. It was deliciously hot and made Minh sweat. He felt fresh, almost happy.

He was talking to the owner-cashier, complimenting her on the steady quality of her house's *pho*, when he heard someone calling his name, someone whose face he could not quite remember.

"I'm Long Van," the stranger told him. "I met you once, ten years ago, at the mid-autumn literary festival at the home of the poet Vu Hoang Chuong. I've read all your works and admire and respect you a great deal. I hope you remember me."

"Of course I do," Minh said apologetically. "My brother wrote me about you recently."

"What did he tell you? May I ask?"

"Sure. He said that you're in some kind of trouble."

"Not just some kind—a lot. As a matter of fact I've been summoned to report to the special police this afternoon at three. But forget my problems. Let's go to the Huong Giang to have coffee. The flavor of any good *pho* must be prolonged by strong coffee, and Huong Giang has the best and strongest in town. Besides, the owner is an interesting woman. She came from Hue a little before last year's Tet."

"Let's go," Minh agreed.

It seemed to Minh that ten years ago Long Van had been a tall, muscular man. Now he looked tired, frail, even emaciated. Only his black, smiling eyes burned with life. His nicotine-stained fingers were like dead branches in wintertime. His voice was hoarse, as if it had to fight through a thick wall of smoke in his throat to be audible. Minh suspected that Long Van was an opium addict. He put his right arm around Long Van's waist as if they were old friends; but actually he was afraid that without assistance Long Van would disintegrate.

The Huong Giang Coffee Hermitage was only a block away. Pushing open the bamboo door, they saw at once through the thick cloud of cigarette smoke that all the tables were filled. A heavy aroma of cigarette and pipe tobacco blended with that of *Con Tien*, considered to be the best marijuana grown in the hills around Hue.

"Well, the Hermitage seems to be a very popular rendezvous. We'll have to wait for some time," Minh said.

"No, we won't. There's a small room in the back reserved for special customers like us. Follow me."

They walked to the counter, where Long Van introduced Minh to the owner. "Madame Luu, this is Professor Tran Van Minh, who just returned from exile in the United States," Long Van smiled. "He's also a native of Hue."

"You don't need to introduce him to me, Long Van. I knew him when he was in high school, and I also know his brother An well," she said, her face radiating pleasant surprise. "Please go to the inner sanctuary, in the back."

There were two small tables there, one occupied by a couple immersed in serious discussion. Minh and Long Van sat at the other. Madame Luu pulled up a chair for herself. She must be in her late thirties, yet she looks like a student, Minh thought. Her face was smooth and serene, her hands immaculate and soft as if she had never had to work for a living. She exuded quiet elegance in her dark blue *ao dai*, brightened at the neck by a gold collar.

"Let's drop the formalities," she said. "I'm going to call you *Anh* Minh. I knew you, *Anh* Minh, in the late 1930s when you were very close to my sister Thai. And, of course, I know that you're Co Tung."

Minh bowed his head slightly. "Yes, elder sister Luu, I remember. Thai and I were high-school lovers. We wrote poems to each other. We used to meet for ten minutes once a month at the full moon, under the banyan tree at the south end of the botanical gardens." Minh looked more closely at Luu. She resembled her sister.

"Do you still think of her?" she asked.

"It's as the poet said: 'After a thousand years, it is still not easy to forget that first moment of attachment.'"

In the brief silence that followed, Minh thought of Thai, but only Jennifer's image came to his mind. He felt almost as if he should ask Madame Luu's forgiveness for not having been faithful to Thai.

"Where is she now?" His voice was almost a whisper.

"She joined the resistance after graduating from the School of Pharmacy. She's in the North now."

"What's she doing there?"

"I don't really know, and when I say 'in the North' I simply mean on the other side. I was told by no less an authority than your brother An that she was identified as the military commander of the Viet Cong zone fifteen around Hue. I asked him how he could be so sure, and he said that with advanced American detection technology, American intelligence knows the location and shape of every blade of grass in the country."

There was a spark of anger in her eyes.

"I'm very glad to hear that she has an opportunity to do something exciting; not something as banal and insipid as teaching."

Madame Luu scrutinized Minh, her curiosity at his remark unhidden.

"What kind of coffee do you want, Minh?" Long Van broke in.

"Are there many kinds?"

"Yes." He turned to Madame Luu. "Shall I describe them to him?"

"Please."

"There are three major and five minor types of coffee in the Hermitage. Each one is known by a poetic name and should be taken at particular times by specific people. But to simplify things, I suggest that we have the *Luu Khach*, for keeping the guests. It's a perfect choice right now because although we just met you a few minutes ago, we want to keep you with us—we need you in these trying times." Long Van's eyes brightened as he turned to Madame Luu. "We need a poet of his integrity and wisdom."

Madame Luu shook his skinny hand. "Long Van, you're a good man. I agree with you. I've read all of Minh's poetry and novels, but I never dreamed I would meet him again after so many years. Years ago," she said to Minh, "there were rumors in Hue that you had left the U.S. and joined the other side, and that your works were being smuggled into the cities by the Viet Cong underground. But never mind. Now that you're here, let's celebrate. That terrible brother of yours didn't even tell me you were returning, or I would have closed the Hermitage tonight and organized a dinner party for you. Of course, brother An is trained to fight and keep secrets. Let me go to the kitchen and prepare a good pot of *Luu Khach*."

Minh stood with her.

"Thank you very much, Luu. I appreciate your thoughts." He felt the warmth of his people, something he'd missed during his years overseas.

"What's in the coffee?" Minh asked.

"I tasted it here once before, and it's exceptionally exquisite," Long Van said. There was a twinkle in his eye; Minh looked at him curiously. "Madame Luu says that it's a mixture of African and Banmethuot coffees blended with ginger powder and fried with coconut milk and lemon grass. The secret lies in what she calls the 'double-filter.' She rearranges two standard French filters into one double-decked filter. It takes at least half an hour to prepare."

Madame Luu emerged from the kitchen. "It will take a few more minutes," she said. "In the meantime, can I offer you some *Banh Phu The* that I just received from Hue? We now have three planes daily between Saigon and Hue, and one can have anything quickly."

It was the first time since he'd left Vietnam that Minh had an opportunity to savor a typical Hue delicacy. It reminded him of all the Tets of his youth. A week before Tet, he would spend hours helping his mother select the greenest coconut leaves for making the identical square boxes that, fitted together, constituted the wrapping of the delicious cakes.

Long Van pushed the cakes toward Minh. "I don't want any. You can have them all. I don't like sweet things."

"Now, Long Van," Minh said, "tell me about the situation in our country as you see it."

"I'm sure that An knows more about the government's policies and the war than I do. All I can tell you is how the intellectuals and students feel about the general situation.

"Of course, intellectuals are not of one heart and mind, neither are students, but they do agree on a number of points. One is that the present government is a national disgrace, not only because it's corrupt to the bone, but also because it's antinational. This government brought 'the elephants to trample on the ancestors' tombs,' it invited the foreigners in to destroy us. Its officials are not only servants of the U.S., but inefficient servants at that! Their wives go to Japan and spend thousands of U.S. dollars to 'correct' their noses and have their faces lifted to look like Vietnamese Elizabeth Taylors and Marilyn Monroes. How disgusting! They've betrayed the national honor!

"The second point of agreement, regardless of what each of us believes ideologically, is that this war must be stopped unconditionally before the whole social and cultural foundation of our country collapses. Recently a Harvard University professor—I don't remember his name— gave a lecture at the Lincoln Library of the United States Information Agency and claimed that the war, destructive as it is, will in the long run accelerate Vietnamese development because it brings the peasants closer to modern technology. What a sick idea! War is an instrument of death; it brings destruction, not development! Modern weapons don't make their victims modern, they just make them dead!

"And last, we all agree that if the war is to be stopped then the present government, which is worse than any previous one, must go. Yet as long as it is supported by the U.S., it will remain—and the U.S. will support it."

Long Van stopped for a second to light a cigarette. "I say these things not out of personal resentment because they censored my work, or because they have made my life impossible, but because as a poet, I can work alone, but not live alone. Poets and writers are not on this earth only to produce, but also to induce. I don't have to tell you that all our great poets of the past were those who participated in the building and preservation of the nation." His eyes reddened with anger. He took Minh's arm. "Although I'm very happy to see people like you here—lotus flowers in a lake of mud—I wonder what good you can do. Perhaps you'd be more useful in the U.S. I don't know. But it's obvious that the root of the war is in Washington, not in Saigon. Don't you agree?"

"Well, yes and no. It's true that money, arms, planes, bombs, defoliation, and 150,000 soldiers all come from the U.S., but it's equally true that the war is being fought on Vietnamese soil, mostly by Vietnamese against Vietnamese. It's affecting all of us, and we must each bear the responsibility. This isn't the first time that Vietnamese have been manipulated by foreigners to fight against each other.

"As you know, when I was in the U.S. I took part in the antiwar movement, but I soon realized that the American people themselves would fight for peace effectively only when their own sons were drafted into the army and their husbands started coming home in coffins. When I read the daily headlines about a hundred or two hundred Viet Cong or 'commies' or 'reds' being killed, I was torn by guilt. I really had no choice but to return. You may be right, it *is* possible that there's nothing I can do here, but at least here I can share in the shame and suffering of our people. And besides, my father is old and in ill health. He needs my company."

"I understand your situation," Long Van nodded, "and I hope you won't be as helpless as I am now."

Madame Luu returned with a wooden tray which she ceremoniously placed on the small table. She poured a jet black, thick liquid into two small cups of "Hue blue" porcelain.

"Please taste this. And let me know later how you like it. Now I must excuse myself to take care of my other customers."

The flavor of the coffee burst into Minh's nostrils with his first sip. He became dizzy. His heart beat rapidly. Then the dizziness left him and he felt a deep relaxation. His mind melted into a multicolored nothingness. He was sure his eyes were dilated and he closed them slowly. When he opened them, Long Van was smiling sweetly.

"How do you feel?"

"It reminds me of LSD—or at least of what I've heard about LSD. I've never taken any kind of drug before."

"Yes, it's a drug. The first time I drank this coffee, I felt as if I'd flown into the air and dropped back to the floor in a matter of seconds. That's why it's named *Luu Khach*. No customer can leave the house after he drinks it. He has to stay for at least half an hour before he can walk again."

Minh nodded, wishing he could lie down for a while.

Madame Luu returned to the back room, shaking her head. She was visibly disturbed.

"What's wrong?" Long Van asked.

"Well, nothing serious, really. The usual police check for draft evaders. They took four to headquarters for questioning. It's routine, I know, but I always feel angry about it. Why don't they leave people alone? Why do they need so many young men for the army? The whole world knows that the real draft evaders are the children of the big shots. And they're all safe in schools in Switzerland, France, and America."

"Why didn't the police come back here?" Minh asked. He was beginning to feel better. Evidently the drug's effects were short-lived.

"They usually don't, except once when they suspected that a very important Viet Cong leader was hiding here."

Now, at midmorning, the place was suddenly quiet. Minh guessed that there was no one in the house except them.

"Why don't we sit in the main room?" Long Van proposed to Madame Luu.

As they entered the front room a military jeep pulled up in front of the coffeehouse.

"Well, well. The dragon is coming to the shrimp!" Luu exclaimed as An alighted from the vehicle and moved toward the door. Long Van stood and shook hands with him.

"Are you coming for late coffee or to take your famous brother away from us?" Madame Luu asked. "I've not seen you since you became a V.I.P."

"Please don't tease me, *Chi*, Sister, Luu. I'm not a V.I.P.," An retorted shyly.

"How did you know I was here?" Minh asked.

"He's an intelligence officer," Long Van interjected, "though he's a harmless one."

"Thank you," An said, "but one doesn't need to be an intelligence officer to know where my brother is. I remembered he always liked to have *pho* in the morning—at the best restaurant—and he liked to follow it up with the best coffee. Excuse me. May I have a few words with my brother alone?"

"Of course. We common people have no business with state secrets," Madame Luu replied.

An pulled two chairs into a corner and whispered to Minh. "The President's aide-de-camp just called me. The President will have to cut his visit to Hue short and return to Saigon this afternoon for a meeting with a very important American coming from Bangkok. The American is with the U.S. National Security Council and he's supposed to arrive about five. He'll see the President as soon as he arrives, and after that the President will see you."

"Fine," Minh answered. "I read in the newspapers that Secretary McNamara and the chairman of the Joint Chiefs of Staff will visit soon. Is it true?"

"Yes, it's true. And that's why I've arranged for you to meet with the President today or early tomorrow. If you don't see him this week, you'll have to wait at least five more days, because next week is McNamara's visit. The aide promised me that he'll try to have you see the President immediately after the American representative leaves. You may not know it, but half of the Vietnamese government and U.S. command personnel spend literally most of their time receiving, briefing, and entertaining visitors from Washington."

"Are you busy this afternoon? Can we spend some time together until my appointment?"

"I'm afraid I'm not free, Minh, but I have taken the liberty of making a date for you with an old friend. I told Pham Ngoc Lam that you're in town, and he insisted you have lunch with him."

"That's wonderful! I haven't seen him since we were in the States, and for some reason he hasn't answered my letters since the beginning of the year."

"I know the reason. It's because of you. The police intercepted his letters and learned of your friendship. They visited him in January and asked the nature of his relationship with you. He wasn't arrested, but he was watched closely for some time. Fortunately for him, he has a friend who is the U.S. cultural attaché. They knew each other at M.I.T. His American friend protected him, otherwise he might have been arrested or dismissed from his job. I found out about it when the police checked with my office."

"What time does he expect me?"

"He has no classes today, so he'll be glad to see you anytime after eleven. I'll drive you to his house. You can stay as long as you wish, but I suggest you return to the hotel after lunch and rest before your meeting with the President—it's going to be tough. Now let me say goodbye to Madame Luu and Long Van before I have to leave."

Minh, An, and Long Van walked slowly back to An's car.

"An," Minh asked, "did you know that Long Van has been summoned to the special police this afternoon? Who are they?" He turned to Long Van. "What address did they give you?"

"906/12 Hong Thap Tu Street."

"Have you been there before?" asked An.

"No. I've been to the central police headquarters on Phan Than Giang Street twice, but I've never been to the special police."

An looked worried, though he spoke lightly. "*Anh* Long Van," he said, "be careful. Take care of yourself. Call tonight and let me know what happened and how I can help. Do you have my number?"

"I'm afraid not."

An handed him a business card.

"Thank you very much," Long Van said softly. "I must go now. I'm very glad that I met you both, and if you stay here for the next few days," he turned to Minh, "we'll have dinner."

"I don't think I'll be here," Minh said, "but thanks anyway." He shook Long Van's cold, bony hand.

Long Van crossed the street and hailed a taxi.

As soon as he was out of earshot An turned to Minh. "It doesn't look good for Long Van," he said. "That address he was given is the office of the Central Allied Intelligence Study Group, the C.A.I.S.G. It's staffed by U.S., Thai, Australian, South Korean, Filipino, and Vietnamese intelligence officers. The nominal head is a Vietnamese major general, the President's cousin. I've never been there myself, but rumor has it that once you enter its gates you leave by way of the cemetery."

"Why do you suppose they want him there?" Minh asked.

"I wish I knew. I really don't know him very well, but he seems like a nice man—not a dangerous subversive. The police told my office that he's suspected of being the secretary of the Saigon Cultural Committee for Liberation, but we've no evidence of that except that he's a much-loved and respected writer and poet. In fact there was a popular rhyme in Saigon last year listing the country's four best writers and he was second: first Tung, second Van, third Tam, fourth Phan. It didn't surprise me that you were first, brother. Of course few people outside of your friends and relatives know that you're Co Tung—except the President and the police."

"That makes me proud," Minh said. "I only hope I can live up to that reputation. But why did Long Van tell me that he has to report to the special police, and not the C.A.I.S.G.?"

"I don't think he even knows they exist! In Saigon, any intelligence or police organization that isn't official and public is called special police. There are at least ten such organizations and they all have the powers of arrest, interrogation, and detention."

"Even execution?" Minh challenged.

"Yes," An answered matter-of-factly.

"And they all report to the President?"

"In principle, yes."

"To the American Embassy?"

"In practice, yes."

.　　　.　　　.

An dropped Minh in front of a modest villa behind the Gia Long College for Women on Duy Tan Street. Professor Pham Ngoc Lam rushed out to greet Minh.

"I'm happy to see you back with us," he cried, "but I thought you wouldn't return home until peace was restored."

"That's what I thought, too, but I realized that peace isn't a gift from heaven or the U.S. We have to work for it, and the place to work is right here in our own country. It's good to see you, Lam."

"I'm glad you came early so we can have a private talk before the other guests arrive."

"I didn't expect a party!"

"It isn't a party, just three interesting people who heard you were back and wanted to see you. One's an old high-school classmate of yours, Ngo Duc Hoa, who's now with the School of Medicine, one is Cung Dinh Chuong, dean of the Law School, and the third is a woman I've been seeing, a painter, Le Minh Thuy."

"I remember Hoa well, and of course I've heard a lot since then about his work with the poor."

"He and Minh Thuy and I were all on the government's blacklist for being founders of the old Committee of Academics for Peace and the Withdrawal of U.S. Troops. The irony of it is that we would all have been languishing in jail for years if it hadn't been for the intervention of the American Embassy. The American government wants to keep a democratic face on the Saigon regime, and Saigon in its turn shows its pro-American position by giving special treatment to graduates of U.S. universities. It's ironic. We're against the war, but our existence is protected by the source of it."

They walked into the sparsely furnished living room.

"Where is your wife?" Minh asked.

"She died five months ago in a plane crash over Nha Trang, about the same time I stopped writing you."

"I'm very sorry to hear that. Where are the children?"

"They're with my parents in Can Tho, but I may have to bring them and my parents here very soon. Can Tho isn't safe. There were two Viet Cong attacks in broad daylight last week." He paused. "Minh, we're in the midst of a national tragedy of such magnitude that somehow, family and personal problems don't seem to bother me anymore. Often I feel ashamed of myself. Here I am, a Ph.D. in nuclear physics from M.I.T., living among the corrupt and the invaders, while a Vietnamese peasant works in the ricefields during the day to produce food for me and takes up the gun at night to fight for me to remain Vietnamese. Maybe I'm excluded from the revolution, coming as I do from a landlord family, but I still want to be included in national history and do my duty as a Vietnamese."

"I understand your feelings, Lam, but you shouldn't be ashamed of your class origins. It's your class position now that matters. With whom do you stand in this war? With the masses of peasants or with the privileged few, the businessmen and generals? As for me, I've chosen my position. I have no stake in this war or in this government, or for that matter in any government that continues the war. The problem for me is how I can find the best way to bring the war to an end."

An old man entered with two glasses of beer. Lam politely thanked him.

"He used to work on my family's lands in Can Tho Province, but his village was bombed three times and his wife and children were killed. He left his home and buffalo and came to Saigon to stay with me. Poor man. Some nights he wakes up and cries like a crazy person. In his dreams, he sees his wife and children coming back, asking for revenge. He's scared. He went to a sorcerer in Cho Lon for several exorcisms. I don't believe in these superstitious practices, but I have to let him do what he wants for his peace of mind."

Lam invited Minh into the small garden. They stood under a blooming frangipani.

"Actually, Minh, I'm doing what I can to bring the invasion of Vietnam to an end. Our committee was officially disbanded, but several of us continue to work in the Association of Intellectual Workers for Liberation, in secret, obviously."

"I've read about the organization in the Foreign Broadcast Bulletin of the U.S. State Department. Isn't it dangerous to associate yourself with it?"

"Yes, of course, but we cover ourselves by associating with people like Dean Chuong. That's why I invited him today. He's blindly anticommunist, and may be the next minister of justice. Actually, he isn't an evil man, but relatively clean and honest. His anticommunist position comes partly, I was told, from the fact that his father was assassinated by the Viet Minh in 1946. He has powerful friends in the United States Congress and he goes over there every year for lectures and contacts."

"I've never met him, but I'd like to see where he stands."

"Obviously, our lunch is a social affair. We can't talk about anything serious. But don't talk only about the weather, or he may get suspicious. I think we should talk about politics in general. But here comes his car. We'd better get inside."

Chuong's car was a Vega; it reminded Minh of Jennifer. He smiled as he entered the house.

"I'm a bit early," Chuong apologized as he entered the living room a moment later.

"You're not early, I am," Minh responded.

Lam introduced them and excused himself.

"Lam tells me that you studied at the University of Paris?" Minh asked politely.

"Yes, and also at Columbia. I've read two of your novels and several of your poems. I've often wondered how a political scientist like yourself can do so well in literature, especially poetry."

"But in our tradition poetry and politics always mix. Look at Nguyen Trai, Nguyen Cong Tru, Nguyen Du, and hundreds of others."

"Do you consider Cu Ho a poet?" he asked, and without waiting for an answer went on, "I don't. He's too shrewd and cunning to be a poet. Besides, even if poetry and politics blend, poetry and communism certainly cannot. One is all heart and the other is all heartless manipulation."

Minh was annoyed by Chuong's observations and puzzled that he used the polite word, "*Cu*," the Honorable, in reference to President Ho Chi Minh. But he was spared having to respond by Lam's return.

"I'm sorry, Chuong," Lam said. "I was in the kitchen making sure that we'll have something to eat for lunch. A widower's life isn't easy. Besides, my cook left suddenly this morning. Her son was killed yesterday in a battle near the airport. He was a lieutenant."

The old man brought a beer for Chuong and asked if Minh wished another. He thanked him, but declined.

"I'm glad you could come, Chuong, regardless of the fact that you must be very busy at your expanding law school," Lam said.

"It's true, I'm very busy, but it's more true that I was very eager to meet Dr. Minh. The problems in my school are not professional; they're political. This morning I had to call the police to disperse about a hundred students who were demonstrating for peace. Most of them are naive enough to believe that we'll have peace if the communists win. Perhaps we'd have peace, but we'd lose all our freedoms. I'm used to these minor incidents, but getting arrested will be good for these students. They'll be drafted and learn how to fight with guns rather than slogans. Incidentally, before you emerged from your kitchen, Dr. Minh and I had started to exchange opinions on poetry and politics."

"A fascinating subject. Please continue."

"I said that poetry and communism can't mix," Chuong said.

"Why?" Lam asked.

"Because poetry is all a matter of the heart and communists have no hearts."

"How can they live, then, without hearts?" Minh asked with a laugh.

Chuong ignored the interruption. "Poetry is like a tree—it can't grow on a rock. Communism is a rock. The communists always claim to observe our principles of *Hop Tinh*, conform to feeling, and *Hop Ly*, conform to reason, but they always use their foreign Marxist *Ly* and never apply the Vietnamese *Tinh*."

"Don't you know, Chuong," Lam interceded, "that there are trees that grow on solid rock and remain green for thousands of years?"

But before Chuong could reply they were interrupted by the arrival of the other guests.

"Minh, this is Miss Le Minh Thuy—Dr. Tran Van Minh; and this is Dr. Ngo Duc Hoa."

"I'm happy to finally meet you," Miss Thuy said in a pronounced Hue accent. "There's nothing more frustrating than to read a person's works without knowing who he is or even where he is."

"Well, here I am. I hope you won't be disappointed." He turned to Hoa. "We haven't met for more than twenty years, but I'd recognize you anywhere. You look the same. Of course, I know all about your fine work, especially your 'popular hospitals' for the peasants and the poor."

"I've tried to do my best under the circumstances, but the real disease is the war itself," Hoa said. "Isn't that true, Dean Chuong?"

"It's true, but in order to cure the disease, one has to go to the root, and the root of the war in Vietnam is communism itself."

There was a dead silence, discomfiting even to Chuong. "Well! Let's not talk about politics anymore," he said briskly. "We're not living in a communist state yet, where we have to speak on one subject only." He turned to Miss Thuy. "I've seen your exhibition at the Central Gallery. It's very good. You're very talented, but I must confess that I don't understand some of your abstract paintings—the one called 'The Rising Sun' for instance. I didn't see any sun, only what looked like profiles of women and men working in the fields and the factory against a red and green background. No horizon, no nature, no trees, no birds . . ."

"Dean Chuong, thank you for having visited my exhibit. You're too modest. I think you understood my painting very well, and that you understand abstract art, too. It's only another form of realistic art—an indirect expression of the Buddhist concept of the impermanence of all things, the absence of a center or an ego, and the transient character of all realities."

Minh was beginning to express his agreement with Thuy when Lam invited his guests into lunch. It was served on a round table in a small room adjacent to the study-library.

With good Vietnamese manners they were silent as they ate, except for an occasional compliment on a certain dish. After lunch Chuong excused himself from coffee and prepared to leave.

"If I drink coffee," he said, "I'll not be able to sleep, and siesta is the most important part of my daily life. Without two solid hours of siesta, I'm half dead, and my mind doesn't function properly. I have to see the President after dinner today. He has an important visitor from the U.S., the White House legal counsel. He'll be discussing plans for future military bases in Vietnam after the war. He wants me present for the discussion."

Thuy and Hoa also prepared to leave.

"Do you take siesta, too? I always thought that only those who are French-educated were siesta-addicted," Minh said to Thuy, "not the U.S.-educated."

"Your observation is true in theory," she responded, smiling, "but once you live in this hot climate, siesta is really necessary. However, I'm not leaving to go to bed. I have to go to the airport to meet my cousin who's coming in from Hue."

"I usually don't take siesta," Dr. Hoa said, "because I have too much work to do. I have an appointment at one thirty with a group of medical students who want to set up a mobile health unit to inform the people about the dangerous effects of defoliation. So far, the government is against the project, but I'm still trying to help them organize it. I'll certainly keep in touch with you, Minh. I may even see you in Hue next month."

"Minh, do you absolutely trust your brother?" Lam asked when they were alone.

"I have no choice. He's my brother, although I've been away a long time and hardly know him anymore. Why do you ask?"

"Because I can't understand why the government gave him such an important job and promoted him so quickly. He's still quite young."

"He's thirty-four," Minh said. "I don't understand it either. Government actions, especially this government's, are not always rational. Perhaps he knows the President's younger brother. Still, he's not an exception. We now have thirty-five-year-old ambassadors and thirty-year-old colonels. The Vietnamese military attaché to Washington is only thirty. He's also the President's brother-in-law, I think."

"You're right. We are living in irrational times, and the most irrational of all is this seemingly endless war."

.　　　　.　　　　.

Back in his hotel room, Minh stretched out on his bed. It was siesta time, and the whole city seemed asleep. He took out his traveling companion, a copy of Dag Hammarskjöld's *Markings*, given to him by Jennifer on his birthday in April. He read:

In our era the road to holiness necessarily passes through the world of action.

Back in the U.S. the thought of taking precise action to stop the war had never really occurred to him. He had opposed the war in the abstract, out of principle. The war was far away from most people in the States, except for those who had relatives killed in action. Of course, the war was brought into living rooms by television, but television didn't convey realities: it multiplied illusions and created fantasies. Now, after less than twenty-four hours on the soil of his ancestors, the war was no longer an abstraction to him but a cruel reality. He heard it in the thunder of the distant guns, saw it in the sad look of the child beggars in the street. It was in the fierce eyes and bony arms of the poet Long Van, in the extravagant lives of the generals in power, in the fear and suffering he saw everywhere.

He read another Marking, one on which Jennifer had asked his views:

> To separate himself from the society of which he was born a member will lead the revolutionary not to life, but to death, unless in his very revolt, he is driven by a love of what, seemingly, must be rejected and therefore, at the profoundest level, remains faithful to that society.

"First of all," he had told her, "I'm not a revolutionary, and therefore the question doesn't arise. Second, suppose I were a revolutionary. Then the very fact that I love an American who must be rejected by Vietnam makes me still profoundly faithful to that society."

His answer was not convincing either to himself or to Jennifer, and they had laughed it off as a futile exercise in semantics. But now that he was home again, he found in himself a strong loyalty to his society. It was a loyalty he had thought impossible, having often described himself as an "internationalist." And he knew that his loyalty would lead to a different life for him whether he was revolutionary or not.

He reached for a pencil to underline the Marking, then hesitated and changed his mind. He closed the book and slept soundly until the telephone rang. It was An.

"I hope you had a good rest."

"I did, indeed. For the first time in years, I slept in the afternoon, from three o'clock until you woke me up."

"I'm sorry, but I have good news. The President's aide just phoned. He'll see you about seven. I'll pick you up in thirty or forty minutes."

"Thanks, An. I'll be ready."

Minh suspected that this meeting with the President would decide his future, yet he didn't feel excited or anxious about it. He had met the President several years earlier, at Gia Long Palace in Saigon. Minh was then Minister Plenipotentiary and Deputy Chief of Mission at the Vietnamese Embassy in Washington, and had returned to Saigon to see the advisor to then-President Ngo Dinh Diem. As he sat in a palace anteroom, there had waited with him a brigadier general commanding the fifth ARVN division in the Delta. The general had held in his outstretched hands a rectangular fish tank wrapped in a piece of red and gold cloth, the colors of the national flag. The general had seemed deeply preoccupied and nervous, so much so that Minh had introduced himself and asked if something were bothering him.

"Mr. Minister Plenipotentiary," the general responded, "I have been waiting almost an hour, and yet I'm holding in my hands the most precious and rarest fish in Vietnam. It's the lemon fish, or the *Ca Chanh*, as it's called in the Delta. This fish grows old to become a Blue Dragon, and whoever has the fortune to eat it will become a great man, an emperor. Knowing this, I mobilized my whole division for one week to search for and catch this fish. When a colonel under my command succeeded in capturing it, I immediately ordered a company of soldiers and brand-new American armored cars to bring me here to Saigon so that I could present it to the adviser. He should be very pleased, and the future of our country will be safe."

"General, why don't you eat the fish and become an emperor yourself?" Minh asked jokingly.

"Please don't joke, Mr. Minister Plenipotentiary. I have never dared to entertain such an ambition. My ambition is to stay where I am now and faithfully serve the President, his brother, the adviser, and the nation. Besides, if you eat the *Ca Chanh* but are not predestined to become a ruler, the fish will turn into a White Tiger in your stomach and destroy you."

"Why don't you present the fish to the President?"

"The President is already like an emperor. The adviser will probably succeed him, but I want to be sure. They have both done so much for our country, for my family, and for me. I was nobody in 1954 when I left the French army as a lieutenant. Now I have stars on both my shoulders."

"I see," Minh said, amused by the general's answer. He turned to the adviser's A.D.C. "Captain, I have an appointment with the adviser for ten o'clock, but I can yield my time to the general, who has a very important mission. Can you let him in first? I'll wait."

"No, sir, I'm sorry. The adviser will be angry if I do that. I've already announced the general's presence, and the adviser said, 'Tell him to wait.' There's nothing I can do."

After nearly an hour with the adviser—an hour of enduring his boring monologue—Minh left his office.

"Good luck, General. I've told the adviser that you've been waiting for hours and that you have a very important gift for him. He'll see you soon."

"Thank you very much, Mr. Plenipotentiary. Thank you."

At first, Minh had felt contempt for the general. Here was a high-ranking officer assigned to the most strategic area in the country, and all he did was use his soldiers to catch a fish to please his superior. But on second thought, he felt sorry for him. His was not a unique case. Most of the ARVN senior officers had served the French colonial army and fought on the side of the French against the Vietnamese independence movement during the first Indochina War of 1945–54. One couldn't expect much dignity on the part of those who were Vietnamese by name but French by conviction and training. Minh had never quite understood why all the Saigon regimes that claimed to be anti-French and independent continued to maintain an army commanded by former Vietnamese junior and noncommissioned officers of the French colonial expeditionary corps.

The whole episode of the *Ca Chanh* returned clearly to Minh's mind as he waited in the reception room of Independence Palace, completely renovated after its bombing by two rebellious air force officers. The palace, once the home of the French governor general in Indochina, was now a modern building and the home and office of the President of the Republic of Vietnam—that same general who had ordered the capture of the *Ca Chanh*, who had led a *coup d'état* in 1963 and ordered the murder of his President-emperor.

Minh was reading the latest copy of the bilingual magazine, The Free World, when the President's aide, an Air Force colonel, called the room to attention.

"Stand up! The President is passing through!"

Minh and An rose. The President was showing his American guest through the reception room to the corridor. From there, his aide would escort the guest to the front door. The President didn't look at them, but the American jumped when he saw Minh.

"Dr. Tran Van Minh! What a surprise to see you here! I didn't know you were back home. I tried to reach you just before I started on this trip. When your office told me you were out of the country, I assumed you were on some trip to Latin America."

"It's a surprise to see you, too, Dr. Hamilton," Minh responded. "How long are you here for?"

"I have to go straight to the airport, directly back to Washington. I won't be able to spend any time with you."

"What a shame," Minh responded.

Turning to the President, who was staring in annoyance at the ceiling throughout this exchange, Dr. Hamilton said, "Dr. Minh is an extremely capable person, Mr. President. A man of great intellectual vigor and moral integrity. Very bright. I met him at a seminar we jointly conducted at Stanford University on culture and politics more than a year ago. Everyone was impressed by his knowledge of Asian cultures. I'm glad he's back to work for you."

The President didn't respond. He shook hands with Dr. Hamilton quickly and walked back to his office without looking at Minh and An.

"Well, I'll keep in touch," Hamilton told Minh. "Take care. Good to see you."

"Yes, have a safe trip home."

The A.D.C. returned from escorting the American to the door and disappeared into the President's office. A few minutes later, he appeared and announced pompously, "Professor Tran Van Minh, the President is now available for your audience."

He took Minh into a huge office with wall-to-wall carpeting. The President was sitting behind a large lacquered desk on an elevated red and gold chair that resembled a throne. He didn't move when Minh entered but asked the aide to take a small chair while ordering Minh to sit beside him.

"Mr. Minh," he said in a grave and solemn tone, "though we've never met, I've had reports from our various agencies regarding your antinational activities in the United States. What you did there was very bad. By opposing the war, which is solely instigated by Moscow and Peking, by criticizing the policies of the U.S., which only wants to help Vietnam become a great, prosperous and democratic country, you aided the communist camp and undermined the heroic efforts of the free world. I would have asked the American government to arrest you, I would never have allowed you to return, if it hadn't been for the repeated requests of your relatives. Also, your brother, Lieutenant Colonel An, and your friend General Vu Binh, have guaranteed your behavior. You must be careful not to violate my conditional trust.

"You may not know it, but I've just signed a decree, Law No. 100/67, regarding crimes against the state, the major one being to propagate the dangerous ideas of peace and negotiation with the Viet Cong. If you respect the law and cease to allow yourself to be duped by communist propaganda, then you can ask me for any job you like. I know that you're an intelligent and capable man."

"Thank you—Mr. President." Minh found it difficult to use the formal title with this man of the lemon fish. The general he'd met in 1962 must have gained at least a hundred pounds since he had become the head of state of South Vietnam in 1965. In his immaculate white sharkskin suit and deep yellow tie decorated with a white eagle, he looked far more impressive than the former skinny general with his fish. Minh had almost laughed out loud when the President had said that he'd never met him before.

Then, without warning, the President grew gracious. He invited Minh into the private study adjacent to his office.

"Doctor Tran Van Minh," he said, "it's more comfortable here. We can talk better."

Minh noticed that he was now referred to as "Doctor." The President pushed a button on the wall and the A.D.C. appeared.

"Bring a drink for Professor Doctor Tran Van Minh," he ordered. "What would you like, Professor? Chivas Regal? Dubonnet? Champagne, if you wish."

"I don't drink alcohol, Mr. President. May I have a lemonade?"

The President looked serious again. "Professor Minh, as I told you earlier, you can ask me for any job. Ah! Before I forget. Do you know Dr. Hamilton well? How much influence do you think he has in the White House?"

"Mr. President, I don't know him very well politically, only academically. Everybody in Washington knows that he's a close friend of Dr. Walt Rostow, President Johnson's assistant on national security."

"Do you correspond with him often?"

"In the U.S., yes, Mr. President. But now that I'm back in Vietnam, I have no need to correspond with him."

"Don't be afraid. I encourage you to write him; put in a good word for our government. We have just made an additional request for one billion dollars for the coming pacification campaign. Dr. Hamilton doesn't seem to be convinced of the urgency of our military needs. I assume that his report will influence Secretary McNamara, who will be here soon for a review."

"Mr. President, I've been back for less than twenty-four hours. I don't know anything to write about. I'm not familiar with the government budget, and I'm ignorant of military matters."

"But think about it, anyway. Well, now that you're home, what do you wish to do?"

"Mr. President, as I understood it from General Vu Binh and Colonel An, I'm to give a series of lectures to the Staff and Command College."

"Forget it. That's no longer necessary. The American Embassy just informed me that two American experts will be here soon to instruct our officers on strategy and politics."

"In that case, Mr. President, may I go to Hue?"

"What do you plan to do there? I was there yesterday and the situation isn't stabilized yet. The Viet Cong infiltrations and the Buddhist agitations are only temporarily suppressed."

"I wish to stay in Hue to be near my father and teach at the University."

"Would you be interested in the governorship of Hue Province? That way you could be near your father and serve us at the same time."

Minh was speechless. A governorship was no small compensation in exchange for his loyalty. With an effort he spoke calmly.

"Thank you, Mr. President, for your generous gesture. But I resigned from the diplomatic service in 1963, to teach and follow the example of my father."

"If that's what you wish, I will order the minister of education to appoint you dean of the school of social sciences at Hue University beginning this academic year. As you may know, your mother's brother has already been named Rector of the University."

"Yes, I know, but I don't wish to be dean or a department chairman. I would be grateful just to teach there in any capacity."

"I rarely see a man without ambition. Without exception, everyone who comes into this office asks me for favors and positions. In case you change your mind, let me know."

He summoned his A.D.C. to show Minh out.

"That was a short visit, *Anh* Minh," An remarked.

The A.D.C. now groveled openly. "Professor, if you need anything at all, please let Lieutenant Colonel An know and he will convey your wishes to me. I shall try my best to make your stay here as comfortable as possible."

"Thank you, Colonel, but I don't need anything."

.   .   .

Out in the humid air of the Independence lawn, Minh felt relieved.

"What happened?" An asked.

"The President tried to buy me off. He actually offered me the Hue governorship! But of course I declined."

"You're kidding! Then what did he say?"

"He wanted me to be dean of the school of social sciences, but I told him I prefer to be a teacher. I guess it was my accidental meeting with Dr. Hamilton that made the President so nice to me. He needs Hamilton's help to get more money for his budget and he thought I could put in a good word for him. Dr. Hamilton's a close friend of President Johnson's assistant on national security affairs. Now," he changed the subject abruptly, "let's go have a good dinner, and tomorrow I'll go to Hue and see father."

"Good. What about the lectures at the Staff and Command College?"

"The President said they were no longer necessary."

"So much the better."

An selected the Ngu Binh restaurant, named for a series of hills and pines in Hue that were thought to protect the former capital from malevolent spirits. The restaurant was located on a short, shady street called Thanh Thai after a Vietnamese king and poet who had reigned from 1889 to 1907 and was a great uncle of Minh's.

King Thanh Thai was famous for having feigned a playboy life in order to distract the French, who had colonized Vietnam in 1884, while he organized the resistance against the invaders. When his plan was discovered in 1907, he was put in restricted residence at a seaside resort in the south and later exiled to Reunion Island in the Indian Ocean. During his short reign Hue earned a reputation for beauty and poetry. Minh had heard many anecdotes from his mother about the King's era.

"Does Madame Nguyen Tuong Tam still own the restaurant?" Minh asked.

"No. She died last January, but the cook is the same. She's an old woman from Hue who still believes that the only way to have peace and tranquility in Vietnam is to bring back the monarchy."

"Why have the police let her alone?"

"They think she's an old, senile, crazy woman and nobody listens to her ideas, although everybody praises her culinary talents."

The Ngu Binh's neon-lit facade was visible from a distance. An drove into the back yard.

"It's dangerous to leave the car in front under an electric lamppost. After dinner, we could have a car minus four tires. There are lots of thieves and gangsters in this area. The cowboys are getting smarter every day."

It was early, but the restaurant was nearly deserted. A girl in a pony tail and blue jeans greeted An. "Hey, Colonel, we haven't seen you for weeks. What happened? Don't tell me you've been busy?"

"No, just lazy, that's all."

"I don't believe you," she laughed.

"Is your grandmother in?" An asked.

"Sure, she's in, and she's waiting to cook you the best Hue dinner you've ever had." She ran into the kitchen shouting, "Grandma, Colonel An is here with another customer."

A woman in her seventies emerged from the kitchen, obviously pleased to see An.

"Why don't you come here anymore?" she scolded.

An took her hands in his. "Auntie, this is my brother who's just come back from America."

"I'm glad to meet you," she whispered. "Your brother is a good young man." She raised her voice. "Now tell me. Why does America refuse to bring Emperor Bao Dai back from France to restore peace in the country?"

"If you cook me a good dinner, I'll tell the American government to do just that," Minh joked.

"You promise?"

"Yes, Auntie, I promise."

"Then I'll prepare the very best. I even have a surprise for you."

She returned to the kitchen and brought out a tray of shrimp paste spread on the backs of empty crab shells, and thin rice cakes in banana leaves. At the sight of the green leaves and the rosy shrimp paste, Minh exclaimed like a child, "I simply can't believe it! It's not Tet, and you offer me such a delicacy!"

The old woman beamed at him. "This morning I went to the market and saw such big, fresh shrimps that I bought them just to treat myself and my granddaughter to a special dish. But now that you've promised to bring the Emperor back, I want you to have them, free. You are happy? Good! Eat now, and when Tet comes and peace is restored, we'll have even better food."

"I'm more than happy, Auntie," Minh said, "I'm very grateful. I'll call America tonight and ask them to bring the Emperor to you."

"You're a good man," she said, showing her few remaining teeth, black-lacquered, through her broad smile.

Minh had not tasted such good food for years. Without a doubt, he thought, Vietnamese cuisine is the most exquisite and delicate in the whole world. He felt stronger, more Vietnamese.

After dinner, An suggested green tea. Minh agreed. "You're right, An. After good *pho*, coffee is best, but after good shrimp, green tea is necessary."

The boiling hot tea made Minh perspire, but it cleansed his lungs. He was so inspired that he thought of writing a poem dedicated to this woman with her imperial dream.

As he left, Minh gave the young girl 5,000 Vietnamese piasters.

"It's too much," she protested.

"No, it's not enough," Minh answered, "but it's all I have now. Can I say goodbye to your grandmother?"

"I don't think so. She's praying to Buddha for the return of the Emperor. She would be very angry if we disturbed her." She took An's hand. "Promise me that you'll come back often with your brother. And bring the Emperor back so grandmother can die happy."

"I will," An said quietly.

III

Wood and Fire

Deep inside wood sleeps primal fire.
Set free, it kindles back to life.
If there's no fire locked up in wood,
Where does the tinder's spark come from?

Wood and Fire
Khuong Viet
959–1011
Translated by Huynh Sang Thong

There were only six passengers aboard the nonstop Air Vietnam Flight to Hue. The plane was an old, converted military DC3 with a special VIP cabin in front and fifty coach seats for ordinary passengers. Minh and An, traveling by special military passes, were put in the VIP cabin. With them was a middle-aged American with curly gray hair. In the rear were three Vietnamese.

The American took a seat opposite them and introduced himself. "My name is James Roger Morgan, but call me Jim. I assume you're going to Hue?"

"I hope so," Minh said. "My name's Tran Van Minh and this is my brother, Lieutenant Colonel Tran Van An."

"It seems that half of the population of Vietnam is made up of members of the Tran Van clan," Morgan commented.

"Not quite half, but many. We divide the country with the Nguyen Vans, who are in power now. The President and one-third of his cabinet are Nguyen."

"That's for sure," Morgan added. They all laughed. "May I ask what you'll be doing in Hue?"

"I just returned from the States to see my father and hopefully find a teaching job at the University. My brother's come along to make sure the plane's not hijacked to Hanoi with me as hostage. That's a joke," he added quickly, seeing Morgan's serious expression.

"I'm pleased to know you're going to join Hue University. It's a great institution in a city with a strong tradition of learning."

"Thank you, but I haven't been appointed yet."

"What's your field?"

"International politics," Minh answered. "What are you doing in Hue?"

"I'm on leave from the anthropology department at Yale. I received a grant to do research on the effects of American technology on traditional Vietnamese culture. Basically, what I hope to accomplish during my two years in Hue is to learn more about the culture and get to know the elite, the old families like the Tran Vans. How old is your family?"

"According to our family records, we came from Hanoi originally. Then, it was called *Thang Long*, which means 'Ascending Dragon.' At that time, about 1600, Vietnam was temporarily divided into two seignories at about the seventeenth parallel, just as it is now. And you, Dr. Morgan, what part of the States are you from?"

"I was born in New Jersey, grew up in Massachusetts, and went to Amherst College. I was in the Marines during the Korean conflict and then I got my Ph.D. in anthropology from Yale. I've taught there since 1960. Nothing as interesting as your family history."

"Are you married, Dr. Morgan?"

"Please call me Jim. Yes, I am. My wife teaches literature at a small community college not far from New Haven. She's from New Jersey, too. Actually, I married the 'girl next door.' I'd like my wife and relatives to visit me here—learn about a country where Americans are dying for the cause of freedom, but the government thinks it's not safe. Of course, that's ridiculous. It's safer here than New York or Washington. I hope the rules are relaxed soon."

Minh was tempted to ask Morgan for his wife's maiden name. He seemed to remember Jennifer mentioning that her older sister was married to a Yale professor, and she too came from New Jersey. But it would be too coincidental, he thought.

Instead, he asked, "What arrangements have been made for you in Hue?"

"Well, as I understand it from our Embassy in Saigon, I'll be attached to the anthropology department at the university, but I won't be teaching. I'll just be researching and learning the language, and perhaps music too."

"I'm sure you'll enjoy my hometown."

"No doubt about it, and I'm looking forward to 'eating Tet' as the Vietnamese say. I understand from my reading that Tet is the most important lunar holiday of the year, a time of joy and celebration. When will it take place this year?"

"January 30, 1968."

"What new year will it be?"

"The Year of the Monkey."

"Is the Year of the Monkey a good one for the nation?"

"I think so. As a matter of history, in the Year of the Monkey, 1789, Emperor Quang Trung, in 'his cotton garb and with his red flag,' as it's described in the records, marched his troops and his elephants from the south to the north during Tet, and in a surprise offensive liberated Hanoi from occupation by the Chinese Ming forces."

"It's interesting that he used the red flag," Morgan remarked.

"That was long before the Bolshevik revolution. I guess the red was more visible. At any rate, he was the first Vietnamese leader to come from the peasant class. Too bad he didn't live longer. If he had, he would probably have installed Vietnam as the first socialist state in the world. But he remains our great hero. The main boulevard in Saigon bears his real name, Boulevard Nguyen Hue. Quang Trung was the name of his short reign."

"Did any of your ancestors serve under him?"

"Two of them were commanders of what were called the left and center columns of his army. They weren't peasants, though, just dropouts from the imperial examinations."

The FASTEN YOUR SEATBELTS sign flashed on. Morgan returned to his seat. "I'll talk to you both again soon. Thanks for the interesting conversation."

"Do you think he's Xia?" An asked when they were alone.

Minh was amused by An's use of the slightly vulgar "Xia" to mean "C.I.A."

"Why do you ask?"

"Well, according to our files, practically all Americans who officially or apparently work as researchers turn out to be important C.I.A. agents. The most famous case was an anthropologist in the Delta."

"I don't know, An," Minh answered thoughtfully.

He looked out the window. The whole city of Hue was like a red sea with waves of green. It was the season of blooming *phuong* trees. A cascade of memories from his youth surged to mind. The *phuong* blossom signaled the coming of summer vacations with all their delights: visits with his parents to neighboring provinces, full-moon festivals on the River of Perfume, hot nights spent on sampans amid the melancholy songs of the graceful boatwomen.

"I thought we would land in Phu Bai," Minh said.

"Phu Bai is still used for commercial planes, but the U.S. Air Force has built a new, modern one on the outskirts of town for military use only."

"But this isn't a military plane."

"Yes, but to assure your safety, General Vu Binh asked the U.S. command's permission for your plane to land on the military field. During the last two weeks, Phu Bai has been mortared almost daily by the Viet Cong."

"For a moment," Minh confided, "I thought we *were* flying to Hanoi." They both laughed.

It was hot when they landed, and the airfield, with dozens of planes side by side, looked like any military installation in the U.S. No Vietnamese were to be seen, only U.S. military personnel. With the other passengers they walked to a small air-conditioned reception room. A youthful, blonde, bespectacled American came forward to greet Morgan.

"I'm Anthony Buckley, United States vice-consul in Hue. Welcome to this beautiful city," he said. He looked curiously at Minh and An.

"This is Dr. Tran Van Minh," Morgan said, "and Lieutenant Colonel Tran Van An. Dr. Minh is just back from the States."

"I've heard a great deal about you," Buckley responded. "I'm glad to meet you and hope we'll meet often in the future. In a friendly city such as Hue, I'm sure of it."

"I hope so," Minh said politely. He didn't know exactly why, but he disliked Buckley instantly. There's something phony about the man, he thought. He and An excused themselves politely and walked out onto the burning asphalt road to a waiting military limousine for the drive to the city.

"Did you know any of the Vietnamese on the plane?" Minh asked.

"The two men are actually military officers in plain clothes, attached to the special counterespionage unit. They're going to Hue to investigate an important case involving the Buddhists."

"Another special unit!" Minh exclaimed. "That reminds me—did Long Van call after he reported to the special police yesterday?"

"No, he didn't. I checked with them this morning. They say they've never heard of him." He lowered his voice. "Brother Minh, I'm afraid he's become what the police call a 'lost file.'"

"You mean he's been killed?"

"I don't know for sure, but he has certainly disappeared. His file is lost, forever."

.　　　　.　　　　.

Hue was still deep in its siesta torpor. The heavy umbrella of heat and silence that lay over the city was pierced at regular intervals by the strident song of the cicadas.

They passed the Trang Tien Bridge and entered the Citadel that walled off half the city, six square miles. Once the residence of kings and their mandarins, the Citadel had been partially destroyed during February and March of 1947 when the Viet Minh, rich in will and courage but equipped only with rudimentary weapons, resisted the French reconquest of the central part of Vietnam. The Citadel's ponds and moats were choked now with fully blooming lotus. The lotus, Minh's father used to tell him, is a symbol of purity. It grows from mud, yet smells sweet. From the lotus he drew parallels about life—that even in the most difficult situations a good person must not succumb to immorality. Minh found he was growing nervous as his meeting with his father approached.

The car turned into Quoc Tu Giam Avenue. The tall, shady *Mu U* trees that lined the street bore fruits known for their hard rind. In 1885, during the French invasion, the people of the imperial capital collected these fruits and spread them on the roads where the enemy was expected to pass. They hoped the French soldiers, wearing nailed boots, would slip on them and become easy prey for the hidden guerillas. The strategem proved useless, but the rows of *Mu U* trees remained a symbol of the desperate struggle against the European "barbarians."

The limousine parked in front of Number 9 Quoc Tu Giam Avenue. This was the family's city residence, an elegant-looking structure partially hidden by a concrete screen decorated with a phoenix mosaic of bits of colored, broken porcelain.

"Who lives here?" Minh asked in surprise. "Not Father!"

"Yes," An answered. "Father lives here now." There was a note of sadness in his voice.

"I thought he was living in Phong Xuan Village."

"Not now. It's not safe there. We invited Father to stay here with my mother and brother. Still, we know that even Hue's relative security doesn't extend beyond a ten-kilometer radius." He paused. "You may not know that my brother, Phong, is stationed with the first regiment of the first ARVN division headquarters. He's a captain. Here he comes now."

Captain Tran Van Phong, a young man in khaki uniform, rushed to the car and opened the door.

"Phong," Minh cried getting out the car, "you've grown so tall and I must say, handsome, too. You were still in college the last time I saw you in 1960."

"I hadn't finished college when I was drafted and sent to Dalat Military Academy. I'm happy to see you back home. Father has been waiting impatiently since yesterday. He was awake practically all of last night asking what time you were arriving."

The first thing Minh noticed was that his father had aged considerably in seven years. His salt and pepper beard and white hair contrasted sharply with his smooth face. But his eyes were unchanged—bright and inquisitive. He sat under a canopy on the right side of the living room, his arm resting on a cylindrical cushion of red brocade. He reached for his glasses with shaking hands.

Minh bowed his head. "Father, I'm home, and glad to see you in good health and spirits."

"I've been waiting many Tets for your return. Are you tired by the long voyage? Have you eaten? You've certainly gained weight, but that's good. It's the right age to become plump." His words came slowly.

"I don't feel tired. I had lunch on the plane." Minh stepped closer. "Father," he said formally, "I beg you to forgive me for staying away from home so many Tets. This time, I promise I'm home for good. I'll stay here, work, and serve you until my old age."

"Well, I'm not sure," Father said quietly. "I'll have to make another study of your horoscope during the coming Tet to find out if your promise is in accord with the will of Heaven." He turned to Phong. "Son, make some tea for me and your brothers. It's in the brown jar on top of the cupboard."

"Yes, Father," Phong answered quickly and left for the kitchen.

"Your uncle," he continued, "recently visited Hong Kong and brought back some excellent O Long tea. Your mother would love it if she were still with us." His eyes were half closed; opening them, he asked abruptly, "Did you know your uncle is Rector of the university?"

"Yes, I heard about it in Saigon." Minh deliberately avoided saying that the President had told him. He knew his father despised the generals who were ruling the country.

Father turned to An. "How long will you be staying with us this time?"

"I have to leave in a few minutes to catch a return flight to Saigon. I got special permission to accompany Minh, but I have to go back because I have so many things to do."

"Too bad. You won't be able to see your mother. She's not home now." He stroked his beard. "Your mother and I are very concerned about you and Phong, not only because you're soldiers in wartime, but because soldiers these days aren't respected by the people." He paused significantly. "We trust you won't do anything to harm the good name of our family."

"Yes, I shall always adhere to your advice. I'm sorry, but I must go now," An said, his eyes fixed on his watch. He stood up, bowed, and said goodbye. Minh followed him to the front gate.

"An, Father has aged so much," Minh remarked.

"Yes. But today he looks happier and younger than I've seen him in a long time."

"I'm glad to hear that. Well, take good care of yourself. Thanks for everything. I'll keep in touch as much as possible. Remember me to General Vu Binh and tell him that I want to eat Tet with him this year."

When Minh returned to the living room, Phong was ready with the tea.

"Where's Auntie?" Minh asked. His father had had two wives: Minh's mother, now dead, and An and Phong's mother. In traditional Vietnamese families, children of the first wife call their father's second wife "auntie," while children of the second call his first wife "mother."

"She went to the Dong Ba market. We'll have a special dinner for your return. She's looking for some spices because she wants to cook shrimp, with fish sauce, one of your favorite dishes."

"That's very thoughtful of her, but she shouldn't have left the house at this time of day. It's still too hot."

In the silence that ensued, Minh reflected how lucky he had been as a boy to have had such love and attention lavished on him not only by his mother when she was alive, but by his father's second wife as well. After his birth, his mother had to undergo an operation that left her permanently infertile. She had insisted that his father take another wife and it was she who had made the selection.

Phong poured the tea into three small white and blue porcelain cups.

"This tea is good," Minh said. "Its flavor reminds me of Tet. It would be even better blended with lotus stamens."

"Yes. I was thinking that myself," Father responded. "I would have kept it for Tet, but your uncle tells me it's not good to blend it with lotus stamens as we used to do before the war. He said the water in the moats and ponds has become so polluted with poisonous chemicals it's dangerous to use them." His eyes flashed with anger. "The Americans have mined the rivers, lakes, and ponds, and put chemicals in the moats. They believe the Viet Cong will hide underwater. Too bad, too bad." He reached for his water pipe. "Son, perhaps it's better for you to rest now. I want to lie down for a while myself. After we've rested, we'll talk. Phong, take your brother to his room on the east side. Minh, I'll see you in an hour or so."

Although the house had belonged to his family for at least fifty years, it had never really been home for Minh. He had come here only for brief visits. As a youth he had lived with his parents on an ancestral farm in the

Phong Xuan Village founded by his clan when it moved from the North to Hue three hundred years ago.

The house had been renovated recently and a new wing added to the east side. His was a large rectangular room divided by a bamboo screen into two similar areas, one serving as a study and the other as a bedroom. The room opened into a garden of jack, orange, custard apple, and banana trees. The warm wind blew a few petals from a blooming flame tree past the opening, a red signal in a sea of green.

On a round, shiny wooden table at the left corner of the study was a large blue vase holding dozens of blooming white lotus, flooding the room with an enticing perfume. Above it, on the wall, hung a portrait of his mother that Minh remembered immediately. It was a painting by the celebrated artist Mai Sa, a friend of the family and one of the first graduates of the Hanoi School of Arts.

Minh stared at her, admiring the fine features of his mother's face. When she died in 1941, at the age of 35, she was known all over the land as an exceptionally beautiful woman and one of the nation's most talented artists. She was a poet and a ballerina with the Royal Ballet during the troubled and declining years of the Vietnamese monarchy. A patriot as well, she refused to dance on any occasion when French officials were invited to court. "We must never reward the invaders with our souls," she had responded once when the King insisted that she perform during a welcome ceremony for the newly appointed French governor-general.

She married in 1926 when she was 20, and Minh was born the following year. In that same year his father accepted the rectorship of the Royal College. In 1919, at the age of 27, his father had graduated as a Doctor of State, first in his class. But his were the last imperial examinations. The French abolished them after his graduation, after 944 years. From that time on Minh's father refused all positions offered by the court and rejected any form of direct cooperation with the French. He accepted the rectorship of the Royal College because he thought education could be a means to uplift the spirit of independence of the people, a spirit especially needed among the children of aristocratic families. But in 1930 he resigned to protest both the French execution of the leaders of the Vietnam Nationalist Party and the Vietnamese court's inability to save the patriots.

He returned to Phong Xuan Village to live as a 'scholar in residence' among the peasants. Minh's mother continued to direct the Royal Ballet in Hue, where she went twice a week.

In another corner of the room hung a framed paper panel bearing a quote from Mencius, a third-century B.C. Chinese philosopher. He recognized his father's "pine style" calligraphy:

To dwell in the broad house which is the world,

Wood and Fire

> *To stand upright, to travel the main highway,*
> *To be uncorrupted by riches and honors,*
> *To remain firm when poor and in low estate,*
> *To be unflinching even when threatened with force,*
> *This is to be a mighty man.*

The quotation was followed by another by Wang-Yang-Ming, a fifteenth-century Chinese neo-Confucian. It was written in the difficult "bamboo and wind" style:

> *Knowledge is the beginning of action.*
> *Action is the completion of knowledge.*

His father had great skill as a calligrapher. Minh remembered that during his childhood, exactly one week before each Tet, on the 23rd day of the last month of the old year—the day *Tao Quan*, the God of the Kitchen, goes to heaven to report on the affairs of earth to the Emperor of Jade— people from all walks of life would wait in front of their houses in Phong Xuan Village to ask of his father a few characters welcoming the new year and spring. On important festivities, especially Tet, Vietnamese homes, rich and poor, are decorated with two lines of poetry or prose written on red cloth or rice paper. When he was only six Minh was initiated into the complicated art of calligraphy. He remembered the pride he had felt when his father entrusted him with the tasks of preparing the ink and cleaning the brush.

Minh lay down on the hard wooden bed, contemplating his mother's picture. Her smiling eyes, full lips, and long delicate fingers seemed to welcome him back and elicit from him a promise that he would not leave again. He lay quietly for a long time; then he heard a woman's voice from the living room. His "auntie" was back.

Minh went out to greet her. "Auntie, how's your health? You look very well."

"Thanks to heaven and Buddha, I'm well; and you, you look healthy too."

For a woman in her late fifties, she was surprisingly youthful, with a rosy complexion and jet black hair. Dressed in a dark-brown *ao dai*, she had a quiet dignity and serene confidence. She was helping his father find his wooden slippers to wear into the front garden for the daily care of his collection of orchids. Minh followed her to the kitchen.

"You can't imagine my happiness when your father told me that you'd be back to live with us," she said. "In the last four years his health hasn't been good at all. He worries about the war constantly, and about you, An, and Phong. I've tried my best to take care of him. Now that you're home, I'm sure he'll feel better. He misses Phong Xuan Village so much, though.

He's distressed at not being able to visit your mother's tomb as often as he wishes."

"Auntie, I'm very grateful for all you've done for my father, for all of us."

"You don't need to say that. Since your mother's death, I've felt it my duty to preserve her influence and authority in the family, although I know I'm lacking her talents and intellectual capacities. No one could really replace her for your father or you, but I try."

She took six *ca ong huong*, another Hue speciality, from her shopping bag. Minh exclaimed, "I haven't seen these fish for years!"

"I went to the An Cu market to buy some shrimp, but I couldn't find any, so I bought these instead. So much the better because I know your mother liked them very much. I'm going to prepare them myself because our new cook can't handle such a difficult job yet. Why don't you go and keep your father company? When dinner's ready, I'll invite you both to come in and make an offering to your mother. She will be pleased in the Golden Springs to know that you're back, and equally pleased to share the *ong huong* with us."

"Yes, Auntie."

The sunset reflected off a small pond in the middle of the garden. Several goldfish were swimming in the clear water. A talking blackbird greeted Minh from a gold and red cage. Father was molding the branches of a bunch of orchids hung on a trellis above the pond.

"Father, you must be tired by now. Let me help you," Minh said.

"I'm not tired yet, and I'm not sure you could be of much help."

Minh was a little offended. His father, noticing it, hurried to finish. "There's nothing difficult about it. It simply takes a great deal of patience and experience. Besides, orchids demand loyalty and are often jealous, like human beings.

"This kind of orchid is particularly sensitive. It's called Moonlight. A peasant I helped financially during a flood two years ago brought it to me last month as a gift. He wants me to keep it a secret. His son joined the Viet Cong and after his training in the North, he came back to the South via the Ho Chi Minh Trail. On the way back, he picked up this rare orchid which grows in the deep jungles of the Truong Son Mountain range. I knew of its existence, but I'd never seen one before. Its color supposedly changes from purple to gold in the moonlight. It's supposed to bloom from the full moon of the twelfth month, throughout Tet, until the end of the first month. I've taken special care of this orchid. It will be another seven months before it blooms. Hand me those scissors on the chair, please. I have to trim the dying roots every day so the new ones will grow stronger."

After awhile, Auntie brought out a basin of water so his father could wash his hands.

"You are both invited in for the offering to Madame Elder."

Nearly an hour of exercise had brought new vitality to Minh's father. His cheeks were flushed as he walked into the house quickly. Minh offered to help him climb the few steps from the garden to the living room, but he declined. "I feel strong now, but if you stay around long enough, one of these days I'll need your strong arms." He glanced at Minh affectionately.

As in all Vietnamese homes, the Ancestors' Altar occupied the central place, hidden from the living room by a silk curtain embroidered with figures of dragons and phoenixes. The beautifully prepared dinner lay spread about the altar. Brass candleholders in the shape of cranes on turtles' backs were set on the altar on opposite sides of a porcelain incense burner. Behind a vase of lotus flowers, in an inlaid pearl frame, was a photograph of Minh's mother. The flowers hid her face so that only her shining, smiling eyes were visible.

Minh's father lit the candles and a piece of sandalwood gave off an intense, religiously sweet smell. Minh took up half a dozen joss sticks, lit them, and, holding them in his hands, bowed his head. Placing the sticks in the incense burner, he prostrated himself four times. As he glanced up, he caught sight of his father behind the curtain. His hair shone whiter in the candlelight.

Sitting on a square carpet in front of the altar, overwhelmed by the emotions this familiar ritual called up in him, Minh prayed silently: "Mother, I'm home now, and I promise never to go away again. I'll stay with you, with father, with your spirit, with my country; and until I join you in the Golden Springs, I shall eat every Tet in Hue. Please help me to do my duty as your son, as a Vietnamese." Tears rolled down his cheeks.

Minh's father moved in front of the altar; the joss sticks were not yet half burned. He recited a short, whispered prayer and snuffed the candles with a small silver stick. Auntie and a male servant removed the food from the altar and placed it in the dining room.

The meal over, Father took Minh aside. "Son, let's go to my study."

"Yes, Father." He followed him into a small studio, the walls of which were lined with books written in Chinese. His father offered Minh a small armchair and settled himself into a larger one. He sat, motionless, looking out into the back garden, saying nothing. Stroking his beard, he glanced at the ceiling and then at a gold and red panel with four large black Chinese characters on it that read: "Just Cause, Nation's Gratitude." His father's calculated, slow gestures signaled to Minh that the conversation would be a serious one. He realized, not without some surprise, that at the age of forty, after many years of living in Western countries, he still felt deeply awed by, even fearful of his father. He waited for him to speak in much the same way a school child might wait for the instructions of his teacher. As a matter of fact, Vietnamese children often called their father "teacher." Minh felt like a novice waiting for ordination by a Zen master.

"Son," Father began slowly, his voice grave. "I've waited a long time for an opportunity to tell you my closely held feelings." He paused, shifting as if to make himself more comfortable. "Since 1963, when you resigned from the diplomatic service to protest the Buddhist repressions by the Ngo Dinh Diem government—an act I was very proud of—I've been longing for you to return home. Of course, I knew that you might be imprisoned or suffer even harsher punishment from the government if you returned, but our public morality, duty, and the just cause demand that a decent person accept every sacrifice." All the anger and frustration he'd been storing for years surfaced in his voice, like an angry whip lashing out at his son.

"First I was disappointed and then angry that you preferred to stay on in a country whose soldiers were raping our women and corrupting our youth, whose planes and ships—whose defoliants—were and are destroying the land of our ancestors, polluting our rivers and depleting our mountains. You chose to live on in a country that supports the worst, most decadent Vietnamese traitors, the Catholics, who are determined to destroy the Buddhist religion. Remember, it's the American wood that sets the Vietnamese house on fire."

Minh was frightened by the flash of anger he saw in his father's eyes. He wanted to tell him that he hadn't supported the American government that committed these horrible acts but had allied himself with the good American people who opposed them. But the argument, which had once seemed so logical, now seemed like sophistry and wasn't convincing even to him. His father might even guess that the whole argument was simply an excuse to cover up his attachment to Jennifer. He hadn't thought of her once since coming to Hue; and now she came so suddenly to his mind that he resented his own thoughts—resented her—as an intrusion in his life. Confused, guilty, unable to speak, he sat nodding vigorously at his father's every word.

His father asked him to bring the brass spittoon closer, spat in it, and continued. "I was told that you were active in the movement to oppose the war, but I fail to understand how you could stop the war by working with the people who are making it. How can you stop planes and guns with speeches and writings? I fully realize that speeches and writings can be very powerful weapons, but they're useless with people who don't understand your thoughts and who lack a humanistic culture, who don't appreciate Buddhist wisdom. The very fact that they allowed you to speak and write against their policies shows that your activities were not effective anyway. When I see and read about what is going on in our land, a land our ancestors have spent four thousand years of sweat, blood, and labor in building and defending from the Chinese and Mongol invaders, my only regret is that I'm no longer young and strong enough to take arms and fight, the way your grandfather did when he joined the scholars movement against the French in 1882."

He glanced back at the gold and red panel. His voice was trembling now. "As you know, your grandfather was executed by the French that year, when I was only ten years old." His voice shook with rage. "And now look! What have I done to merit this punishment from heaven? You, my son, living in America, the land of the enemy! Oh Heaven!" He took his head into his bony hands. "It is said that parents give birth to children, but that heaven gives them personality and character—still ... And in all those years you never returned to see me, not even when you were in Saigon five years ago!"

He stopped, and taking up his water pipe, inhaled deeply. When he spoke again, his voice was calmer.

"I unburdened myself now, not only because you are my son, but more because you are your mother's son. It was a great mistake on my part not to tell you the truth about her death in 1941, long after the Tet in the Year of the Snake."

Minh felt a chill of apprehension. "Didn't she die because of a heart attack as you wrote when I was away in Saigon?"

"No. At that time I didn't want you to know the truth because I thought, mistakenly, I now realize, that it would upset you too much. No, Minh, your mother died from a French bullet." Tears rolled down his father's cheeks. Minh took his hand. Shocked and shaken, he felt his own eyes fill.

"After she ate Tet," he continued, "she left for the Chinese border with three men and a woman. They were going to contact the underground Viet Minh party. I begged her to allow me to go, but she convinced me that I must stay home and care for the family. I was suffering from severe asthma. Her group was ambushed by the French. She was wounded at the same time that two of the men and the woman were killed. The other man brought her back to Hue. It was a difficult journey and your mother died soon after she reached home. Before she passed away, she made me promise that I wouldn't reveal the circumstances of her death to anyone, not even your uncle. She said I should tell you the truth only after you had finished your studies—which you never seemed to do."

Minh wiped his face. He was sobbing openly, like a child.

"Father, you don't need to tell me any more. I understand everything. You won't have to be ashamed of me any longer. I shall be a good Vietnamese in whatever I do from now on. Please trust me and give me a chance. My mother's example will be with me always now."

"Son, you're now forty. Half your life is past, but you still have time to continue the tradition of our family, and our clan."

With an effort Minh stood up and helped his father walk out of the studio. He felt drained, but relieved, as a child does when a long-dreaded scolding has cleared the air. He had thought for months about this reunion with his father, but it had been an abstraction, a fantasy. The reality of an angry, disappointed, but forgiving father and the depth of his own feelings of guilt amazed him. And his father, too, he reflected, seemed to be more at peace now that, after so many years, he had finally confronted his son.

.　　　　.　　　　.

Minh and Phong dined the following night with their uncle, the Rector, his wife, and two daughters at their home near the Bach Ho-White Tiger-Bridge on the southern outskirts of the city. The family had lived in the house, which was known as one of the ten best in town, for only two years, but Minh had often seen it from the outside and was familiar with the location.

As schoolboys, he and his friends used to tell each other stories about "ghosts wandering over the White Tiger Bridge." He had heard from his father that according to the concepts and configurations of logic of the earth, or geomancy, Bach Ho represented bad influence and treacherous character. When Minh had asked why a tiger, known for strength and independence, was in this case bad, his father had answered, "Because it's white. White things are not auspicious things. Don't we use white for funeral dress and red for weddings?" Minh hadn't pursued the conversation further.

According to the most popular version of the story, there was once a very beautiful Vietnamese woman who was forced by her impoverished parents to marry an old and ugly, but wealthy, French businessman. She consented, but on the wedding night she tried to kill her husband. Failing in the attempt, she jumped from the Bach Ho Bridge. When fishermen found her body floating under the bridge one moonlit night, it was as transparent as a piece of jade. Since then, her jaded form appeared nightly on the bridge, laughing hysterically at passersby and insulting only the men, in perfect French.

"Does the ghost still appear on the Bach Ho Bridge?" Minh asked Phong as they crossed it.

"No more," Phong answered. "War has driven away ghosts and people alike. Except for a few houses like Uncle's the area is practically deserted, and now the community center of Bach Ho Village is occupied by an ARVN company. Two years ago when I was with that company, I passed the bridge often, but I never saw a ghost, even on moonlit nights."

Their car was stopped at a police control station, a small hut made of scrap-metal sheets salvaged from a downed helicopter. Phong showed his army identification card. The officer took a casual look and let the car pass.

"I'd be in trouble," Minh said, "if he had asked for my I.D. My passport was retained by the immigration authorities in Saigon and I've no other Vietnamese identification of any kind."

"When you have time, let me know and I'll go with you to police headquarters to register and get an I.D. for you. You're sure to be in trouble if you're checked and found without it. The new I.D. is supposed to be foolproof—it's made in the United States. For years, the Viet Cong have been able to produce fake ones and move about the city easily."

A soldier with his bayonet at the ready kept guard in front of the Rector's residence. He saluted Phong and removed the roll of barbed wire to let the jeep enter. The Rector was at the front door waiting for them.

"Welcome to the new dean of the school of social sciences of Hue University," he shouted.

His wife and daughters were standing behind him. They were all wearing western-style clothing, the mother in a long, yellow satin gown, the daughters in T-shirts and blue jeans. The girls looked like American teenagers. The Rector gently pushed them forward.

"Loan and Mai, say hello to your cousin, Doctor Professor Dean Tran Van Minh."

"Uncle," Phong interceded, "why do you address Minh as 'dean' when he doesn't even know if he has a job?"

"Come into the living room and I'll tell you."

The spacious living room, with its leather chairs and couch, was furnished like a suite in a Hilton hotel and dominated by a Picasso reproduction. Below the painting, on a pedestal, a large TV set reigned majestically. A uniformed servant entered with a tray of drinks. Minh, not seeing lemonade, asked for a Pepsi. Loan and Mai chose Bloody Marys.

"You see, Minh," the Rector's wife remarked, "coming from the States you prefer a nonalcoholic drink, while your girl cousins, raised in a traditional Vietnamese family, ask for Bloody Marys. Does that surprise you at all? Have you noticed how Vietnam has changed since you were last here?"

"I'm not surprised," Minh answered curtly, unable to keep a note of disdain from his voice.

"Uncle," Phong persisted, "what is this about Minh's deanship?"

"Yesterday morning the Minister of Education in Saigon called to say that the President wanted me to immediately prepare papers naming Minh dean of the school of social sciences. If he refuses—and I hope he won't," he smiled, looking at Minh, "he'll be appointed full professor of political science beginning next month, the day after tomorrow. I was very pleased to receive that order, but I didn't want to tell Minh yesterday in front of your father. I know how much he despises the government, even though the generals invited him to become the government's supreme advisor. The generals have always kept up a show of respect for his moral and intellectual prestige in the country."

The Rector leaned back in his chair and reached for a cigar. "I must confess," he went on, "I don't know what happened to alter your situation, Minh. I'm at a loss to understand it. Not long ago, you were persona non grata, the *bête noire* of the regime, an 'overseas Viet Cong.' Now you're the President's favorite, and from what the Minister of Education told me, highly regarded by the government. What happened? Did you make a secret deal?"

"No. No deal, no secret," Minh replied bluntly. "My guess is that the government's getting such bad reviews in the American press that it's under pressure from Washington to create a good image of liberalism and democracy by co-opting the opposition, especially those with American connections, like myself. But that's just a guess. Whatever the motive behind the government's sudden change of attitude, I've already made up my mind. I told the President when I saw him in Saigon that I want only to live in Hue and teach, in any capacity."

"If that's all you want, things will be very easy for me. I can sign a decree tomorrow appointing you as a full professor to the school of social sciences. It will have to be countersigned by the Minister of Education to be valid, but that's just a formality. Starting tomorrow, you will be a member of Hue University's faculty, and you can start work any day. Of course, you can take a few days to browse around and become familiar with the city."

"Thank you, Uncle."

"Cousin Minh, why didn't you stay in the U.S.?" Loan asked. "Life's much more pleasant and interesting there. Here everything is lousy. The TV programs on the government station are terrible. The U.S. Army channel is excellent, but it only comes on three times a week." She paused to light a Salem cigarette, then turned to her sister. "Did you know that tonight they're showing 'I Love Lucy?' We mustn't miss it. What time is it, Dad?"

"Almost seven."

"It's time, Mai. Let's go watch it in your room." Turning to Minh, she asked, "Will you excuse us?"

"Of course," Minh answered, almost relieved that his cousins were leaving. He still couldn't believe how un-Vietnamese they had become after only a decade of American influence in the country. The Rector sensed Minh's reaction.

"You see, we have another generation in Vietnam—the American Pepsi generation."

His wife laughed and added, "I don't know if the behavior of the new generation is good or bad, but there's little I can do about it. Your uncle's too permissive with the girls. His excuse is that we live in an uncertain time and we should let them enjoy life as much as they can. By the way," she said, turning to Minh, "now that you're home and have a good position, are you thinking of getting married? Your father would be happy to have grandchildren. And you, too, Phong. Why don't you get married? You shouldn't wait for your older brother An. From what I know, he'll never marry."

"Auntie," Phong answered, "I'll marry only when the war is over."

"I agree with him," Minh added. "Uncle, what's the situation at the university now?"

"You've probably heard that the university was closed early this year, at the end of March, because of student agitations. But we plan to reopen at the end of July instead of September. We'll probably have an enrollment of about three thousand."

"Do you think there'll be protests again?"

"I don't really know. It all depends on the Buddhist monks. They have a great deal of influence on the students. Also, there's a new law under which any student suspected of political agitation is drafted into the Army. It's supposed to deter them from antigovernment activities. We'll see."

"Are the students politically conscious in general?"

"Yes, all of them are. They're divided into several factions, although they're all antigovernment. And of course the Viet Cong infiltrations into the student body complicate everything."

"Why did you agree to be Rector? I'm sure you didn't accept the job for the money."

"You're right," the Rector answered happily. "You know, all my life, ever since I returned from working for the Eiffel Company in Paris, I had just one thing in mind: to make as much money as I could so I could retire early and enjoy life. And I did make a lot of money with my construction firm in Saigon. But I didn't like life in Saigon at all. There was too much confusion and pressure, too many soldiers and prostitutes. Besides, it was unsafe for my daughters.

"Then, last year, after the turmoil in Hue, the generals approached me and asked me to take this job. I hesitated, but they forced me, subtly of course, and I had no choice. They thought I'd be a good administrator and they knew that as the first Vietnamese to graduate number one from the Ecole Polytechnique, and with honors from law school, I enjoyed some respect among the intellectuals. They also knew that I come from Hue, from a well-known Buddhist family. Sometimes I wonder if your mother, if she were still alive, would have liked my taking this job ... but, here I am."

Minh was tempted to say that his mother wouldn't have wanted him to have anything to do with the government and the war, but he held his tongue.

"By the way," the Rector continued, "you should go and pay your respects to the Patriarch at the Thien Mu pagoda. It's your pagoda you know. Your mother entrusted you to the protection of Buddha there. Mine is the Tu Dam."

"Is it safe to go there?" the Rector's wife asked Phong.

"There's no place in the whole country absolutely safe," Phong answered, "but it seems to be Viet Cong policy, at least for the present, not to disturb the Buddhist pagodas. If Minh wants to go, I can go with him, but not this week. I have to fly to Da Nang for a military conference. Next week is good."

"I'll probably go there by myself tomorrow," Minh said. "Who's the Patriarch now?"

"Hoa Thuong Thich Dai Hai," the Rector answered. "He's a distant relative of ours. His father was a cousin to my mother, your maternal grandmother. He left home for the monastery when he was eight. He was very close to your mother. He's widely respected by everyone, and there-fore feared by the government. He's well informed—reads French, English, Chinese, Japanese and Sanskrit—all self-taught. He's still a very vigorous man. The best time to see him is about ten o'clock, after his morning meditation. Bring him some tea and be sure to tell him your Buddhist name. Do you remember it?"

"I think it's *Tam Linh*, Pure Heart, but I'm not sure."

"Then ask your father."

"I will."

The lavish dinner consisted of ten dishes, but none of them was prepared in typical Hue fashion. The cook, the Rector's wife said proudly, came from Saigon and had worked for the American ambassador. Minh tasted all the dishes so as not to offend his hosts, but he had little appetite. The contrast between the luxurious lifestyle of his uncle's family and the unhappy state of the country in wartime depressed him. He was shocked by the behavior of his teenaged cousins, who ate their TV dinners alone in their private room. The strident voice and loud laughter of Lucille Ball could be heard through the closed door, dominating the dull sounds of mortars and howitzers at work across the river. Once, a loud explosion rattled the dining room windows.

"Military operations at night?" Minh asked.

"Not quite," Phong answered. "The new U.S. command's strategy is to fire a lot of mortars and howitzers in the free fire zones around the city during the night to prevent the Viet Cong from infiltrating the city."

"We're used to the cacophony of war," commented the Rector's wife as she invited them to return to the living room for liqueurs and coffee.

.   .   .

The next day, Minh woke at six to prepare tea for his father—a habit he had acquired when he was very young. They talked about dinner at his uncle's.

"I've never been to his house," Father said, "but I'm told it's very large and beautiful. Your mother would frown on his way of life. He's very different from her. When he brought his family to visit recently, his daugh-ters' behavior was shocking. They have no manners. They spoke French to each other and their parents answered them in French."

"I'm planning to visit Thien Mu pagoda today, Father, to see the Patriarch. My Buddhist name is Pure Heart, isn't it?"

"That's right," Father answered, pleased. "Would you like me to tell you a little about the pagoda's history?"

"Of course."

"In 1558," he began, "a quarrel developed within the reigning Le family in Ascending Dragon, Hanoi's old name. Lord Nguyen Hoang was exiled and became governor of Thuan Hoa in the South. In 1601, wandering west of Hue, he noticed a hill emerging from the landscape in the form of a dragon turning its head to the center of the city. He was told by people living in the area that a mysterious lady dressed in a red gown visited the hill nightly and announced that a 'king will be born from this auspicious land.'"

Father paused and sipped his tea. "Lord Nguyen Hoang then decided to secede from the North," he went on. "He founded a dynasty, the Nguyen, and made Hue the capital. He ordered a pagoda to be built in honor of the mysterious lady. The pagoda, called *Thien Mu*, Heavenly Lady, or sometimes Holy Lady, has since become Hue's most celebrated landmark as well as its oldest religious center. The most prominent feature of the pagoda, the octagonal, seven-storied tower in front of it, was built much later, in 1855 by King Thieu Tri. The present Patriarch is a relative of your mother's—a remarkable man."

"Yes, Uncle reminded me of that."

"I'm glad he remembers his family, despite all his years of study in France and money-making in Saigon," Father observed sardonically. "How do you plan to go there?"

"Phong volunteered to drive me next week, but I prefer to go today. I'd like to see a little bit of the city, too."

"I don't think there's any danger in going there. The Viet Cong have never attacked religious centers. Perhaps you can use Phong's bicycle to save time. It's too long a distance to walk."

"I plan to do just that."

"You should take half of my O Long tea and offer it to the Patriarch. He's known for his taste for good tea. He even grows some in the little garden behind his pagoda. He's a learned man, and you'll benefit greatly from his knowledge and advice. But be sure to return before curfew time. If you're asked to stay overnight, try to contact Phong and let him know so that we don't have to worry about your safety."

"I won't stay overnight this time. Maybe next time."

IV

Words and Action

However many holy words you read
However many you speak
What good will they do you
If you do not act upon them

The Dhammapada
The Sayings of The Buddha

Minh was amazed at the crowds that thronged Hue as he set out on his bicycle the next morning for the pagoda. He knew the city's population had swelled from 50,000 to over 100,000 in a few short years, but he had continued to imagine the city as it lived in his memory.

Streams of bicycles surged out of the Citadel through the Thuong Tu Gate and towards Tran Hung Dao Boulevard, the city's main thoroughfare—young men in shirtsleeves; young women wearing silky trousers under long, split dresses, with their black hair hanging down their shoulders. Minh stopped at the foot of the Truong Tien Bridge. Beneath it, the River of Perfume sparkled deep blue under an already blazing sky. Hundreds of boats, sampans of all sizes, disgorged passengers from outlying villages, who carried with them all kinds of commodities for the Dong Ba Central

Market. On the pavement, lines of women in peasant pajamas balanced bamboo poles on their shoulders, from which were suspended baskets filled with fruits, ducklings, chickens, and vegetables. In the botanical garden on the right of the bridge, a huge government poster trumpeted anticommunist slogans, including the familiar warning of a future Viet Cong "bloodbath" that Minh had so often heard from conservatives in the United States. But the people seemed busy and happy. No one glanced at the poster.

Riding along the west bank of the river on the narrow road outside the city limits, he saw tanks fanning out into the bushes, searching for Viet Cong mines and booby-traps. A truckload of singing soldiers passed by and drowned him in a cloud of rosy dust. After an hour of hard, uphill pedaling, the bicycle rolled downhill smoothly. The air was pure, tranquil and serene. On the distant horizon, silhouettes of a squadron of jet planes reminded him that the northern part of Vietnam was receiving American bombs daily, but he heard no noise. The planes were probably flying back to their Pacific Ocean bases.

Turning left sharply, Minh saw before him the seven-storied tower of the Thien Mu pagoda. As he bicycled toward it he hummed two lines from a popular boat song:

> *The breeze gently balances the bamboo branches,*
> *The bells of Thien Mu toll,*
> *The roosters at Tho Xuong hamlet crow.*

He thought of his mother and tried, unsuccessfully, to remember details of his dedication to Buddha, when he was five. He would ask the Patriarch if the occasion permitted.

He entered the grounds, passing through several rows of blooming frangipani, then a garden full of banana, guava, breadfruit, and coconut-palm trees. A swarm of dragonflies hovered over a small, square lotus pond.

A young monk in a dark brown robe was walking toward him. He seemed to be a novice, Minh thought: he carried a basket of grapefruit and dragon eyes, a kind of litchi whose pupil-like dark seed and surrounding white flesh inspired its local name. Minh raised his hands above his forehead and greeted the novice in the Buddhist manner.

"*Nam Mo Phat*, pray to Buddha," the young monk murmured as Minh approached him.

"I would like to ask permission to pay my respects to the Patriarch," Minh whispered.

"You are welcome. Please proceed to the main building and a monk will help you."

The central room of the main building served as a reception center for the faithful who brought offerings or sought advice. There were already a dozen men and women sitting on the floor talking quietly together. Minh removed his shoes and sat down in a corner. His eyes traveled slowly over a poem mounted on a long piece of yellowed rice paper:

> *Nothing is born*
> *Nothing dies*
> *When one understands this*
> *Buddha appears*
> *The round of avatars end*

"I've never seen you here before." An elderly monk spoke to Minh. "Are you just visiting, or are you looking for someone in particular?"

"My wish, if it's not too presumptuous, is to have an audience with the Patriarch ... to pay him my respects."

"Very good. May I have your Buddhist name?"

"Pure Heart," Minh answered.

The monk left and returned shortly. "The pagoda is pleased to know that you still remember us. You were dedicated here, according to our records, on the fifteenth day of the first month of the Year of the Buffalo, thirty-five years ago. We know from the records that you come from an old, devout Buddhist family and that your late mother was a relative of the Patriarch."

Minh was impressed by the pagoda's accurate recordkeeping.

"Do you read Chinese characters?" the monk asked, then went on, before Minh could reply, "Of course you would, coming from such a scholarly family."

"Yes. I learned Chinese when I was very young, from my parents."

"Do you know the source of the sentences you've been reading?"

"I'm not sure I do. Please instruct me."

"They come from a Zen work written during the Tran dynasty, the Khoa Hu Luc Scriptures, which also state, 'So long as you have not reached Buddha's heart, practice abstinence and recite prayers. But when you reach it, you will see that neither Buddha nor the Bodhisattvas exist. Abstinence and prayers then become useless.' This was the principal teaching of the Bamboo Forest Sect founded by King Tran Nhan Tong of the Tran dynasty at the end of the thirteenth century after his victory over the Mongol invaders. Now, if you will wait here a moment, I'll see if the Patriarch is free. I'm sure he will be pleased to receive you if he is."

In about five minutes the monk reappeared and signaled for Minh to follow him.

"Come in and wait for the Patriarch in the anteroom of his private chamber. He'll see you very soon. You're fortunate. Only rarely does he receive guests in his private chamber."

The anteroom was very small and unfurnished. Through its unusual moon-shaped window he saw the bough of a flame tree moving in the breeze. A door opened and a tall monk, holding a fan, came out. Minh knew it was the Patriarch.

"Are you disciple Pure Heart?"

"Yes, Venerable, I am."

"Come in."

The Patriarch's chamber was a large, rectangular room without chairs or carpeting. In the left corner were a cushion and a small mattress that served as his bed. In the middle of the room was a square table with one thick book, an inkstand, and two brushes on it. The Patriarch sat behind the table. Hanging on the wall behind him was a long piece of yellow brocade on which a couple of verses were written in powerful, lean strokes:

> *Escorted by the wind, the sound of the horn slips through the bamboos.*
> *With the moon riding behind, the shadow of mountains climbs the*
> *   ramparts.*

"Son, I've been waiting for you to visit me for many years." The Patriarch lowered his eyes. "When I look at you, I remember your mother. She didn't live long enough to serve the Dharma and the nation, but that's not very important for true Buddhists. The important thing is to have a pure heart, and your Buddhist name is Pure Heart."

"Teacher, I'm honored to bear that name, but can you tell me more about it?"

"Pure Heart means Buddha Heart, which means intelligence, compassion, steady courage, and enlightenment. Yes, courage and determination are much needed today when the religion is in grave danger. Religion is in danger because the nation, itself, is in danger. Perhaps you know the story about King Tran Thanh Ton of the original Tran clan, from which your family descended. His reign lasted from 1225 to 1258. One day, he asked the Great Master of Truc Lam's opinion on his intention to retire to the mountains to seek Buddha's teaching. The Great Master advised, 'No Buddha is to be found in these mountains. Buddha is in your heart. When the heart is at peace and lucid, Buddha is there. Since you are king, the will of the kingdom must also be your will, the heart of the kingdom must be your heart. The whole kingdom is waiting for you to return. How can you refuse?'"

Minh listened attentively to the Patriarch's every word. A few rays of sunlight passed through the window and shone on his clean-shaven head. An aureole seemed to surround his body, like those Minh had seen in paintings of Christian saints.

"How long have you been back home?" the Patriarch inquired. "Where do you live? What are you doing now?"

"I returned to Hue only two days ago. I'm living with my father, aunt, and brother, and I'm going to teach at Hue University when it opens—soon, I hope."

"Very good."

The mention of his father reminded Minh of the offering of tea.

"Teacher, my father would like to offer you some tea." Minh set the tin can, wrapped in red paper, on the table.

"Tell your father that I think of him often. How is he?" But before Minh could answer, he continued, "Your father's a very good man. Since your mother died, he's been sad and unhappy. He visited me a few months ago and spent the night at the pagoda. I noticed then that his health wasn't very good. He's too attached, too deeply frustrated and unhappy. That's why courage is an important Buddhist quality—the courage to be detached from honors, from wealth, from memories of fleeting moments of bliss. The courage to serve the religion and the nation."

"Teacher," Minh asked, his interest caught, "if Buddhism is a religion of detachment, how can Buddhists serve the nation?"

"A Buddhist shouldn't remain attached to suffering as if it were a religion, but he should remain with the people, and the people make the nation. If there are no people, and no need to bring an end to suffering, there's no need for any religion, for Buddhism. Buddhism is concerned with human suffering. Buddha, himself, after his enlightenment, resolved to renounce Nirvana, to remain in the circle of existence and continuity in order to serve others. That's why Buddha and the *bhikkus*, his disciples, wandered from village to village throughout the year—except during the three or four months of rains—preaching to the people ideas conducive to their wellbeing here and in the hereafter." He paused for a moment.

"Not long ago, a young man came to this pagoda in the middle of the night and asked for a place to rest. The monk in charge of the hospitality service sought my opinion. I told him that the doors of the pagoda as well as the heart of Buddha are open to everyone. The young man came to pay respects to me. He looked very intelligent, but his complexion told me that he came from a poor peasant family. When I asked him what he'd been doing, he told me, without hesitation, that he was a cadre for the provincial committee of the National Liberation Front. When I asked him what he was doing as a cadre of the front, he answered, 'Except during the very heavy rainy months, I travel from village to village telling the people about the causes of their sufferings and explaining to them the ways to end their misery.' I told him that what he was doing was no different from what Buddha and his disciples have been doing for over twenty-five hundred years. He was pleased to hear that and told me that his uncle had been a monk but died when his pagoda was bombed by the Americans. I gave him a blanket that had been given to me by a rich merchant from Saigon. He accepted it, and when he left, he said, 'The blanket will keep me warm so I can travel even during the rainy months.'

"The next day, the police came to look for what they called a 'Viet Cong infiltrator.' I told him that for me and the pagoda, there's no difference between a Viet Cong and a Vietnamese. The pagoda, like the heart of

Buddha, is a refuge for all, including police officers should they need it." He stopped, then ended in a whisper: *"Nam Mo Phat."*

There was a pause. Then, getting to his feet, the Patriarch asked, "Son, would you like to walk in the garden with me?"

"Yes, Teacher."

Minh followed him onto a path that led to a cottage alongside the River of Perfume. In the cottage, there stood one bamboo bed.

"I often come here during the hot season to rest and compose poems while looking at the river. In the main pagoda, even in my private chamber, I'm often disturbed."

"I apologize for also having disturbed you," Minh said.

"Not in your case. I was waiting for you. You're one among few whom I would invite to spend a moment with me in this humble cottage."

Outside, the water was so clear and limpid that Minh could see fish of all sizes swimming, some fast, some slow; at the bottom of the river an eel lay sleeping.

"Son, in that underwater world the big fish swallow the small, while small ones eat up millions of miniscule living things our eyes can't see. It's often said that the world of human beings, at the moment, isn't very different. When the sun sets and the water is opaque, you can't see the fish, but the cycle of destruction continues and continues. Now you can see the bottom of the river. You can see the fish, big and small, because of millions of rays of sunlight. They dispel illusions and reveal their realities as they are. With pure heart, with Buddha Heart, one can see. With eyes, one cannot always see."

A gunshot cracked through the stillness. Minh looked at the other bank of the river. A group of five or six soldiers, their helmets glinting sunlight, were installing a machine gun, the muzzle of which pointed threateningly in the direction of the cottage. One soldier waved to Minh while another pursued a rabbit. A second burst and the rabbit was dead, its red blood spattered over its white body.

"Nam Mo Phat," the Patriarch murmured. "Son, come inside. If you like, stay and have some lunch with us."

The palpitating noise of a helicopter approached steadily. They walked silently, returning along another path through a small forest of pine trees. The narrow track led to the dining hall. Twenty monks sat on long wooden benches, facing one another across two tables. At the far end, a small table with one chair was reserved for the Patriarch.

The food was simple: rice, pounded sesame mixed with salt, vegetables, and bean curd. Though they ate slowly and silently, the lunch was over in less than half an hour. It would be the monks' last meal until a breakfast of rice porridge the next morning.

The Patriarch signaled a monk. "Give some fruit to the professor."

He turned to Minh, "Follow this monk, who will give you a gift from the pagoda for your father. Tell him to come and visit me from time to time."

"Yes, Teacher."

Minh walked behind the monk, turning his head to follow the figure of the Patriarch now disappearing behind the frangipani.

.   .   .

The sun was at its zenith; it was too hot to return to the city, Minh thought. He sat down under a banyan tree. He wanted to remember every word the Patriarch had spoken to him, to understand the meaning of courage, of religion, of nation. He wanted to sort out the overwhelming impressions of the past days.

As a Buddhist, Minh knew well the cardinal teaching of the Master: "Accept my words only after you have examined them for yourself; do not accept them because of the reverence you have shown me . . . you yourself must make the effort. Buddha only points the way, and the Buddha's teachings are only a raft on which to cross the stream. Once the stream is crossed, you can even forget the raft, or leave it for another's use."

Alone now, under the same kind of tree that had witnessed Buddha's enlightenment more than 2500 years earlier, Minh wondered how he would cross the stream, what effort he should make, what he should do. Perhaps the central direction for his life lay in his Buddhist name. Yes, he thought, he must focus on the present, not anticipate the future or regret the past. He must marshall his courage to take the next step. But what was the next step? He hadn't even made the first step; he lacked the courage to take any step at all! And how could he be sure of his present situation until he found the courage to take that step? He thought of his mother's heroic death. Her act, he knew, had required more than courage: it required sacrifice. For him, no sacrifice was required, only the courage to be himself, to act in accordance with his religion, his nation.

He followed the meandering of the River of Perfume as it flowed effortlessly under an immaculate blue sky, disappearing into distant groves to reappear in a cacophony of rocks. He thought of another river, the Ben Hai, which since 1954 had divided Vietnam into two zones, each one claiming to represent the whole of Vietnam, the unity of 4000 years of culture and civilization. A mosquito landed on his ear. He didn't bother to swat it. Everything seemed to come to a standstill. Even the distant song of the cicadas had stopped. He leaned against the banyan tree and closed his eyes.

When he awoke, it was three o'clock. He had slept for almost two hours. The sleep of an untroubled Pure Heart, he thought, and smiled to himself.

As his bicycle rolled effortlessly down the path from the tower to the main road, he murmured two lines of a poem that seemed to him to describe the state of his mind:

The wind carries the prayers through the pine trees,
dispelling the impurities of the dusty world.
The butterfly's soul, the fairy's dream, drive away the affairs of this
   earthly life.

The wind blew through his hair. He half-closed his eyes and let the bicycle roll. By the time he saw the barricade, it was too late to stop. As he was thrown against it, two soldiers jumped on him, one pressing his bayonet against Minh's chest. They searched him and took his watch and the bag of custard apple and grapefruit, the Patriarch's gift to his father.

"Stand up! Raise your hands and follow us!" one of the soldiers shouted.

One of them rode Minh's bicycle while the other walked behind him, eating the round custard apple voraciously. For a moment, Minh thought he had been kidnapped by gangsters dressed as soldiers, but when they reached the top of a small hill he saw below a small military bivouac: two tents under the trees surrounded by antennas. In front of one of the tents stood a lieutenant, his uniform sporting two gold plum flowers on each shoulder. At the sight of the soldiers, the young Vietnamese officer cried out, "Soldiers, have you arrested a Viet Cong sapper? Bring him here so I can have a good look at him."

"Yes, sir. We don't know who he is, he hasn't any papers."

The lieutenant pulled out his revolver, pointed it at Minh's head and said, "Who are you, where do you come from, how many times have you mined this road and where? If you tell me all I want to know, you'll be free. If you lie, you'll join your ancestors in the Golden Springs tonight."

His hands still raised above his head, flanked by two threatening soldiers on both sides, Minh summoned some of the courage the Patriarch had taught him only a few hours ago and answered coolly, "I'm returning from a visit to the Thien Mu pagoda."

The lieutenant was furious. "Ah, *now* I know who you are! You went there to meet with the leaders of the Viet Cong provincial committee. The Thien Mu pagoda is no longer a place of worship. It's a communist headquarters and the Patriarch is an agent of Moscow and Peking. One of these days we'll have to bomb the pagoda to save Buddha."

Angrily, Minh looked straight into the lieutenant's face. He thought of his mother, her body bleeding on a jungle path at the Chinese border. "You're insulting the most sacred institution in our country! You'll pay for your criminal behavior!" Minh raised his voice. "You're a Vietnamese without religion, without country. A mercenary!"

"You dare threaten me, insolent Viet Cong!" the lieutenant shouted.

Without warning, he hit Minh full in the face with the butt of his revolver. Minh felt the warmth of fresh blood in his mouth and nostrils.

"I have taken my first step," he thought. A fly buzzed around his bloody face. He swiped at it with one hand.

"Keep your hands up, or I'll shoot!" one of the soldiers commanded. The lieutenant walked behind his tent. He came back with another soldier, a sad-faced corporal with thick reading glasses and a notebook in his hands. The lieutenant was now all smiles.

"Now, for your own sake, cooperate with us. You may be just a misled intellectual, and if you tell us the truth, we'll let you return to your family. Don't force me to be tough with you. I don't want to. After all, we're both Vietnamese. Now, tell me the truth."

"If you just want the truth and consider yourself a Vietnamese, why do you treat me with such brutality?"

"Don't be insolent! Sit down, lower your arms, and cross them over your chest."

"All right," Minh said slowly. "The truth is, I just returned from the United States two days ago. I'm going to teach at the university. That's why I don't have an identity card yet, but my address is Number 9 Quoc Tu Giam Street in the Citadel. I live there with my father, Doctor of State Tran Van Quang, and my brother, Captain Tran Van Phong of the second bureau of the staff of the first regiment of the first ARVN division."

The lieutenant, whose accent betrayed his Southern background, laughed heartily. "You, a Viet Cong professor from the United States? That's the biggest joke I've ever heard. Is this the latest Viet Cong trick? But we have a way to prove you're a liar. You'll regret using such an obvious stupid trick." He raised his voice. "Lieutenant Bradley, I've got a gift for you. A Viet Cong who claims he's just returned from America."

From a tent adjacent to the lieutenant's emerged a tall, thin, serious-looking black American in a sweatshirt.

"What's the problem, Lieutenant Vi?"

"Come here, please."

They walked several yards away from Minh and conferred between themselves for a few minutes. Lieutenant Vi eyed Minh suspiciously and returned to the front of the command tent. Lieutenant Bradley approached Minh.

"My name is Bradley," he said in English. "Lieutenant Arthur Bradley, U.S. Marine Corps, adviser to the third company of the first regiment of the first division of the Army of the Republic of Vietnam. Would you please step into my office?"

The lieutenant's firm but polite demeanor was reassuring.

"My name is Tran Van Minh. I've just returned from the United States where I taught school in Massachusetts. I'll be teaching at Hue University when it opens."

Lieutenant Vi, who was eavesdropping nearby, seemed startled and embarrassed that his suspected Viet Cong "sapper" spoke fluent English. "Art," he called, "I'm going down the road to do some checking before it gets dark. This V.C. is yours; do whatever you like with him."

"Don't worry, I'll take care of him," Lieutenant Bradley assured him. "You take care of yourself," he warned Vi gently.

Lieutenant Vi quickly disappeared down the winding road. Inside the tent, Bradley said, "I just got a pound of Louisiana chicory coffee from home yesterday. Can I offer you a cup, Professor? And if you'll permit me, I'll clean that blood off your face," he offered.

"Thank you, Lieutenant," Minh replied softly.

Bradley brought out styrofoam cups and poured a thick, black liquid into them.

"I've got cream and sugar if you like, but chicory's popular back home straight," he grinned.

"That's fine."

They sat down, sipping quietly, scrutinizing each other and smiling occasionally. Under the glare of a lightbulb dangling from a long cord hung a framed picture of Dr. Martin Luther King, Jr..

Bradley took a washcloth, drew a bowl of water and proceeded to clean the dried blood from Minh's face. "It's not serious, thanks, Lieutenant," Minh said apologetically.

"I guess," Minh began cautiously when Bradley had finished, "that Lieutenant Vi thought I lied when I told him I came from the States. He wanted to test me and prove I was lying."

"A black man in America learns to tell truth-tellers from liars. By the way you speak, your conduct, I know you're not a liar, professor. It's just damn unfortunate. The problem is, you haven't any I.D. to prove who you are. In war, that can get a man accidentally killed." He paused.

"Don't you know anyone in Hue who could vouch for you? That's all we need. This whole thing could be over in a New York second."

"My father lives in the Citadel, my uncle's the Rector of Hue University, and my younger brother's a captain in the Army."

"Did you tell all that to Lieutenant Vi?"

"I did, but he laughed it off."

Lieutenant Bradley shook his head in dismay. "What's your brother's name and address?"

"Tran Van Phong. He's on the staff of the first regiment, first ARVN division."

"What! Is that Captain Phong, a real no-nonsense serious type with the second bureau?"

"Yes, it is."

Lieutenant Bradley's face became animated for the first time. "I know him! Hell, I work with him. I'll give him a ring right now and have him pick you up and that's that!"

"This is a happy coincidence, but I'm afraid I don't have his phone number," Minh apologized.

"I do," Bradley exclaimed, grabbing the telephone.

In a moment, the mild, gentle lieutenant was transformed into a model of military efficiency. "Give me the second bureau, first regiment," he ordered briskly. "Captain Phong, please. Oh. Yes. Well, please ask Captain Phong to call Lieutenant Arthur Bradley at XYI-2000. And lieutenant, tag that urgent."

He hung up and turned to Minh. "I'm really sorry about all this," he said sorrowfully.

"You're not responsible."

"That's the big problem with this war. Officially, we American advisers aren't responsible for anything. We're just supposed to advise ARVN. But hell, for all practical purposes, we're in charge of everything—fighting, advising, building, destroying . . ." He trailed off and lit a cigarette.

"Lieutenant, where's your home in the U.S.?"

"As a matter of fact, I come from Massachusetts," he responded. "Springfield." He took a puff from his cigarette and exhaled deeply. "And where did you teach in Massachusetts, Professor?"

"Please, if you will, just call me Minh."

"Fine. My name's Art."

"I taught at Thomas Paine College in Amherst."

"I've heard of it. It's supposed to be an expensive place. Not for me. I was too poor for that. I went to Springfield College on a basketball scholarship and enlisted in the Marines in 1964, before I could get drafted. I've been in Nam for a year now."

Minh was deeply impressed by Bradley's character and behavior. He didn't try to impress Minh with a phony facade like some Americans Minh had met. He regretted that he had had so few opportunities to really get to know blacks while he was in the States. He felt an immediate rapport, even a brotherly affection, for this unusual American officer.

"Art, can you explain to me why Vietnamese officers act so brutally? I shudder to think of what happens to poor peasants without connections who are arrested and detained. I must confess I've been away for several years, and I'm surprised at the changes in the language and behavior of my people."

Bradley inhaled on his cigarette. "I've only been in your country a short time and I haven't had time to learn about your culture or your people. But one thing is increasingly clear: most of the soldiers and officers, American and Vietnamese alike, are getting more and more frustrated every day with this damn war. Frustration causes brutality. I've seen suspected V.C.

flung from helicopters. It seems they're everywhere and nowhere. We don't know their organizations, their commanders, their headquarters—we've been told many of them are actually women and children. Once I remember asking your brother Phong and he said that the Viet Cong are the Vietnamese. He's right, but it doesn't help us at all to know that. Just to give you an example: recently, the C.I.A. and ARVN counterintelligence working together uncovered a clandestine V.C. radio operating in the basement of the residence of a senior American officer."

"How was that possible?"

"The American officer, a colonel fresh from the Staff and Command College, was assigned as chief of staff to a brigade near the seventeenth parallel. At a party in Saigon, he met a beautiful Vietnamese who, according to the story, was educated in the States. Radcliffe, of all places. They lived together in a house not far from Hue for over a year until it was discovered that she was the operator of the V.C. radio. Strangely enough, when the secret hideout was found, she suddenly just up and disappeared into thin air. It was rumored the colonel himself helped her escape. Of course, he's back in the States now."

The telephone rang loudly. Bradley answered it quickly, scooping up the receiver.

"Phong, you won't believe it, but your brother Professor Tran Van Minh is right here with me in my tent on Hill 86."

"What's happened!" Minh heard Phong exclaim excitedly over the phone.

"It's not a pleasant story, but I assure you he's well and under my personal care. I'd rather he told you himself what happened."

Minh took the phone. "As Lieutenant Bradley said, it's not a pleasant story, but Art, your friend and mine, has rescued me. If you don't mind, I'd prefer to tell you everything when I get home."

"As long as you're well, I'm happy. Let me speak to Art, please."

Minh handed the phone back to Lieutenant Bradley, who listened for a moment and then said, "Sure, Phong, I'll be glad to take him home. I have to go to the city anyway.... Right.... Right.... Goodbye."

Later, when Minh shook hands with Bradley in front of his house, he remembered that Lieutenant Vi hadn't returned either the bicycle or the fruits. He can have them as gifts of Buddha, Minh thought.

.   .   .

Father was in his study when Minh came into the house. Auntie heard his steps on the threshold. From the kitchen she called out, "Are you ready for dinner? I've prepared some soft-shelled crabs for you and your father."

"Thanks, Auntie, I don't think I'll have dinner."

His father walked into the living room. "I heard you say you're not having dinner. Phong won't be home until very late. Did you meet with the Patriarch?"

"Yes, Father. I had a long conversation with him and had lunch. He was very kind and asked about you. It's been a very long day. If you'll permit me, I'd like to go to bed."

"As you wish. Perhaps you're not used to the hot weather yet."

It started raining heavily. A blinding flash of lightning was followed by a deafening roar that shook the house. His mother's picture fell to the floor. Minh picked it up but didn't rehang it. He put it on the table near his bed. Lying down, he stared at her, his head to the side. He listened to the rain falling on the tiled roof. It alternated in regular intervals of heavy and light. The rain and wind soothed his nerves. He repeated a few lines from the poem *Nightly Rains* by poet Huy Can, now in North Vietnam:

> *... My ears tuning to the rain dropping from the roof,*
> *I heard that nature is cooler and cooler and*
> *I heard that I am sadder and sadder ...*

But Minh wasn't sad. He was confused, shaken, even terrified. The events of the day—his meeting with the Patriarch, the Patriarch's comparison of a Viet Cong cadre and a Buddhist monk, the brutal treatment he had suffered from his own countrymen, the unexpected kindness he had received from a black American officer—appeared to him now to be a series of Zen *koans*, each pointing to a different path. Perhaps an understanding of their collective, related meaning would help him to understand his situation, decide what to do. Unconsciously he prayed: *Nam Mo Phat.*

Outside, the rain had temporarily stopped. It had washed away all the dust of the land, he thought, cleansing his soul. He recalled two verses from the "Hymn to the Buddha of Infinite Compassion and Wisdom" in the Satapancastka of Matroceta of the second century A.D. They were an answer to his prayer and a summation of all that had happened to him since morning:

> *An island you are to those swept along by the flood,*
> *A shelter to the stricken,*
> *A refuge to those terrified by be-coming,*
> *The resource of those who desire release ...*

Minh realized that he was terrified by be-coming, by transformation, by his own growth from a position of uninvolved observer of Vietnamese history to a participant in that history. He was becoming a committed Vietnamese, a Buddhist Vietnamese at that. Now he wished he could return to the pagoda, following the streams left by the rain on the soft soil, to kneel in front of the Patriarch and receive still more instructions. But he knew the Patriarch would tell him to look into his heart to see reality and face reality in order to know his heart. Seeing the Patriarch was unimportant. His infinite wisdom, his defense of religion and the nation, his sympathy, if not support, for the Viet Cong cadre, these were the keys that would decipher the *koans* Minh was struggling with.

He heard his father coughing in the next room. Minh wondered if he should confide in him. "I'll confide in him only after I've become a true Vietnamese, his true son, not now," Minh rationalized to himself. He glanced at his mother's picture. He felt immensely grateful to her without knowing why. He cried quietly, tears warming his throat. He imagined her proud. How beautiful and serene she must have been that day when she brought him to the Thien Mu pagoda for the dedication rituals. Buddha would have blessed her and her infant son with his enlightening smile and compassionate love.

Minh didn't know when he fell asleep, but he knew why he awoke suddenly in the middle of the night. He'd had a dream. In it, he saw his mother. Blood dripped from her face, her black, disorderly hair fell to her shoulders, her white *ao dai* dress was torn at her breast, revealing a red brocade bra. She seemed to be dancing furiously, but Minh couldn't see her feet. He implored her to hug him. She came to him, her eyes as beautiful and loving as ever. She touched his face, held his hands. Minh felt reassured.

"Mother, what happened to you?"

"Son, your father has already told you. What happened to you today is my concern. I came back to tell you that you're becoming my son again. You needn't worry, you need only see the truth and face it with courage. If you see clearly, the path of action will be obvious to you. I shall always be near to help you. Buddha and the Patriarch will guide you."

Crystal clear water seemed to drop from nowhere, washing the blood from her face. She looked angelic now; her white dress became an elegant red silk gown. She walked away slowly. A cloud at her feet lifted her towards a violet horizon. Minh cried out for her to come back. A thunderclap woke him. He heard a knock at his door.

"Minh, are you all right? I heard you cry out."

"Is that you Phong?"

"Yes, I just came in a few minutes ago."

"I'm all right. I just had a dream. I'll see you tomorrow."

.   .   .

When Minh got up, his father had already finished his morning tea. Phong was cleaning the tea set.

"Did you sleep well?" his father asked him. "Did you hear the rains? The monsoons are starting up early this year. It's good, because we'll have cooler, drier weather for Tet and my orchids."

"Yes, Father, I slept well." Minh looked at Phong, hoping he wouldn't contradict him. He didn't want to tell his father about the dream. It might make him unhappy and concerned.

"Professor Le Duc Loc came to see you yesterday afternoon, Minh. He said he'd be back this morning about ten-thirty. Do you know him at all?"

"I don't think so. Who is he?"

"He's teaching literature at the university. He returned from Paris about four years ago. His father, who died last year, was a good friend of mine. We both graduated the same year from the Imperial examinations and belonged to the same 28 Constellations Club. He was the best scholar on Taoism, and that's the way he lived and died. Professor Loc would come to visit me from time to time with his father. He told me he's doing an anthology of Buddhist and Taoist literature. His family, particularly his mother, contributed to the restoration and renovation of the Tu Dam pagoda. It's more popular now than the Thien Mu."

"His students like him very much," Phong added, "but he's not liked so much by the government."

After a breakfast of spiced beef and noodles Phong invited Minh to walk in the garden.

"I'm sorry about what happened to you yesterday, Minh," he said.

"How did you know?"

"After he brought you home, Lieutenant Bradley came to see me at my office and we went out to dinner. He's an exceptionally sensitive man, not like most of the other American officers whose only concerns are Viet Cong body counts, promotions, and R and R in Hawaii or Bangkok. He told me once about the conditions of his people, the history of slavery. He says it's ironic that while he's fighting for freedom in Vietnam, his people at home haven't any."

"Phong, they also stole your bicycle. Can you reclaim it?"

"I'll try. But forget about it. It happens often to many people." He paused for a long moment and lit a cigarette. "I have something important to tell you."

"Please."

"I have to go to Da Nang tomorrow for a conference but I'm also receiving orders from the I Corps commander about a new assignment." He stared at the ground.

"What assignment?"

"I'm being transferred to Quang Tri to command a company of Rangers. I don't want Father to know about this yet because he might worry about my safety. I'll tell him when I come back from Da Nang."

"You don't seem very happy about your new duty."

"Well, I'm happy enough now that you're back to take care of Father. Otherwise . . ."

This was the first time Minh had had an opportunity to talk with Phong. He hardly knew his half-brother.

"Phong, I know you were drafted into the army, perhaps against your will. How do you see this war?"

"I hate it. I don't believe I'm on the right side, the people's side. They despise us soldiers. People want to stay alive and they think we're responsible for their death. They're not afraid of communists because communists are Vietnamese too. They say *we* bring the elephants to trample upon the ancestors tombs. They don't care about freedom, they care about life and their families. All of this makes troop morale very low. Anyway, even though I hate this war I've no choice but to be in the army, partly to protect the family, especially Father, from the government's harassment. Without me and An, Father might have been arrested and jailed already. The government suspects him in spite of his integrity and popularity."

"I understand," Minh said, putting his arm around Phong's waist. "I admire you, but I'm afraid there's nothing I can do to help. We're all victims of this war, prisoners of our own situation."

"Thanks for your kind words. I'm old enough though to see for myself what I can do."

"When do you leave for Quang Tri?"

"Soon. I also want to tell you that Professor Le Duc Loc is being watched closely by the police. They have no evidence against him, but they're convinced he's a Viet Cong underground leader. They have to leave him alone for the time being because he's strongly supported by the monks at Tu Dam pagoda and besides, he has a large following, especially among the young. You can trust him, but be careful of the eyes and ears of the police. Perhaps you can protect him."

"How can I do that?"

"Because you come from America, and regardless of your activities there, the authorities here think that you have a channel to the Americans. And in Vietnam today, the Americans are the *real* masters. I think you should keep up your friendly relations with them, both at the consulate and the university. That way you can protect yourself, your friends, and our family against the government."

"I don't know if I can play that game, Phong, but I'll give it some serious thought."

"By the way," Phong said, "yesterday when I went to dinner with Lieutenant Bradley, I met the chief of Hue police and told him about the incident. He seemed very happy about it."

"Why?" Minh asked, surprised.

"Because there's a great deal of jealousy and rivalry between the army and the police. The chief said the incident proves that if the army had power over civilian affairs it would commit excesses."

"I see."

"He wants you to mail him a picture of yourself with the usual information, place of residence, occupation, and so on, and you'll be issued an I.D. right away. He promised he'd send it in no time. I don't think he has any file on you yet. He asked me to tell you that he wants to meet you sometime and find out if you can introduce him to the Americans."

Minh smiled. "I'll do just that."

The brothers turned to stroll back towards the house. "I don't suppose you've heard," Phong asked, "about the woman who immolated herself two days ago in Saigon to protest the war."

"No! How come I didn't hear anything about it on Hue radio? Who is she?"

"The government tried to suppress the news, but I'm sure you could get the details on Voice of America or B.B.C. Her name is Nhat Chi Mai. She's a teacher who worked part time in the Buddhist School of Social Work. She told newsmen to come to the Tu Nghiem pagoda for an important happening, and when they arrived they found her seated in the lotus position, meditating, with pictures of the Goddess of Mercy and the Virgin Mary beside her. She poured gasoline all over her body and then, reciting a poem she'd written for peace, she lit the match. The fire consumed her very quickly."

"That's terrible!"

"Yes, I know. I'll try to get her poems for you. I know you'd like to have them."

"Yes, I would, but don't risk yourself to get them."

Minh vividly remembered the evening of June 11, 1963, almost four years ago. He had been alone in his apartment in Washington when on to the television screen had flashed the image of a monk seated on a street corner, clothed in a column of orange flame. He burned for an endless moment, then fell backward, his blackened legs pointing towards heaven. It was the venerated monk Thich Quang Duc. Minh had watched his body settle into stillness while the other monks held banners demanding peace. It was that scene, more than any other event or argument, that had moved Minh to resign from government service. Minh and Phong walked in silence to the house.

.   .   .

"Minh, Professor Loc's here," Father called from the living room.

In his early forties, with a round, open face, his hair cut short, Loc looked like a student. He wore khaki pants and a light brown shirt that went well with his tanned complexion and was brightened by his big, lively eyes.

"I'm glad to meet you at last, Professor Minh. I used to come here often with my father when he was alive but that was when you were away."

"Yes, my father told me. I'm glad to know you, too."

"I'll leave you to talk," Father said. "Nephew Loc, you are welcome to stay and have lunch with us if you have time."

"Thank you, Uncle, but I have to leave at noon for a meeting. Thanks again for your kindness."

"Then come again and stay as long as you wish."

"Yes, I will, Uncle."

"When I was in Saigon two days ago," Loc began, after Father had left, "Professor Pham Ngoc Lam told me that you were back home in Hue for good. He also said he'd told you that he's with the Association of Intellectual Workers for Liberation. I'm pleased he did."

"To be honest, I was a little surprised that he was so open with me. Of course we knew each other before, but I've been away from home for so long to be worthy of such trust . . ."

"Sure, you've been away, but he was aware of your resignation from the diplomatic service and your antiwar activities in the U.S. Also, some if not all of us were impressed by the progressive and humane feelings you expressed in your books and poetry."

"Thank you."

"The fact that your pen name is Co Tung doesn't mean that you're lonely or without friends," Loc smiled. "In my case, I trust you completely because, among other things, I know and respect your father. He represents the best in our traditional culture."

"But you also know that my two half brothers are with the Saigon army and my uncle's the Rector of Hue University."

"Of course I do, but the fact that a Vietnamese is in the Saigon army or heading a university doesn't mean that he's no longer patriotic, especially when his fatherland is being occupied by foreigners. You may be surprised to know that several high-ranking officials in the Saigon government are working secretly with the National Liberation Front."

"Loc, shouldn't you know me better before you trust me with such important matters?"

"No, we trusted you before today."

"What do you mean, 'we?'"

"I mean the Hue chapter of the Association of Intellectual Workers for Liberation, which, as you can tell by its name, is part of the National Liberation Front of South Vietnam. I've discussed the matter with the association's national committee in Saigon and they've asked me to invite you to join us. If you agree, and I hope you do, you'll be one of the three members of my cell. I'll introduce you to the other person in our next meeting. Obviously, the association operates in secret."

"Loc, thank you for trusting me, but let me think it over." What is this, Minh thought. He's never even met me. Why is he trying to recruit me?

"Of course, but please make your decision as soon as you can. We have very little time. We've received instructions from higher echelons to work harder because we just learned that Secretary McNamara will make his ninth visit here sometime in early July for an on-the-spot review before

Washington sends fifty thousand more troops. We must organize the entire population to resist the U.S. escalation. May I ask you a few questions?"

"Go ahead."

"What's the strength of the antiwar movement in the U.S.? Not only the masses but among the universities and colleges, too."

"Well, as you may know, the movement started first with university teach-ins and gradually spread to the general public. Its strength increased in proportion to the increase of U.S. troops here and to the draft, which of course increased the number of U.S. casualties. Then there's another and I think much more fundamental direction in the antiwar movement—the identification by black leaders with the issues of war and peace. Also, the women's liberation movement has had some effect. Most importantly, though, the movement in general gets stronger with the strength of the resistance led by the national liberation movement here at home and with Hanoi's refusal to be bombed into surrender."

"That's what I thought. The Johnson administration is being caught between two fronts: one here in our mountains, plains, and cities and the other in New York, Chicago, and Birmingham."

"How's the situation at our university?" Minh asked.

"Well, you know, your uncle wanted to reopen the university in early June. As a matter of fact, I just received a note of convocation for a faculty meeting the day after tomorrow to discuss the reopening plan. Did you receive one?"

"No, not yet."

"I'm sure you will sometime tomorrow. In case you don't, come anyway. Because you're new, the secretariat might not have your name on the faculty list." Loc stopped suddenly. "If by then you've decided to join us, then when you meet me, shake my hand. If it's no, just wave, smile, and forget the handshake. I usually like smiles," he added, flashing his own bright grin, "but not in this case."

"All right."

"One more thing. If the decision is yes, then we'll meet the day after the faculty meeting, at the Moonlight Tea House on the left of the Thuong Tu Gate at four o'clock. If I don't show, it means that I think I'm being followed by police agents. In that case, we meet again the next day, same time, same place. It's easy to underestimate the efficiency of the police and fall into a trap. Many agents are trained in the U.S., England, or Australia and shouldn't be taken lightly. On the other hand, we try not to overestimate them either, and become paranoid. The police know about my general political attitude—antiwar, antigovernment, pro-Buddhist—but as far as I can ascertain, they've no knowledge of my connection with the National Liberation Front."

"Why?"

"Because our organization operates officially and openly as the National Buddhist League for Peace and Democracy, which, again officially, has no connection, with the National Liberation Front. I'm also adviser to the Buddhist Youth Organization, headquartered at Tu Dam pagoda."

"Do you think the police are naive enough to believe that the League has no connection with the National Liberation Front?"

"I don't know. However, it's always dangerous to assume your enemy doesn't know you. Therefore, all precautions have to be taken. But since we're engaging ourselves in legal and semi-legal struggles to sustain and support the illegal armed struggle, it's necessary to operate behind a front within a front. Again, it may not fool the enemy but it's a tested strategy to educate the masses on our minimum program of democracy and peace."

"Minimum program? What do you mean?" Minh asked.

"Democracy means the overthrow of the Saigon regime, which even Washington recognizes as undemocratic. Peace means the end of the war and the withdrawal of all U.S. troops and civilian personnel. Of course these two goals are actually one, because they're interrelated. If the regime were overthrown, the U.S. could hardly continue its present limited war in the South and the destructive war in the North, unless it occupied our country outright as it did the Philippines in 1900. But that would take at least two million troops in the South and probably *twice* that many in the North, and the U.S. would never commit itself that far. The U.S. is a neocolonial power, not an old-type imperial one. So for both internal and external reasons, it needs a local, native, puppet regime to carry on its policies. Conversely, if the U.S. were to withdraw its troops, the Saigon regime would collapse under its own weight of corruption and inefficiency."

Loc was on his feet now, his voice ringing with intensity. He must speak often in public, Minh thought. He looked at Loc's strong hands, his wide shoulders and muscular arms. They seemed to complement his exuberant face and optimism. "At a higher level, democracy and peace are the mighty tides of our time. People all over the world, including Americans, are demanding it. These two imperatives will allow social revolutions to take place even in industrialized countries. They will transform the world!"

Minh wasn't impressed by the ideas Loc expressed, nor were they new to him. After all, they were only the essence of his course on the politics of national liberation. He was amazed, though, at the ease with which Loc explained them in the Vietnamese language, which was not, Minh thought, a tongue well suited to expressing political ideas, however beautiful it may be for poetry and fiction. Loc was an intellectual who had earned a Ph.D. at the Sorbonne, but he used clear, simple terms, not jargon and rhetoric, to convey his political views.

"Any more questions?" Loc asked.

Minh hesitated. "Do you mind if I ask a rather personal, maybe irrelevant one?"

"Anything."

Minh hesitated again.

"Go ahead, Minh!"

"Loc, are you a communist, a member of the Workers Party?"

"Yes, I am." Loc answered matter-of-factly. He paused. "I know, after years in the U.S., even with your family background and progressive ideas, you might find that disturbing, but I'm glad you asked. The question's neither personal nor irrelevant. I didn't join the Party for personal reasons, but for national and historical ones. Marxism is relevant to our history and the nation at this stage, the same way Buddhism was during the Tran dynasty in the thirteenth century. Without Buddhism then, we would have been unable to defeat the three successive waves of Mongol invasions. Without Marxism today, both in Vietnam and internationally, we'll have difficulty combating U.S. imperialism, which is clearly analyzed by Marx and Lenin. At the same time, any ideology, whether Marxism today or Buddhism in the past, will take Vietnamese forms and content if and when it becomes an effective tool in our struggle for freedom and independence. It'll become 'Vietnamized.'"

Loc laughed. "Not long ago the White House and the Pentagon and their 'gurus' at the Rand think-tank came up with a plan to win through 'Vietnamization' of the war. What arrogance and ignorance! For one thousand years the Chinese failed to 'Vietnamize' Vietnam, that is to say, pacify our country and annex it to the Middle Empire. After nearly one hundred years, the French attempt was blown into ashes at Dien Bien Phu. How do the Americans think they can do it when all the others, Chinese, French, Japanese, have failed miserably? How? By using every conceivable advanced weapon they have to kill all the Vietnamese, defoliate our forests and poison our rivers?"

Irrationally, Minh felt that because he had been in America, he was partly responsible for American policy.

"I'm sorry," he said.

"You've no reason to be sorry for things you weren't responsible for. But still, I'd like to know why the Americans entertain such irrational dreams."

"I really don't know. In their innocence—I shouldn't use that word—in their total disregard and ignorance of other nations' historical experiences, they believe that armed with guns, a copy of the Declaration of Independence, and a Constitution, they can propagate a 'melting pot' policy around the world."

"But," Loc interrupted, "how can they expect the melting pot to work in other countries when their own pot can't melt the Blacks, Puerto Ricans and Indians! How can their unmelting pot pretend to melt the Vietnamese into a Vietnamese pot? I get lost in their thoughts."

"I do, too," Minh said uncomfortably. "I'm much more interested in what you were saying about the Vietnamization of Marxism."

"Well, let me explain, if I can. Marxism, a humanist philosophy basically, is made up essentially of two interrelated foundations that we Vietnamese have discovered and lived with for thousands of years. These are *Tinh*, feeling, and *Ly*, reason. At the present time, our *Tinh* is grounded in our culture and our *Ly* is rooted in our just struggle for independence, freedom, and socialism. *Ly* helps us clarify our *Tinh* and devise appropriate strategies and tactics for the revolution. *Tinh*, in turn, humanizes our *Ly* and transforms our strategies into understandable, popular, workable programs of action. *Tinh* and *Ly* form the unbroken circle in which our national communication operates.

"In Marxist terminology, *Tinh* represents the 'superstructure' and *Ly*, the 'economic base,' or the 'economic infrastructure.' Looking back at our history, we can see that from our original culture we've drawn the necessary strength to absorb and Vietnamize Confucianism, Taoism, and Buddhism. There's no reason to suppose that we can't Vietnamize Marxism as well, especially when Marxism is basically the same humanistic philosophy as the others were. Moreover, Marxism was developed in Europe at the height of its capitalist and imperialist expansion, so it assists us very effectively in correctly analyzing our enemy, which is *not* the American people, but American capitalism and imperialism. It all depends on our actions, though. A fifteenth century Chinese philosopher, Wang-Yang-Ming, once said, 'Knowledge is the beginning of action and action is the completion of knowledge.'"

Minh sighed. Perhaps Loc's ideas weren't new, but he had integrated them into his life in a way that he, Minh, had never been able to do. Almost in spite of himself, Minh was impressed.

"Would you like some tea?" Auntie called from the doorway.

Loc stood up. "I'm sorry, Auntie, that I didn't have a chance to greet you when I came in. How are you? My mother told me that you and she are going to the Tu Dam pagoda next week to pay your respects to the nun Thich Lien Hoa who's in from Saigon for a visit."

"Yes. But I don't want to disturb you. I know how eager you are to talk with each other. If you want some tea, just let me know."

"Thank you, Auntie," Loc said, "if and when we do, I'll go to the kitchen and make it myself."

"Minh, what courses do you plan to teach?"

"I was thinking of one on the American Revolution emphasizing the internal conflicts within the revolutionary leadership, namely the ideological differences between Thomas Paine on the left and Thomas Jefferson on the right, and the influences of the American Revolution on the French Revolution of 1789."

"That's a very good idea. Our students are rather familiar with the French Revolution, but they need to know more about the American one."

"The other one," Minh continued, "will be on the American presidential elections and presidential power."

"I'm glad you thought of that. Our colleagues here spend a lot of time discussing the same subject, guessing who will be the next President of the U.S. and what his Vietnam policy will be. We're ignorant of the forces at work, or to put it bluntly, the money behind these forces. In fact, I'd like to sit in on your classes along with my students."

"By all means," Minh said. "And then I plan to have a seminar on the U.S. military-industrial complex, ideally with a colleague from the economics department. Do you know of anyone who can do that?"

"Offhand I don't, but I'll think about it. Perhaps you can ask your uncle. But with or without an economist, go ahead and plan it."

"What do you teach, Loc?"

"I teach three courses. One on popular literature, including sayings, proverbs, theater, and so on; one on Buddhist literature from the thirteenth to the fifteenth centuries; and one on Vietnamese newspapers and magazines under the French regime. The last is really a communications course, but since we have no communications professor on faculty, I take care of it. I did it last year and the students were fascinated to learn about the debate in the early thirties between 'art for art' and 'art for life and society.' The debate, as you probably know, was started right here in our hometown by Nguyen Khoa Van. He was then a member of the Indochinese Communist Party. I was told he died not too long ago in Hanoi."

Loc glanced at his watch and stood to leave. He shook Minh's hand warmly. After saying goodbye to Minh's auntie, he walked with Minh to his father's study.

"Come back again for lunch," Minh's father said.

"I will. Thanks again Uncle."

After lunch, Minh took a walk along Quoc Tu Giam Street. His head was whirling with a thousand impressions. *Tinh* and *Ly*, he thought. What a brilliant exposition Loc had given him of their relationship to communism—and how different from Dean Chuong's insistence that communism was all *Ly*, with no heart. Loc's evident confidence in him at their very first meeting was based mostly on *Tinh*, on the close contacts Loc had had with Minh's family. There was some *Ly* of course—mainly his antiwar activities in the States—but Loc was anything but heartless and unemotional. Minh was flattered that this exuberant, thoughtful man trusted him, for whatever reason. Work with him would be exciting, inspiring.

But he couldn't help feeling uneasy that Loc was a communist. He hadn't realized how deeply the anticommunist climate in the U.S. had penetrated him, though in theory and appearance, he had never been anticommunist himself. He considered himself a progressive, even a radical. But now, in practice, wondering whether to join an organization most likely set up by communists, he was confused. He remembered all the studies and research papers, the documents he'd read in the States about the effects of a communist victory; the possible bloodbath, the 'domino theory,' the betrayal of national causes, the 'darkness at noon' and suppression of individual liberties. When he was there, he had ridiculed those theories and assumptions. He had even written essays and articles to denounce them as superstitions and fabrications. But now, here, talking with an avowed communist, he wasn't so sure any more. Was Loc trying to use him? Was he sincere and patriotic? Or was he himself the dupe of communists plotting in the Politburo in Hanoi?

In a communist regime, would intellectuals be forced to follow the Party line as they had been in 1956 in the North, after a short period of a "hundred flowers blooming?" Were the Vietnamese communists puppets of the Soviet Union and China, just as the Saigon regime was a puppet of the U.S.? Minh had always respected President Ho Chi Minh, who was above all a patriot, the 'George Washington of Vietnam,' the father of the Dien Bien Phu victory, of which Minh was so proud. But what if he died? Rumors had been circulating in the States that he was in poor health. Would his successors be divided into a pro-Russian faction and pro-Chinese faction, as some American scholars had predicted?

It was only a week ago, Minh thought, that he'd left America—and Jennifer. In the few days since, he'd been wined and dined in Bangkok and Saigon, entertained by prostitutes, interviewed by the President. He had seen his aging father for the first time in seven years and learned the truth of his mother's death. In just one day he had been welcomed as a prodigal son by the Patriarch and beaten by Vietnamese soldiers. And now this. Was this step that Loc offered the "first step" he was seeking? Yesterday he had been inspired by religion; by day after tomorrow he might join a communist front. It was all too much. Too many *koans*, too many choices. And yet, he thought, Loc offered action . . .

V

Gold Caskets and
Cosmic Order

. . . Our country's purged a thousand years of shame.
Inside gold caskets deathless deeds shall live.
The cosmic order now has been set right.
To heroes does the world still give a thought?

Inscription on a sword
Nguyen Trai
1380–1442
Translated by Huynh Sanh Thong

Minh had been walking for hours. Siesta was nearly ended; the streets were still quiet and deserted. He stopped at a stand where an old man was selling refreshments.

"Uncle, can I have a glass of coconut milk?"

"Sure. Would you like it with ginger and sugar?"

"Just plain, thanks."

"It may not be very good. The coconuts are rather sour this year."

"Why is that?"

"I was told it's caused by chemicals the Americans use to defoliate some areas along the coast where the coconut trees grow. That's why I suggest the ginger and sugar, to neutralize possible toxic effects. You're still too young to die."

"Thanks for the advice. Add the ginger and sugar."

Minh stared at the old man's wrinkled face. His toothless mouth made him look very old although his hands were still strong and smooth and his eyes sharp.

"How's life with you, Uncle?"

"Not very happy. Two years ago, I was living in Phu Loc."

"I used to live there!" Minh interrupted.

The old man's face brightened. "How long have you been in Hue?"

"Only a few days," Minh answered, hoping the old man wouldn't ask him where he'd lived before. He didn't want to explain that he'd spent seven years among the people who sent defoliants to ruin his country.

The old man continued. "I was a farmer. Then one day the government troops came to the village to clear it of Viet Cong. I'd lived there for years and never seen any Viet Cong, but there was a battle and many died. After that the whole village was declared a 'free fire zone.' That meant I couldn't go to the fields except during certain fixed hours. One can't farm that way. Growing rice is 24-hour work! One of my neighbors was shot dead when he went back to the field after six o'clock to fetch the shovel he'd left behind.

"About that same time, my son was drafted. He was a good boy. A good farmer, too. He could predict the rains and fix the roof on our cottage. I'd raised him for twenty years by myself after his mother died. He brought me to Hue to live with him and even found me a job with his superior, a colonel who entertained a lot of guests, mostly Americans. That's how I learned to make drinks. Last year he was sent to the front and died in a battle near the Ben Hai river at the seventeenth parallel. I've never seen his body. His soul must be wandering now all over the place. Poor son!" The old man sobbed, tears rolling down his toothless mouth, which he tried to dry with his tongue.

"I'm sorry to hear that," Minh said softly.

The old man continued his story. "After my son died, the colonel left for Saigon and I lost my job. Then a relative of mine gave me this cart and I started selling refreshments for a living."

"Do you make enough?"

"Barely. I have to pay the family whose garage I live in practically all I earn. But it's all right. I don't have a long time to live or any children to leave my fortune to, so just a place to sleep and rest my body is fine with me."

Minh had heard enough. He handed the old man a banknote of one hundred piasters.

"That's too much. It only costs twenty piasters with ginger and sugar."

"Keep it, please, and thank you very much."

"Thank you, sir," the old man whispered as Minh hurried away.

The old vendor's life story seemed to Minh to sum up everything he'd seen and heard since he'd been home. Vietnam must have peace if it is to survive, he thought. This war must end and the U.S. troops must leave. No doubt the Saigon regime would then collapse as Loc predicted, and the communists would come to power, but whether they brought with them democracy or new dictatorship seemed to Minh of secondary importance.

"I'd do anything for peace," he thought. "I'd work with anyone, devote all my efforts to bring peace to the remaining years of that old man who sold me coconut milk." Peace was no longer an abstraction to him like some doctrine or aspiration. It was a human and national imperative, as necessary as the rice a Vietnamese eats daily.

In front of his house, Minh saw a postman trying to open the gate Minh had closed before his walk. The postman handed him a brown envelope. In it was a decree appointing him professor of social sciences at Hue University, with a note of congratulations from his uncle, and an invitation to attend the faculty meeting the day after tomorrow, May 21.

Minh arrived at the university ten minutes before the faculty meeting was to begin. Following a sign directing him to the second floor, he entered a large lecture hall, where he saw his uncle talking and gesticulating animatedly with a group of about 30 professors, five of whom were women. On the far side of the room he spotted Loc, surrounded by a group of colleagues. He knew no one else.

His heart pounding, Minh approached Loc. "Professor Loc?" he murmured. "I'm Tran Van Minh." He extended his hand. Solemnly Loc took it in a firm handshake; but his dark eyes sparkled as the two men gazed at each other. Well—that's it, Minh thought. I'm committed.

The Rector opened the meeting by reading a prepared text.

"Although I'm new, my face at least is known by some of you whom I met in March at the mayor's reception in honor of my appointment. By order of the President—or more exactly, the chairman of the national leadership, whom I'm sure will be confirmed as President during the coming September elections—and on the instructions of the Minister of Education, the university, which was closed because of political distur-bances in early March, will be reopened on June 8. I have asked the faculty to begin work immediately on the preparation of curricula and also to set up a committee to write a code of academic freedom for the institution. Although

I have the utmost respect for the sanctity of the university and for the freedom of speech and publication, I will not tolerate sabotage, infiltration, or agitation by faculty and students misled by Viet Cong propaganda."

About fifteen in the audience stood and applauded. Minh glanced furtively at Loc, who was seated in front of him in the second row. He seemed totally undisturbed and showed no sign of displeasure or surprise, although some of the others were visibly upset.

The Rector concluded his statement by introducing to the faculty the deans present in the audience. They stood as he called their names.

"Dr. Hoang Anh Hung, dean of the faculty of law." Dr. Hung had led the applause when the Rector had spoken of "faculty and students misled by Viet Cong propaganda." And his name means "hero," Minh thought wryly.

"Dr. Le Tan Giap, dean of the faculty of humanities. Dr. Nguyen Manh Ky, dean of the faculty of medicine and pharmacy. Dr. Thai Van Mau, dean of the faculty of letters."

"Except for Dean Hoang Anh Hung," the Rector went on, "who just came from Saigon to lend more prestige to our university, all these men have been with the university for the last five years." He paused a moment, glanced at Minh, and continued.

"As you've all noticed, we don't have a dean for the faculty of social sciences because Dr. Tran Van Minh, my nephew, has declined the position. He remains, however, the senior professor on the faculty and is *de facto* its dean whether he likes it or not!"

The audience applauded. Minh wanted to protest but he thought it useless. Besides, he wanted no confrontation with his uncle, whom he had begun to dislike as an opportunist.

The Rector was still speaking. "Are there any questions?"

"Will there be any guidelines governing curricula?" someone asked.

"All curricula will have to be approved by both the Minister of Education and the Rector of the University."

There was a stir among the faculty. Dean Nguyen Manh Ky got to his feet. "With all respect, Sir," he said, "that would violate the university's autonomy."

"We are in a struggle for life and death against the communists, the worst enemy of the free world," Dean Hoang Anh Hung retorted emotionally. "It's not proper or patriotic for us to talk about the 'autonomy' of the university. We'll talk about that after we defeat the Viet Cong!"

The Rector intervened. "All this debate is irrelevant, because none of us here can change the orders of the government. I advise you to accept the reality of our situation and try your best to live with it—especially when you prepare the code of academic freedom, which must also be approved by higher authorities in Saigon. I suggest we adjourn for lunch. Thank you."

The professors were still heatedly discussing the issue as they filed out of the hall.

·   ·   ·

The Moonlight Tea House was only five minutes from Minh's house. He had passed it often in the last few days but hadn't noticed it before. It was a long, narrow room on the ground floor of a three-story building. The entrance was covered by a screen made of small, multicolored, split-bamboo fragments strung together to form a moonlight scene: a sampan gliding on the River of Perfume, and above, the full silver moon shining through a solitary, blooming peach tree branch. Only one of the room's ten tables was occupied. In the back corner sat a couple with their heads together, their hair a black cascade falling against the yellow wall.

A stereo was playing *Twilight on the Imperial Landing*, a song Minh had listened to often when he was in the U.S. Its melancholy, haunting melody had reminded him of the beauty and poetry that reflected the tortured soul of Hue. He stood in the doorway and listened.

The singer was accompanied by a *Dan Bau*. Minh had never quite understood how one string and a little box could render so many varied tones. His mother had been well known as a *Dan Bau* player in her time. Once, he remembered, a poet friend of his father's had commented: "When she plays the *Dan Bau* in the daytime, the heat wave turns into a cool breeze, the grass sings, and the rain moistens the dry earth; when she plays it in the nighttime, the moon descends from the sky to embrace its reflecting face in the river, nightingales mate, and Heaven opens its gates for a festival in honor of all the artists and poets of the world." The music Minh listened to was not, perhaps, as enchanting and beautiful as his mother's, but it was lovely; he had heard nothing like it in years.

Looking around, Minh spotted Loc talking to the owner of the tea house. He joined them.

"Professor Tran Van Minh has just returned from America to join the university's faculty," Loc told her. "He's also a poet, a writer, and a friend of mine."

"Welcome," she said. She arranged her hair with her hand. "But I can hardly believe that Loc's telling the truth about you."

"Why not?" Minh inquired.

"First, your dress. Those who return from the States either dress smartly like models in the Sears catalog, or very sloppily, with torn shirts and jeans like a hippie. Second, your hair. It's neither too short like a U.S. Marine's nor too long like an intellectual's. Third, you don't have your sunglasses hung on your belt, and fourth, you don't shake my hand, you're shy."

"And fifth?" Minh asked.

"Fifth," she continued, "a poet and writer could not at the same time be a friend of Loc's, a reputed bon vivant who always insists on the best tea and the best pastry." They all laughed heartily. "Why don't you sit at that table next to the entrance? And what kind of tea would you both like?"

"The best you have in the house," Minh said.

"I can drink any tea," Loc added.

"You see," she said, "I told you. Loc drinks anything, eats anything, and sleeps anywhere. He's a peasant, but he's a good person. You can trust him with your wallet or your sister. I have some excellent tea from Banmethuot, but you have to drink it at your own risk. I was told recently that the U.S. Air Force has sprayed the highlands with defoliants and it might affect the tea grown there."

"I'll take the risk," Minh said.

"I'll be back in a few minutes. I'll bring you some fresh lotus seed cakes too," she said.

"Thank you," Loc and Minh answered at the same time.

"You know her well, Loc?" Minh asked.

"Yes, very well. Her husband used to be with the university as a registrar. About two years ago, on Tet, he was killed by a stray bullet during a street brawl between drunken Vietnamese Rangers and Police. I started a collection among the students and faculty to help her. The money allowed her to buy this tea house, make a living, and raise her three teen-aged children."

Loc looked around. "And now, before she comes back with our tea, here's my plan for the meeting. After we leave here, say about five o'clock, we split up. I'll tour the city on my motorbike and you walk to the Dong Ba Gate. You know where it is?"

"Of course. I'm not a stranger to this city."

"Good. There's a bookstore on the left-hand side of the gate called Tu Do, which specializes in English-language publications. It'll take about ten minutes for you to get there. Usually there are two women in charge. One, middle-aged, is the owner, who always sits at the counter. The other one, who is much younger, is the saleswoman. She'll greet you and ask what book you're looking for. You say, 'The Making of the President, 1964, by Theodore White.' She'll answer that she has to look for it in stock at the back of the shop. Follow her. I'll be there at exactly five-thirty."

The owner returned to the table with a pot of tea and a small dish of yellow lotus seed cakes. She sat down.

"It's on the house. I would like to welcome Professor Tran Van Minh back to Hue."

"No, that's not fair," Minh protested. "Coming from America where money grows on trees, I should pay double. If you don't let me, then I'll go out and sit in the street and wait for Loc there."

"Then Loc will drink all the tea and eat the cakes!"

"Let's not quarrel over this insignificant matter," Loc intervened. "I have a solution. I'll pay."

It was the best tea Minh had tasted for years, better than the O Long tea his father treasured, and the cakes were superb. They melted in Minh's mouth, the flavor gradually "penetrating his lungs."

Suddenly there was a noisy moving of chairs as the couple in the back corner stood up to leave. Minh could see them now: the young man wore big dark pilot glasses that hid almost half of his thin pale face. His very tight shirt and pants, his pointed shoes and hesitating step, made him look like a small bird on a rainy day. He held the woman's hand. She had long black hair that fell to her waist. She looked bluish, almost moribund, in a low-cut blouse that revealed half of her breasts and a leopard skin mini-skirt that barely covered her. They passed Minh's table, whispered some inaudible words to the proprietor, and left.

"Don't they pay you?" Minh inquired, disgusted by what he had seen.

"Sometimes he does. He's the son of the police chief in Hue. She's the daughter of the provincial prison warden. He's a drug addict."

"You mean he smokes opium at that age?"

"No. He takes heroin."

"That's terrible!"

"It's not unusual."

"Tell me, Madame," Minh began, but she interrupted him. "You can call me what Loc does. *Chi* Loan."

"Thank you, Sister Loan. Tell me, wasn't this place the Dream Flower Studio years ago?"

"Yes, it was."

"The owners of the studio were a painter and her two brothers, weren't they? They were well known for the pre-Tet parties they gave for the artists in town. Where are they now?"

"According to the woman from whom I bought the place, they left the city for the Marquis when the French reoccupied Hue in early 1947. Nobody knows exactly where they are now, but rumors circulated some time ago that they were imprisoned during the crackdown of intellectuals in the North in 1956."

"I see," Minh said and glanced at Loc; but he seemed unperturbed.

. . .

Minh paced the pavement of Tran Hung Dao Boulevard. He passed a fortune-teller who sat stoically under a tamarind tree. He was tempted to stop and talk to the old man, who seemed lonely, but he was afraid he might be late for his rendezvous.

The street became busier by the minute. Bicycles, motorcycles, army trucks, pedestrians, all seemed to be rushing into the Citadel. Down the street he could see the Tu Do Bookstore with its English name, Freedom, above the door. It stood out confidently from a row of small shops. It was indeed a large bookstore for a city like Hue.

He went in. A middle-aged woman was sitting at the counter, sipping tea; a younger woman was busy talking to a customer. Minh spotted a shelf, labeled "Politics and Government," containing familiar books like Morgenthau's *Politics Among Nations* and Deutsch's *The Nerves of Government*, but he saw no copy of White's *The Making of the President*. The young woman guided her customer to the counter and came back to Minh.

"What book are you looking for, sir?" she asked politely, raising her voice for everyone to hear.

"I'm looking for Theodore White's *The Making of the President, 1964*, paperback edition."

She looked up and down the shelf as if looking for the book. There were no customers in the store but Minh.

"I have to look in the back storeroom to see if we have any copies left. Please follow me, sir."

They crossed a small yard and climbed a steep stairway to a large living room on the second floor. She smiled.

"Please sit down. We close in a few minutes and won't reopen until seven-thirty. I'll be right back. There are some newspapers that just arrived from Saigon, and a few magazines."

The room overlooked a large moat covered with lotus in bloom. Because the house was on stilts—to raise it above flood level—Minh had a clear view of Hue from the window: the Citadel's zigzagging ramparts, the canals paralleling the walls of the fortresses. Beyond, on the Phu Van Lau esplanade, the South Vietnamese flag with its three red stripes on a yellow background waved in the wind. The River of Perfume flowed quietly, like a ribbon of blue silk. The city was lush with blooming flame trees dotting the green scenery like so many red carpets. On the horizon, the silhouettes of several airplanes looked like stray birds flying home before nightfall.

In the May issue of Literature and Arts Magazine, Minh noticed that Trinh Cong Son, a native of Hue and a composer, singer, and musician who was known even in some circles in the U.S. as the "Bob Dylan" of Vietnam, would visit his hometown, Hue, in June, to celebrate the fifteenth day of the seventh month of the lunar calendar. Minh marked the date in his pocket calendar notebook.

At 5:30 on the dot, Loc and the young bookseller came into the room.

"You're very punctual," Minh observed.

"He always is," the young woman replied.

Loc seated himself and leaned back comfortably.

"I assume you haven't had the chance to introduce yourselves properly to one another. This is Minh, and this is Lan. Lan is a part-time teacher at the Dong Khanh Women's School. She's from Da Nang. Her husband was killed during a bombing raid in 1965, and she is helping her aunt take care of the bookstore during her spare time." Then, after telling Lan a little about Minh, he went on:

"I'm happy that Minh has decided to join us in this cell, which hasn't been fully functional for a few weeks since one of our members was transferred suddenly to Saigon. Now we can operate at full strength again. I would like to discuss with the two of you our general plan from now until Tet—eight months from now." He stopped to take a notebook from his pocket, glanced at it quickly and continued:

"Let me give you an analysis of the present situation. The Johnson administration is more determined than ever to use more force to carry out its so-called Vietnamization of the war, that is, the pacification of Vietnam with U.S. money and guns and Vietnamese manpower. He's set up an organization called C.O.R.D.S., Civil Operations and Revolutionary Development Support, at the American Embassy in Saigon. He's sending more troops, up to five hundred thousand, by the end of this year, and has escalated the bombing of the northern part of our country. The D.M.Z. has been occupied by U.S. troops, and thousands of our countrymen have been removed from their ancestral land. Naturally, in the long run, with more troops and casualties, the U.S. will encounter greater opposition, not only from our people but from the American people as well. But in the meantime, certain segments of our population, especially those crowded into the cities, will be demoralized, then bribed and coerced into cooperating with the enemy.

"The U.S. has decided to sink or swim with the Saigon military regime, which will attempt to legitimize itself in the September elections. Regardless of how the elections are organized, the Saigon generals will get at least ninety percent of the votes, even if only ten percent of the people vote. For us, the elections mean nothing, but we must exploit the opportunity to expose the bellicose and corrupt nature of the Saigon regime and the imperialist, neo-colonial designs of the U.S. Our policy must be, then, to oppose the U.S. policy *and* to overthrow the Saigon regime in favor of peace and democracy. Our national Buddhist League for Peace and Democracy must increase its activities by organizing teachers and students, not only at the university and the high schools, but at the elementary schools too. We must organize cultural, religious, and literary events with clear peace and democracy themes.

"I've received instructions from our National Central Committee," he went on, "to mobilize for a large-scale but peaceful demonstration on the fifteenth day of the seventh month, which is August 10, a Thursday. The committee has been able to persuade the singer Trinh Cong Son to come for the occasion. He has a large following among the youth. Although there will be demonstrations all over South Vietnam that day, our committee thinks that the main event should be in Hue, the intellectual and Buddhist center of the nation. That means that as quickly as we can we must build a broad coalition with all the organizations and all the well-known people who support peace and democracy. I have already secured the cooperation of the head monk of the Tu Dam pagoda." He looked again at his notebook.

"Today is the 22nd of May. That means we have ten weeks to prepare for the largest demonstration ever held in this city. We'll meet here again, if the situation permits, on June 3rd, at five-thirty, to review our plan. As Minh and I will see each other practically every day at the university, we'll have no problems coordinating our work. As for you, Lan, if you need to contact me for anything urgent, let my niece, Mai, who's your student, know. She's a very serious and responsible young woman."

"Yes, that's the most natural and easiest way."

Loc asked if either of them wished to ask questions. Neither did, so he continued in the same formal, businesslike tone:

"Now, to a more precise division of our work. For myself, I'll take charge of the Buddhist Youth, as I have in the past. I'll also help Minh contact faculty and students at the university, and act as liaison with other groups and organizations. Minh, I suggest that besides your work at the university, you should try to get on good terms with the Americans in town, particularly the vice-consul. Since you're not too well-known here yet, it would be good if you were in charge of external affairs, that is, contact with the Americans, and intelligence. Of course, we must be aware of the Rector's attitudes to our activities." Minh nodded.

"Lan," Loc went on, "you will continue your work coordinating all the women's groups." He stopped for a moment. "The main point we should all stress is that the demonstrations must be absolutely nonviolent. Even if they are provoked by the army or the police, the demonstrators should refrain from any violent act. We have no idea how the authorities will react. In the past, they haven't hesitated to shoot to kill. If violence does break out, the committee will have a plan to deal with the situation and will communicate with me by a special courier." He paused and again invited questions.

Minh felt a little annoyed by the authoritative way in which Loc conducted the meeting. He had attended many meetings while he was in the U.S. but they weren't like this one, he thought. Still, he refrained from expressing his complaint. Instead, he said, "Brother Loc and Sister Lan, I am new, and I've never had any experience in mass organization, but I'll do the best I can. I'm sure you'll both help me."

"You'll get experience while you're organizing," Loc told him, "and you'll work out better ideas and learn how to develop collective action. It will take time."

"*Anh* Loc," Lan said, "My experiences during the demonstration in March showed me that we have a serious weakness. Most, if not all, of our brothers had a very dictatorial attitude towards our sisters. Many of the women found that we always had the same chores—typing, or making tea or coffee. This is in contradiction with the practices prevailing in the liberated zones and in the North."

"*Chi* Lan, your observation is correct, and the fact that our sisters complained about this inequity shows that their consciousness is higher now. That's encouraging. But it's important that we study this matter seriously and act on it. I suggest that within the next two days you give me, through Mai, a list of suggestions as to how we can remedy the situation. After the August 10th demonstration, we'll plan a campaign to bring the issue to public debate. But remember—we're living among all the vices of a decadent feudal and bourgeois society, not in the socialist North or the liberated zones. Unlike the lotus, we can't bloom in the mud."

"Maybe after the demonstration you should broaden your contacts with the women's schools," Lan suggested. "From what I know, especially from faculty and students at the Dong Khanh Women's School, you're very well liked and respected."

"I'll think about that. But in my opinion, the question fundamentally lies in the difference between the bourgeois-feudal concept of love, and the revolutionary concept of comradeship. As long as men still entertain bourgeois values based on competition and private ownership, they will only act as protectors of women—or as lovers, which is just another form of domination and private ownership of property. They will see women only as sexual objects, or servants or temptresses labelled as *femmes fatale*. I don't know if I always have a correct attitude towards women, but I know that when women work with me in the same project, in the same organization, I always consider them as comrades. They're part of me and I of them. Comradeship transcends love, sexual or otherwise, and it overcomes jealousy, competition, and intrigue. We all have our biological demands and desires, but we don't have to hide them behind such hypocritical labels as love. After August 10th, we'll discuss this question again and educate ourselves."

Loc glanced at his watch and stood up. "I'm sorry," he said, "but we'll have to finish up now. I know the meeting has been rather short, and we won't have time to go through our usual period of criticism and self-criticism. But in any case Minh is new and needs some time to grow with us, with our revolution." He patted Minh affectionately on the back.

"You'd better leave the bookstore before me and take the Dong Ba Gate on the way home," he told Minh. "It's actually a short cut. And be careful, although nobody watches us as far as I know. I'll see you tomorrow at the university."

Lan shook hands with Minh.

"Incidentally, have you read Daniel Bell's *Cultural Contradictions of Capitalism* yet?" he asked her. "I saw it in a catalog downstairs. I bought a copy at the airport when I left the U.S. but I haven't read it yet. I'll let you have it after the demonstration."

"Thank you," Lan said. "Goodnight."

Minh felt a glow of comradeship as he left Loc and Lan, and a sense of pride that he would be working with them, for a cause he was beginning to believe in. Perhaps it was her businesslike, uncoquettish manner, he thought, but he realized as he headed home that he had hardly noticed Lan's physical appearance. Yet Jennifer could be just as businesslike, he reflected. Was his love for her exploitation? He put her out of his mind. She was beginning to seem irrelevant.

.   .   .

The June 3rd meeting did not take place at the Freedom Bookstore as planned. The day before, Loc had sent word to Minh to meet him after dinner at the Phu Van Lau Pavilion, facing the River of Perfume, south of the Citadel. One of Hue's landmarks, it was built in 1818 as a center where royal decrees and proclamations as well as lists of laureates of triennal examinations were posted.

It was an unusually cool evening. An afternoon torrential rain had swept away all the heat and dust of the day. A half-moon shed its milky light on the city. The wind blew intermittently, pushing broken pieces of white cloud further and further up the dome of a dark blue sky. Minh came a bit early. He wanted to have a few minutes alone at a place he had visited often in his youth, especially during those lingering post-Tet days. He would spend the evening with his friends, looking idly at the river and listening to the melancholy songs of the boatmen and women.

Two perpendicular stone tablets stood at the sides of the pavilion, inscribed with the command, "*Khuynh Cai Ha Ma*, Down from the hammock, off the horse." They were a reminder of a time when the population was required to show respect for royalty.

One of Minh's high school friends had once tried to express his antiroyalist feelings by adding the word "Phong" to the command: "*Khuynh Cai Ha Ma Phong*." "*Ha Ma Phong*" was the name given to a fatal attack suffered without warning by men who attempted to make love after too much wine and food. The victim, his body pressed against his woman, would feel his temperature rising quickly as if he were sunburned; his penis would become as erect as a rod of steel; and within a minute he would be dead. But if his partner was experienced, she could save him. Instead of letting him down "off the horse," she would thrust her hairpin like a needle deep into his pelvis until the blood ran out—whereupon the man slowly returned to life.

Minh heard a song from a distance.

Evening after evening, at the Phu Van Lau landing stage,
Who is seated there, an angling-rod in hand?
In his mind, hope alternates with anguish while on the River, boats go to
and fro.
Boatmen and boatwomen songs rise, and his heart aches as he thinks of
mountains and rivers.

It was about a nineteenth-century patriot, Tran Cao Van, who plotted to drive the French occupation troops out of the capital. He failed and was executed in the public market.

"A beautiful, cool night, isn't it?" Minh had not seen Loc's approach.

"You look very comfortable in that sweater, Loc. I didn't know it would be so cool after the rain."

"You've lost touch with Vietnamese weather. I thought you might have, so I brought an extra one for you." Loc pulled a dark yellow sweater from his paper bag.

"Thank you very much, Loc. That was thoughtful of you. As a matter of fact, I have goose flesh all over." Minh paused to put the sweater on. "Where's Lan?"

"You'll see her the minute you hear a boatwoman's song about the desolation of Hue after the French reconquest in 1947. Do you remember that famous song?"

As Loc finished his sentence, the song arose from the river:

No tree is left on the Imperial Screen:
Birds perch on bare earth,
No passenger on the River of Perfume:
Songstress weeps at the empty sky.

Lan's sampan appeared at the end of the landing. Loc and Minh jumped in.

"I didn't know you were a boatwoman and a talented singer. But you've changed one word in the song. The original one, I think, was 'prostitute,' not 'songstress,'" Minh commented.

"A boatwoman, yes; a talented singer, I doubt. And I changed the word 'prostitute' for aesthetic reasons," Lan answered, smiling. "But now that I've sung a song that is pessimistic and depressing, I'll have to undo it by singing another more optimistic and inspiring one."

Here is the River, there is the Mountain,
They are still the same
Our land is as beautiful as brocade,
Why then worry, comrade?

Right now, we are going to rebuild our future,
To provide a tree for the bird and a sampan for you to cross the River.

Minh knew this song too. He had heard it for the first time during the Tet of 1957. Again, Lan had changed the original word "lover" and replaced it with "comrade," but this time he refrained from comment.

"On that note, *Chi* Lan," Loc saic, "let's row to the middle of the river and anchor."

The River of Perfume was not as busy as Minh remembered it to be. A bumboat-woman asked Lan if she would like to buy some food, but Lan shook her head. They held their meeting inside the sampan, which was lit by a kerosene lamp hung on a suspended altar. Minh was shocked to see on the altar a nude photo of a blonde woman, taken most likely from a spread in Playboy magazine. Loc noticed Minh's surprise and embarrassment.

"Minh, you must know that our Hue sampans are no longer for poetry and music as in the old days before the Americans descended. They're floating houses of prostitution now, mostly to serve our new, unwelcome guests. The government makes some profit out of this, too, by registering the boats and taxing them according to size. Anyway, conducting a meeting on a sampan with a woman isn't a bad cover at all."

"I see," Minh nodded. He glanced at Lan, who seemed to be completely undisturbed.

"This meeting mustn't end any later than 9:45. You may not know it, Minh, but curfew time is eleven on land and only ten on the water. Any sampan moving after ten will be shot at or accosted by the river police."

Loc sat down, gestured to the others to do the same, and began. "Tonight, we're going to discuss two items, unless Brother Minh and Sister Lan have some special problems to raise. No? O.K. The first item is the fourth anniversary of the self-immolation of the Venerable Thich Quang Duc, and the second is our preparations for the demonstration and celebration on August 10th. Both events have been complicated by the self-immolation in Saigon of a young Buddhist woman, Nhat Chi Mai, on May 16. The government has tried to hush it up in Hue, but I'm sure many people already know about it from the Voice of America and the B.B.C. I knew it, but I didn't bring it up at our last meeting because we needed to study the event first and find a proper way to deal with it. Had you heard about it?"

"Yes. I heard it a few days ago from a friend in Saigon who came to visit me," Lan said.

"My brother Phong informed me," Minh said. "He told me that she had left some poems. I think it's important that we have them."

"Yes, I have them," Loc answered quickly. "I'll give you a copy to translate into English and one to Sister Lan for her own use.

"Now. The question we should discuss is this: The Buddhist Institute for the Propagation of the Faith, in Saigon, has tentatively decided to hold demonstrations on June 11th, in both Saigon and Hue, for the anniversary of Venerable Thich Quang Duc's self-immolation and as a memorial for Nhat Chi Mai. When the monks contacted our national committee, we advised them to keep a very low profile on June 11th, that we should all concentrate our efforts on organizing the national demonstration on August 10th, because that's a universal, traditional Buddhist day. It would be very difficult, if not impossible, for the government to ban it.

"Well, we've not had a firm agreement with the Buddhist Institute in Saigon on this matter yet. I *have* reached an understanding with the Patriarch of Thien Mu pagoda and the head monks of Tu Dam and Dieu De, which is that there will only be quiet indoor ceremonies on June 11th, no public, outside demonstration. We won't participate in this event as an organization. In fact I don't think we should be there even as individuals, except for me. My absence would arouse suspicion because of my official position as advisor to the Buddhist Youth Association. Do you have any questions?"

"I agree with you, Loc," Minh said.

"But suppose," Lan interjected, "that the population in general, and particularly the students who think of Thich Quang Duc as a national hero, were to spontaneously demonstrate? What would be our position then? Some of my students have already asked me about the possibility of commemorating the event. After all, they see the Venerable as the man who saved both religion and the nation and whose courageous act led to the overthrow of the Diem regime."

"The question you raise," Loc interrupted, "is being studied very carefully by the committee. As a rule, spontaneity is always bad, even dangerous, in politics. Any political public manifestation that is part of the legal struggle must be well prepared ideologically, strategically, and tactically. On the other hand, of course, disregard for the people's spontaneity can also lead to suppression of revolutionary fervor and put a political organization behind the people instead of with them, or a little bit ahead of them, where it should be."

"In my opinion," Minh interposed, "we should do all we can from now until June 11th to convince people of the greater importance of the August 10th national holiday, of its historical and religious as well as its humane significance. But we must act so as not to antagonize the leadership of the Institute in Saigon. I think we must convince the Venerable Thich Tri Quang, who is no doubt the most charismatic Buddhist leader, of our position. He's well known in the United States; he was even the subject of a cover story in Time magazine. If he opposes us we'll be seen in a very bad light, both at home and abroad."

"*Anh* Minh," Loc answered, "your point is very important. In fact, our national committee in Saigon is in close contact with the Venerable who incidentally is related to my mother. But our principal concern is right here in Hue. We'll follow a two-pronged policy—show our respect and admiration for Thich Quang Duc and Nhat Chi Mai while at the same time promoting our long-term political goal, the mass mobilization struggle for peace and democracy." He paused. "If you have no more questions about June 11th, we can go on to the preparation for the August 10th national mobilization."

Both Lan and Minh nodded in agreement.

"First, we'll maintain the division of work we agreed upon at our last meeting. Don't forget, Minh, that you should be concentrating on building contacts with the American officials in town. Make sure you're invited to the July 4th celebration. Anthony Buckley, the U.S. vice consul here, always has a reception on that day for the big shots. Have you met him yet?"

"Yes, I met him at the airport the day I came home. Another American introduced me to him."

"Who was he?" Loc asked.

"Professor James Morgan of Yale. He'll be doing research in anthropology at our university."

"Very good. You must contact the American vice consul as soon as possible, or at least leave your business card at the consulate so you'll be invited to the reception. From what I know, Buckley is a very cunning person. He's not a regular foreign service officer but a C.I.A. agent. Not a very big difference, though. He speaks no Vietnamese though he has studied French and Chinese. He's single, and close to a Vietnamese woman who's generally sympathetic to our cause. I know her well. She tells me from time to time about what happens at the consulate. She works there as an administrative secretary."

"I'll do what I can to get invited to the reception. Were you invited last year?" Minh asked Loc.

"Not last year, but the year before, because I was acting then as the chairman of the department. The consulate usually invites only the Rector, deans, and department chairpersons of the university. You should also invite the vice-consul for a private dinner and keep in close touch with him." Loc lit a cigarette.

"The second thing I want to discuss with you," he went on, "is the list of suggestions Sister Lan sent me about how we can remedy the inferior and unequal position of women in our organization as well as in any other collective work. Of course our discussions can only be preliminary because the question is so important, not only to our present work but also for the future of our nation. Eventually I'll write a report on our talks to the national committee.

"Now, Lan, about your first suggestion that we should circulate some basic literature on the woman's question. I've thought of two documents. One is a study by Frederick Engels that analyzes the origin of the family, private property, and the State, and the other is a compilation of documents by the propaganda department of the Vietnam Workers Party. The Engels has been translated into Vietnamese, but I haven't seen a recent print. The second one was published in Hanoi last year. Of course neither can be freely circulated in our zone.

"I'll suggest to the national committee that they compile a list of readings on the subject, in Vietnamese and in other languages. In the meantime, Minh should help with the compilation of such a literature for our immediate use locally, bearing in mind that there is a fundamental difference between the feminist movement and the women's liberation movement. Remember, too, Minh, that it's the woman's *question*, not the woman's *problem*. Men and repressive political and economic systems are the problems, not women. There are also some differences between the struggle of women in industrialized countries and those in third world countries. What's your opinion, Sister Lan?"

"I think the best way is to start with a simple booklet that would include topics like the original Vietnamese culture, women and Confucianism, women and Buddhism, women and Taoism, women in resistance wars against foreign invaders, women and socialism, women in the North, and women in the liberated zones. The important point is to build, or rather rebuild, women's self-confidence. With self-confidence and basic information, women can carry out any task. After all, equality is a question of self-confidence."

"I agree," Minh concurred, "and all of us should start working on it, not right now, but after August 10th. I taught a course on the politics of national liberation while I was at Thomas Paine College in the States, and based on my research, I've come to the tentative conclusion that a national liberation movement would win if forty to fifty percent of women participated. Of course, I do make a distinction between representation, which is the essence of feminism, and participation, which is the essence of women's liberation. There is some significant literature on this subject, I think. I'll try to contact friends abroad, in Paris and the United States, to get some of it."

"I'm sure you both know that in the National Liberation Front women are sharing equal and full power and responsibility with men," said Loc. "Madame Nguyen Thi Dinh, for instance, is president of the Women's Union and deputy commander in chief of the liberation armed forces, and Madame Nguyen Thi Binh is in charge of foreign affairs and is vice-president of the Women's Union.

"Now, on Lan's second suggestion, that we try to get courses on women at the university, I think it's a good idea, but we'll have to find out how to get the university's approval. What's your opinion, Minh?"

"Realistically, I don't think we can get separate courses on women under the present circumstances, but we can accentuate the role of women in all our courses. Nobody can prevent us from doing that informally."

"We'll try," Loc said. "Her third suggestion, that we start a campaign to educate the population on the importance of women in society, is obviously crucial, but we can't do it without the direction and approval of the national committee. In any case we can't do it before August 10th, but we'll talk about it again.

"As for the suggestion that I should broaden my contacts with women's schools, again, the idea is excellent, but I don't know how I can find time to do it regularly. Sister Lan has recommended that I visit her school sometime in the near future. I'll be glad to do so and I'll confirm the date soon.

"The suggestion to invite Nun Thich Lien Hoa for a speaking tour in Hue needs some preparation. As *Chi* Lan might not know, Nun Hoa was recently here on a private visit but had to return yesterday to Saigon because of urgent business there. My mother and brother and Minh's auntie have seen her. I have met and talked with her here and in Saigon. She's quite a remarkable person, dedicated, an excellent speaker and intellectually advanced. She's studied both in Japan and France. I'll try to contact her and make arrangements for her to make another trip to Hue."

"How come only a very few people know about her visit?" Lan said.

"She's on the government's enemy list and is being confined to restricted residence," Loc replied. "She came here with special permission from the Saigon police and she had to sign a promise that she would attend to purely religious matters."

"I see."

"Well, that's all your suggestions. Do either of you have any more questions?" Loc asked, looking at his watch. "We still have about twenty minutes before curfew. If you don't, then we can conclude the meeting. The time and place for our next meeting will be communicated to you in the near future. Now we can go outside to be in the company of our sister moon."

The River of Perfume seemed to be exploding in light. It was more lively than it had been earlier, perhaps because the passengers on the river knew they had only a little time left to enjoy the night. A large sampan filled with laughter and music floated by. Loc stopped a boat to buy some hot, sweet lotus seeds.

Under the moonlight, Minh noticed how beautiful Lan was. Her brown eyes, black hair, and long neck reminded him of a Modigliani portrait he had once admired in a museum in Boston. He knew he shouldn't respond to her physical beauty, but he told himself that his reaction was artistic, not sensual.

After they had eaten their lotus seeds, Loc read a poem, "*The Song of the Sampan-Woman on the River of Perfume*," written over thirty years earlier by To Huu, the poet laureate of North Vietnam and a member of the central committee of the Vietnam Workers Party:

"The moon rises, and then wanes:
All my life I shall sail on my sampan.
My sampan is empty:
When shall I be able to leave this stream of depravation?
How could one talk of love when all of it is hypocrisy and shame?
My sampan has grown derelict:
Could it ever be young and fresh again?

Loc rowed the sampan down to Dong Ba market to return it and pay its owner. He let Minh and Lan disembark at a landing near the Trang Tien Bridge. Before he left, he handed Nhat Chi Mai's poems to Minh.

"Please try to translate them into English and send them to some magazines or newspapers in the U.S. Their effect could be tremendous."

Minh walked silently with Lan to the Freedom Bookstore. He took leave of her with a handshake and hailed a rickshaw to return home.

.   .   .

Everyone in the house was deep in sleep. He tiptoed to his room, and turning on the light found a letter in an army envelope. It was from An.

Saigon, June 1st 1967

Dear Brother Minh,

I have not written you or talked with you for some time but Phong tells me that you are well and busy. I myself have been very busy. The army and police are taking precautions for an anticipated Buddhist antigovernment demonstration June 11th, on the 4th anniversary of the self-immolation of the Venerable Thich Quang Duc. However, I'll be in Hue sometime after June 11th to visit with you and father and say goodbye to Phong before he leaves for his command in Quang Tri.

You will find enclosed a letter addressed to you in care of myself. As you will notice, I was promoted by the person who wrote you, to Lieutenant General and Deputy Chief of Staff. This error could have cost me heavily if it had come to the attention of my superiors. Fortunately, the lieutenant in charge of military postal service knows me and knows you're my brother. He detected the error and rushed the letter directly to me without going through the routine screening process. Perhaps it would be better for your American friends to write you directly at the house or your office. But in case they like to use my address, be sure they identify me as Lieutenant Colonel and Deputy Director of Military Intelligence.

I'll see you soon.

Affectionately,
Tran Van An

Minh was sure that the enclosed letter was from Jennifer, although the address was typed and the postmark unclear. He turned it over in his hands. Though she couldn't have known the possible consequences, her error annoyed him. He was reluctant to read her letter, he realized. It came as an intrusion from another world. Instead, he started translating Nhat Chi Mai's poems. They moved him to tears; each sentence sent a lump to his throat.

By midnight he had finished the first draft. The first poem, which she had hung nearby as she was preparing for her self-immolation, was titled, *My Intention.*

> *I wish to use my body as a torch*
> *To dissipate the darkness*
> *To waken Love among men*
> *And to bring Peace to Vietnam.*

The second one she had recited as the fire consumed her body. It was called, *I Kneel Down and Pray.*

> *Why do Americans burn themselves?*
> *Why do non-Vietnamese demonstrate all over the world?*
> *Why does Vietnam remain silent And not dare to utter the word Peace?*
>
> *I feel helpless And I suffer.*
> *If alive I cannot express myself,*
> *I will offer my life to show my aspirations.*
>
> *Is appealing for Peace a crime?*
> *Is acting for Peace communism?*
> *I am appealing for Peace in the name of Man.*
>
> *I join my hands and kneel down;*
> *I accept this utmost pain in my body*
> *I hope that the words of my heart be heard.*
> *Please stop it, my fellowmen!*
>
> *Please stop it, my fellowmen!*
> *More than twenty years have elapsed,*
> *More than twenty years of bloodshed;*
> *Do not exterminate my people!*
> *Do not exterminate my people!*
>
> *I join my hands and kneel down to pray.*

> *Signed: Nhat Chi Mai*
> *The one who burns herself for*
> *Peace.*

The third was in the form of a letter she had mailed to her father and mother before she died:

I have decided by myself to offer my life, not because I hate this world, but because I love it. I love the country, the people and mankind.

Minh reread the translations, put them into a folder, and threw himself on his bed. He couldn't sleep. He watched the moon's rays as they filtered into the room. He opened the window. A gentle breeze scattered diamond-like drops of water from the banana leaves. He thought of Lan and tried to push back in his mind any kind of sentimental attraction for her. "She's my comrade," he said to himself. He got out of bed and opened Jennifer's letter.

321 Hampshire Street # 5
Amherst, Mass. 01002
May 25, 1967

Dearest Minh,

It's been almost a month since you left and although I haven't received any news from you, I'm sure you're well. I can imagine how busy you must be with your family and friends. Your absence makes me realize how much I love you and perhaps no one can express better my feelings at this moment than the Japanese poet Buson whom you admired:

Old weary willows . .
I thought how long
the road would be
when you are away.

It's very hard for me to forget you. Every night the TV brings scenes of war and death from Vietnam and every day's newspaper headlines tell of bombings and body counts. Last week, I attended a lecture given at the local Unitarian church by a woman who had just returned from Vietnam. She served as a social worker for three years with the Vietnam Christian Service. She showed slides of the "free-fire zones," of defoliated forests and children grotesquely disfigured by napalm. The audience was generally sympathetic to her pacifist position, but I was horrified when a man came to shake her hand and said he "enjoyed the show." Also, there was a huge man in the room who challenged her, claiming that he'd been in Vietnam for four years as an adviser to the South Vietnamese Special Forces. He said she was a dupe of the clever propaganda by the Viet Cong who committed the atrocities, killing village chiefs, burning down schools and hospitals, and kidnapping the peasants. He was convinced that the Viet Cong and the North Vietnamese were increasing their attacks because the South was making enormous economic progress, thanks to American financial aid and military protection. I don't know how much he impressed the audience. They didn't react one way or the other to his short speech. After the lecture I approached the woman speaker, (her name is Dorothy Robinson), and I asked her if she had been in Hue. "That's the most beautiful city in Vietnam," she answered, "but unless the war is ended soon, it will be destroyed the same as the others, physically and culturally. And if Hue is destroyed, the soul of Vietnam is destroyed." She told me that she visited Hue from time to time, but worked in a smaller community about fifty miles south of it. She impressed me as a very dedicated person and said she was going back to Vietnam within three months. She didn't ask me why I was interested in Hue, though, sparing me a very difficult explanation.

My school was over yesterday and I felt so relieved. For the first time, the idea came to me to leave school, temporarily of course, to do something else for a while. I don't know what the school's reaction will be, but it seems that all my life literally has been spent going from school to school and I'm tired of it all. What do you think? I'n going to Canada for a two-week vacation after June 15th, and will be back in Amherst about July 1st. If you have time, please drop me a note to let me know what you've been doing. I'll write to you again after vacation. Please take good care of yourself and let me know if there's anything I can do for you here. I miss you a lot, but somehow I know we'll be seeing each other again, perhaps before the war is over, so I'm not very sad.

> As always,
> Love,
> Jennifer

Minh reached for an airletter and wrote an immediate reply:

> Hue, June 3rd, 1967

Dear Jennifer,

Thank you for your note of May 25th, addressed to me through my brother who is NOT a Lieutenant General but a Lieutenant Colonel, NOT a Deputy Chief-of-Staff, but a Deputy Director of Military Intelligence. Next time, please write me directly at this address: No. 9 Quoc Tu Giam Street, Hue, via Saigon, South Vietnam.

I have been very busy since I returned, and beginning next week, I will start teaching at the University and will probably be busier.

I understand how you feel about school but I hesitate to give you any advice except to say that to leave school even temporarily is an important decision and you should think about it more. Perhaps you should consult your parents.

Have a pleasant vacation.
Best wishes,

> Yours,
> Tran Van
> Minh

Minh knew his letter was cold and formal and that he had not signed with "love." Love is like an orchid, he thought, it grows only in certain climates and with certain specific care. Jennifer seemed unreal to him. His main concern was that she should have his address so she wouldn't repeat the error that might harm An.

VI

Heaven's Truth

To read is quite an act in these foul times.
To teach was even hard for wiser heads.
By knowledge freed, the mind flows like a stream.
With few desires, the body fears no threat.
Purge man of greed, and Heaven's truth will shine.

Advice to students
Phung Khac Khoan
1528–1613
Translated by Huynh Sanh Thong

Minh was scrutinizing two large yellow banners bearing red characters that were hung at the gate of the university. One read:

Study to fight atheist and obscurantist Communism.
Study to serve the winning Free World.

The other said:

Remember what the Communists did, not what they say.
Remember the 1956 Nhan Van Affair and the Communist suppression of
Freedoms of Speech and Publications.

Loc came up behind him. "So you're studying government slogans?"

"Yes. I wonder how many students are paying attention to these?"

"I doubt very many. As a matter of fact, last year I asked my students to write a paper in class about slogans they saw in the city's buildings and streets, and to my amazement, only two out of fifty remembered exactly what they said. Generally they dismiss them as meaningless."

"Where are your classes?" Minh inquired.

"On the ground floor."

"Mine are on the second."

"I'll see you," Loc said, running after another man who had passed by.

It was Minh's habit, when he taught in the U.S., to come to school early on opening day to watch the students, and also to reflect a little. Coming from a family of Buddhist scholars, he believed that a teacher's vocation was comparable to that of a *bhikku*, a Buddhist monk, and that the beginning of an academic year was like the beginning of a retreat. No matter how long one has taught, Minh thought, on the first day there are always the same anxieties, a feeling of humility, concentration, and the same openness of heart. And too, the realization of the fragility, the indefinable relations between human beings and the Unknown and the Unseen, whether one thought of the Unknown as Buddha or as education. The start of a school year calls for a renewal of discipline and compassion, precision and toler- ance. The teacher justifies his existence with faith in the possibility of human enlightenment, elevation, purification, and liberation.

But here the similarity between the *bhikku* and the teacher ends. In silence—light in body, heavy in soul—the disciple of Buddha contemplates eternity and salvation, while the teacher, in the same room with dozens of unfamiliar, cynical-looking men and women of undeclared intentions, pressured by time and squeezed by space, must perform immediately. Against a blackboard—symbol of the dark state of human knowledge—on stage but without a platform, the teacher has to rise above his audience and at the same time treat each student as his partner and confidant. In this sense, his task is lonelier than that of an actor. He has no warmth of lights, colors, music, or cues to rely on. His only resources are his physical presence and the theories, paradigms, and footnotes he assimilated years ago in graduate school or in his reading of dull articles in professional magazines.

But no matter how well the teacher prepares during those hot, lazy summer months, it takes time for theories and paradigms to be developed coherently so they can be explained clearly. Ideas from specialized journals need to be tested and verified, and experience is no real help, being most often a combination of exaggerated successes and suppressed failures. The teacher is saved only by an eager face or a meaningful question. But somehow students, at least American students, are sad-looking and strangely mute at the beginning of a semester. Most of them don't know that it is the eager face and the meaningful question that create communication, that establish for the rest of the semester the common bond between student and teacher. Without that bond, there is no education, only mutual tolerance, deception, moral and intellectual destruction.

When he was teaching in the United States Minh had devised a number of strategies to engage his students. The best one was "to draw the tigers out of the mountains." It was a guerilla strategy used by leaders from Mao Tse-tung to Ho Chi Minh. Its main tactic was to take the offensive right away by asking a provocative question disguised as an opinion: "I wonder why people go to college at all?" Minh thought of Jennifer. It was her eager face in a sea of blank ones that had first endeared her to him.

Earlier that morning his father had given him some advice. "In the present Vietnam," he had said, "people must be taught the sense of shame. Without it, education is a disguise for corruption and servitude. Without it, teachers and students are criminal accomplices in the destruction of public and private moralities, of national traditions and individual courage. Without the sense of shame, one is unable to understand tradition, one is afraid of change, of revolution, of taking risks." Yes, education is both tradition and revolution, Minh was convinced of that. But who represented tradition and revolution in Vietnam in the 1960s? The Buddhists? The communists? The nationalist anticommunists?

Standing in front of the university, Minh was almost frozen with fear for a moment by the quick comings and goings of hundreds of young women and men, all so serious and determined. Carrying his attaché case he slowly walked to the second floor for his class on the American Revolution.

Although he was ten minutes early, the room was packed and the 50 seats were all taken. At first glance, he saw more women than men. Perhaps the men are in the army, Minh thought. He wondered why there were so many students, what had attracted them to his course. And unlike American students they seemed eager, even intense.

The room was hushed.

"I would like to welcome all of you to this class and I'm glad and grateful that so many of you came."

There was no answer, no visible reaction, except for a few discreet smiles in the front row. To cover his stage fright Minh began to distribute copies of the syllabus, apologizing for their insufficiency. He had expected 30 students at most.

Minh had never lectured before in Vietnamese. He looked forward to finding out whether the Vietnamese language, so expressive in literature and poetry, could be as fit for politics as Loc had demonstrated during their first meeting. He began to explain his methodology, saying that while he hoped the students would read the books he recommended, he would not lecture on them but on such concepts as "life, liberty and the pursuit of happiness"; the influences of Confucianism on French philosophers like Voltaire, Montesquieu, and Diderot, who in turn had influenced American revolutionaries like Thomas Jefferson; and the role of Thomas Paine in the 1776 revolution. And he would require the students, he said, to form groups of ten to conduct specific projects that would be presented collectively in class as final papers. At this, one student raised his hand.

"Professor, could you explain a little bit more about group projects? We're not familiar with this method. We've always written individual papers." Many heads nodded in agreement with the questioner.

"The fundamental idea behind a group project is that history, revolution, or any event of significance is the result of collective work, of many people cooperating with one another. You all probably learned about our resistance against the Mongol invasions in the thirteenth century. Our victories against what were probably the most powerful armies then on earth weren't brought about by the leadership of the Tran monarchy, enlightened as it was, but mostly by the collective determination of all Vietnamese, expressed thunderously at the famed popular convention at the Dien Hong Palace in 1284. In learning together, researching together, you will, I hope, discover the collective meaning of historical events rather than the individual qualities of a certain hero. I shall go into detail in another session after you form your groups and decide on your research topics."

He realized that his answer was vague but he wanted it that way. Then, to "draw the tigers out of the mountains," he asked the students why they had come to his course. "What do you expect to learn here," he asked, "and to what specific use do you expect to put what you learn?"

A woman wearing thick reading glasses raised her hand. "Professor, I came to this course to find out the relationship, if there is any, between the principles of the American revolution and those dictating the present American foreign policy in general and the American policy in Vietnam in particular. Also, as a scholar who has been in the U.S., I'm sure you can tell us also how the American people are faring in their 'pursuit of happiness.' And one more thing. Why is it that all revolutionaries in the third world, from President Sukarno to President Ho Chi Minh, denounce what they call American imperialism, while praising the American revolution? Is there a contradiction here? Is it possible, as the Hanoi leaders claim, to fight against the American soldiers and love the American people?"

"Miss . . . what is your name?" Minh asked.

"My name is To Ngoc."

"Thank you, Miss To Ngoc. I'm very grateful for your question. It contains most of the issues I'd like to raise and discuss in this course."

A tall, long-haired man in a Hawaiian shirt spoke.

"Professor, my name is Vo Van Buom. I came to this course to learn more about America, to prepare myself to continue my graduate studies in physics in the U.S. I have great admiration for America and I'm grateful for the American soldiers who leave their comfortable homes to come here and help us fight for democracy against communism. I was in the army in 1963 and had an opportunity to visit the Philippines and see with my own eyes how America has built that country into a free and prosperous nation. Moreover, I heard that you have been teaching in the U.S. and therefore you must understand that country better than some of our professors who were educated in France and prejudiced against America."

There were scattered chuckles in the room. Minh raised his voice.

"Please let Mr. Buom speak."

"Thank you, Professor, that's all I want to say."

Judging from their reactions, Minh thought, the majority of his students were curious about America. Some were discreetly sarcastic about the American revolution, some openly pro-American; but it would be a very interesting class.

Suddenly there was a knock at the door; before he could open it his uncle burst in. The Rector handed him a brown envelope stamped "SECRET" in fat black letters.

He whispered to Minh, "Could you introduce me to your class? I'm new here and most of the students don't know who I am. I've some announcements to make."

"Of course, Uncle. May I have your attention?" Minh asked, turning to the class. "I have the honor and the pleasure to introduce to you the new Rector of the university, Dr. Hoang Luong."

All the students stood up. Annoyed at their automatic expression of respect—all too common among Vietnamese students, Minh thought—he motioned them to be seated.

"I'm glad that so many of you have chosen to attend this class," the Rector said. "Your professor is a relative of mine, but he didn't get the job because of nepotism"—he stopped and smiled, but the students remained unmoved as he continued—"but because of his perfect credentials. However, I came here today not to introduce my nephew to you, but to welcome you, and have a few words with you.

"As you all know, our university was closed for a few months because of political disturbances and I'm sure none of you would want it to happen again. Therefore I strongly advise you to devote all your energies and time to study, not to political activities, on or off campus. If there are things you dislike or disagree with, you can talk them over directly with your professors or make an appointment to see me. The government has made it very clear to me that if disturbances occur again, the university will be closed for good. I assume that you male students realize that if that happens, you will all be drafted." He paused and paced the floor for a moment.

"I received a request from both the mayor of Hue and the Hue district military commander asking for weekend volunteers to help our less fortunate compatriots. There are two projects. One is to go to the hospitals and spend time with our wounded soldiers to give them comfort and encouragement. There is increasingly heavy fighting in Quang Tri and other areas north of our city, and hundreds of wounded are being evacuated here. The other is to go to any of several new refugee settlements on the outskirts of the city to help families who have had to leave their villages because of the Viet Cong attacks. In both cases, you should contact the Revolutionary Development personnel in charge. Leave them your name, address, and student number, your major, and the names of your instructors and the R.D. office will send the list back to me at the end of each week. Although the government doesn't wish to make this service compulsory, it did say to me in no uncertain terms that it's an obligation which cannot be shirked. If you have any questions, please contact the vice-rector in charge of public affairs.

"Also, be sure to get your student identification card, as well as your regular citizen I.D., of course. The university will stay open Saturday and Sunday this week to assist you. The Hue chief of police has emphasized that without your student I.D., you will have a lot of trouble with the military police, who check regularly for draft dodgers. Thank you for your attention."

The Rector shook hands with Minh and left. Again, the students stood up, and again, Minh quickly asked them to sit down. Looking at his watch, Minh said, "You can go now. I'll see you next Tuesday, and remember the Rector's instructions." He didn't look at the students as they filed out.

Alone, Minh opened the envelope his uncle had given him. It contained lists of all the students in his classes, two copies of each. On one, marked "SECRET" in red, there were signs in front of some names. A note explained that a cross signified a suspected Viet Cong agent, a circle, a suspected Viet Cong sympathizer, and a square, a person suspected of doubtful morality or drug addiction. Out of the 125 students enrolled in his classes, 62 bore symbols beside their names.

Minh was disgusted. He couldn't imagine any professor in an American university accepting such a list without protest. He wanted to tear up the pages, rush to his uncle's office, dump the pieces on his desk, and tender his resignation. But he was in Vietnam, not the United States, and he knew that as Rector his uncle had no choice but to yield to government and police pressures.

He was amazed at the speed with which the lists had been compiled. Registration had closed only two days ago, yet the lists were already completed and computerized. The police must have files on every student and citizen, he thought. I'd better be careful myself.

With more than three hours free before his next class, Minh had just set out for a walk when he heard someone calling his name.

"Professor Minh, can I see you a minute?"

Jogging toward him was a well-dressed middle-aged man. "Minh, don't you recognize me?" the man asked.

"But of course, Trang, what are you doing here?"

"I've been teaching economics here for the last two years. I just came back from Saigon yesterday from my father's funeral. That's why I wasn't present at the preregistration faculty meeting and the first classes. I was so happy when the Rector told me that you and I would be team-teaching the seminar on the U.S. military-industrial complex."

"I'm glad too, but I'm sorry to hear about your father's death. It's been a long time since we saw each other. The last time was five years ago, and then only for a few minutes, on a street in Saigon."

"Yes. You were a big shot then and very busy. I was just starting to teach economics at Saigon University after my return from Tokyo."

"How long did you stay in Japan?"

"It took me three whole years to finish my Ph.D. in economics at Waseda University. Let's walk to the Imperial Landing Market and have lunch there so we can talk."

"I'll have to tell my uncle first. He was supposed to pick me up at noon to take me home. I always use his official car for my transportation."

"You don't need to. I just saw him and he actually suggested that I invite you to lunch."

"Very well."

They walked along the canal, on a shady avenue that bore the name of Phan Boi Chau, a patriot-poet whom Minh's father—indeed, all Vietnamese—greatly respected. He had died in 1940 after years of forced residence in a simple cottage on a hill north of Imperial Landing.

"How did you like Japan and the Japanese?" Minh asked. "I passed through Tokyo once and I must tell you that I didn't like either the country or the people. I know I'm biased, but I can't forget the atrocities they committed against our people when they occupied our country. And they've often betrayed us. All our patriots who flocked to Japan after it defeated Russia in 1905, hoping to learn how to defeat Western colonialists, were betrayed to the French. And I don't like their individual characteristics, either. They always look sleepy, and walk like automatons. The women are treated like toys or servants. I must admit, though, that they have produced artistic things, some beautiful poetry. And of course, they've succeeded in a short time to build a very powerful economy," Minh said. He surprised even himself with this outpouring of anti-Japanese feelings.

"Well, Minh, I too suffered a great deal mentally and biologically while I was in Japan. I don't like their food. It's insipid, simplified, and bland. Come to think of it, Japan is the only country in Asia whose people eat raw fish. They've not learned how to spice their meals the way other Asians do. They're really very different from us. We're openly romantic, they're sentimentally repressed. We explode, they internalize; we eat well, they work hard; they are brutal and we are . . ." Trang paused, embarrassed.

"You mean, we are violent," Minh finished for him. "Is that what you had in mind?"

"Yes, Minh, that's what I had in mind. A few months ago, I went to the delta in the South. I never witnessed so much war and destruction in my life. I saw violence and death everywhere. At the hastily built cemeteries, at the crowded refugee camps. I saw our racial discrimination against the Cambodian minority and was told about the slaughter of Cambodians at the border by the Saigon soldiers. I saw defoliated forests and cratered rice fields, children burned by napalm and women disfigured by mine explosions or just by sheer sufferings . . ." Trang stopped, his head lowered.

Minh spotted the sign of a restaurant he remembered for its famous pancakes. "Let's go to the Exile's Dream Restaurant," Minh said, glad to change the subject.

"Anyplace. I know very little about Hue's restaurants, although my father lived here several years before we moved to Saigon."

"I like this place not only because of its delicious pancakes, but also because of its name."

"You are an incurable romantic," Trang commented. "Where did the name come from?"

"From a poem in memory of the late patriot Phan Boi Chau. Part of it goes, 'the bells of Dieu De pagoda recall the exile's dream, The nightly rains over the River of Perfume weep over the poet's soul.'"

Although Minh had only just met Trang again after so many years—they had been high school classmates—he liked him: his open face and uncombed hair, the dimples on his cheeks, his sincerity and sensitivity.

The restaurant's interior decoration had not changed. The same large painting depicting the Eight Immortals of the Taoists still dominated the room with its magical and colorful mythology. Chung Ly Chuyen, the senior among the eight, was shown holding the Elixir of Life, which, possessing the power of transmutation, symbolizes longevity. He was followed clockwise by Ha Tien Co, the only woman, with her lotus flower and her fly-whisk; Lan Thai Hao, the patron saint of florists, carrying a basket of flowers and a flute; Tao Quoc Cuu, the patron saint of the theater, playing his castanets (Minh's mother disliked him; she thought the theater should be represented by a woman); Han Luong Tu, the protector of musicians, who besides his musical powers can make flowers grow and bloom instantaneously; Ly Thiet Quai, a magician, with his iron crutch and a gourd, shown standing on a crab; Lu Dong Tan, the guardian of barbers, worshipped by the sick and the poor, armed with a sword and a fly-whisk with which he drove away evil; and Truong Qua Lao, with a bamboo drum on his lap, riding a mule backwards.

"You seem to like the Eight Immortals." Trang interrupted Minh's absorption in the painting.

"Yes, I do. I'm always impressed by the intellectual powers of the Taoists, their sense of magic and fantasy, mixed with irony."

"Unfortunately they can't do anything for us mortals in a mortal war."

"How do you feel about our war Trang? Can we win?" Minh asked.

"Our war is hopeless. It has lost all its meaning and we're going to lose it soon."

"Why?"

"Because the Vietnamese army, the Saigon army, doesn't want to fight an American war, the Americans don't know how to fight a Vietnamese war, and the peoples of both Vietnam and America hate the war."

"What can we do to stop it?"

"I don't know. To be honest, I'm in a cruel dilemma. I'm convinced that if the war is stopped, it'll mean the Viet Cong are winning, and I have no illusions about what they'll do afterwards. They'll impose socialism, which is not going to work, curtail all individual liberties, and put people like you and me, the intellectuals and the bourgeoisie, in re-education camps. At the same time, as an economist, I realize that socialism can bring a better life for the masses—the workers, the peasants, and the poor—though at a very heavy price, of course. Yet I've often thought that we will all have to join the Viet Cong if we're ever going to stop this senseless war and get rid of our external enemy, the Americans."

"But what about the internal enemy?"

"We can't deal with both at the same time," Trang answered unconvincingly. "Let's talk about school and what we can do together in our seminar."

"You've been teaching here for two years, you should be able to tell *me* what we can do, what kind of situation we're in."

"Well, let me finish this delicious pancake before it gets cold," Trang responded. He applied himself like a child at a Tet dinner to devouring the steaming pancake with its savory filling of shrimp, mushrooms, bean sprouts, and flavored leaves. He wiped the brown sesame sauce from his mouth with his handkerchief before he spoke.

"I'm not a cynic, never, but the situation here and at Saigon University is really sad, even absurd. We have a war in our midst, yet we pretend that it doesn't exist because we don't see the Viet Cong and his bazooka in our streets. Young people from privileged families go to school to avoid the draft. And what do we teach them? Not only here but at Saigon University and elsewhere? Economics, in a country that has no economy of its own, only foreign aid. Law, when we don't even have a legal code or a constitution. Politics, when there is no political life here, only intrigue, manipulation, and a rotten, corrupt administrative apparatus set up and ruled by illiterate generals. We teach them humanities when they see around them only degradation and violence. We teach them medicine, preparing them to be medical doctors in seven long years, when millions of our people need only good sanitation and nutrition. I could go on and on. You and I are in a tragic, if not a comic, situation. We have no choice, of course, because we're afraid of making choices, so we keep on pretending."

"I suppose that what you say is true. Still, we have to continue our life and teach."

"Obviously."

"By the way, have you received the students' lists for your courses?"

"Why do you ask?"

"I just received mine. It's the first time I've ever seen such a thing—a secret student list with all the students' political beliefs identified."

Trang broke into a cynical smile. "Minh, you're new in this system and you take it too seriously. The lists mean nothing, they're not even secret. I'm sure the students will have copies of them, and the Viet Cong already have. Just a game to threaten the students and the faculty, who I know couldn't care less about them either. Just forget about the whole thing and enjoy your lunch."

"I see."

They crossed a small bridge over the canal and took a different route, parallel to Phan Boi Chau Avenue, to return to the university. The city was hushed at siesta and they both walked quietly. Minh broke the silence.

"Trang, do you observe siesta?"

"Sometimes I do, sometimes I don't. In a few minutes I'll have to go to An Cuu to meet with a Redemptorist Father who just came back from Canada. He's a Japanese expert who taught me Japanese before I went to Tokyo."

"So you're a Catholic?"

"Sort of. I was born a Catholic but I've never confessed. My confessions would take a year to complete and neither Jesus nor a priest could have that much time." He smiled. "You might like to while away your time in the library until our seminar. The library isn't well stocked but it does have a very good collection of historical records in Chinese of the period from 1600 to 1900, that might interest you. Some of them are already translated into Vietnamese. In case the library's closed, just go downstairs and ask for the key at the security office."

"Thank you, I might just do that. I'll see you at two."

·　　　　·　　　　·

The library was open, but except for the librarian there wasn't a soul in it. The librarian let Minh in without asking for his faculty I.D.—probably because I'm wearing a tie, Minh thought. He went directly to a shelf marked "History" and quickly located the 1600–1900 archives. He read the anecdotes about *Bac Tien*, the March to the North, in 1789, the year of the French Revolution, when King Quang Trung, during Tet, attacked a Chinese invading force of 200,000 that had occupied *Thang Long* (Hanoi). The king defeated the Chinese in a brilliant victory, and the Chinese commander had to flee Vietnam without having time to organize his troops' retreat.

That period had always absorbed Minh's interest. For one thing, Vietnam was divided then, as it was today, at the seventeenth parallel. Besides that, Minh was fascinated by the personality and policies of King Quang Trung, who was the first king to have come from peasant origins and who, "with a red flag and cotton garb," defeated all of Vietnam's external enemies and started the most radical land reform in the history of Vietnam thus far. His short reign (he died at the age of 40) provided the best evidence of the revolutionary power of the peasantry. One did not have to wait, Minh often thought, for Mao Tse-tung's famed 1927 "Report on an Investigation of the Peasant Movement in Hunan" to understand that power.

Minh sensed that someone was looking over his shoulder. Looking around he saw James Morgan, whom he had met on the plane coming from Saigon.

"What a surprise to see you here, Professor Minh!" Morgan exclaimed.

"What a surprise to see you here, too, Professor Morgan!"

"We shouldn't be surprised. We're probably the only two in the city who aren't addicted to siesta. Even our vice-consul has taken up the habit. I hope the Viet Cong are observing siesta too, otherwise this city and the consulate could be overrun easily. I think there are two holy observances in this country: the daily siesta and the yearly Tet."

"You're right."

"Incidentally, I saw Vice-Consul Buckley the other day and he asked about you. He suggested that we get together some time for dinner with him at his place."

"I certainly would love to do that," Minh replied.

"Let's go sit on the grass on the back lawn and look at the River of Perfume and talk. Can I go back to my office and bring you a coke?"

"No need. Let's go."

They sat under the only tamarind tree on the lawn. The grass sloped gradually down to the river, where only a few sampans were moving idly.

"Well, Professor Morgan, how have you been? Are you settled? Where do you live? Where's your office?"

"Call me Jim. I'd feel more comfortable."

"If you wish." Minh had never quite become accustomed to the American habit of quick informality and now, back in his own country, he was reluctant to ask Morgan to call him Minh. He liked to let a situation develop by itself, but Morgan didn't seem to notice that subtlety. Morgan continued.

"I've been enjoying my stay so far. Hue is a quiet, cultured, attractive, and interesting city. I've been living at the Capital Hotel, but I'm looking for a house. I hope the government relaxes the regulations so I can bring my family here. I just bought a second-hand Renault and my office is in the university annex, just a room and a typewriter. I've already developed good relations with my colleagues in the anthropology department. The only unhappy thing is that the chairman, Dr. Que, whose works I'm most interested in, is in Saigon for treatment of his wounds."

"What happened to him?"

"I was told that about two months ago, against the advice of everyone, he bicycled to the Thien Mu pagoda to see a monk. On his return, while he was riding down a slope, a mine exploded and he was badly wounded. They had to evacuate him to Saigon for better facilities. He might be away for several months. Too bad, because without him I lose a precious guide, especially since I was told that he was about to finish a study on the human and cultural dimensions of Tet."

"I'm sorry to hear that. I hope you can find other scholars to help you. If I remember correctly, you're interested in studying the effects of the introduction of American technology on Vietnamese traditional culture, and in knowing the old Vietnamese aristocratic families?"

"Correct, and all my inquiries so far have led me to believe that to understand the Vietnamese culture, one has to understand the essence and meaning of Tet. I've not yet seen anything like it. It seems to me that the Vietnamese are living and working 364 days a year to wait for one day of Tet. I have to wait eight more months."

"We used to celebrate Tet," Minh interrupted, "not just for a day, but a whole month or at least two weeks. But now it's only five days."

"Yet I've not seen any study on Tet in English. Have you?"

"It seems to me there was a long article in the special Tet issue of the Saigon Courier two years ago."

"Is the Courier an English paper? Who wrote the article?"

"Yes, it's English owned by an American. I can't recall the name of the author," Minh said. He was reluctant to tell Morgan that he himself had written the article under his pen-name, Co Tung.

"I'll look up the paper in the library, and if it's not there, I'll send for it at the Lincoln Library in Saigon." He brushed an ant from his arm.

"Another conclusion I've come to—actually I knew it before I came here—is that your family is the oldest in Hue and your father is nationally respected and recognized as a leading authority on Buddhism. Do you think you could arrange for me to see him and have a talk with him?"

"Well, I'll try, but I can't guarantee anything. You know, he's old and his health isn't very good. That's one of the main reasons I returned here, just to take care of him," Minh explained, knowing well that his father would never consent to meeting a foreigner, an American at that, to talk about the family's history.

"Perhaps I can interview *you* about your family," Morgan persisted, a faint smile brightening his face.

"I'm not authentic, nor a very good source. I've been Americanized and Europeanized, what we call in Vietnamese *Mat Goc*, losing roots," Minh said.

"That's not true. I was told that you're one of the four best writers and poets of the Vietnamese language."

"That's disinformation." Morgan laughed. Minh had used a word commonly employed in the U.S. to describe misleading information planted by intelligence services like the C.I.A. or the K.G.B.

"Minh, can I count on you for dinner with Vice-Consul Buckley?"

"Of course. I'd be delighted. What about this Sunday?"

"Strange, when he mentioned it, I suggested Sunday too, but he said it's impossible, he has to work the whole day. It seems he expects some political disturbances on Sunday, which I was told is the fourth anniversary of the self-immolation of a well-respected monk whose name escapes me."

"His name is Thich Quang Duc."

"Did you know him?"

"Not personally, but every Vietnamese has heard about him and respects him. He's even better known outside Vietnam."

"Yes. I read about him and his self-immolation in a Time magazine cover story." He looked at Minh apologetically. "Minh, I don't want to ask you too many questions during this chance meeting, but I've never quite understood why Buddhist monks commit suicide, or self-immolation, as you call it. To my knowledge, neither Confucianism, Taoism, nor Buddhism approves of suicide. How do you explain it?"

"Have you read the book, *Vietnam: Lotus in a Sea of Fire*? It was published in February this year in the U.S."

"I've heard about it, but I'm afraid I haven't read it. Who wrote it and what did he say?"

"It was written by Thich Nhat Hanh, an antiwar Buddhist monk living in Paris now. He visited the U.S. often for lectures. The book's about Buddhism and the war, and he explains the monks' self-immolation. Actually, the explanation was contained in a letter he wrote to Reverend Martin Luther King, Jr. In the Vietnamese Mahayana Buddhist tradition, you see, the candidate monk is required to burn one or more small spots on his body while he takes his vow to observe the 250 rules of a *bhikku*, monk. There is nothing more painful than burning oneself, and by burning and suffering, the monk says to the whole world that he is serious, that his message must be heard.

"I don't know if this explanation is convincing enough for you, but to me, self-immolation by fire, the way it's being committed by the Buddhist monks and nuns, is neither a suicide nor a negative protest, it's a positive way of sending a message. It's very difficult to give a correct definition, though, because Buddhism is undogmatic, or as Thich Nhat Hanh himself says, 'pervasive but formless.' He compares Buddhism with a drop of mercury: 'You can strike the mercury and it will disintegrate into many smaller parts, but as soon as you remove your fist, they run together.'"

"That's a very interesting and beautiful comparison. I'll look for the book in the library."

"I doubt if they have it. The author is persona non grata with the government and I don't think they allow his book to circulate in Vietnam. Perhaps you can order it from the U.S." Minh changed the subject. "What about that dinner with Buckley? Is Tuesday O.K.?"

"It's O.K. with me. Let me check with him and I'll let you know. What's your phone number?"

"I have no telephone. I live with my father at Number 9 Quoc Tu Giam Street."

"It doesn't matter. If you don't hear from me, then I'll pick you up at seven. If there's any problem, I'll drop a note at your office at the university."

"Very good. Thank you. I really am looking forward to meeting with him and you in a relaxed atmosphere so we can talk," Minh said, hoping he hadn't shown too much enthusiasm for the meeting. He wanted to arouse no suspicion as he pursued his task of keeping tabs on American officials in Hue.

"We'd certainly like to see you often to discuss matters of mutual interest and importance and get to know you better," Morgan replied. He seemed sincere.

Small groups of students, chatting and laughing, began to enter the university. Minh looked at his watch and stood up.

"I have to go to my class. Good to see you again, and I'll see you Tuesday at my place."

"Oh, can you write your address for me in my address book, please?" Morgan asked. "I'm not familiar yet with Vietnamese names."

"With pleasure," Minh said.

.   .   .

Minh woke early on Sunday. It was June 11th. He prepared tea for his father and had breakfast with him and Auntie. Phong was still sleeping. Phong had been coming home late recently, after midnight. One evening, as Phong had tiptoed past Minh's room, Minh had smelt alcohol. He had never before known Phong to drink more than a small glass of wine that reddened his face quickly.

After breakfast Minh excused himself and retreated to his room. He planned to follow the events of the day on the radio, but there was no news yet on Hue Radio, the B.B.C., or the Voice of America. Perhaps the demonstrations had not yet begun.

He kept the radio going at a low volume and took out his diary. He wanted to keep a record of his experiences as a professor at a Vietnamese university. One thing seemed absolutely clear to him. Most students were respectful of their teacher, were eager to learn, and looked to him as a dispenser of truth and advice.

He remembered how a woman student had run after him after his seminar, and, in a sure but shy voice, had said, "Professor, my name is Xuan. I'm taking your seminar as well as your course on the American Revolution just to find out one thing; what is the future, if there is any, of our country? That's all."

Before Minh could take in what she had said, she turned her back and walked quickly away. She wore a violet *ao dai*, she was much taller than average, and her hair was cut short to her neck, which was unusual. Now, pondering her question-statement, he tried hard to remember her face, as if knowing her face would allow him to understand her thoughts better. He wasn't sure whether she was prowar and pro-American—although he realized that it was unfair to equate the two—or antiwar and anti-American. Why did she think that Vietnam's future was linked to an understanding of the American Revolution and the U.S. military-industrial complex? Perhaps she thought that if America were true to its revolutionary heritage, and if it were strong militarily and economically, it could win the war and build a bright future for Vietnam on the ruins of the war.

He took the student lists from his attaché case and found her name at the bottom of both lists. On both, her name was preceded by a cross: she was, according to police, a Viet Cong suspect. Was she really? Or were the lists themselves meaningless fabrications as his colleague Trang had insinuated? If she was a Viet Cong agent, was it her intention to learn everything she could about America and report her findings to the Viet Cong high command in the jungles of South Vietnam or Hanoi? But Minh was sure that the Viet Cong and Hanoi and their Americanologists already knew everything he planned to teach, that they received major newspapers and magazines from antiwar activists in the States. Minh imagined Xuan to be pretty. He smiled at the thought that he would concentrate on her, provoking her to ask questions that would reveal her identity.

His door opened. It was Phong, wearing a well-pressed military uniform. For the first time, Minh saw him with a revolver dangling at his waist.

"Please sit down, Phong. You look like a policeman on a beat. I've never seen you with a revolver before," Minh said teasingly.

"I'm on special duty today at headquarters. The army expects trouble and all officers are required to carry weapons. But I don't expect anything but tranquility on earth and rain from heaven."

"Why?"

"Experience. In the past, whenever our intelligence predicted disturbances and riots, we had nothing but quiet, and whenever we forecasted calm, we had nothing but violence and confrontations. That's what happened on June 1st, 1965, when students broke out and attacked the U.S. consulate and burned down the U.S. cultural center."

"Do you have to go now, right away?"

"In about half an hour. I'm waiting for a military jeep to come and pick me up."

"Phong, when are you leaving?" Minh asked in a whisper.

"I was about to tell you. I talked with An three days ago and he said that he will be visiting us sometime Monday afternoon. He'll stay overnight in town and the next morning he's going to Quang Tri for official business with his boss, who's already here visiting. He suggested that I should go with them on the military plane, although I don't have to join my new post until Friday. He thought it would save time and the dangerous trip with armed convoy. Also, my being seen with him and his boss would impress my superiors and create more respect for me in my new job."

"What is your new job, actually?"

"Fighting. And there's a lot of it now," Phong answered without the slightest emotion. "In the last two months, the North Vietnamese have accelerated their infiltrations from Laos along the Ho Chi Minh Trail. They already occupy all the hills dominating the Khe Sanh airfield and the special forces camps at the Laotian border of Quang Tri Province and south of the D.M.Z. The Marines have been flown in and reoccupied some hills and cut some infiltration routes. The U.S. army has penetrated the D.M.Z., too, which in fact is no longer demilitarized. Both sides violated the Geneva Agreement a long time ago anyway. I'll be commanding a combined special unit of 350 soldiers selected from among the best of the rangers, special forces, the Marines, and the paratroopers. Our mission is to conduct harassment, interdiction, and destruction operations. We call it HID-Op. It's clear that the war is spreading to the North and this year and next will be decisive and crucial for both sides."

Minh listened to Phong's description of his job and the military situation with amazement. He had thought that Phong hated the war and would be reluctant to talk about it, yet he talked with a sure professionalism.

"I forgot to ask you if you've told father and your mother about your departure."

"Yes, I told them a day or so after I told you. I thought it would be bad to hide it from them. Also, An suggested that I do it."

"What was father's reaction?"

"He didn't say a thing, but I knew he was unhappy, mostly because of his deep opposition to this war."

"What was your mother's?"

"As you might expect, she was also unhappy, but for a different reason. She's afraid I could be killed. But she's a woman of great courage. Even when she's crying inside, she doesn't show it on the outside. She simply advised me not to take any unnecessary risks and told me to write home often. She even hoped that after my Quang Tri tour of duty I would come back to Hue and get married."

"Can I ask you a personal question?"

"*Anh* Minh, I've always respected and trusted you. You can ask me any question, even about marriage," Phong said with a broad smile.

"Thank you. I've noticed the last few days that you've been coming home very late, and once you smelled of alcohol. Please don't misunderstand me. I'm not saying that you shouldn't drink, you're a grown man and an army officer, but I'm curious to know why, because I've never seen you drinking heavily before. Are you unhappy? Are you trying to drown your troubles in alcohol?"

"Not at all. You may not believe it, but I'm not unhappy at all. It's true I don't like this war much, but as an army officer, I've developed a certain pride in my profession. It's just that there were lots of farewell parties for me. Also, I've spent a great deal of time with my girlfriend."

"I didn't know you had one."

"Only since four months ago. Actually she's a student of yours and she told me that you're different and an excellent teacher. Also, that you're very handsome."

"What's her name?"

"Xuan, Vu Thanh Xuan."

Xuan! Could this be the woman who had asked him the tormenting question about the future of Vietnam? Minh tried to hide his curiosity.

"What does she look like?" he asked.

"She's tall, as tall as I am, which is very tall for a woman. She wears her hair short, almost like a boy's, and she's considered the most beautiful girl in town."

It must be the same woman, Minh thought. "Does she know you're my brother?"

"No, I don't think so. I thought it would be better if she didn't know about our relationship."

"It really doesn't matter. What's her background?"

"She's from the North, born in Hanoi. Her parents came here in 1954 after the partition. She was about ten years old then. She's 23 now. Both of her parents died last year and she's living with an aunt. Her parents were relatively wealthy, her father was an engineer and her mother taught at the

Dong Khanh Women's College. A year ago, she ran into trouble with the police. They suspected her of being a Viet Cong agent and believed she incited the students' attack against the U.S. consulate. She was in jail for a month and released without trial, thanks to the intervention of an uncle of hers who's a colonel in the Air Force. The police have told us that when she was eighteen and a high school student, she had a baby with a classmate of hers who was later identified as a Viet Cong cadre.

"I first met her last year when we went to Saigon on the same plane. Then I forgot about her for a while. I met her again four months ago when she came to my office to ask permission to fly on a military plane to see a relative of hers, a major stationed in the highlands. We recognized each other immediately and have seen each other often ever since."

"She must be unhappy to see you leave Hue now."

"Yes, but she has an enormous capacity for self-control. She's resourceful and I have no doubt she'll manage to come and see me from time to time. She's very well connected and knows a lot of important people here and in Saigon. The police continue to follow her activities, but so far they've not come up with any evidence of her Viet Cong affiliation. Funny! One police officer who was assigned to watch her fell in love with her, wrote her long, romantic letters which she collected and sent to his superiors. Then she denounced him in a magazine article. The officer was transferred.

"Well, I'm sorry I've taken so much time talking about my girlfriend. You'll find her a good, interesting student, well-read. Incidentally, her English is excellent."

"Phong, the jeep is here." Auntie called from the kitchen. "Will you be back for dinner?"

"I don't think so, Mother," Phong said, and ran out into the street.

.   .   .

Minh tuned the radio louder and listened to a news bulletin from Radio Australia:

> Today is the fourth anniversary of the self-immolation of the Venerable Thich Quang Duc. Although the South Vietnamese government had anticipated violent Buddhist demonstrations, everything seems to be quiet both in Saigon and in Hue, the Buddhist stronghold. However, the army and the police in both cities remain on alert. Thai and Australian contingents continue their successful mopping-up operations in the Viet Cong infested province of Quang Ngai, south of Hue.

Minh went to the kitchen to talk with his auntie.

"Minh," she said, "today your father has asked for a vegetarian lunch, although it's neither the first nor the fifteenth of the lunar month. Perhaps he wants to commemorate the self-immolation of the Venerable but he didn't say so. He simply suggested that we have a vegetarian lunch for a change. I hope you don't mind."

"Of course not," Minh replied. "But I wanted to talk to you about Phong. He's leaving us soon, but I'm not worried about him. He's strong and intelligent. He'll take good care of himself."

"I don't know. I hope so. I just pray to Lord Buddha to protect him. There's nothing we can do in a situation like this. What really concerns me is your father, not Phong. You know he hates this war and despises the Saigon army, which he believes is a band of mercenaries. Yet he has to swallow the irony that his two sons are army officers who protect him from the government's harrassment. Now with Phong gone to the war, and An in Saigon, we can only rely on you. Regardless of what your father says sometimes, I know he loves you very much." She wiped a tear from her cheek with her sleeve.

"Yes, Auntie. I shall do everything I can to make my father forget the unpleasant things, and you can be assured that I'm with both of you, always."

"Thank you," she said, sobbing.

His father called him. "Minh, did you listen to the radio? Is anything happening in Saigon or here?"

"Yes, Father, I just listened to Radio Australia and they said everything is quiet."

"Continue to listen and if you hear anything important, let me know immediately. I'm in my studio, reading."

"Yes, Father."

Minh went back to his room. At noon, he listened to a B.B.C. relay from Singapore:

There are no major disturbances in Saigon or Hue as were anticipated by government sources. In Hue, a stronghold of Buddhism, thousands, under a pouring rain, came to the Dieu De and Tu Dam pagodas to pray for the late Thich Quang Duc. There were scattered antigovernment leaflets in the streets, but no violence reported. In Saigon, one incident took place. Here is the report from our correspondent, Malcolm Fitzgerald:

At half past eleven, a nun came to the front door of the American Embassy and asked to see the ambassador. Refused entry, she left a note for the ambassador with a Marine guard and walked away. A few yards from the Embassy, she sat down in a lotus position, poured gasoline upon herself, struck a match, and was quickly engulfed in flame. She was rescued by a police patrol. There are no reports on her condition at this time.

Minh went at once to his father's studio. "Father, they have just reported the self-immolation of a nun in front of the American Embassy in Saigon."

"*Nam Mo Phat*," Father murmured. "Did she die? What's her name?"

"They said she was picked up by a police car and no one knows about her condition. They didn't mention her name."

"No name! The Vietnamese have no name any more. The whole of Vietnam ceases to have a name. We are a battlefield, pawns for the greedy and the powerful," Father muttered. He didn't look at Minh, who tiptoed back to his room, leaving his father alone to his bitter thoughts.

At eleven that night Minh listened to the Voice of America's roundup of the news:

Despite worse predictions, the fourth anniversary of the suicide of Thich Quang Duc passed without major incident. In Saigon, a nun who attempted to burn herself in front of the U.S. Embassy this morning died at 6:50 p.m., according to a spokesman for the Saigon Ministry of Information. She was identified as Thich Lien Hoa, Venerable Lotus, a prominent Buddhist leader who studied abroad and was known in the past for her antiwar and anti-American activities. In Hue, the Buddhist stronghold, thousands of Buddhist faithful met despite heavy rains at three major pagodas in the city to pray. No inflammatory speeches or violence were reported, and there were no Viet Cong acts of terrorism. On the military front, at the D.M.Z., Operation Mighty Eagle, which started earlier this week, ended with complete victory for the allies. The final body count: 341 Viet Cong killed in action, no prisoners; 30 G.I.s. dead, 30 wounded; 65 ARVN dead and 129 wounded. The smashing success, according to an army bulletin, will frustrate the North Vietnamese plan to invade the D.M.Z. The victory was made possible, according to the same bulletin, by precise pounding of enemy positions by B52s.

Minh rushed to his father's bedroom to tell him the news but he was asleep. He thought of announcing it to his Auntie, but there was no light in her room. The news of Thich Lien Hoa's self-immolation would, he was certain, grieve his father and auntie, who had met her so recently, but it didn't affect him any more deeply than anyone else's. Perhaps he was becoming hardened. He was waiting eagerly for the next day when he could go to his classes and have a good look at Vu Thanh Xuan, Phong's girlfriend. He was also looking forward to seeing An, who would be coming later in the day.

.   .   .

Minh left for the university before his father was awake, skipping breakfast. He deliberately avoided the unpleasant duty of telling him and Auntie about the death of Thich Lien Hoa. "I'm sure they'll learn about it when they listen to Hue Radio morning news," he thought.

It was already hot. Portions of the streets were still flooded from the rains of the day and night before. He intended to stop by the Moonlight Tea House to have breakfast, but a sign on the front door disappointed him: "Open 7:00 a.m.—Close 10:30 p.m." Feeling hungry, he continued to walk along Tran Hung Dao Boulevard until he saw a Chinese restaurant that was already open. He asked for a bowl of chicken noodle soup, but he couldn't finish it. It was a mistake for him to have even tried it. He should have waited and gone to Ben Ngu for a steaming bowl of *pho*. To fill his stomach, he ordered two breadcakes with meat stuffing, which he consumed without much appetite.

Minh had never liked Chinese food. While he was in the U.S., he'd force himself sometimes to go to Chinese restaurants just to avoid the monotony and blandness of the daily American food, especially hot dogs. He had tried those once and promised himself that he would never try them again.

He recalled the story about the Vietnamese from an area in the North where dog meat was considered a prime delicacy who visited the United States for the first time. Passing a restaurant one day that advertised hot dogs, he rushed in and order confidently, expecting a delicious hot meal of dog meat cooked with lemon grass, the way it was prepared in his village. Instead, he was served an American hot dog which at first he thought was an appetizer. He ate it quickly, not liking it, and sat waiting until the waitress asked him, "Is there anything else you'd like to have?" "I'm still waiting for my dog meat delicacy!" he answered angrily. The waitress gave him a stunned, unfriendly, suspicious look. Realizing that he must have been misled by the words "hot dog," he paid reluctantly and left without giving her a tip.

Whether the story was true or not, the fact still remained, Minh thought, that the hot dog, American-style, was an unaesthetic and uneatable dish. And Chinese food, too, was not only inferior in taste but also vulgar in preparation compared to Vietnamese cuisine. Yet when he had to describe Vietnamese food to his foreign friends, it was simpler to say, "It's somewhere between French and Chinese." But in truth that was cultural treason. He thought Vietnamese food much more subtle, more delicate, and less fattening than the Chinese, a "poem for the tongue, the eyes and the throat." He agreed with a friend of his, a Vietnamese who had tried unsuccessfully to open a restaurant in New York City, that the fundamental difference between the Chinese and Vietnamese cuisines is that the Vietnamese use fish sauce, and the Chinese use soy sauce to salt and aromatize their dishes. Minh often wondered why the Vietnamese had remained so un-Chinese after a thousand years of Chinese domination while so many today, especially the city youth, were so quickly being Americanized. Someday, he thought, Vietnamese scholars or Americans like Morgan would find an answer to that fascinating question.

It was early when Minh reached the university. The main gate was still closed. There was a new poster on the wall. It showed a dog with a face resembling that of the President of South Vietnam, running after a huge European who brandished a machine gun and a flame thrower marked 'Made in U.S.A.' at a Buddhist monk sitting with eyes closed on a bed of lotus flowers. The caption at the bottom read: 'The enemies of our Nation and our Religion.' Minh was looking at the poster, which seemed to him to be in poor taste, when a policeman came along and tore it down. The policeman neither noticed him nor asked for his I.D.

"Why do you tear it down?" he asked.

"Don't you see, Professor, that it's a Viet Cong poster?" The policeman crumpled the poster and threw it away. "Last night," he said matter-of-factly, "the Viet Cong infiltrated the city and plastered hundreds of these all over the place. We have to tear them down before eight-thirty so no one will see them."

"How do you know I'm a professor?" Minh asked him.

"Easy. The way you dress, your suit, your tie, even your face. I'm right, aren't I?"

"You're right. I'm teaching here."

"I wish I could go to school myself. That's why I don't understand why these fortunate men and women who have the opportunity to go to school don't spend all their time studying. Instead they smoke marijuana and listen to Viet Cong propaganda. It's bad."

"How long have you been with the police force?"

"About three years. I'm the only son and I live with my mother. My father died when I was very young. My mother had to pay some friend who knew some big shot in town 10,000 piasters to get me a job in the police department. Otherwise, I would have been drafted into the army, sent to the front, and killed. No one would have taken care of my mother."

"I thought the government didn't draft people who have to support a family."

"That was true several years ago. Now the government needs more soldiers and they have to draft everyone, except those who are lucky, rich, and powerful, or go to school."

"I see."

"I have about half an hour to finish two more streets, the two longest in the city. Goodbye, Professor, and if you need me, let me know. My name's Hai, Corporal Hai."

"Goodbye, Corporal. Stop by and sit in on my class whenever you wish. My class is on the second floor and my name's Minh, Tran Van Minh."

"And my name's Loc."

Minh turned around, startled and pleased. "You're early," he observed.

"I usually am. I watched you with the policeman from a distance. I thought at first you were in trouble, but then I decided you were just having a friendly conversation."

"We were. Actually he's a very nice man. Very candid."

"Well, maybe because he's new in the service."

"Three years, he told me."

"A few more years and he'll become heartless and cruel like all the others. But I don't hate them."

"Did you hear about the death of Nun Thich Lien Hoa?" Minh asked.

"Yes, I did. My mother cried all night. You know, I respect such acts but I don't think they have any effect any more. People are already getting used to it. Leaders should live for the people, not die for them. Still, I feel very sad. She was quite a remarkable person, well liked, respected, and a good scholar. I'm sure your father and auntie were upset too."

"I didn't tell them last night when I heard about it but I'm sure they'll hear about it this morning on the radio."

"I'm not sure if Hue Radio will carry the news, though. Remember Nhat Chi Mai's death? It was never officially announced. She was not officially dead!"

"How was the situation at the pagodas?"

"All three pagodas were packed with people, at least 15,000 in all. They came to listen to the monks' religious discourses and pray. The sermon by Patriarch Thich Dai Hai was quite impressive and to the point."

"What did he say?"

"He linked the defense of Buddhism with the defense of the country. He gave a very simple example that moved a lot of people. He said that Buddhism is like a tree and the nation is the soil. The soil nourishes the tree which in turn gives back its life to the soil. The tree dies if the soil is turned up—he actually used the word bulldozed, and if the tree is defoliated and loses its life the soil dies off to drought and heat."

Loc seemed to be lost in his thoughts, but he continued after a moment. "After the ceremony at Thien Mu, the Patriarch recognized me and came over to talk. He asked about my work and mentioned that you paid him a visit recently."

"Yes, I did. I was dedicated to Buddha there. How many people were there?"

"A big crowd, at least eight to nine thousand, squatting all over the front lawn in the rain. I saw some of our students and some plainclothes policemen and a few men who may have been army intelligence officers in civilian clothes busy taking pictures. Some people decided that one young man was a police informer and attacked him, but a monk and I intervened. We didn't want any trouble."

.   .   .

Students began to assemble in long files. The Rector's shining Mercedes drove by and Minh's uncle waved to him through the bullet-proof windows of his chauffeur-driven car. Minh smiled back. He shook hands with Loc and slowly walked to his classroom.

It was ten minutes to nine and Minh was happily surprised to see Vu Thanh Xuan already there, reading a book. As he would have in the U.S., Minh broke the classroom's silence.

"Hi. Good morning. How are you? What are you reading?"

She stood up, answering him in Vietnamese with a Hanoi accent charmingly blended with the soft one from Hue. Minh asked her to sit down.

"I came early because I had to bring my aunt to the hospital in a friend's car," she said. "He dropped me on his way to work."

Minh was tempted to ask if it was Phong who had brought her, but he refrained, having promised himself that he would never tell her that he was Phong's half-brother.

"I'm sorry to hear that. Is it anything serious?"

"No. She has chronic asthma and this morning her condition was a little worse than usual. She's had a heavy cold the last few days, but she'll be all right soon, I hope," she said. Her voice was filled with a distant sadness. Then she handed him the book she'd been reading. It was Dag Hammarskjöld's *Markings*, its cover wrapped in a piece of green parachute cloth.

"*Markings*! I'm very glad you're reading this! I've read it once a year since it was translated into English."

"I like the book very much. I'm on my second reading. I have to return it to my friend, though, who's leaving town either tomorrow or the day after."

The book must be Phong's, Minh thought. "You don't have to worry. I have a copy of it and I'll let you borrow it next time I come to class."

"Thank you, Professor, but not this week. I won't have much free time and my mind will be too preoccupied to read it. As you know, it should be read in complete serenity, 'Marking' by 'Marking.' It's like savoring a good piece of candied ginger with hot tea on the first cold morning of Tet."

"I agree with you," Minh murmured, blushing a bit as her eyes met his. There was something in her oval, smooth face that reminded him of his mother, and a little of Jennifer, too. The same full lips, the same mole on the left corner of the delicate nose. Her short hair contrasted sharply with her long, almost vulnerable neck. He was relieved when the first group of talking, laughing students entered the class.

He had to make a real effort to concentrate on his first major lecture on the differences between revolution, rebellion, revolt, uprising, riot, and *coup d'état*. He tried to emphasize the point that revolution is not a total, sudden change as it is popularly believed to be, but rather a transition, albeit a radical one, from one socioeconomic stage to another in a given society, through collective action. He deliberately refrained from too strongly criticizing the *coup d'état*, which he had once described as "the division of labor and profit among armed hooligans."

Minh noticed that To Ngoc, the girl who had asked if it was possible to fight American soldiers and love the American people, was absent. He glanced furtively at Xuan, who was assiduously taking notes like the rest of the class—something he rarely saw among his American students. During the fifteen minutes reserved for discussion, he hoped that she wouldn't ask any questions; but hers were the first.

"Professor, you have said that revolution is the product of a collective action. I fully agree with that. My question is: what is your opinion of Dag Hammarskjöld's statement that 'in our era, the road to holiness necessarily passes through the world of action.' If the world of action leads to the road of holiness, can we say that revolutionaries, men of action, are also holy men or even mystics?"

Minh was delighted at her question. Because she had asked it in such a low voice, he repeated it. Then he asked the class how many of them knew of Dag Hammarskjöld and had read *Markings*. Five students raised their hands, an impressive number to Minh, who never expected any American students to have read the book. He pointed to a male student who looked as if he was the oldest in the class.

"I think he was a European communist leader."

Xuan chuckled and hid her mouth behind her hand. Several others smiled.

"No, I'm afraid he was not a communist leader," Minh commented. "He was a Swedish aristocrat, diplomat, and statesman, who was Secretary-General of the United Nations from 1953 to 1961, when he was killed in an air crash in Northern Rhodesia at the age of fifty-six."

Another male student stood up. "I have read somewhere that he was killed by the American C.I.A."

"There were rumors to that effect but no hard evidence to support it," Minh told him. Then he turned to Xuan.

"Your Vietnamese translation is excellent, especially your use of the Buddhist expression *giai thoat*, liberation or nirvana, for 'holiness.' In that sense, I think Hammarskjöld's statement *is* true, in that men of action believe that their actions transcend their lives, or go beyond their lives. As for mystics, I have some difficulty in finding the connection between mysticism, which is the negation of revolution, and revolution itself, although it is possible to say that within each revolution there is transformation and within each transformation there is negation. However, as a Buddhist, I'm against all kinds of mysticism. Buddhism is a philosophy, a religion if you wish, of truth and reality. Buddha himself has said that you can find the truth only in yourself; and nothing is more real, more material than one's self. This is just an idea that came to my mind with your question. I'll think it over and do some research on it. Incidentally, there's a good book on mysticism titled *Mysticism: East and West* by Rudolf Otto. You may as well look into it. I hope this long answer is satisfactory to you, Miss Xuan."

"Thank you, Professor. I'll think it over myself."

Minh felt exhilarated when the class was over. He thought of Jennifer and the way she had sparked his class on the politics of national liberation back at Thomas Paine. Xuan was the first to leave the class and Minh was sure she was rushing to see her aunt at the hospital, or Phong, who was probably waiting for her at the gate.

.   .   .

Minh waited at the university's main entrance for a lift home from his uncle. "Sorry to make you wait." The Rector's car pulled up beside him. "As I was about to leave, the chief of police came to see me about an urgent matter."

"What urgent matter, Uncle?"

"A number of students, eight to be exact, have been arrested. One of them was yours."

"What's his name?"

"*Her* name. To Ngoc. Cong Ton Nu To Ngoc. Do you recognize her? Perhaps you don't. She's in your largest class on the American Revolution."

"Oh yes, I do. But I didn't realize she's from the royal family; I didn't know her family name was Cong Ton. It's surprising. You don't expect Hue royalty to have such a clear Hanoi accent. She seemed very bright. She wore thick glasses and even in the first class, she asked some meaningful questions."

"Such as?" the Rector interrupted.

"Let me remember. She asked about the relationship between the principles of the American Revolution and the principles dictating the present American policy in Vietnam.Also, why third world revolutionaries like Ho Chi Minh denounce American imperialism and at the same time praise the American Revolution. She asked another question about the American pursuit of happiness or something to that effect." He paused for a moment. "What did the chief of police tell you?"

"He told me that she was arrested last night with seven other students who belong to the Viet Cong's Association of Intellectuals for Liberation. They were organizing students and even faculty for the Viet Cong campaign for peace and democracy."

"Is she among the suspects on the students' lists?"

"I think so."

"What are they going to do with her—or the others? Is she going to be tried soon?"

"I really don't know, but I doubt if she's going to be tried. One thing is sure. She's going to stay in prison for a long, long time."

To Minh's surprise and pleasure his uncle's tone sounded sympathetic. He asked, "Is there anything we can do? Can our law school help?"

"Well, I just called the dean of the law school and he thinks there's nothing we can do, since the country's practically under martial law now."

"How many women students were arrested?"

"It's amazing to me. Out of the eight, six were women."

"Can I see her at the prison?"

"I don't think so. Prisons are overflowing with suspects and most of the time nobody, including immediate family members, knows where a suspect is detained."

"Can I tell my students about the arrests?"

"Absolutely not. But I'm sure the students will know about it one way or the other." He looked through the window, reflective. "Minh, you shouldn't interfere with any political business, just go about your teaching. Vietnam isn't America, war isn't peace, and the best thing one can do is to learn not to see or hear certain things. Have a good time whenever you can. Get to know a few women. Go to Saigon, Nha Trang, or Dalat on the weekends and enjoy yourself. And if you don't like to do any of those things, then get yourself married. There are still nice girls from good families in town." He patted Minh on the back. "What are you doing tonight?"

"I want to stay home." Normally Minh would have told his uncle that An was coming from Saigon and they were having a farewell dinner for Phong, but he hesitated, not knowing if his father would like his uncle informed about all these family affairs. If he had wanted him to know, he would have invited him for dinner.

"Too bad," his uncle said. "I was going to ask you to join us for dinner. We've invited the new director of Hue Hospital and his wife, an American."

"Thanks anyway. Give my regards to Auntie and love to my cousins."

"I'll do that. You should come and see us more often."

VII

A Hollow Shell

A hollow shell, it needs man's touch.
Light it-the smarty will go off.
The louder cry the bigger burst,
And it all ends with just one bang.

Firecracker
Nguyen Huu Chinh
?–1787.
Translated by Huynh Sanh Thong

An was with his father in the garden when Minh entered. "An, I'm glad to see you again. You look so dignified in your new uniform. Oh! You've been promoted! You're a full colonel."

"Not really. Just a temporary promotion. My boss is a lieutenant general now and he and the Minister of Defense insist that his deputy be at least a colonel."

Their father interrupted irritably. "You're late this afternoon," he said to Minh. "How was school?"

"Uncle was a little late picking me up. School's fine. The students seem eager to learn."

"Are they eager to act?"

"I really don't know, Father."

"Have you heard the terrible news from Saigon?" Father asked.

"No, I haven't," Minh lied.

"An just told us that the nun who burned herself in front of the American Embassy yesterday was Thich Lien Hoa. Your auntie met her recently—she was terribly shocked when An told her about it. As a matter of fact, she's inside the house now, crying."

"Oh, I'm sorry. I'll go inside to be with her."

"No. Leave her alone for a while."

"Yes, Father."

"I think I had better go inside. You two can stay here and wait for Phong's return."

"Yes, Father."

His father's brusqueness seemed to Minh a reproach. Did he think Minh should know how the students were reacting to Thich Lien Hoa's death? Was he comparing her sacrifice to An's new rank in the government's army, to Minh's indecisiveness?

"Let's walk a little before we go inside," Minh suggested.

"An, I must admit that I did hear about Nun Hoa's death on the late news last night but I didn't tell Father and Auntie because I didn't want to wake them. I left home very early this morning so I didn't have a chance to tell them about it then."

"They say 'Fortune does not come in pairs, disaster never arrives single,'" An observed. "Between Phong's leaving for the front and the death of the nun, my mother's really in terrible shape."

"Yes, indeed. Phong told me that you'll be accompanying your boss to Quang Tri and that you asked him to join you. That was very thoughtful of you."

"This way people in Quang Tri, especially the military there, will have more consideration for Phong and won't make life too difficult for him."

"What do you mean?"

An looked worried. "I must tell you the main reason why Phong is being transferred, but keep it to yourself and don't tell Father or Mother."

"I promise."

"Well, even though military operations at the D.M.Z. are being intensified and more officers are needed at the front line for combat, Phong would not normally be sent. He's regarded as a very gifted staff and intelligence officer with all the qualities to be a general by the time he's forty-five. But something happened recently. The military intelligence's counter-espionage section received reports from the police saying that Phong is close to a woman whom they suspect, without any proof yet, of being a Viet Cong agent. When I warned Phong about it he laughed the matter off. But the general staff, with my concurrence, decided that for his own sake he must be transferred. I've talked with my boss and General Vu Binh about the matter and they both agree that the best solution is to have Phong assigned to the front so he'll forget about her. They both promised me that he'd return to Hue in a few months, at the latest by Tet."

"Phong told me about his girlfriend, too. Is her name Xuan?"

"Yes."

"She's very intelligent, a student of mine, taking both my courses. Besides, she's a very beautiful woman and quite articulate. I'm not at all certain the police are right about her."

"I've never met her, though I've seen her picture in the police file that was transmitted to us. She's very beautiful indeed. I don't know either if the police's suspicions are correct. The matter is delicate and it isn't wise for me to challenge the police's information, especially because I'm Phong's brother."

"Well, anyway, I'm glad that his transfer is of short duration and I hope nothing happens to him before Tet."

"I really don't know. I'm a little bit concerned. Right now the Quang Tri front is the most dangerous one. Our casualties and the Americans' are unusually high. Yesterday alone, sixteen Americans were killed, 25 wounded, and ten missing. We lost 25 soldiers, 65 wounded, and 29 missing. Practically all the officers killed are company leaders like Phong. So, I just pray and tell him to be very careful and not take any unnecessary risks. That's all I can do, I'm afraid."

"I'm worried too, but there's little either of us can do. Let's talk about something else. How much do you know about Viet Cong infiltrations among the students? The reason I ask is that I've just received my class lists, and some of the students' names are marked by a cross, meaning they're Viet Cong suspects. And just this morning I was told by Uncle that several students were arrested yesterday, among them a woman student of mine."

"Not Xuan, I hope."

"No, another one. Although Xuan was absent. I had a hunch she was spending the day with Phong."

"Well, if by Viet Cong we mean antigovernment, anti-U.S., then the majority of the students are Viet Cong because most of them are nationalists. But if by a Viet Cong we mean a communist cadre, then nobody knows exactly how many.

"Of course, the communists aren't strong because of their num-bers—it's very difficult to be admitted into the Party—but because of their dedication and ability to mobilize well-meaning people to work for them. It's a terrible dilemma for the government. If we don't arrest suspects, it's possible we let the real communists among them go free. If we do, we're even more likely to be putting noncommunists in jail, thus creating more resentment and more support for the communists. Many security agencies operate on the principle, which I don't support, that it's better to make a mistake and arrest the innocent than let one communist go free."

An sighed. "That's only one of the complications of fighting what the communists call a 'people's war.' Another is the killing of civilians. In my office, we know of hundreds of cases of women and children being killed in military operations, cases that the Viet Cong exploit for their propaganda. And when we investigate these killings, all the officers in charge admit that it's impossible to avoid them. They can't tell who the real fighters are. In fact the women fight better than the men, they claim, and the children are the best scouts and spies the Viet Cong have. It's a nightmare, but we're going to have to face it, and soon. If we're going to win, we're going to have to kill millions, and if we won't do that, we will lose. I remember in your novel one of your characters says, 'To stop an idea which has found its temporary home in the hearts of millions is like trying to stop water. Either you get wet by it or you are submerged by it.'"

Listening to An's analysis, Minh was struck by the contradictions in his soldier brother's life. Sensitive, thoughtful, even romantic, An was known among his friends as a poet and a playboy, although he never shared his poems or talked about his romantic adventures with Minh.

A taxi stopped with a shriek behind them. It was Phong, dressed casually in civilian shirt and khaki pants. His face was partially sunburned and his hair was uncombed.

"I hope you had a good day. How's Xuan?" Minh asked mischievously.

"She's well and hopes you'll understand why she missed your class."

"How can I understand it," Minh teased, "when she didn't tell me where she was going and you didn't tell her that you're my brother?"

"I don't know, but better let things go that way," Phong said vaguely. They both laughed.

"Why don't you invite her to have dinner with all of us?" An interjected.

"No, I wouldn't dare do that. As a matter of fact, I haven't told Father and Mother about her at all."

"Oh, I was just kidding," An said. "Let's go inside. Mother's very unhappy over the death of Nun Thich Lien Hoa."

"Yes, I know," Phong said. "I heard the news this morning when I stopped by my office. Very few people in Hue know about it, though. The population seems very quiet. How did Mother find out?"

"I told her. As for the population, they probably know about it too, but without orders from the monks, they won't react one way or the other."

The farewell dinner for Phong was not a happy gathering. No one talked about either the death of Nun Thich Lien Hoa or Phong's departure. Sadness permeated everyone, like an evening mist, or summer humidity. Minh tried to taste all the marvelous food on the table: chicken cooked in coconut milk and chili sauce, vermicelli sauteed with fresh mushrooms, rolls, but he couldn't muster enough appetite. The only dish everybody concentrated on was the *kim cham* soup; *kim cham*, a dried flower, reputed to make one sleep well and forget unhappiness.

Frozen in silence and pain, Auntie was swallowing her food with tears. Father's eyes were red and wet behind his glasses, which were blurred by his vaporized tears. He wiped them hesitantly with the sleeves of his dark blue gown. Only An and Phong broke the silence from time to time, inviting their parents to taste this dish or that delicacy.

Minh's father retired immediately to his studio after dinner, without uttering a word to anyone. Behind his stooped shoulders, Minh could see his wrinkled face ravaged more by repressed anger than by sadness. An and Phong helped their mother bring the dishes to the kitchen before the servant came to serve tea. They spent a long time with their mother. About ten, they came to Minh's room to talk.

"*Anh* Minh," Phong began, his face unusually serious and drawn, "I can go to the front without worrying, knowing that you will take good care of Father and Mother. Mother's especially grateful for the sincere love you've shown her. As for me, I'll take good care of myself, and when things get settled, perhaps I'll be able to take a short leave and return for a visit. Now I'd like to say goodbye and thank you for all you've done for all of us. Please help Xuan in case she needs you, but I think it's better that she doesn't know you're my brother."

"Of course I'll look after all of them, Phong. But why are you saying goodbye now? You're not leaving until tomorrow morning."

"Yes," An interjected, "we're leaving at dawn, but it's better for all of us, especially Father and Mother, not to be disturbed too early in the morning. I asked their permission to leave tonight and they agreed. Phong and I will spend the night at the officer's clubhouse downtown and leave by plane from there about five in the morning. I'll be back in Saigon by late afternoon."

He stopped suddenly. "Oh! Before I forget. I've made arrangements with the army communications center in Hue to have a telephone installed in the house tomorrow. Father objected, but he's agreed to have it in your room, now that Phong is away and I can't communicate with home through his office telephone."

"That's a very good idea."

"It's probably best if you restrict its use to unimportant affairs, as all telephone conversations through the army network are monitored by the counter-intelligence and also by the C.I.A."

"I'll remember that. I hated the telephone when I was in the United States."

Minh walked them to the gate where a military limousine was waiting.

.   .   .

Minh was pleased to find Xuan already in class when he came in fifteen minutes early. She greeted him.

"Professor, an American just stopped by and left this note for you."

"Thank you." It was from Morgan, confirming dinner that night with the American vice-consul.

Minh was surprised to notice that Xuan was as serene as if it were just another day. He had expected her to wear the unhappy look of someone whose lover had just departed for a long, dangerous mission.

He was tempted to ask her why she had missed the class yesterday, but instead he asked, "How's your aunt? Has she recovered? I was worried about her when you didn't show up for class yesterday."

"No. No," Xuan replied, "she's all right now and back home. I didn't come to class because I was busy with a friend who had to leave town unexpectedly last night."

"Is that the same friend who let you borrow *Markings?*"

"Yes, sir."

"I'm sorry I forgot to bring the book today, but you said you're too busy this week to reread it. I'll bring it sometime next week."

"Thank you, sir. I promise I'll take good care of it."

"Can I ask you something, Miss Xuan?"

"Please, sir."

"I'm still surprised that you're interested in Dag Hammarskjöld, and more so by the fact that you have a friend who shares the same interest. Is he Swedish?"

Minh immediately regretted this feeble stab at humor, but Xuan seemed not at all displeased.

"No, sir. He's not Swedish. He's Vietnamese, from Hue, born into an aristocratic scholarly family. I've never asked him why he was interested in *Markings.*" Her eyes became a little dreamy. "The book attracted me because I'm deeply concerned about politics. And politics, at the individual level, is the action and reaction, contradiction and harmony, between the public and the inner person. Dag Hammarskjöld personified and expressed this better than anyone I know. Besides, there's an element of tragedy and beauty in politics that was reflected in his life."

"Yes, a Marxist would call it the dialectical relationship between the individual and society," Minh said, deliberately using the word "Marxist" to see how Xuan would react. But she listened attentively and responded calmly.

"It's that contradiction which draws me into politics, even . . ." She stopped. Unwilling to push her to say more than she wanted to, Minh moved to the front of the room to start his class.

.   .   .

Vice-Consul Buckley lived on the second floor of a white-washed house that Minh remembered as having once belonged to a Vietnamese popularly known as Mr. One Hundred Thousand, because he was the first Vietnamese ever to have won the first prize of 100,000 piasters in the national lottery. The second floor of the house now served as an office and the third was the special guests' quarters.

Besides Minh and Morgan, Buckley had invited only a few guests, who seemed lost in the immense living-dining room. There was a consular officer named Marvin Turlington, with a beautiful Vietnamese woman, and an American, Colonel Charles Leclerc, who had in tow a painted, moon-faced giggling woman called Madame Dai.

Towards the end of dinner, Buckley, in a solemn voice, proposed a toast to Minh.

"Welcome to Professor Tran Van Minh. Welcome back to Vietnam and to Hue. May we all work closely with each other so that peace can be restored to the heroic people of Vietnam in the not-too-distant future, and may we celebrate the coming Tet in peace and victory."

"Welcome, Professor Minh." The guests raised their glasses, while Minh said repeatedly, "Thank you, thank you."

After the toast, guests began to leave, but Minh and Morgan stayed on for a while. A faint "rara-rum, rara-rum," combined with less distinct noises, could be heard in the distance.

"Is that artillery shelling?" Minh enquired.

"Yes," Buckley answered. "It's around Phu Bai, about eight miles south of here. In the last few months, there's been an increase in Viet Cong infiltrations around the base. But the fire is simply harrassment and interdiction fire, not real fighting. I've gotten used to it. Actually it makes me fall asleep more easily."

"You expect more fighting in the coming months?"

"I think there'll be increased fighting around Hue and up north at the D.M.Z. The Viet Cong and the North Vietnamese have to protect the Ho Chi Minh Trail and extend their control in order to survive. But the military situation isn't important; it's the political one that's decisive. The government must broaden its base and successfully organize the general elections on September 3rd. And based on the results of recent elections in the hamlets in several provinces, things are getting better. The peasants seem to understand the meaning of democracy. After all, this is a peasant country, this is Vietnam's war, and war and peace will be decided by the peasants."

"In your opinion," Morgan asked, "do the peasants support the government in Saigon?"

"Yes and no," Buckley answered. "The peasants want to be left alone. In areas where they are bothered by corrupt officials—and corruption is what finally kills a country, not communism—they had no choice but to side with the Viet Cong, who exploit them too, but more intelligently."

"I have been told constantly," Morgan objected, "that peasants want to be left alone. But if that's so, who's fighting on the Viet Cong side? Who's been fighting for Vietnam against all the successive Chinese invasions of the past? In my view, peasants everywhere will fight for their land. That's fundamental to the understanding of wars and revolutions. They'll accept the leadership of those intellectuals they intuitively trust, those who have developed an organic link with them. Strange as it may seem to some, peasants have a great deal of respect for morality and honesty. They admire honest and moral people, and that's the major weakness in Vietnam at the present time in my opinion. The present leadership is neither intellectual nor honest and elections won't change the picture. Elections, even in developed industrialized countries like the U.S., have become a ceremonial, with less and less meaning to more and more people."

"But, if that's true," Buckley retorted, "why wasn't the Ngo Dinh Diem regime in the early 1960s popular? Diem was intellectual, aristocrat, honest, yet . . ."

Morgan interrupted. "Because he was a Catholic, and a Catholic is not authentically Vietnamese. Catholicism is a recent intrusion in the Viet-namese culture and it has yet to find a home here. That's the subject I'd like to study during the next two years, the role of culture in politics. I want to select a few prominent old families that have participated in the building and defense of Vietnam, such as the Tran Van family, from which our friend Professor Minh comes."

"Thank you," Minh said. He had followed their exchange with interest, wondering again, as he listened, whether Morgan was after all Jennifer's brother-in-law. It would be almost too coincidental, he knew, but she did have a brother-in-law from New Jersey who was an anthropologist—and Morgan had the same clear mind, the same intensity and humanistic bent that Jennifer had . . . Minh brought his attention back to the conversa-tion.

"I agree with much of what you've said, except that the structure of the Vietnamese society itself has changed. In the past, scholars who failed in their examinations would return to their villages and become teachers, and as teachers they were the moral and intellectual pillars of the community.

But they are disappearing now, so we no longer have intellectuals in residence among the peasants, with whom they can develop organic links. In any case, the general question of why people revolt and why people fight, and for what and for whom, still needs more scientific study."

Buckley changed the subject. "We're pleased to have you back here with us," he told Minh, "but on the other hand we're deprived of the pleasure of reading the articles you wrote while you were in the U.S. I've read several of your pieces, especially those in the New Republic. Many of us agreed with some of your views and proposals. I hope somehow you can continue to do it here in Vietnam, but then again, I don't know . . ."

"If I continue to write here the way I did while I was in the U.S., I'd like to know where I could publish my articles. Unless you promised to give me asylum in your consulate in case of trouble, I would never dare," Minh said, only half joking.

"You're still in some ways protected by the U.S. Constitution and your status as a permanent resident of the United States."

"I didn't know that Minh was a critic of the government," Morgan interrupted. "Does that mean that the government is more liberal than many of us in the U.S. think?"

There was a silence; Buckley broke it by asking Minh to sign the consulate guest book. "We want to be sure that you're invited to our Fourth of July reception."

Minh and Morgan left the consulate exactly at midnight, violating in principle the curfew regulations, but both of them knew that in Vietnam, in practice, regulations didn't apply to Americans and their friends.

· · ·

For almost ten days Minh hadn't met with Loc. He spotted him one day at lunchtime and they went for a walk.

"Minh," Loc said, his face unusually serious, "I was in Saigon on Saturday and Sunday and met with our underground national committee. They want us to accelerate our activities as quickly as possible. Of course, our priority still remains the August 10th celebration, but after that we're to expand our organization into an Uprising Committee. We'll receive detailed instructions on how to go about it. One thing they've already told me. They want you and Sister Lan to start your own groups. In fact, they think that from now on you and I should meet only on very urgent matters. Of course, we can still meet casually at school and social functions, behaving ourselves as naturally as possible. Anyway, organizationally, you'll be on your own after August 10th. I'll stand ready to help you if you need me. They also cautioned us that we must be extremely careful. The government will increase its repressive measures as the military situation deteriorates." He paused. "By the way, have you made any connections yet with the U.S. consulate?"

"Yes, I have. Through Morgan. I was invited to dinner there by Vice-Consul Buckley, a week ago."

"Excellent. That kind of work is highly regarded by the committee and I shall recommend to them that you stop your mass organization work and concentrate more on this."

"Intelligence work, you mean?"

"And you're the only one who can do it. Our committee would agree with my assessment. We've had some contacts at lower levels, but yours are much higher and will be very important for our cause."

"But how can the American officials trust me or tell me anything important when they all know my position on the war and the government? Buckley himself told me at dinner that he had read articles I had written in the U.S. He even said that he agreed with a number of my views, though I don't know if I should believe him."

"He probably does agree with some of what you say. That's precisely why they trust you, *because* you're liberal. The only thing is, you must not be suspected as having direct or indirect contacts with the National Liberation Front. You see, the Americans are frantically looking for a liberal third force in Vietnam, to replace the generals, whom they secretly despise. They would dump the present regime the same way they had Mr. Diem and his brothers killed, provided they could find a third solution to save their long-range interests. Most of the U.S. civilians here would love to have someone like Magsaysay of the Philippines, who was on the one hand a liberal, even a progressive, and on the other, a dedicated, effective anti-communist. They are embarrassed in the eyes of the world by the support they give to the present Saigon regime. Deep in their hearts, many of them respect the opponents of the government and would cooperate whole-heartedly with anyone who was critical of it—so long as he wasn't commu-nist or procommunist or neutralist or affiliated with any front organization of our Party."

Loc put his hand affectionately on Minh's shoulder. "Were there other guests at the dinner besides you and Morgan?"

"Yes, there were. Marvin Turlington of the consulate and his Viet-namese language teacher, Miss Phuong, a quite decent woman whom Sister Lan mentioned at our last meeting. And a colonel named Leclerc, who's in Civil Operation and Revolutionary Development in Quang Tri. He brought along a Vietnamese woman who looked cheap to me—called Madame Dai."

"Is she the one with a mouthful of gold teeth, plump, about 45 years old?"

"Yes. How do you know?"

"If you stay long enough in Hue, you'll surely know her. She is what is called a procurer. She owns a high-class house of prostitution, mostly for Americans. Hue is off-limits for U.S. military personnel, so only American civilians and high-ranking officers in civilian dress can visit her place. Was the conversation interesting?"

"Mostly academic. I think Marvin Turlington is an interesting man, could be C.I.A. His Vietnamese is quite good and he seems serious in his work."

"I've never met him so I don't know. You should try to meet other Americans outside of the consulate's personnel, like the advisers to our university, and in particular, some of the visiting journalists. The more you're seen with the Americans, the better for us. The police will guess that we're working for the Americans and leave us alone. At the same time, not all of us should be seen with them. We'd be suspected by the people then, especially the students, as American agents. Above all, though, you should make sure that you're invited to the Fourth of July reception. All the Vietnamese V.I.P.s will be there and when they see you, they won't bother with your political activities."

"No problem. Buckley asked me to sign the consulate's guest book just to make sure I get an invitation."

"Good. Now, I'd like you to write regular reports about all your contacts with the Americans, starting with the dinner with Buckley last week. Do it in diary form, mentioning names, places, and details of conversations. You can handwrite it or type it, but do it in duplicate and keep the original. The other copy you can put in one of the books you carry to class and pass it to me casually at school. Insert some frivolous and trivial observations along with the serious stuff, so that if the diary falls into unfriendly hands, it won't be taken seriously. For example, in your report about the dinner at Vice-Consul Buckley's, you could remark that 'the woman with the colonel was quite sexy.' Or along with political and military information you could pass a few well-known verses from the *Kim Van Kieu* to distract the casual reader from the real intelligence. Our national committee will be very happy to receive your first diary. I shall transmit it through very safe channels."

Minh was a little upset by these new directives from the committee. Not only was he being asked to form a group of his own—and how was he to accomplish that?—but now he was being ordered, in effect, to become a Viet Cong spy. Loc conveyed the order, it was true, in his usual gentle, polite, and convincing manner. But Minh had thought that in his commitment to the cause of peace he could be an outsider, a "liberal" as Loc had said, not the leader of a cell and certainly not an informer!

To be fair, Minh had to admit that Loc had never lied to him. During their first meeting, Loc had told him he was a communist. He knew he had no choice. He had maneuvered himself into a position where he could not refuse Loc's request. And yet he could not bring himself to say yes, either.

Loc seemed to read his mind. "Minh, you know that we all serve our country, our people, in different ways, and we each do what we can do best. One thing I'm sure you'll agree with: we're not doing anything immoral. On the contrary, we're following the logical dictates of our just cause." Minh was silent.

"O.K.," Loc said. "Do you have any questions before we meet again on August 1st at the bookstore? It's a long time away, but we must think ahead of all the details to discuss before the August 10th manifestation. Of course, we can meet casually at school but we shouldn't be seen together too long, not more than five minutes at a time. If there is any change about the August 1st meeting, I'll communicate with you through the usual contact."

Minh nodded. The subject was closed, the matter, he supposed, decided.

"Loc, do you know anything about the arrests of students on June 11th? One of my students was arrested. Were any of yours?"

"None. But I was aware of the arrests, and I'm contacting influential friends who can help. Not all the arrested students had anything to do with us or even with politics, but there may be cases on which we have to act quickly before the suspects are sent to provincial interrogation centers in Da Nang. As far as I know, the arrested students are still being detained at the Hue police station pending the completion of their files. Who's your student who was arrested?"

"Cong Ton Nu To Ngoc."

"Beautiful name. From the royal family, too. I don't know her, but if I have any news, I'll certainly let you know. Often these arrests are harassment tactics, a kind of warning for others. The arrested persons might be released after a month or so. The most important thing is that you yourself should not be involved in any way in this whole matter. Let me handle it."

"Oh, before I forget. Do you know Trang, a professor of economics who's teaching with me in my seminar?"

"I don't know him personally, but he has a reputation on campus as an honest, blunt man who publicly expresses his opposition to the war and contempt for the government. He's been left alone because of his family connections. Two of his cousins are generals in the army. Also, he's an anticommunist nationalist. Perhaps you can cultivate his friendship, bring him into your organization. Use your own judgment. I must go now, we've spent too much time on the street and that's not good. So long."

.   .   .

The Fourth of July reception was held at the American Perfume; the newest and biggest hotel in town, on the left bank of the River of Perfume. The consulate had rented the whole ground floor from six to eight for a reception buffet for over 200 guests. As early as five o'clock all the streets leading to the hotel were blocked by the police and traffic was diverted through Trang Tien Bridge to the right bank. Those few hotel guests who were not invited were requested not to use the front door until nine o'clock. A cordon of U.S. Marines and Vietnamese paratroopers in full battle gear surrounded the hotel. Once a guest passed the cordon and his invitation had been verified and collected, he was issued a small pass in red, white and blue bearing a computer code whose meaning only security officers knew. By 5:30 a steady stream of Mercedes, Cadillacs, Lincolns, Peugeots, and military vehicles was arriving at the hotel.

The darkening sky was threatening rain when Minh arrived with his uncle and aunt and their two daughters. The Rector had misplaced his invitation card, causing a rush of negotiations between Vietnamese and American security officers. Vice-Consul Buckley, in black tie, starchy white coat, black trousers, and shiny black shoes, stood, visibly nervous, at the door to receive guests.

Buckley's monotonous greetings and compliments—"How splendid you look, How beautiful you are, It has been a long time since I saw you last"—repeated automatically as he shook hands with his guests, reminded Minh of the first time he had given a reception at the Vietnamese Embassy in Thailand, the year before he went to the United States. Exhausted and relieved when the reception was over, he had left the messy Embassy to his third secretary, taken the midnight train to Chiengmai, a hill resort north of Bangkok, and spent three days at a hotel with a prostitute he had picked up at the Hualamphong train station. He had wanted to forget everything: the clownish role he had played for the occasion, the meaningless grandiloquent words he had spoken about the eternally special relationship between Thailand and Vietnam.

There was something degrading, sad, even tragic, Minh felt, in fulfilling a public role one didn't sincerely believe. It was a form of prostitution more despicable than selling one's body. Minh sympathized with Buckley, who looked so lonely and miserable. Poor man, because of war regulations he wasn't even allowed to bring his wife along to share his burden.

When Minh, the Rector, and his family finally entered the reception room, it was filled nearly to capacity. About two thirds of the guests were Vietnamese, the rest American, in civilian black tie or white military uniform. At one end of the room a platform was erected in front of a red, white, and blue curtain. On each side of the platform stood two huge flags, one American, the other that of the Republic of Vietnam. To the right of the U.S. flag a podium with a microphone was installed and on the left stood a six-man band of Vietnamese and U.S. Marines, as rigid as toy soldiers, ready to play martial music. In the middle of the room, on a long table decorated with several bouquets of gladiolas, was laid out a combination of Vietnamese food, mostly rolls, and American dishes, predominantly hot dogs.

Minh noticed that practically all the Americans tasted the rolls while the Vietnamese were eager for the hot dogs. Twenty or so waitresses, wearing white aprons over their red, white, and blue uniforms, circulated among the guests, offering them trays of drinks: whisky, gin, Vietnamese-produced La Rue and "33" beer, Coca-Cola, Pepsi, ginger ale, Florida orange juice, and a new brand of soft drink Minh hadn't seen before, Viet-Cola. It was a Vietnamese imitation of Coke except that it was too sweet.

Minh knew practically no one among the guests present except his uncle's family; the deans and department chairmen from the University; Morgan; and two of the people he had met at Buckley's—Turlington, without his Vietnamese teacher, and the prosperous-looking Madame Dai, without Colonel Leclerc. She was escorted by a youthful American in civilian dress who looked and behaved like her bodyguard. Minh watched her from a distance. She was certainly very popular with the Americans, who greeted her like an old mother. Buckley conspicuously avoided being seen in her company.

At seven on the dot, Vice-Consul Buckley, holding a glass of champagne came to the platform and tested the microphone. Following him were four American lieutenants, representing the Army, Navy, Air Force and Marines, who grouped themselves in a row behind him.

"May I have your attention, please?" He repeated his words until the noisy crowd quieted and directed its attention toward him. The band played the "Star Spangled Banner."

Buckley raised his glass. "To the President of the United States." He had a sip of champagne. Then the band played the *Thanh Nien Hanh Khuc* Youth March, the Vietnamese national anthem. Buckley again raised his glass. "To the President of the Republic of Vietnam." He finished his champagne.

Minh wondered how many in the room knew the ironic history of the Vietnamese national anthem. It had been written in 1941 as a marching song for the youth groups organized by the French colonial administration, which later switched its allegiance to the French "traitor" Marshal Petain. In the 1950s, the Saigon government picked up the song as the national anthem. The ultimate irony was that the song's author, Luu Huu Phuoc, was now a member of the presidium of the National Liberation Front of South Vietnam, and the chairman of the Association of Intellectuals for Liberation, the organization to which Minh indirectly and secretly belonged.

After the short ceremony, Buckley took a folded paper from his breast pocket and prepared to read it. Suddenly the sound system shrieked, then went dead. He tapped the microphone with his forefinger, embarrassed, perhaps, by the glaring failure of American technological superiority. There was some commotion; then Turlington appeared from nowhere and fiddled with something inside the podium. The microphone returned to life.

"I can assure you it was not an act of Viet Cong sabotage," Buckley remarked. There were few chuckles.

He adjusted his reading glasses, put his right hand in his trouser pocket, and more solemnly than ever began a "message from the President of the United States of America to the Vietnamese and the Americans in Vietnam."

On the occasion of the 191st anniversary of the independence of the United States of America, I send to all of you my greetings. One hundred and ninety-one years ago, the American people fought valiantly for their independence, just as the heroic people of the Republic of Vietnam are now fighting for theirs. The only difference is that today the Republic of Vietnam is not alone. It has the complete material and moral support of the mightiest country on earth, the United States, and of its allies all over the Free World; today, the enemy of Vietnam is not a colonial country, but an international conspiracy which defies the laws of God and respects only brutal force. But I am confident that very soon the communists will be defeated and the people of Vietnam will be able to enjoy the first peaceful Tet after so many years of war. The American people will help the Vietnamese to build a prosperous democratic society. I congratulate all Americans in all capacities who have temporarily left their families behind to come to the land of Vietnam and to carry out, ten thousand miles from home, the noble ideals and the best traditions of our country. To them, and to the Vietnamese people, the government and the people of the United States, I will give all the material and moral support needed for final victory. God bless you all.

Buckley raised his glass. "To the President of the United States." He had a sip of champagne. Then the band played the Youth March, the Vietnamese national anthem. Buckley again raised his glass. "To the President of the Republic of Vietnam." He finished his champagne.

From the crowd emerged a short, stocky, middle-aged man with a well-trimmed mustache. He wore a white army uniform with a sword dangling at his waist. His grease-shined black hair and small slanted eyes, barely visible under a brush of brows, complimented a protruding chin that swallowed half his bow tie. He pulled out a white handkerchief, dried the drops of sweat from his forehead, rested both his hands on the podium, and read in a slow but clear American-accented English:

"Your Excellency the Vice-Consul of the United States" (Minh noted that some Americans and quite a few Vietnamese were having a hard time repressing their laughter. They knew that according to protocol only the ambassador is addressed as "Your Excellency." Buckley had a faint embarrassed smile), "officers of the armed forces of the United States and the Republic of Vietnam, ladies and gentlemen. On behalf of the people of the city of Hue, I have the deepest honor to convey to Your Excellency, and through you to His Excellency the President of the United States, my most respectful and warmest congratulations. The United States is only 191 years old, yet it has become the most powerful nation on earth. Vietnam is four thousand years old, but it is weak and beset by an international communist conspiracy, the agents of Peking and Moscow. Together, our countries are 4191 years old, and together we shall annihilate all our enemies, internal and external."

He stopped and raised his eyes, obviously expecting either applause or a gesture of appreciation for his clever comparison, but the room remained silent. He continued:

"The Vietnamese people will be eternally grateful to the government and the people of the United States for their assistance and sacrifices. With your country's support, Your Excellency (he turned to Buckley, who wore a half-grin), we will eat Tet this year in peace, with no enemy guns to disturb our meals. And with God's blessing, with the courage of the American and Vietnamese soldiers, we shall march North and eat Tet in Hanoi the year after. Thank you." He put the text of his address back into his pocket and quickly left the podium. There was scattered applause.

Minh followed his uncle to a group of V.I.P.s near the platform. His uncle introduced him to Colonel Thang, who shook his hand firmly.

"I heard about your return to Hue, and I'm very pleased with your participation in our struggle against communism. If you need my help for anything at all, please let me know through the Rector here. We must do all we can to prevent the students from being used by the Viet Cong agents and creating disturbances. You know," he went on, "two years ago when I was in the U.S. to study at the Staff and Command College in Leavenworth, Kansas, I visited several universities and colleges, and I was impressed by their size and wealth. I was told that the budget of just one American university is as big as or bigger than our national budget. But one thing I've never quite understood: why so many professors and students in the U.S. oppose our war. They are intelligent, they have everything, and they must know that if we don't defeat the communists here, then the U.S. will be finished too. The frontiers of the communist world will extend from the Atlantic to the Pacific, from Hong Kong to San Francisco."

Minh listened politely. "I don't know either," he said resignedly.

Then Colonel Thang introduced him to a number of Vietnamese who formed a small court around him.

"Professor Tran Van Minh, I would like you to meet Major Chinh, our chief of police; Mr. Ngai, the chief warden; Major Nhan, commander of the Hue military sector; and their ladies."

Minh passively shook hands with them and bowed slightly to their wives, who were all overdressed in brocade and expensive silk. He thought of the arrested students, especially To Ngoc, and he itched to ask the chief of police about them; but remembering Loc's advice he merely remarked, "Major, you must be having a very busy time."

"I can tell you, Professor, I've never been so busy in my life. We have to deal with all kinds of enemies: communists, procommunists, communist dupes, drug pushers, sex deviates. My job would be easier if we had a clear situation in which all the communists and their followers were on one side and we, the freedom fighters, were on the other. But our situation is complex. It's like pepper and salt, or rice and beans."

While Major Chinh was talking Minh was remembering the time he had seen Chinh's son and Ngai's daughter, at the Moonlight Tea House. He looked closely at Major Chinh's face. It somehow inspired sympathy.

Chinh pulled from his pocket a crocodile skin wallet, took out his business card, and handed it to Minh.

"Professor, here's my card. If anyone in this town tries to create trouble for you, or if you need my help on any matter, private or official, just call me either at my office or home. Someday soon I'd like to invite you to my house for dinner with some American advisers. My English isn't good and I'd like you to help me explain to them some delicate aspects of my job and my urgent need for help, especially in methods and instruments used to extract information from Viet Cong suspects. Will you help me?"

"If I can. You can contact me at my home or office at the university. Do you have my address?"

"A police chief must have the addresses of everyone, even of those 'whose files get lost.'" He glanced at Mr. Ngai, a graying, thin man with tobacco-tainted teeth and cold eyes. Ngai was unmoved.

Major Nhan, who had been listening patiently to Minh's conversation with Major Chinh, cut in. He spoke in English. "Professor, welcome home. We all need people like you. The army and the police are fighting one war, you and the people like you are fighting another—the war against lies, distortions, immorality, and falsehoods." His English was so good that Minh was prompted to comment.

"Major, your English is perfect. You even have a Yankee accent."

"You're right. I went to Bowdoin College in Maine as an undergraduate. When I returned to visit my family, I thought of going back to continue my graduate studies at Princeton—I'd been accepted to the Woodrow Wilson School of Foreign Affairs. Instead, I was drafted and went to Dalat Military Academy. After Dalat, two years as a company commander, and special training at the John F. Kennedy School of Special Warfare in Fort Bragg, North Carolina, I was transferred here as commandant of Hue military sector."

"But you're not originally from Hue?"

"No. I'm from the South, born in Can Tho. But I lived most of the time in Saigon. I went to Lycee Chasseloup-Laubat High School. Stop by and see me sometime. My office is about ten blocks from the university. Perhaps we can have dinner someday and talk about the good old days in the U.S. There's a new restaurant that has excellent beef in the traditional seven different styles. Excuse me please, I have to take my sister home," he said, indicating a strikingly beautiful young woman standing nearby. "I have a lot of work to do tonight. Good to see you, Professor."

Minh was impressed by Major Nhan's background and friendliness. If he had had more time with him, he would have asked if he knew An and Phong.

On his way to the food table, Minh spotted Lieutenant Bradley, the American officer who had saved him from arrest the day he had visited the pagoda. He was with a blond woman. Minh dashed over and grasped his arm.

"Professor Tran Van Minh! I'm so happy to see you! Would you believe we were just talking about you? How have you been? May I introduce you to Miss Carolyn Pendleton? She's with the A.F.S.C. in Quang Ngai and is visiting here for awhile. I'm sure you must know what A.F.S.C. stands for."

"It stands for 'America, for friendship, service and community.' Right, Miss Pendleton?"

"That's the best definition of A.F.S.C. I've ever heard!" she said, her pale skin reddening. "I wonder if we deserve it."

"Did you say that you were talking about me?" Minh asked Bradley.

"Yes. We were talking about the university because Carolyn plans to visit a friend there tomorrow and I mentioned your name and told her that I know your brother. She said she's read your articles and heard you lecture once in the States."

"I must confess," she added, "I've long been one of your numerous admirers. Many of us back in the States were surprised that you were allowed to return. I've read practically *all* of your articles and if I'm not mistaken, I met you in 1964, when you came to Philadelphia to speak at Temple University. The same evening you met with a group of antiwar activists at the A.F.S.C. headquarters."

"Oh, yes, I remember now. And where is Stewart Anderson now, who organized the meeting? He was the Friends peace secretary then, and a very good man."

"He's their representative in Singapore now. I saw him recently. When I write to him I'll tell him I met you here. He'll be happy to hear about you. You may not know it, but you're the subject of intense discussions among people involved in the antiwar movement in the U.S. They're confused by your attitude. Some even accuse you of selling out to the government."

Minh was amused. "I decided to come home for a simple, fundamental reason: food. It had become evident that without fish sauce, my brain wouldn't function properly. Besides, I missed eating Tet at home." He turned to Bradley. "What have you been doing since I last saw you?"

"I'm being transferred to Quang Tri. I've been promoted to captain."

"Congratulations!"

"And in addition to that, I'll be assigned as adviser to your brother Phong's company."

"That's good news. I'm certain the two of you will get along very well."

"No question about it. Your brother's a fine man. But it's rather strange that I, a foreigner, am advising your people instead of being advised by them."

"Better to have you as an adviser than somebody else."

"Money talks," Carolyn commented dryly.

"Well, good luck, Lieutenant, I mean Captain, Bradley. I hope that when you and Phong get settled, I can come and visit you."

"There's no such thing, unfortunately, as being settled in military life on the battlefront, but you'll be welcome whenever you feel like coming. Let us know, and we'll roll out the red carpet for you."

"Thank you," Minh said. "So long, take good care of yourself. Good-bye, Miss Pendleton."

It was getting late. On his way to the other end of the room to join his uncle, Minh saw Buckley talking animatedly with a three-star American general and a two-star Vietnamese general. Minh stopped to say goodbye to him.

"Thank you, Vice-Consul. It was an excellent reception, and again, my congratulations."

"Actually, it's my first experience. Last year on the Fourth of July I was in Manila for a regional diplomatic conference."

"You did very well."

"Can you spare a minute to talk with my friends?"

"Sure," Minh answered, "but I can't stay too long. My uncle and his family are waiting for me."

Buckley took him by the arm. "This is Professor Tran Van Minh, who just returned from the United States to teach politics at Hue University. He comes from the most prestigious family in this aristocratic city. Minh, this is General Jackson of the Third U.S. Marine Division; General Le Song Manh, commander of the I Corps; and Mr. Henry Williams the Fourth, of our Embassy in Saigon. They're just here for a few hours on their way to Quang Tri."

"I'm honored to meet you gentlemen."

General Manh, a tall, tanned officer in his late fifties, with a deep scar on his forehead, spoke in English with a French accent. "You should come and visit me at my headquarters in Da Nang and teach me some American politics. I know nothing about it. I only know about American weapons, generals, diplomats, and some American women, but I need to know more about American politicians so I can explain our plans to all the visiting Washington big shots."

"The general's too modest," General Jackson interjected. "He's an excellent general and a shrewd politician. He has survived all the changes in governments, and Vietnamese politics is much more complicated than American."

"*Ce n'est pas si compliqué,*" General Manh said. Turning to Minh, he spoke in Vietnamese, "What I just said is true. There are too many American politicians visiting, from the Vice-President and the Secretary of Defense to members of Congress. They all have thousands of questions to ask, they want to *check* everything. I have to spend more time briefing them than fighting the Viet Cong."

"I don't know much Vietnamese," Williams commented, "but I understand the General's complaint about too many visitors from Washington. I sympathize, because we have exactly the same problem. The war in the Congress is often more difficult to fight than the operations on the Ho Chi Minh Trail." General Jackson nodded in agreement. Williams continued, "Professor Minh, you might not know it, but at the Embassy we've read practically everything you wrote while you were in the United States. We didn't necessarily agree with you on everything, because we thought you were out of touch and listened to American leftists too much, but we admired your frankness and appreciated your background analyses. A friend of mine at the Embassy, Frederick Adams, spoke highly of you after meeting you a few months ago in New York." Williams must be a C.I.A. man too, Minh thought.

"Yes, I've met him. I hope to see him again."

"He's in Saigon most of the time. Anytime you come, stop by and see us."

"Thank you. I will." Minh turned to General Jackson. "How long have you been in Vietnam, General?"

"A little over five months and already I'm in love with your country, professor. Vietnam will be the most powerful in Southeast Asia after we beat the Viet Cong, which I hope is soon. President Johnson plans to send more troops so we can clean up the North Vietnamese infiltration at the D.M.Z. Once that's done, General Manh and his soldiers can devote all their time and energies to pacification."

The room had cleared of guests, and Minh noticed that his uncle was waiting nervously for him. He shook hands with General Manh, who whispered in his ear, "If you're not married, or even if you are, we'd like to have you join us later tonight. We're having a private party for General Jackson." He smiled suggestively. "You know what I mean by party?"

Minh knew what he meant: women, liquor, drugs . . . "Thank you, General, but I have to go home."

"You're a good man," General Manh said sardonically as Minh walked away.

Minh and his uncle stood in front of the hotel, waiting for the chauffeur to bring the car around. It was raining hard. Little streams of red water, like blood from a wounded body, ran down from the American and Vietnamese flags and disappeared into the sewers of the street.

.   .   .

On a Sunday morning two days before their long-planned August 1st meeting, Loc visited him at his house. He brought tea for Minh's father, who had had a serious case of influenza for over a week. Minh had been spending most of his time after school keeping his father company, reading him books and newspapers. After the three had talked for a while, Loc invited Minh to walk with him in the backyard garden. "The meeting on August 1st has been cancelled," Loc began. "Also, I met yesterday with a special messenger from the national committee, and one of their recommendations is that you and I should keep our contacts as normal and open as possible. You'll understand better when I've told you everything they said.

"To begin with, they were very pleased with the reports of your contacts with the Americans. Although the information you conveyed apparently wasn't secret, it was vital to our specialists because it verifies other intelligence sources and gives us background on important people. For example, an item such as a party organized by General Manh for General Jackson in a hotel suite after the reception proved to be of great importance to us. General Jackson has just been assigned by Westmoreland to lead an allied team of senior officers, Americans, Vietnamese, South Koreans, Australians, Thai, Philippinos and New Zealanders, to study the feasibility of a partial invasion and temporary occupation of the North, a repetition of General MacArthur's landing at Inchon during the Korean War.

"And by the way, the committee has passed along some information about some of the others. Turlington seems to be an important C.I.A. agent and Buckley just a regular foreign service officer. Turlington is known as a homosexual, immune to women's influence. And we suspect that Morgan might be working with the C.I.A., but we have no evidence yet.

"Anyway, the committee, on my recommendation, has suggested that you cut your political mass organization work to a minimum and concentrate on your work on the Americans. Specifically, continue to maintain the "Faculty-Student Caucus for Peace and Democracy" that you and Trang set up last week. That was a very good move, Minh. The caucus can be useful and it shouldn't arouse suspicion. And it's good to have Trang with us at this stage of our struggle even though he's anticommunist, because he's well connected."

Minh was startled. "How did you find out about the caucus so soon? We've barely decided to set it up."

Loc laughed. "It's not my intelligence network this time," he replied. "I've heard a number of students talking about it. But to continue. You shouldn't get too close to Xuan, just maintain normal relations. I wasn't given any explanation for that. To Ngoc will be released soon and you can safely enroll her in the caucus. She has no direct or indirect relations with us, just some influential relatives who protect her.

"Your role during the August 10th manifestation, which is still going according to plan, will be exclusively that of an intellectual and Buddhist scholar. You will recite Nguyen Du's *Calling the Wandering Souls.*

"We expect government security forces, the army, and the police to be very tough, but we cannot back down. It would be bad for the population's morale. Besides, the occasion will give us a chance to study the latest methods of control the police and the army are using while recruiting future cadres for the Uprising Committee. You and I and Sister Lan will all be members of the steering board of the committee, along with a few others, under different names. Actually, we've chosen a name for you: Nguyen Quang Giang. Any questions?"

"Yes!" Minh said. "I don't understand what you mean about the possibility of police and army reactions during the demonstration. Do you expect them to kill people, and we should look at it as a drill and a chance to recruit cadres for the Uprising Committee?" Minh could not completely conceal his shock and anger.

"Minh," Loc replied, "I understand your question and concern. We know from the past that the police and the army can be very tough and cruel. Of *course* we don't wish to see people killed, but after all, we're at war with the government and they with us." He spoke calmly, reasonably. "What we hope is that out of every confrontation, bloody or bloodless, we learn something and profit from it. You use the word drill and I must say that's correct, although it might sound inhumane to you. But think of it: life is a constant drill. Without practice, exercise, training, without drill, one cannot effectively deal with dangers and crises. The more one drills oneself and observes others, the better are one's chances of victory.

"In fact, strangely enough, constant alertness and practice contain an element of peace, nonviolence if you will. To prevent violence from taking place, one has to thoroughly understand its nature and manifestations. I know your life until now has been free of all drills and dangers, but living in present-day Vietnam, you're left with no choice but to train yourself to confront realities. Actually, you're left with a very good choice, the choice to serve the masses. But enough politics for now. Shall we return to the house? I'd like to chat with your father for a while before I go."

Minh was not convinced of Loc's assessment. Rational as it was, it sounded heartless and cold to him. *Tinh* and *Ly* he thought, but he said nothing.

He sat passively, listening to the conversation that his father and Loc were having about the role of poetry in Buddhist literature. He has a more intimate relationship with my father than *I* do, Minh thought sadly. He was deeply suspicious of Loc's brutal and dogmatic approach to politics and of his total, serene obedience to a "we" that represented not the two of them, not the Buddhists, not the Vietnamese people, but Loc's party, the Vietnam Workers Communist Party. Still, his unselfish kindness inspired confidence and admiration, and these went a long way towards allaying Minh's doubts.

Following Loc's instructions, Minh cautiously but energetically developed his contacts with the Americans. He had dinner twice with Turlington, once at Morgan's home on August 8th. The discussion that night centered on the historical role of Buddhism in national resistances against foreign invasions.

Turlington asked Minh his views on the similarities between Marxism and Buddhism claimed recently by some prominent Burmese politicians. At first, Minh suspected that Turlington wanted to find out his connections with the Viet Cong; on second thought, and accustomed by his training and profession to such academic discussions, he decided to give him a reasonable and honest answer.

Minh explained that the fundamental similarities between Buddhism and Marxism were that they both rejected the existence of a Supreme Being, a God-Creator and arbitrator of all things and peoples on the planet earth; both traced the roots of human unhappiness and alienation to greed, class conflict, and acquisition of property; and both believed in the impermanence of all things and in the possible transformation of people to a higher, happier stage. Minh coined the word "psychomaterialism" to describe Buddhist materialism as opposed to Marxist historical materialism. He agreed with Turlington that the Buddhist way to the liberation of man was through nonviolence and the "middle-way," while the Marxist way was through revolutionary violence and the dogmatic belief in the laws of the motion of history. The price to pay for Marxist "nirvana" would be the loss of the human personality and individual liberties, he said, while for Buddhism it would be the disappearance of the "self."

But as he spoke Minh found himself, to his amazement, wishing that Loc were there, so that he could be sure his answers didn't contradict the Party line. He hadn't realized how dependent he'd become on Loc, not only politically but intellectually as well.

VIII

Buddha's Gate

Cross Buddha's gate and wander free at last,
The bonds of seven passions all cut off.
Why shoulder loads and carry burdens still?
What joy in human love can you expect?

A plaint inside the royal harem.
Nguyen Gia Thieu
1741–1798
Translated by Huynh Sanh Thong.

August 10, 1967, the fifteenth day of the seventh month of the Year of the Goat, started auspiciously. The rain which had begun eight days earlier, on the seventh day of the seventh month, and that normally lasted for several weeks, had stopped the night before. Rain that began on that day was known as *Mua Ngau*, the yearly tears of separation rolling down from Heaven from the eyes of the lovers Nguu Lang, a poor buffalo herdsman, and Chuc Nu, a heavenly princess, who were condemned by the Emperor of Jade to meet each other across the Milky Way only one night a year, on the seventh day of the seventh month.

According to a schedule of events printed on yellow bamboo paper, the program would start at noon with a "Ceremony of Prayer" to be held in all Buddhist pagodas for "wandering and lost souls." At one o'clock there would be a symbolic release of birds and fishes at the River of Perfume and distribution of food and clothes for the needy. A service for the remembrance of the dead and a national appeal for peace, to be conducted at the Linh Mu pagoda under the patronage of the Patriarch of the Buddhist Church, would begin at three and last until sundown, to be followed by a lantern procession through the town.

Minh had fasted the day before, to cleanse his body and mind of impurity, but on August 10th he ate vegetarian dishes prepared by his auntie. His father advised him to take along a lot of fruit and candied ginger for strength. He left home at ten, with his stepmother, after half an hour of meditation in front of his mother's picture.

About a mile before they reached the pagoda, the road was blocked, lined with uniformed policemen equipped with walkie-talkies and reinforced by paratroopers and rangers in full battle gear. All the vehicles were ordered to stop and everyone, even very old people, had to walk the last mile to the pagoda.

The front lawn of the pagoda was overflowing with people—at least 50,000, Minh guessed. There were many children in the crowd; most of them carrying lanterns, usually in the shape of a lotus flower. Members of the Buddhist Youth Organization, dressed like Boy and Girl Scouts and proud of their armbands of yellow with a red Buddhist wheel, circulated cheerfully among the crowd, answering questions and helping the younger children. In front of the pagoda, by the banyan tree, a wooden platform had been erected. It was covered with a yellow cloth and decorated with ten big vases of lotus flowers.

"Auntie," Minh observed, "where does the pagoda get all these lotus flowers? The season is long over, isn't it?"

"Yes, the season's over," she answered, "but these bouquets come from a hamlet called Ten Thousand Year Lotus, which was founded over three hundred years ago by a monk who with his own hands dug a large pond in which to grow them. It took him twenty years. Unlike ordinary lotus, these bloom every season of the year, and in five colors. I visited the hamlet once with your father a long time ago. It's inaccessible now. Phong told us that it's a Viet Cong stronghold. There's a story circulating among the farmers here that about a year ago an American plane attempting to bomb the hamlet suddenly lost altitude, fell into the pond, and was miraculously sucked into the mud without leaving a trace."

A thunderous sound of *"Nam Mo Phat"* broke out. The people bowed their heads. Silence fell.

The Patriarch, holding a staff, dressed in deep yellow garments, and accompanied by nine other monks, climbed the platform and seated himself, crosslegged. In a grave voice he began:

"On this, the fifteenth day of the seventh month of the Buddhist Year 2511, the Year of the Goat, we ask all of you to look into your hearts, to remember all the wandering and lost souls of the dead, and to meditate on the unhappiness of the living. Pray to Lord Buddha, the Compassionate, implore Him to bestow His infinite wisdom upon all men and to restore peace to our land, cruelly ravaged by so many years of war and conflict. *Nam Mo Phat.*" The crowd responded, "*Nam Mo Phat.*"

Then, raising his staff, he recited "The Hymn of the Buddha of Infinite Compassion and Wisdom," from the Satapancasatka of Matroceta. Minh knew the hymn by heart. The Patriarch recited the first two verses alone; then the other monks joined in. The crowd repeated the last sentence after them: "There is nothing that is not wonderfully true in Buddha's dharmas." "*Nam Mo Phat,*" the Patriarch intoned again. The ceremony ended with the Prayer of Repentance.

The Patriarch stepped from the platform and, accompanied by his retinue, he moved among the faithful, his hands joined above his breast, his shaven head shining to the afternoon sun. He recognized Minh and his auntie and stopped to ask about Minh's father's health. "I shall pray to Buddha and ask His protection for your sons," he told Auntie. She bowed and whispered, "*Nam Mo Phat.*" Trays of fruits and cones of cooked, artificially colored glutinous rice were passed among the crowd, who accepted this "gift of Buddha" with gladness.

When the Patriarch and the monks retired to their chambers, the "lay" portion of the ceremony began. An amateur Buddhist Youth Movement band played several traditional religious songs; then a stout middle-aged man in a blue gown and black turban came to the rostrum beside the platform and stood behind the microphone. The audience recognized him immediately as the president of the Hue Buddhist Layman Association. He welcomed the crowd, observing that the "number of participants is as large as the compassionate heart of the Buddha"; then, after speaking of the essence and meaning of the day and the importance of praying for peace so that "the wandering souls will not wander any more and will return to our midst and enter our homes," he invited Minh to the rostrum.

"We are proud on this day to have with us Professor Doctor Tran Van Minh, the descendant of the oldest Buddhist family in our city, a great scholar, a prominent writer, and a beloved poet. He has returned home after long years overseas to be with his family and his nation and to serve Buddha."

A wave of applause interrupted him. He continued, "It's appropriate that he will declaim today the *Calling the Wandering Souls*, which was composed by the greatest poet of all times, Nguyen Du, the immortal author of the immortal *Kim Van Kieu*, the candle to the darkness of our soul and the light of compassion of Lord Buddha."

The people fell silent and without any instruction bowed their heads to the ground. Minh was frozen with emotion. Never before in his life had he faced such a large audience on an occasion of such national importance. He closed his eyes and invoked his mother's assistance. Gradually his serenity returned. Opening his eyes he saw in the front row his auntie and Loc, who flashed a smile of encouragement. In the traditional Hue style, blending the high tone with the low at the beginning of each sentence to leave a flat note between, Minh declaimed the poem.

In this seventh month the rain is endless.
The cold penetrates into the dry bones.
The autumn evening is mournful and sad.
The reeds are livid, the leaves withered.
In the twilight, the birches droop.
The pear trees are shrouded in mist.
Who can remain unmoved?
If the world of the living is so sad
Much sadder must be the world of the dead.

In the utter darkness of eternal night,
Appear, lost souls, like will-o-the-wisps, reveal your presence!
O poor beings, creatures of the ten categories.
Your abandoned souls are roaming in strange lands!
No incense is burning for you.
Nobles and plebeians, scholars and ignorant,
You wander, helpless, in the night.

There were those who pursued glory,
Who dreamt of conquest and power.
Why evoke the days of epic battles
When later misfortunes brought great sorrow?
Their golden palaces crumbled
And they envied a humble man's lot.
Power and riches make many enemies.
Blood has been shed, the dry bones are molding.
Helplessly, the abandoned souls are roaming.
Headless ghosts in the rainy night are wailing;
Success or failure depends on one's fate.
Will these lost souls ever find deliverance?

There were those at the head of proud armies
Who sacked palaces and overturned thrones
In a display of might like storm and thunder.
Thousands were killed for the glory of one man.
Then came defeat and the battlefield was strewn with corpses.

The unclaimed bones are lying somewhere in a far-away land.
The rain lashes down and the wind howls.
Who now will evoke their memory?

There were those who pursued riches,
Who lost appetite and sleep,
With no children or relatives to inherit their fortunes,
With no one to hear their last words,
Riches dissipate like passing clouds.
Living, they had their hands full of gold,
Departing from this world, they could take with them no single coin.
At their funeral, hired mourners feigned sorrow,
The cheap coffins taken away hastily in the night.
Lost souls, they roam the flooded fields
Without offering of incense or water.

There were those who sought academic honors leading to high places,
To the cities they went, forsaking their native land.
But do arts and letters always bring success?
One day they lay sick in a roadside inn,
Without the love and care of their families.
Dead, they were hastily buried, far from dear ones and ancestral lands,
In abandoned burying grounds they lie.
Their lonely souls wander without being honored by offerings.

There were those who, conscripted,
Left their families for the service of the king,
Taken to distant lands, they lived a life of privations and sufferings.
In war human lives are cheap
Sword and fire sow death
Roaming will-of-the-wisps, apparitions of their lost souls,
Make the scene still more mournful.

There were those who spoiled their lives,
Selling their charms and smiles,
Abandoned by all when youth was gone.
They had no husbands or children to support them.
In life, nothing but humiliations and sufferings.
With death, only offerings from kind strangers.
Pitiable was the fate of these women.
Why this was destiny, no one knows the reason.

There were those who spent their lives begging,
Sleeping under bridges, on the ground.
Yet, like others, they were human beings.
They lived on charity and now lie in the roadside graves.

There were the victims of injustice,
Year after year they languished in jail.
Dead, they were buried somewhere near the prison wall,
For their shrouds, only tattered mats.
Will their innocence ever be revealed?

There were babies born at an untimely hour
Who lived only a few moments.
There's no one now to carry them,
And heart-rending are their feeble cries.
Struck by fate midway on the path of life,
They followed each other to the other world.
Each with a different destiny.

Where are they now, those lost souls?
Somewhere they hide, maybe among the trees,
Maybe alone the streams or among the clouds,
Maybe in the grass or in the bushes;
Or they wander aimlessly
By the roadside inns or under the bridges;
Or they seek shelter in temples and pagodas.
Perhaps they haunt markets or river banks
Or the barren lands, the knolls or the bamboo groves.

Misery was their lot in lifetime.
In the cold their corpses are now withering.
Year after year exposed to wind and rain.
On the cold ground they lie, sighing.
At dawn, when the cock crows, they flee,
Only to grope their way again when night comes.

Like a person possessed by a powerful spirit, Minh felt the words flow from his mouth. He knew that he had finished the recital only when he heard a wave of murmurs: *"Nam Mo Phat."* No applause destroyed the solemn dignity of the moment.

Then the president of the layman association stepped to the microphone. "I'm sure that through the memorable and unexcelled rendering of the Calling by a great Buddhist son of our city you have all penetrated the sacred meaning of this day," he said. The applause now was prolonged and deafening.

"And now," the president said, "I will introduce to you another son of Hue, a great musician who has refused to be silent and who will sing for us the aspirations and the agony of the Buddhists, of all Vietnamese, and of peoples everywhere."

The crowd clapped and shouted for five full minutes when Trinh Cong Son appeared. Thin and pale, he was dressed in a white shirt and dark blue pants. He looks too fragile to live, Minh thought, as if a wind could blow him away.

Accompanying himself on his guitar he first sang his popular "The Heritage of Our Motherland," followed by "I Shall Go Visiting":

When my land has peace
I shall go visiting
I shall go visiting

Along a road with many foxholes.
When my land is no longer at war

I shall visit the green graves of my friends;
When my land has peace
I shall go visiting
I shall go visiting
Over bridges crushed by mines,
Go visiting
Bunkers of bayonets and pungi sticks;
When my people are no longer killing each other
The children will sing children's songs
Outside on the street

When my land has peace
I shall go and never stop
To Saigon, to the center,
To Hanoi, to the south,
I shall go in celebration
And I hope I will forget
The story of this war.

When my land has peace
I shall go visiting
I shall go visiting
The many sad graveyards
To see the epitaphs on tombstones
That have sprung up like mushrooms.

When my land is no longer at war
The old mother will go up into the mountains
And search for the bones of her son.
When my land has peace
I shall go visiting.
I shall go visiting
Villages turned into prairies,
Go visiting
The forests destroyed by fire;
When my people are no longer killing each other
Everyone will go out in the street
To cry out with smiles.

Trinh Cong Son unstrapped his guitar, bowed his head, and stepped from the platform. But the audience, rising to its feet, shouted for more until he returned. He sang a refrain composed of the choruses of both songs; the crowd, still standing, sang with him:

A thousand years of Chinese reign,
A hundred years of French domain,
Twenty years of American intervention
The heritage of our Motherland

The sad country of Viet Nam.
When my land has peace
I shall go visiting
I shall go visiting
Villages turned into prairies,
Go visiting
The forests destroyed by fire;
When my people are no longer killing each other
Everyone will go out in the street
To cry out with smiles.

The crowd would not let him stop. Again and again they sang the combined refrain, until the artist and his audience melted into a *ying-yang* harmony, the listeners echoing in their hearts the feelings of the artist, the artist in turn transforming their feelings in his voice and face. The pagoda's lawn and the hilly land beyond were a sea of singing beings. The air was charged with alternating currents of sadness for "the sad country of Viet Nam" and vibrations of hope that someday it would be true that "my people are no longer killing each other." Minh had never seen such display of emotion by the people of Hue, who were known throughout the country as reserved and introspective.

Finally the red sun began to sink slowly behind the pagoda's tower, bathing the eager crowd with its softening golden rays. The temperature dropped sharply as a cool breeze rose from the River of Perfume; mothers reached for sweaters for their children. The president of the layman association climbed to the platform and begged the audience to stop singing at last.

"Esteemed and affectionate friends-in-Buddhism," he said, "I'm sure that you all agree with me that never before in our country have we witnessed such a unity of hearts and minds in Buddha and in peace. Now I ask you to demonstrate to all Hue people, to the people of Vietnam and of the world, our firm determination to restore tranquility to our long-suffering country. Please prepare yourselves for the procession into the center of the city. And please remember that our demonstration of the Buddhist Will for Peace should not turn into violence and disorder. The procession will be placed under the compassionate guidance of the Patriarch himself and other venerable monks. Order will be maintained by special teams of selected members of the Buddhist Youth Organization, under the direction of Professor Loc who is respected and known by our Buddhist community. The procession will commence within half an hour."

Lotus-shaped lanterns were distributed by members of the youth organization; some had brought multi-colored moon-shaped and carp-shaped lanterns of their own. Like a human tide, the faithful descended the pagoda's hill to the dirt road that zigzagged toward the city. As darkness fell, the long, moving column looked like an army of fireflies silently following the monks in yellow robes that blended with the early moonlight.

They passed the spot where Minh had been arrested and humiliated by the government soldiers. He glanced at his stepmother. Never had he seen her so serene and confident. He was silent.

Like a myriad of lost wandering souls who had at last found a refuge in the compassionate heart of the Buddha, the lantern-holding columns flowed silently on. From time to time a prolonged murmur arose from their lips: *"Nam Mo Phat."*

The moon was rising now in an immaculate dark blue sky. At the intersection between the dirt road and the paved main street that ran into the city, a few hundred more Buddhists, who had been assembling at a nearby temple, joined the procession.

Suddenly the frightening palpitating sound of a police helicopter broke the stillness. Without warning, soldiers with bayonets at the ready appeared on both sides of the streets. The helicopter descended to treetop level. A tank, like a crawling tiger, moved up the road towards the monks at the front of the crowd.

At an order, probably from the Patriarch himself, the mass of human beings lay down in the dusty earth. The arrogant tank stopped a few inches from a line of monks seated in the lotus position. At the head of the line was the Patriarch, his eyes closed in prayer.

An uneasy silence prevailed. The noisy helicopter had left. In the confrontation between the machines of war and the men of peace, there was no sound or movement.

Minh raised his head from the dust. He saw the threatening gun from the tank's turret hovering over the shining shaved heads of the monks, like a gallows in a Western movie. Suddenly, from the rear of the column, an ear-splitting explosion shook the earth, followed by a distant burst of machine-gun fire and the whistle of rifle shots. Now two helicopters appeared. Cruising low over the now panic-stricken and milling crowd, they broadcast a command to disperse because of a Viet Cong ambush. Distant ambulances wailed, children cried, parents shouted for their children as they ran for cover. Minh pulled his stepmother to the other side of the street. They ran for almost half an hour before collapsing in exhaustion.

They rested for a while, leaning against a wall in the shelter of a doorway, then started walking again, southward. A few blocks farther on they spotted a taxi parked in front of an isolated house. The driver noticed their dirty and torn clothes at once.

"Are you all right?" he asked. "You want some water? What happened?"

"We don't really know," Minh said, "we were in a procession coming

from the Linh Mu pagoda to the city when we heard an explosion. Everybody was frightened and ran for their lives."

"My wife and I heard the explosion, too," the cab driver said, "We
saw several helicopters passing over the house but we thought it was a
military operation against the Viet Cong."

"No, it wasn't—at least not as far as I can tell. Can you take us home?"

"Of course. I'll avoid the main avenues and take a detour to the Bach
Ho Bridge."

"Thank you very much." Minh and his stepmother climbed gratefully
into the cab.

.   .   .

Minh's father was visibly happy to see them back early, but his face
reddened with anger when they told him what had happened. "That's
typical of the way the government destroys a peaceful demonstration," he
snapped. "They mount an attack and then accuse the Viet Cong of the
crime!" He retired to his studio.

Lying on his bed, Minh tuned in the Hue Radio evening news:

"At 7:30," the radio announced, "several thousand Buddhists were
marching from the Linh Mu pagoda to the center of the city for a night rally,
when they were ambushed at the city limits by an unidentified group of Viet
Cong sappers. According to the police, the Viet Cong succeeded in fleeing
from the scene of the crime, leaving behind five dead and dozens wounded,
among them the Patriarch of the Linh Mu, who is now resting in his private
chamber at the pagoda."

It couldn't be possible that the Viet Cong would ambush a Buddhist
demonstration for peace, Minh thought. Or could it? Was it possible that
they did it to show the people that the government was unable to protect
them, unable to guarantee the security of a peaceful Buddhist demonstration? On the other hand, what made his father so sure that it was the
government's doing? Could the government be as cynical as to attack its own
people and blame it on the Viet Cong? He wished Loc were with him at this
moment to clarify all the conflicting versions of the incident. But he had
seen Loc only once, and briefly, at the pagoda. As far as Minh knew, he had
not been at the procession at all.

Minh waited for the more reliable B.B.C. news at eleven, which
started with a special bulletin on the incident. The newscaster, a woman
with a Hue accent, read the news:

"An explosion took place at about seven this evening during a peaceful
march of about fifty thousand Buddhists from the Linh Mu Pagoda outside
the city limits to the city's center. The bloody incident took place at the
intersection between the dirt road and the paved street that leads to the
town, an intersection often called Red and Black Junction because of the

colors of the red dirt road and the black asphalt street. In the ensuing panic, five persons were killed and dozens wounded. The Hue police have accused the Viet Cong of the ambush on the civilian population. But in Saigon, a spokesman for the United Buddhist Church said that 'although we have to wait for a detailed report from Hue, we have no doubt that the work was done by government agents and not by the Viet Cong.'"

Minh tried to think seriously about the Church's interpretation, which was the same as his father's comment, but he was too tired. He fell asleep, hoping that by tomorrow his head would be clear enough to understand the tragic incident.

Early the next morning Minh tuned in again to Radio B.B.C.

"A final count," the announcer said, "reveals that ten people were killed in the attack instead of five, as earlier reported, and one hundred and twenty were wounded, most of them students and members of the Buddhist Youth Organization. The injured are being treated in the crowded Hue Hospital."

The Hue police, the announcer continued, had taken into custody a young woman student from Hue University who allegedly was with a Viet Cong sapper. She was being sent to Saigon for further interrogation. In the meantime, the President had dispatched a special team of military investigators to Hue to help the local authorities track down the perpetrators of the incident.

The President also was calling on the people to observe calm, and he reiterated, the newscaster said, that although he was a Catholic, he held the authentic peace-loving Buddhists in high respect; on the other hand, he would be very firm against those who claimed to be Buddhists but who were actually working with the Viet Cong. The government's allegation had been strongly denied by a spokesman of the United Buddhist Church, who insisted that government agents disguised as Viet Cong had provoked the incident. The Church issued a call for a massive demonstration of sympathy for the "Hue martyrs" at an appropriate date. "Incidentally," the B.B.C. commented, "the United Buddhist Church's denial is similar to a version of the event given on a Viet Cong Radio Liberation broadcast monitored in Singapore."

The news was followed by an exclusive interview by the B.B.C. correspondent in Saigon with the head of the Strategic Intelligence Office, General Con, who was a cousin of the President and had recently served as army deputy chief of staff for external affairs. According to the General, who like Minh was a member of an aristocratic Hue family, "the bloody Linh Mu incident" was engineered by the Viet Cong as part of its preparation for what they called, in a "captured document," the coming "general uprising." The Viet Cong organization in charge of this preparation in the cities, he said, was the Intellectuals for Liberation, "which includes among its rank and file, professors, artists and students."

The telephone rang. It was An.

"I called to find out if everything's all right."

"Yes, it is. Your mother and I were at the Linh Mu pagoda for the ceremony. I read the *Calling the Wandering Souls*." Remembering the cautious advice An had given him regarding telephone conversations, Minh stopped short at describing how he and his stepmother had escaped the incident and continued. "Everything's fine. I just listened to Radio B.B.C. to find out what actually happened."

"Yes, the B.B.C. is usually objective and accurate. I think you should stay home and be careful. In an emotionally charged situation, the solution is inaction," An counseled.

"I think so too," Minh concurred, "but I do have to teach today. I hope the situation isn't going to affect the university."

"I really don't know, Minh. We have to wait for the presidential investigation team's recommendations. How's father?"

"He's well, except for a bout of cold a few days ago."

"I'm glad to hear that. And mother?"

"She's well. She's still sleeping, I think. She was quite upset by yesterday's incident. Do you want to speak to her?"

"No, I don't think so. Whenever they wake up, please tell them I called. Goodbye. I'll call you sometime next week."

"Goodbye, An, and thanks for calling."

It was frustrating not to be able to question An over the monitored phone line. He wanted to believe that the government was behind the incident; perhaps An knew something. If only he could get some clarification from Loc! If the government was lying, he reasoned—if it had *not* captured a Viet Cong document—how did it know so precisely the Viet Cong plan for a general uprising, and the role of the Association of Intellectuals for Liberation? But then, why on earth would the Viet Cong kill people as a preparation for a general uprising? Didn't the people hate the government enough already without the necessity of such a measure? And could the Viet Cong possibly be so brutal, so cynical itself, as to kill the people it was committed to save?

.   .   .

From a distance, Minh could see that the university's compound was surrounded by cordons of police and army soldiers. Hundreds of posters on the walls and along the street called for a general student strike. Police agents were busy taking them down.

"What happened?" he asked one of them. Noticing the policeman's suspicious eyes, he added, "I'm a professor here and I'd like to know if I can get into the school." When he showed him his I.D., the policeman became more cooperative.

"Professor, the United Buddhist Church has issued a call for a general strike and demonstration. We have received orders to be ready. You surely can enter the university."

"Thank you. But I see no one here for a demonstration."

"You never know about these clever Viet Cong. We simply wait and see."

The Rector drove slowly up the street. In the car with him were two men in uniform. Small groups of students began to filter in. All were searched by uniformed police officers.

A crowd began to gather near the library. One student, his forehead wrapped in a white bandage with spots of dark brown dry blood, exhorted his friends, "I was at the peaceful procession yesterday and I saw how the government agents disguised as Viet Cong turned it into a massacre, a bloody pacification campaign. I urge all of you to demonstrate against the U.S. and its Saigon puppets. Down with U.S. imperialism!" he shouted. "Down with the Saigon puppet government! Long live Buddhism! Long live peace!"

A soldier seized him. Other soldiers herded his listeners, about 50 of them, into a military truck. Now the police forbade all students to enter the university's grounds.

Minh looked in Loc's office, then Trang's. They weren't there. He stopped by the Rector's reception lounge. His uncle waved him in. He was having a discussion with two uniformed officers whom Minh recognized as Colonel Vu Tat Thang, the province chief and mayor of Hue, and Major Chinh, the police chief. They both greeted Minh coldly. They didn't seem as friendly as they had when they'd met him at the Fourth of July celebration. They stood up to leave.

"We've done our job. It's yours now!" Chinh told the Rector curtly. Their faces were determined and angry.

The Rector asked Minh to sit down. "The decision has been made to close the university for an indefinite period pending investigations of faculty and student involvement in Saturday's violence," he announced in a flat voice. "Thang and Chinh just told me that they have plenty of evidence to prove that the incident was provoked by the Viet Cong, and that the principal organizers of the demonstration know it. They also said that some faculty and students are being arrested and that there's a presidential team in town to conduct an enquiry and decide what's to be done."

"What did you say to them, Uncle?" Minh asked anxiously.

"What could I say? The successful strike this morning, the small demonstration you just witnessed, all prove that they're right, that the whole thing was organized by a centralized group right here on campus, acting on orders from the Viet Cong."

"Do you mean to say that the Viet Cong engineered the killing of people themselves?"

"I definitely think so. It's not unusual for the communists to do that. Their classic tactic is to create hatred and make martyrs, then exploit the situation for their sinister interests. Don't you think so, Minh?"

"I don't know. It's hard to believe. For one thing, the United Buddhist Church has denied the whole thing and has accused the government of perpetrating the violence. I believe what the Church says."

"I'd like to believe the Church too," the Rector replied. "But experience tells me that our monks, who may be intelligent and sophisticated in matters of salvation and suffering, are terribly naive when it comes to politics. They can be easily used and I think they're being used by the Communists." The Rector smiled sardonically. He thinks I'm as naive as they are, Minh thought.

"What can we do now?" he asked.

"What I do now is close the university and wait. You should stay home too, relax and wait."

"How come no faculty showed up this morning? Did the police chief tell you who they arrested among the students and faculty?"

"Most members of the faculty, unlike yourself, come to school late, and they may have been turned back by the police. Some may have been arrested already. The police chief promised me that he'll give me the names of any faculty and students who were arrested, but for my personal information only, he emphasized."

"I would appreciate it very much," Minh implored, "if you could let me know if any faculty or student of mine gets arrested. Please call me. Incidentally, I forgot to let you know that we have a telephone now. The number is 222-3567."

"That's a military line," his uncle observed.

"How did you know?"

"All army telephone numbers begin with 222. I'll let you know, for your personal information only, if any faculty or student of yours is arrested. In the meantime, take it easy. Take care of your father, and if I were you I'd just stay home and not try to see anyone. Of course, if you don't know what to do with your time, you're always welcome to come to my house and have a drink, or dinner, and watch TV. Now, I must write a statement to be read tonight on radio and TV about the university closing. I'll see you soon, I hope." He shook Minh's hand warmly.

With no word from Loc, and nowhere to go, Minh stayed home. Days passed in inactivity and unease. He called the Rector once or twice but was told that there was no news from the authorities about any arrests of faculty or students. Minh spent his time reading. After a couple of weeks, his stepmother returned from the market one day with the news that Loc had gone to Saigon. Minh was puzzled and hurt. Why hadn't Loc been in touch before he left—if he had left?

Minh's father, who seemed to grow more and more bitter, had little to say to him. It seemed to Minh that his father didn't think he had done enough to fight the government and stop the war. The day he had told him about the university's closing, his father had remarked sternly, "You should have stayed at the university and helped the students organize and demonstrate. The duty of a teacher is not only to dispense knowledge, but mostly, in the situation we're in now, to provide moral, political support and guidance to the young."

"But Father," Minh had replied, "there wasn't a single student around. Those who came were turned away by the police." But his answer was evidently unconvincing, for his father remarked sharply, "You could find them if you wanted to," and turned his back on him.

Minh had never before undergone such a long period of inaction. He went to the Rector's twice, but became even more disgusted than he had been with his uncle's cynicism and his cousins' constant questions about American movie stars and TV programs. He went out to dinner once in town with James Morgan, but the visible hostility of the Vietnamese when they saw him with an American made it obvious to him that Hue's mood had turned ugly: anti-American, antigovernment, antiwar. As in the past, whenever a national crisis existed, Hue withdrew behind its arrogant silence.

.   .   .

Towards the end of September there was a call from the Rector.

"Minh, the police just told me that your friend, Professor Trang, was arrested."

"But he's anticommunist! I know it for sure!"

"He's also antiwar."

"Yes, he is."

"That's enough reason to be arrested."

"Where is he now? Can I see him?"

"Like everyone who's arrested here for political reasons, he's been sent to Saigon for further interrogation and detention. I guess he's there by now." He paused. Minh heard the crackle of turning pages. "Just a minute," he said. "Yes. One of your students was arrested, a woman. Her name is Xuan. She, too, is being sent to Saigon. As you know, she was a Viet Cong suspect on the students' lists you got at the beginning of the semester. According to the police, she was seen with a Viet Cong sapper who threw the bomb into the procession."

"I see," Minh said, and hung up.

For the first time Minh began to feel afraid. If Trang was arrested, he thought, anyone could be arrested, anyone who was for peace, Buddhist or not. It was hard for him to believe that Xuan was a Viet Cong militant, directly involved in the bloody incident. A beautiful woman like her, a member of a terrorist ring? And yet she had been arrested. Were his reputation, his contacts with Americans, enough to protect him? Minh wondered. Could he be arrested too?

How anxious he was to see Loc. Had he been killed? Where was Lan? How much he needed Loc's leadership now! Not for the first time he realized that by himself he was unable to decide what to do about his own safety and security.

His fears were not allayed by an announcement on the news that evening that the National Buddhist League for Peace and Democracy, to which he openly belonged, had been declared subversive and illegal. It was a cover, the proclamation said, for the Association of Intellectuals for Liberation—which in turn was termed "a Viet Cong organization directly under the control of the Workers Communist Party."

.   .   .

The next day, Minh received a letter from Jennifer, dated September 1st and postmarked Washington, D.C.

c/o Richard T. Sloane
State Department
Washington, D.C. 20500

Dearest Minh,

I got your letter of June 3rd on July 2nd when I came back from my vacation in Canada. I was shocked when I read it: it was cold, it was so unlike you that I couldn't believe it was yours. Of course, I was stupid enough to make mistakes in the address, but you should understand that I am unaware of subtleties in matters of ranks and position. Was it a message for me not to write you? If so, why don't you say it directly and clearly and I shall try to forget all that happened between us as if it was a sequence in an imagined Hollywood movie. But I refuse to believe that it was your intention. Or was it? I read and re-read the few short lines to try to find out what really it was all about. I thought I knew you well, but I'm not so sure anymore. Anyway . . . As you can see by the letterhead, I'm in Washington now with a cousin of mine who just came back from a tour of duty at the U.S. Embassy in Taiwan. Although he's nearly ten years my senior, we're very close to each other. I told him about our relationship and showed him your letter and asked his opinion. He told me that "Asians get red very quickly when they drink (which is true with you) and get cold and formal when they write." He advised me just to forget the whole thing and not to worry about my wrong, American interpretation of your letter. Instead I should continue to write you and this is what I'm doing. On August 11th, I read an account in the New York Times about a "bloody Saturday Buddhist demonstration" on August 10th in Hue. The story wasn't very clear as to why and how it happened. I was interested in the whys and hows only if you were involved in it as I'm sure you were. I'm anxious to know if you're safe. I asked my cousin Dick to contact the American Embassy in Saigon to find out about you and let me know if I can call you. On August 13th, Dick told me that the U.S. Consulate in Hue was sure that you weren't among the killed or wounded, that your university was closed for an indefinite period, you have no telephone, and even if you had, I shouldn't contact you by phone as it might harm you. I don't know why, but I have no choice but to listen to their advice. You cannot imagine how relieved I was to know that you were unharmed. I was so happy that I went to the nearby grocery store, bought a bottle of wine and cooked a Chicken a la King for Dick and his wife to celebrate the occasion with me. You didn't know that I'm a good cook too! When I see you again, I shall cook for you ... still, it would be wonderful if I could talk directly with you about all my plans and feelings. Dick promised to send this letter to a friend of his at the American Embassy in Saigon through a diplomatic pouch. His friend, in turn, will mail it to you, to your home address in Hue. This way, you'll surely get my letter which I hope will find you happy and healthy. As for my plans: after I got your cold—I shouldn't mention it, should I?—letter, I visited my parents and told them that I wished to leave school for awhile. To my great surprise, they agreed and understood why I made the decision. The school also had no objection, except that if I stayed away for more than a year, I should repeat one or two courses before graduation. I then contacted Dorothy Robinson, whom I wrote you about in my letter of May 25th, to ask her if there's any way I can be useful in Vietnam for peace and the suffering Vietnamese people. She directed me to the American Friends Service Committee in Philadelphia. I went down to Philadelphia and had an interview with them. They were very kind to me. They accepted me as a social worker and medical assistant in a hospital they are building in Hue! Can you believe it? The only thing that dampens my excitement is that I can't go before the end of November or the beginning of December, when their hospital will be ready for service. This means that I have to wait another three months before I can see you. But I've learned to be patient the way you are. In the meantime, they suggested that I read all the material they make available on Vietnam, and there's a lot of it! I'm now reading Wilfred Burchett's *North of the 17th Parallel*, and I've also volunteered to work with the Friends' committee on national legislation in Washington. So here I am, in the nation's capital. I often visit congressmen and senators to talk with them about Vietnam and influence them not to vote for any increase in the war budget or for the Saigon government. The experience is interesting, but also frustrating. Too many legislators are so ignorant about Vietnam that it's frightening! But again, I'm patient, and Dick is of great help. He's not involved in the day-to-day affairs of Vietnam, but as an "assistant to the deputy assistant secretary of state for East Asia," he's aware of the general developments in your country. Before I forget, by now I'm sure you've met Professor Morgan on leave from Yale University to do research in anthropology at your university. He's my brother-in-law and a good person. Say hello to him when you see him but please, don't tell him about the exact nature of our relationship. I'll do it myself, whenever I arrive in

Hue. I'm still worried if you've changed since you left the U.S. If you have, then please tell me so in no uncertain terms. There's nothing worse than guessing another person's feelings from ten thousand miles away. It would be bliss if we could see each other again and continue our love, and our dedication and service to your people, and to freedom and peace. I'm eagerly waiting for your reply. Dick told me that you can send your letter to his friend at the American Embassy in Saigon, to Mr. Henry Williams IV, who in turn will forward it to Dick through the diplomatic pouch. I hope this letter finds you busy, healthy, happy, and still loving me. I'll write you again as soon as I receive a letter from you. In the meantime, keep well, dearest Minh, and think of me as much as you can.

> As always,
> Your loving,
> Jennifer

Minh was overwhelmed. The letter brought Jennifer back to him as nothing else could have done—her spontaneity, her warmth, her honesty, her idealism. And she was coming here—to Hue. In the months since he had left her, Jennifer had been displaced in his thoughts by his absorption in the struggles of his homeland for peace. And by his efforts to find a way to aid that struggle. But this letter was like a shower in the midst of a long drought. It came at a moment when Minh felt alienated from his people, estranged from the land he so deeply loved, and close to the end of all his dreams.

Isolated and frightened, he felt that the letter was his only intimate link to the world: to Jennifer, ten thousand miles away. Not only did she continue to love him, but she forgave him for his "cold" letter. He had not meant to hurt her. He had written it to break that link, caught up as he was in the demands of his life in Vietnam.

Minh was tempted to call Morgan and confess to him the love he felt for his sister-in-law. Then, through Morgan, he could ask Vice-Consul Buckley for protection. But he dismissed all these passing considerations as reflections of his own insecurity. He reread the letter. Jennifer's decision to come to Hue shamed him into mustering all his courage and determination to continue the struggle.

.   .   .

It was noon and suffocatingly hot. Minh walked into the garden and watched the fishes swimming in the clear pond. He remembered how the Patriarch had spoken to him of the fishes that devour each other in the limpid water of the River of Perfume. "The world of human beings, at the moment, is not very different," he had said. His words were an echo of an old Vietnamese popular saying that Minh always believed was too pessimistic:

> *Nuoc trong leo leo ca nuoc ca*
> *Troi nang chang chang, nguoi giet nguoi,*
> *In the clear water, fishes swallow fishes*
> *Under the hot sun, people kill people.*

Minh lapsed into a profound pessimism about human beings, about life itself. Another two days had passed since he had heard from Jennifer, and he was beginning again to feel lassitude and discouragement. Where was Loc? Perhaps he could find an excuse to give up the struggle, to leave Vietnam and go back to Jennifer's arms. Just then he heard a voice calling him from the street: "Professor Minh, please come out here. I have something for you."

An old woman carrying a basket of grapefruits was waiting for him. Looking quickly around, she gave him an envelope and walked away. Minh hurried back to the garden, opened the letter, and immediately recognized Loc's handwriting.

Dear Minh,

I regret not being able to contact you earlier. I hope you understand the situation and are able to keep your courage intact and your determination high. As you can imagine, in the present climate of increasing repression, I'm unable to function openly. I'm now in our liberated zone. I'm grieved to let you know that our comrade, Sister Lan, was arrested and is now in prison in Saigon. The day after you receive this letter, please go to the Moonlight Tea House at 9:30 a.m. Dress casually and carry a large book with you. Be sure you're not being followed. If you suspect you are, take a walk downtown and return home. Repeat the same for two more days and if you're still being followed, then stop. I will contact you at some appropriate time. Once at the teahouse, you will see a middle-aged woman in dark brown clothes with a white mourning turban. When she leaves and proceeds toward the Citadel, follow her. At the middle of the Thuong Tu Bridge, she will stop and ask if you know how to get to Serene Heart Lake. You will show her the way. Keep following her. If she should stop and head back to the center of the city, please continue on your way to the lake and go home afterwards. That means she knows you both are being followed. If this happens, come back to the teahouse the next day. Stop if during the second try you're still being followed. If everything goes well, you will meet another woman at the Serene Heart. She will tell you that her name is Phan, and you introduce yourself as Tho. She will give you all the necessary instructions for your future activities. Please read this letter carefully and after you're sure you remember every detail, destroy it. Burn it, put the ashes in a pot of water, stir it up and throw it in your garden. I hope that I can see you soon. As we both work for the same objectives, we will meet again in our common path. Be careful, Minh, extra careful, and always keep your courage intact, your determination high.

Fraternally,
Loc

Minh felt that Loc's and Jennifer's letters had brought him back to life. Even the news of Lan's arrest didn't bother him much—he knew that she was strong. With renewed confidence he waited for the next day to begin; but time had never passed so slowly.

Minh didn't follow the straight route from his home to the teahouse. He walked north for half a mile, then turned south and crossed the Thuong Tu Bridge. He was sure he hadn't been followed.

At the meeting place he ordered tea and pastry. He was relieved that Loan, the teahouse owner, to whom Loc had introduced him some months earlier, wasn't there, sparing him an untimely and unwelcome conversation.

Almost immediately a woman wearing a white turban entered and made herself comfortable at a corner table. Minh glanced at her. She glanced back and continued reading her newspaper. Sipping his tea, Minh noisily opened his thick *History of Vietnam*. She smiled meaningfully at him.

After half an hour or so, she left. Minh followed her. She stopped at the middle of Thuong Tu Bridge as planned and asked him directions. They walked slowly toward the southwest of the Citadel.

Shortly they entered a well-maintained residence on Serene Heart Lake. A younger woman came out, greeted Minh, and introduced herself as Phan; Minh identified himself as Tho. She looked every inch a typical woman from a Hue aristocratic family: slender, with an ivory-pale complexion, quietly dressed with a carved golden collar around her neck. The woman in the turban vanished.

There was no one in the large living room but him and Phan. After a polite exchange of greetings, she came to the subject, using the word "we" constantly to make Minh understand indirectly that she was a member of the Intellectuals for Liberation. In a soft, clear voice, she began.

"We think that the situation existing in Hue now isn't good for your activities, although we have no evidence yet that you're in immediate danger of being arrested. You may be safe because you're the Rector's nephew, or because of your father's moral prestige, or maybe because of your American connections. Still, we've come to realize that the Americans won't trust you as much now. And we know that the Saigon administration provoked the Linh Mu incident so they'd have an excuse to carry out more repressive measures against the forces of democracy and peace. If they do have anything on you they'll feel free to arrest you. So, after careful deliberation, taking into account your interests and ours, and at the suggestion of comrade Loc, we've decided that you should leave the city by October first, for the liberated zone, where you'll have better security. That's one week from today. Do you have any questions? Would you like some tea?"

"No thanks. But I would like to know why you say the Saigon administration provoked this incident to carry out repressions. Isn't the Saigon administration already repressive enough?"

"By its nature," she answered confidently, "the Saigon administration is fascist and cruel. But it has to *justify* its repressions. It needs to manage public opinion, especially opinion in the United States, in order to pursue its crimes. So it tries to discredit the progressive forces within the Buddhist church at home, and abroad it attempts to divert the attention of the world from its successive military defeats to other matters."

Her convincing voice and serious face, even more than her arguments, reassured Minh. "I agree with you, and I'm willing to leave whenever necessary to continue our struggle."

"We expect that your patriotism will help you to accept the hardship of life in the liberated zone. Now that you've agreed with our decision, here's what we must do. First, don't let anyone know of your decision to leave town except your father, and don't tell him about it until the day you leave. From what we know of him we're sure he'll be happy and proud of your commitment."

"I'm sure of that," Minh interrupted. And it's true, he thought, Father will be; but he had promised An and Phong he would look after home. What would Father and Auntie do with all three of their sons gone?

"Keep in touch in the meantime with Professor Morgan—by phone, which of course, is tapped by the Saigon security agencies. Make an appointment with him for dinner on October 2nd. Of course, you'll be gone by then, but we hope this will delay police action in case they plan to arrest you before October 1st.

"Now for the procedure for your trip to the liberated zone. On the first take the five o'clock bus, which is the last one, to Phu Loc. But get out at Huong Thuy, halfway. You should be there no later than six. There won't be any army checkpoints between Hue and Huong Thuy, so you have nothing to worry about. But in case there's a police search, just show them your faculty I.D. and everything will be fine. Tell the police that the university is closed and you're using the free time to visit an old friend working in the Huong Thuy administrative offices. His name is Na. He's our friend and will know how to get you out of trouble if it's necessary.

"At the Huong Thuy stop, go to the refreshment kiosk for a lemonade. The owner will be a woman about my age. She'll direct you in the next steps. At this moment, we don't foresee any difficulty with your trip, but as always, be very, very careful. If you feel you're being followed from your home to the bus station, return to your house and take the same bus one week later. If it happens again, then wait until we contact you. Now, if you don't have any further questions, we'll say goodbye. We're struggling for the same cause, so I'm sure we'll see each other again, somewhere, sometime, in this heroic land of ours."

.   .   .

After his weeks of doubt and stagnation Minh felt relieved and happy that he was part of the struggle again, part of Vietnam. He was grateful to Loc for making all the arrangements and was eager to see him again. Instead of going home after the meeting, he walked quickly to the botanical gardens. He sat on a wooden bench and watched the cruising sampans on the River of Perfume. He thought of Jennifer, of how he would write her, explain indirectly to her his decision to join the liberated zone.

It was noon when he reached home. There was a military jeep parked in front of the house. For a minute, he thought that the police had been sent to arrest him. But if the jeep belonged to the military police, it would have a Q.C. (Military Police) sign on it. It wouldn't have a chauffeur watching over it, either, which this one had. He rushed into the house. Before he opened the door, he heard An's voice. Minh was surprised to see not only An but Phong seated in the living room, talking with their parents.

An explained. "Yesterday I flew to Quang Tri with a group of American officers who were visiting from the U.S. War College. This morning on their return to Saigon, they insisted on seeing Hue. So we stopped here for a few hours. The Mayor and the U.S. Consulate's taking care of them. And since there were a few empty seats on the plane, I asked Phong's commanding officer to give him permission to come with us. So here we are. I'm afraid we don't have much time to spend with you, though. We have to leave in half an hour."

"Oh," Minh exclaimed, "you don't know how pleased I am to see both of you at the same time!"

"Let's go outside for a bit," An suggested.

In the garden An spoke with unusual gravity. "Minh," he said, "I'm a little concerned about your situation. An officer I know from General Quang's office told me a couple of days ago that the police in Hue suspect that you're very close to a number of faculty and students who were arrested recently in connection with the Linh Mu incident. They're also looking for Professor Loc who *they* say is a high-ranking communist cadre and a good friend of yours. According to the officer, they're studying your case now. I've no idea what they'll do next. The whole thing depends on the President and on General Quang, who unfortunately doesn't like me at all. What do you think?"

"Frankly, An, I don't have any opinion," Minh replied, as calmly as possible.

"I'm not sure about your case, but as a general rule the government is careful not to touch people close to the Americans. Perhaps it would be good if you could see Vice-Consul Buckley as often as possible. I'll warn my friend Mr. Adams, the C.I.A. station chief you met in New York. Perhaps you should make a trip to Saigon, even Bangkok, to have some fun, create the impression that you're a harmless person. Whatever you choose, you can be sure that I'll do anything I can to help you."

"Thanks, An, but I personally don't think the situation is urgent yet. Let me think a little bit more and I'll get in touch with you in a couple of weeks."

"Sure, take your time. If I hear something more definite, I'll find a way to get here so we can discuss the best way to assure your safety."

"Thanks again, An."

Minh was sure now that his arrest would come soon, but he was no longer afraid. He had connections and connections meant security. He was a part of the revolution, and revolution meant the creation of choices and options. Fear, he thought, was a lack of options, an inability to choose the means for survival. Although many important events had happened in the last two days, he had never felt so much at peace within himself. He was no longer detached from the historical movement of his people, and he was about to become part of a force that would pull that historical movement to a higher stage of civilization, to a more glorious chapter of Vietnamese history.

He called Morgan and made an appointment for dinner on October 2nd. Morgan was visibly excited about the invitation. "That's the best thing that's happened to me since the university closed!" he exclaimed enthusiastically. Minh smiled to himself as he hung up. He liked Morgan—there was a physical resemblance between him and Jennifer. But at the same time he savored in advance the gossip that would circulate in town when he disappeared. He recalled a story he had read when he was in high school about a man who tried to find out who really loved and cared about him. He went into hiding and asked a friend and co-conspirator of his to spread the news that he had been drowned while going to the beach, his body unrecovered. From his hideout, he kept track of the reactions of those who had known him well. To his sad amazement, those who had been closest to him were the ones who fabricated the most lies and propped up accusations against him. He finally disappeared, the second time for real.

In the days ahead, the only important thing he had to do was write to Jennifer. Two nights before "D-Day," he sat down in his room beneath his mother's picture, and began:

Dearest Jennifer,

I'm writing you while it rains heavily outside, one of those rains which seem to challenge eternity itself. I'm almost sure that by tomorrow morning the banks of the River of Perfume will be overflowing and Hue will be transformed temporarily into a little Venice of the Orient. When I was very young, I loved these floods. They provided me and my friends with the cool pleasure of walking knee-deep in water all over town, or floating on improvised rafts made of banana trunks. I didn't realize then that the floods, which gave us kids of rich families so much joy and excitement, created so much havoc to thousands of peasant families, harvests destroyed, buffaloes drowned and carried out to the high seas ... indeed, our dreams were our peasants' nightmares and our hopes, their despair. Morality, public or private, always means to me to be sure that whatever brings us happiness shouldn't create suffering for others. The war raging in my country now is a good illustration of that. It's bringing wealth and power to a few in Saigon, Washington, even Hue, but it's also bringing death and misery to millions. This is also to tell you how much I admire and appreciate your decision to come here and serve my suffering people. Your personal hardship will bring happiness to hundreds, if not thousands, of Vietnamese. I wish you were here right now. There are definite indications that the war is being escalated in the North *and* the South. Your presence in my city would be an eloquent testimony that the just cause the Vietnamese people are fighting for has the concrete support of progressive peoples of the world, particularly the Americans, and that our love transcends national and racial boundaries. Let me answer now, once and for all, the questions and uncertainties you raised in your letter of September 1st. First of all, I would like to apologize for my "cold" letter. It was not meant to be that way. Perhaps I was suffering from the transition from a cold climate to a hot and humid one, from Amherst, Mass. to Hue, Vietnam. I can assure you that "all that happened between us" was not a "sequence in an imagined Hollywood movie," but the beginning of a long, lasting, and meaningful relationship which neither time, space, nor death can disrupt or destroy. Your cousin Dick was only half right. It is true that my face reddens quickly when I drink wine, as you yourself have witnessed, but, I'm not always cold and formal when I write. Maybe I'm an exceptional Asian, I'm Vietnamese. At any rate, forget my letter. Burn it one night when you sit by the fireplace and think of me. Dick and his friend's advice is sound. South Vietnam is under a very repressive regime now. The government is suspicious of any contact by Vietnamese with the outside, and strangely enough, more so with Americans. I have a telephone, an army line, which is tapped by security services. As my university was closed for an indefinite period, I'm planning to use my free time to travel all over the country. Therefore I suggest that unless something extremely urgent happens to you, you shouldn't write me. In case something should happen, ask your cousin Dick to contact his friend in Saigon by phone, who in turn will contact me. Please don't see any indirect, inscrutable message in this. I simply hate the idea of having your letter arrive in Hue when I'm not here to read it and answer you. This in turn might cause you unnecessary and unfounded worry. I hope you understand. We can wait for two months. That's ony two full moons and sixty days. I count on your patience. Obviously, by this letter you can see I'm safe, busy, and healthy. When I see you in Hue, I'll tell you all about that bloody Linh Mu incident. It's too long for me to describe here. At this hour, while I'm finishing this letter, I remember every detail of that night in early spring following our dinner at the House of Crepes in Amherst, the "memorable night" as you wrote in a note you left on the pillow. I have a dream, the same dream I had that night, of having a child with you. I have a strong feeling now that the dream can be a reality. When peace and democracy are restored to Vietnam, we will share our lives together, we will have a daughter with your beauty and my intelligence (excuse my lack of modesty!) and devote ourselves to working for the happiness, not only of the Vietnamese, but also of the Americans and all the "wretched of the earth." In our common efforts, we shall build a work without exploitation of man by man, for all. I'm eagerly waiting for you. In the meantime, please take very good care of yourself. Your health is mine. Be also assured of my love for you.

Yours always,
Minh

Minh mailed the letter the day before he was to leave. He would have liked to have been a little clearer about his leaving the city, but he hoped that Jennifer, who had that unique ability to read his mind and intentions, would see what he really meant when he wrote that he was "planning to travel all over the country."

.   .   .

Minh got up a few minutes before six, a little earlier than usual. He intended to prepare tea for his father and tell him about his leaving while serving him. He tiptoed to his father's bedroom. He wasn't there. The door to the garden was ajar. Minh went back to his room, put on a heavy sweater over his flannel shirt, and walked out into the garden. In the last two days there had been a change in the weather. The nights were cooler, the mornings chilly with clear skies. He had even spotted a few yellow leaves on the streets.

His father was in the garden, wearing the light blue cashmere topcoat Minh had bought for him as a Tet gift while he was in London over ten years ago. His silver-haired head was bent over the pot of his most treasured Moonlight orchids. Seeing Minh standing behind him, he spoke both to himself and Minh, "I'm afraid autumn's come a little late this year. That means the winter will be late too. The cold months will last longer and delay the arrival of spring. And that means that my orchids, especially these, will not bloom on the full moon of the twelfth month as I expected, but much later. If and when they do bloom, they won't last until the end of the first month, as I had hoped, either. It's too bad. These weather disturbances are surely caused by the war, by all the chemicals, and bombs. Terrible, terrible." He turned to Minh. "You're up a little early this morning. Did you sleep well?"

"Yes, I did, but I wanted to be sure to be on time to prepare tea for you."

"Very good. We haven't had tea together for a long while. But first, let me visit a few more orchids before we go back inside. If I fail to touch them and talk with them, they miss my presence and resent it and turn nasty on me." Minh saw a childlike smile on his father's face. He talked to the orchids the way one talks to a lover. "Now, what's on your mind?" his father enquired.

"I'm leaving the city today for the liberated zone so I can better continue the struggle for our people's freedom. I wanted to inform you, and only you, of my decision and ask your permission."

Minh's father raised his head, his face glowing with a joy Minh hadn't seen since his return.

"Son, I'm very pleased. I'm happy and proud to know that you've taken this step. Your mother will be rejoicing at your decision in the Yellow Springs. I wish I could go with you, but I'm satisfied that you can represent me and our family among the best sons and daughters of our land." He took Minh's arm. "Now we can go into the house and *I* shall make tea for *you*."

"Father," Minh mumbled, "I'm very grateful that you've given me your permission. I never doubted that this is what you want me to do at this juncture in our country's history."

As soon as he got into the house, Minh's father went directly to his study. He brought back a small, lacquered box. He beamed, "This is the best chrysanthemum tea I've ever tasted. It was sent secretly to me by a close friend who lives in Hanoi now. I kept it in a special place for a special occasion like this one." He looked tenderly at the box. "Up in the North, they have the best chrysanthemums, big and fragrant. They know how to make chrysanthemum tea for autumn festivities. They have real, lovely, lasting autumns." He paused to look at Minh and gravely raised his voice. "Spring rejuvenates people, summer excites them, autumn refines them, and winter hardens them. Such is the law of nature, such are the conditions of human growth."

Like an artist at work, Minh's father slowly, ceremoniously, boiled the water, cleansed the tea cups, and warmed the dark brown teapot in his hands. He treated Minh not as a son whose patriotism he had suspected, but as a friend, a *Tri Am*, one who knows your sound.

"I've not told this to anyone," he confided, "but for the last ten years I've been writing the history of our family, starting from the thirteenth century. It will take perhaps five years or more to finish. This month I've gotten as far as the reign of Emperor Quang Trung in the eighteenth century, and the careers of our ancestors who participated in the victorious

Tet offensive of 1789 against the Chinese occupation forces. The one I'm dealing with now was the General commanding the front army, *Thiet Loi,* Steel Thunder. He got the name from the Emperor himself, because in battle he always directed his unexpected, powerful strikes like thunder against the enemy's main concentration and smashed its defenses. But his real name, I discovered only recently, was Tran Van Minh! I didn't know that when I named you, but now I can be sure you'll live up to his name. I do hope that we don't have to fight the Chinese again after we defeat the Americans, but no one can be sure. I don't like nor trust them."

Minh was fascinated by his father's revelation. He listened as enthralled as an attentive pupil receiving a history lesson from an erudite teacher. His father had never seemed so alive, so sharp and enthusiastic. Minh didn't want to disturb him with questions and comments. His father turned thoughtful.

"Son, you should take a warm sweater with you. I expect that you'll be going North, although the liberated zone could be as close by as our native district of Phu Loc. However, I don't really think I have anything to worry about. The experienced, responsible leadership of the revolution will take good care of you. With luck you may even see autumn in the North. I remember when you were in America, you sent me some pictures of autumn landscapes in the city where your college was located. It was so beautiful, like a Taoist painting, full of sensual colors."

"Yes, it's beautiful." Minh thought of Jennifer.

"What time are you leaving?"

"I leave the city at five."

"I don't think it's good to tell your Auntie right now. I'll tell her later. I'm sure she'll be as happy as I am. But too much happiness at the same time, under the same roof, can upset the harmonious balance of the home."

Minh didn't quite grasp his father's meaning, but he replied, "Yes, I can leave home with little worry, knowing very well her dedication to our family."

At noon Minh's uncle, the Rector, called.

"Can you come to dinner with me tomorrow? There's something very important I have to tell you," he said, his voice grave.

"I have a dinner date with Professor Morgan tomorrow," Minh replied. "Could we meet on the third instead?"

"All right, but no later than the third, because the matter's very urgent," the Rector insisted.

Minh guessed that his uncle had gotten some king of warning from the police about him, but it hardly worried him now.

At lunch, Minh's stepmother noticed his father's unusually happy mood. "Minh," she said, as he helped her bring the dishes into the kitchen, "your father looks so happy today. I don't know what's happened, but I'm glad he's happy and I don't need to know why."

"Mother." This was the first time he had called her "mother" instead of "auntie." He wanted to convey to her all his gratitude and affection before his departure. "I know why. This morning I saw him in the garden. He was talking to the orchids. They probably promised him they were going to bloom exactly on Tet for his enjoyment."

"Maybe, Minh," she said, and smiled at him tenderly.

IX

People and Water's Strength

Wood stakes in rows on rows stems not the tide.
Sunk iron chains yet fail to shackle waves.
The people's strength, like water, tips the boat.
No rugged terrain frustrates Heaven's will.

Blocking the River's Mouth
Nguyen Trai
1380–1442.
Translated by Huynh Sanh Thong

It would take half an hour at most to get to the bus station downtown, but Minh left home at 3:30. He walked slowly through the inner Citadel and stopped at the Moonlight Tea House. He was the only customer in the quiet room, and the tea was so bad he could hardly drink it. The lingering subtle taste of his father's morning tea at home would make everything else taste like insipid water anyway, Minh thought.

There were two buses parked at the station, the Dong Ba landing on the River of Perfume. One bore a painted sign on the front reading, "Bus 3:

Hue–Phu Loc via Huong Thuy. Maximum capacity: 40." Several police officers milled around the station, flirting with young women vendors. By five o'clock bus number three was packed to capacity, but the driver showed no signs of leaving.

"Are you waiting for someone?" Minh enquired.

"Not for anyone in particular, but I can still squeeze another passenger in the back. You can take the front seat with me."

At that moment a soldier came running up, shouting, "Wait, wait, I'm going to Phu Loc!"

"I should have left on time," the driver whispered in Minh's ear. "You can't charge soldiers these days. If you make them pay, they blow up the bus with hand grenades and blame it on the Viet Cong. It's already happened several times this year."

The soldier, perspiring and breathing heavily, installed himself in the front, next to the driver, taking the seat the driver had reserved for Minh. Minh prudently moved to the back. The driver flashed him a smile of understanding.

Minh found himself pressed to the end of a wooden bench, near the rear door. On his left was a young woman whom he guessed was a student.

"Where are you going? Phu Loc?" Minh asked her.

She wore short hair like Xuan, but she was thinner, with a darker complexion and a more angular face.

"Yes, I'm going to see a friend who's working in the district office there. I'm a student at the university, but it's closed for an indefinite period. So I use my free time to visit friends."

Her explanation, so similar to what Phan had advised him to say, made Minh wonder whether she too was going to the liberated zone, even whether she had been organized by Phan.

"When are you returning to Hue?"

"I don't know," she answered curtly. She pulled from her handbag a thin novel titled *Delayed Autumn*, and began to read. Minh was relieved after all that she hadn't asked him who he was and where he was going. He stopped looking at her. If she were a student, she might recognize him.

Only three of the 41 passengers got out at Perfumed Water, a small district town southwest of Hue: a young man in khaki dress, perhaps a soldier on leave; an older man who looked like a bureaucrat in some government office, dressed in a white shirt and brown sharkskin pants, with neatly combed hair; and Minh himself. He walked to a small booth that bore a sign over its front door: Perfumed Wind Refreshment Kiosk. The young man in khaki and the older man disappeared in opposite directions.

Minh asked for a lemonade. The woman vendor asked him, "Are you Mr. Tho?"

"Yes, I am."

"Please come inside the kiosk. I'll close in a few minutes. This is the last bus stop of the day. We'll go together."

"Thank you," Minh said and finished his lemonade in a single, prolonged gulp.

.   .   .

They walked silently on a tortuous rocky path, she carrying a shoulder pole with a basket at each end, in which she transported all her merchandise, he following her like an obedient child. After about ten minutes she stopped and suggested that he take off his shoes, which she threw into one of the baskets.

"From now on, until the next kilometer, the road is slippery. We'll be going through some flooded land," she said. Squares of fields with newly transplanted rice seedlings lay before them. He spotted a few water-filled bomb craters; in one a lone water-lily flower grew. He had difficulty keeping pace with her. She walked very fast, balancing her pole and baskets elegantly, like an experienced dancer.

Noticing his embarrassment she slowed down a bit to let him catch up. He glanced at his watch. Only six o'clock and he was already feeling tired! But she pointed to a group of thatched houses behind tall, arching bamboos. "We'll be there soon now."

The rice fields ended in a grassy elevation. Cutting along a short trail, they approached a group of five huts set apart by hedges of hibiscus. She gently pushed open the gate. "Here I am, here's Cam," she announced.

The house was dimly lit by a small kerosene lamp set on a broken pedestal in a corner. An old man with a gray wispy goatee sat on a plank bed, reparing a sickle. Cam greeted him.

"How are you, grandpa?"

"I'm well," he mumbled. He continued his work without paying any attention to Minh.

A woman in her thirties, holding a baby, ran from the kitchen, "I'm so happy to see you," she said and touched Cam's face affectionately.

"One stage in my trip is over," Minh thought.

"Mr. Tho," said the young woman, "you'll spend the night here. You're still in the temporarily controlled enemy area. From time to time the local militia comes around at night to check the identities of everyone in every household. When the dogs bark, we know they're coming. But you don't have to worry—we have a place for you to hide, in the garden, outside the kitchen. And besides they're unlikely to come tonight—they were here yesterday. But one can never be sure. After dinner, you'll sleep in the kitchen. Tomorrow, at dawn, you'll continue your trip to the *xoi dau* zone, which as you know is claimed by both the Saigon government and the

National Liberation Front. The trip will take the whole day, but at the end of it you'll be in the liberated zone."

She turned to Cam, who was leaving. "Please tell Bac Da to meet us tomorrow at the hamlet well at the first cock crow."

"Yes, I will, *Chi* Ta."

Minh was impressed by Ta's complete self-confidence, an attitude he rarely saw in the city's women. Obviously in charge of things, Ta didn't show any of the reserve women often had in front of men. She was a peasant, but her political language was no less knowledgeable than that of any political activist in Hue.

Minh slept so soundly that he had to be shaken by Ta several times to be awakened before dawn. Ta herself must have gotten up long before, because everything was prepared for his long journey: rice wrapped in banana leaves, fried sesame and salt in a small pack, a canteen of hot water, a used but clean indigo pajama-like suit, a pair of strapped rubber sandals (the same "Ho Chi Minh slippers" that radical students in the United States craved), and a heavy pellet-proof straw conical hat. She handed him a typewritten half-page paper certifying that "Mr. Tho is a special agent of the intelligence unit of company C, battalion five of the Army of the Republic of Vietnam, stationed in Huong Thuy, on mission to military sub-zone four of military zone one. All responsible authorities, military and civilian, are requested to help him accomplish his mission and for all matters relating to him, refer to Captain Na at Huong Thuy administrative district." The certificate was obviously fake and it made Minh smile at the ingenuity of the Vietnamese revolutionaries.

She asked him to change into his peasant dress in the garden and reminded him to leave everything behind, his Hue University faculty I.D., his pen, his wallet, any papers he carried with him. The only exception was his watch.

When every detail was taken care of, she slipped out of the house, carrying a revolver in her hand. Minh followed. At the first cock crow, they were at the hamlet's well. A man was there, waiting.

"Bac Da, this is Mr. Tho. You conduct him to the next zone, according to the plan we decided on. Have a good day, Bac Da, and I'll see you tomorrow night at our meeting."

Bac Da was a robust-looking man of above-average height. He walked as if he were jogging and Minh soon had to beg him to slow down.

"The quicker we walk, the sooner we arrive," he commented, but he eased his pace.

They followed a wandering route, pocked at intervals with bomb craters, through numerous slippery, narrow footpaths lacing the rice fields, crossing small forests of defoliated trees that looked like sinister sentinels on the way to Hell. They had marched for nearly three hours before Minh was finally compelled by hunger to ask Bac Da to stop.

"Mr. Tho, I am sorry," Bac Da said. "I didn't know you hadn't eaten yet. Ta didn't tell me." His voice was compassionate, but tinged with anger. "This is a serious lack of caring for which I apologize."

They descended a packed earth road leading to a mangrove. Minh sat down and ate his breakfast heartily, while Bac Da scrutinzied the terrain.

Having finally breakfasted, Minh looked around with some anxiety for a place to relieve himself. Bac Da seemed to anticipate his need. "You should go to the bamboo thicket over there," he advised, pointing his finger northward, "and be sure not to show your behind in the open. A cousin of mine lost his life doing that several months ago. An American helicopter pilot saw his bare bottom and cut him down with a rain of machine gun bullets. Those barbarians!"

It was the first time since he was born that Minh used an open-air toilet, with "heaven above, earth below, and genitals in the middle" as someone once said. But although he felt a new, exhilarating sensation of freedom, his bowels refused to obey his feelings. After nearly ten minutes spent observing two sparrows mating on a broken branch nearby, Minh gave up. In any case, he realized, even if he had succeeded he wouldn't have found any toilet paper around or even a sizeable leaf. Bac Da smiled at him.

"Now that you're relieved of the burden of hunger and waste, let's move on. We have to be at our destination no later than sundown." They had barely set off when Bac Da stopped. "Listen!" he whispered. "I hear helicopters coming! Two of them, I think."

"Shall we run?"

"No! You should never do that. We'll go inside the mangrove and stand immobile against the biggest trunk. Cover your head and body with branches and leaves so the helicopters can't see you. We still have about two minutes."

Sure enough, within two minutes two helicopters roared overhead. Strong winds from the rotors blasted into their faces. But they left as fast they came, their silhouettes huge against the sky like two oversized dragonflies.

"These kinds of helicopters are very dangerous," Bac Da said almost to himself. "They're well armed and shoot at anything that moves."

If this man, Minh thought, with his experience, his judgment, and attention to my well-being, is typical of the peasantry, then the Vietnamese resistance will never be defeated.

Now they hurried through fields of corn. At the edge of a rocky-bottomed stream they rolled up their pants. Minh noticed that Bac Da's left leg was pockmarked with long, deep scars. He was sure now that Bac Da must have been a soldier for the revolution who had been wounded and now served as a liaison.

The sun was going down. A light, cool breeze sprang up, bringing a sweet, enticing smell of glutinous rice. Bac Da's face brightened, but Minh saw nothing.

"We are at our destination," Bac Da mumbled, "a little before time. Very good."

They ducked their heads under an arch of bamboo trees and found themselves on a zigzagging path. Under the cover of another arch of leafy bamboos a thatched roof was buried—a masterpiece of disguise, natural camouflage. Minh sensed that he had now entered what was called *Ben Kia*, the other side, by those living under the Saigon government. From behind a clump of betel-nut trees a soldier sprang up, his machine gun on his shoulder. He immediately recognized Bac Da.

"I'm pleased to see you again, Uncle. You look well. Did you have any trouble on the way here? You're a little early this time. It's only 5:30."

"No trouble at all, nephew. No trouble except a couple of helicopters hovering over. No problem."

"Good. You must be hungry. We'll be having dinner soon."

Bac Da pushed the door. In the dim light of a kerosene lantern hung from the ceiling Minh saw a woman in her fifties and two younger men.

"Comrade," Bac Da reported formally, "we have escorted to your liaison station Mr. Tho, on the order of executive committee of hamlet number 29." He handed her a piece of paper. The woman glanced at it and turned to Minh.

"Are you tired? You must be hungry. We'll have dinner right away and talk later about your next destination."

"Thank you," Minh said, not knowing how to address her. Since being in contact with "the other side" he noticed that the word "I" had disappeared from their vocabulary and was replaced by "we"; that he was called *Ong*, Mr., instead of *anh*, brother, as he had expected; and that *dong chi*, comrade, was clearly reserved for party members only.

One of the two men rose, went to the kitchen, and brought out an earth pot filled with rice mixed with dark brown beans, and a large dish of fried carp. The other man left to relieve the front guard, who came in and joined the dinner being served on a small rectangular table with two benches on each side. Minh noticed that they used one end of their chopsticks to bring food from the serving dish into their rice bowl, and the other to move food from the bowl into their mouths. A practical and more hygienic way, Minh thought, and adopted the new style. After dinner, a large pot of boiling green tea was passed. Minh didn't see any glutinous rice. He guessed that it was prepared as travel rations for liaison people who had to cover long distances. Glutinous rice was known to be more filling and slower to digest than ordinary rice, and stayed in the stomach longer.

Bac Da now sat crosslegged on the floor. He pulled a wad of tobacco from his pocket, stuffed some into the neck of his water pipe, lit the pipe, and took a long sustained draw. He inhaled the smoke, retaining it in his lungs for a second, and puffed the smoke away as he closed his eyes. He seemed to enjoy the simple reward of having accomplished his mission.

What discipline, Minh thought. During the whole trip, Bac Da hadn't touched his pipe, probably fearing that the smoke might attract enemy detection. Minh respected him still more.

The woman watched Bac Da for a moment, then said affectionately, "*Dong chi* Da, you'll have to leave early tomorrow. Why don't you retire to the usual place? There's a blanket for you. The night has turned cold."

Bac Da stood up, murmuring, "I will." He moved to Minh and with both of his hands, shook Minh's right hand. "I hope to see you in the future. Have a continuing safe voyage." He bowed slightly to the woman and disappeared into a room in the right corner.

"Would you like some more tea?" the woman asked Minh.

"No, thanks," Minh answered quickly. The strong green tea had made him feel dizzy.

"You must be tired," she observed, this time using the reassuring appellation *Anh*. She adjusted the wick of the lantern to show more light.

"Yes, I've never walked such a long distance in my life."

"You'll get used to it." She paused for a moment. "Until we chase all the foreign aggressors and local puppets out of our land, we will have to march and march. But we will win!"

"I'm sure of that," Minh added.

She raised her voice a bit. "Now. Tomorrow a comrade will take you to the *Bo Chi Huy*, command headquarters. It's not very far from here, half an hour at most. Tonight you'll sleep in the room with comrade Da."

She stopped to roll a cigarette. Minh scrutinized her open but determined face and her sharp eyes. Her hands were strong and calloused and she wore her graying hair tight, rolled into a chignon.

"It's safe here, you're in the liberated zone," she continued, "still, the enemy's everywhere. In case an emergency arises—that is, in case the enemy should discover our liaison station—the comrade guard in front will alert us. If that should happen, you should run to the kitchen and take out the straw mat on the floor. Underneath there's a tunnel leading to another tunnel into the forest. You do the same in case of bombing. So far, we've not been attacked since we built this station. Perhaps it's because we change locations so often." She didn't tell Minh her name, nor did she ask for his. She motioned him to Bac Da's room.

"You don't have to get up at the same time as comrade Da. You can sleep as late as seven. You'll have breakfast with us and leave at eight o'clock. I'll see you in the morning."

Minh's muscles and bones hurt. He ached all over, but his pains were soon overwhelmed by a healthy exhaustion that put him to sleep as soon as he stretched out by Bac Da's side.

He didn't know when Bac Da left. When he opened his eyes, it was ten minutes past seven. He washed his face and ate his breakfast of rice and salted fish. While he was smoking the cigarette the woman offered him after breakfast, he heard footsteps at the front door. The woman told him that a soldier was ready to take him to the command headquarters.

He followed the soldier from one mangrove to the next. Suddenly the dirt road ended in a gully, only to reappear again at a flat hill covered with dense foliage and tall trees. And there, standing under what looked like a jack fruit tree, was Loc. Minh ran to him, embracing him warmly. There were tears of joy in his eyes.

"Minh, welcome to the liberated zone," Loc said softly.

"Oh, Loc, I'm so happy to see you here."

"I am too." Taking Minh's arm, he said, "Let's go inside. The enemy can detect our presence here. They can even pick up our voices."

Minh looked around. There was no house or building of any kind. Loc pulled a thick string attached to a tree and a grass-mat door opened up from the ground a few feet from where they stood. A three-flight solid-earth stair led them inside, to a large bunker, as large as a two-bedroom house, dug deep into the earth. Its roof and walls were made of layers of heavy bamboo and earth; it was lit by a range of kerosene lanterns hung against the walls. About twenty meters from the door an opening on the left wall led to another system of tunnels, larger, deeper, and brighter.

Noticing Minh's astonished eyes, Loc commented, "These bunkers and tunnels were built with the sweat and intelligence of our people, especially our peasants. They can stand up against any heavy bombing. Actually, we now have at least two Vietnams: one above and one underground, and if the war continues longer, maybe one under the underground. I only know a small part of this construction."

He made a detour to the right. "I'll show you my office. It's right here." There was a sign in front of a bamboo partition: "Regiment 45-Command Headquarters—Office of Foreign Intelligence." The furniture consisted of a wooden table and two chairs.

Minh heard a purring noise coming from the next room. "It's our generator for our radio-transmitter and receiver," explained Loc. "Here, sit down and have some tea with me. I hope you had your breakfast."

"Yes, I did, and a very good one. Better than in the city and certainly better than at the Moonlight Tea House."

"Minh, you're lucky," Loc said as he sat down with his tea. "We just got the news that the police came to your house to arrest you at midnight on the day you left. Your father courageously told them to get out, saying that you had left that morning for Saigon. They must have believed his story because they're looking for you in Saigon."

"I am lucky. As the saying goes, ' when loyal people are in danger, fairies come down from heaven to help them.'"

"Well, I don't know if there are any fairies left in our heaven, but I know our liaison people have done a very good job getting you here. And now that you *are* here, let me tell you a number of things you have to bear in mind in your new situation. First, some 'dos' and don'ts.' Don't ask where you are; don't enquire what other people are doing here; don't discuss your past activities in Hue, including the August Linh Mu incident; and don't attempt to communicate with the outside without authorization. Then, we expect you to follow orders, especially security regulations, and respect collective discipline, attend the political courses regularly, maintain the highest vigilance and determination, and observe absolute secrecy."

He paused. "Have you any questions so far?"

"No, I don't. They're fair and necessary rules."

"Good. Now we go to your assignment and duty. But before we define those, remember that you're what we call a political sympathizer and expert. You're neither a cadre, nor a party member. You'll be addressed as *anh*, not *dong chi*, which is only for party cadres and members. As an expert your job will be to translate English-language documents, listen to foreign broadcasts, in particular those from Voice of America, and read the foreign press, particularly American publications. You'll be surprised to know that we get all the major U.S. newspapers and magazines here, not later than ten days after their publication. You may be better informed here than if you were living in Hue or Saigon. Especially, you should read very carefully the Congressional Records. Also, you are to prepare a daily synopsis of foreign news and a weekly analysis. Normally we get up at five, eat breakfast at six after calisthenics, and work from 6:30 to 12:30, with a fifteen-minute break at 9:30. After lunch and siesta we work again from 2:30 to six. After dinner there's political education from 7:30 to ten every evening. The sessions on Thursdays and Sundays are devoted to criticism and self-criticism. Think you can handle all that?"

"I think so. Fortunately, I'm an early riser."

"I'll help you. All my comrades will help you to improve your work and discipline. Precision is the motto and you'll learn it by practice."

"Who will I be working with?" Minh asked.

"You're directly under my supervision as an expert in the Office of Foreign Intelligence. I'm one of the cadres on duty in the office, an executive director, if you wish. Our office is part of the Command Staff of the Command Headquarters of Regiment 45 of the People's Armed Forces for the Liberation of the South. The regiment commander is Comrade Thai Son, a veteran of the resistance war against the French. The political commissar is Comrade Thanh Van. She's from our home town."

"Is Thai Son from Hue, too?"

"Not exactly. He was from Huong Thuy and was repatriated to the North after the Geneva Agreements of 1954."

Minh hesitated. "I was told in Saigon by a woman called Madame Luu that her sister is now a Viet Cong commander somewhere around Hue. Is it the same woman?"

"Minh," Loc retorted, visibly disturbed, "that's one of the questions you don't ask around here. But because you're new I'll answer you this time. Yes, it's true. It's the same woman."

"Then she's changed her name. It used to be Phan Thi Thai. We were very close to each other when we were in high school. One of those first . . ." Minh's voice trailed off.

"I know what you mean," Loc cut in, "but time, situations, and therefore people change. We're fighting a revolution now, we're in the midst of the most decisive and difficult war in the history of our country. We can't use our time and energy remembering high school sweethearts. I sincerely hope that you don't continue to display your romantic bourgeois longings for women here. It wouldn't be good for you, or for us." He looked earnestly at Minh, his expression softening.

"I may sound harsh to you, Minh, but you must remember that I'm responsible to the party and to the regiment's command for having made the recommendations and arrangements for you to come here to work with us."

"I understand that, Loc. I do."

"I know you do. Anyway, tonight after dinner, I'll introduce you to her formally."

"What about commander Thai Son? Shall I see him too?"

"No, he's not here at the moment. He's on mission."

"Shall I start working today?"

"No, you can begin tomorrow. Right now why don't you go to my quarters for some rest. It's a few steps from here. We sleep practically where we work and we sleep on hammocks, not beds. The first few nights you'll feel uncomfortable, but you'll get used to it. Until further notice you'll share quarters with me. We'll learn to know each other better and help each other."

"I'm very pleased to hear that." Minh was reassured that in this new milieu he would have a friend to rely on.

Loc took a large wooden box from under his desk and pulled from it a green zippered plastic bag, which he tossed to Minh.

"Here are the basic tools for your work and life here."

Minh threw the contents of the bag on the table: pencil, eraser, pencil-sharpener, pen, notebook, toothbrush, toothpaste, soap, razor, towel, two handkerchiefs, multi-vitamins made in Czechoslavakia, and an identification card. He read the card carefully. The Regiment 45 Command of the People's Armed Forces for the Liberation of South Vietnam certifies that bearer Phan Viet Dieu is an expert attached to the Office of Foreign Intelligence. For all matters relating to bearer, refer to Comrade Truong Sanh of same office. Thanh Van, Political Commissar.

"You've chosen a very interesting and flattering name for me, *Viet Dieu*, Vietnamese Bird," Minh remarked. "I'm sure you know the quotation:

'*Viet Dieu Sao Nam Chi*, the Vietnamese Bird perches on the southern branch.' But then you've chosen a good name for yourself, too—*Truong Sanh*, Long Life." The two men smiled at each other.

.   .   .

Minh lay on the hammock in Loc's quarters, deep in thought. The whole labyrinth of bunkers and tunnels, made entirely of bamboo and earth, amazed him and he had no idea where it was. Based on the amount of time he had spent on the way, he estimated, it must not be too far, no more than fifty kilometers, from Hue. But fifty kilometers from that narrow stretch of central Vietnam could equally well have put him in Laos. Was he now in that world-famous Ho Chi Minh Trail?

At six o'clock he walked with Loc through a T-shaped tunnel to a well-lit dinner hall large enough for at least fifty people. Rice and fish were served cafeteria-style; each person brought his or her own pair of chopsticks and a plate made of aluminum salvaged from downed American planes. There were about twenty people, mostly women, seated on long benches when Loc and Minh entered the dining hall. They all seemed to be enjoying the dinner, eating, laughing and talking.

"The food looks good," Minh commented.

"Yes. We eat fish twenty-five days of the month—the remaining days we just eat rice," Loc said, half jokingly.

After dinner they walked through another tunnel, this one Y-shaped, to Political Commissar Thanh Van's office, in a partition similar to Loc's. A hammock hung near her desk.

"*Dong Chi*, Political Commissar," Loc greeted her.

"*Dong Chi* Truong Sanh. How are you?"

"I'm well. I'd like a few minutes of your time to introduce *Anh* Viet Dieu to you. He just arrived this morning from the temporarily occupied enemy zone to work in my office, as the regiment party committee decided last week."

"You're welcome here, Brother Dieu," she said, showing no sign whatsoever that she recognized Minh as her old high-school sweetheart. "Was the trip from the city difficult for you?"

"Not at all, Political Commissar Thanh Van. As a matter of fact, it was well organized, even pleasant."

"Comrade Truong Sanh will tell you, if he hasn't done so already, about your life and work here. Of course, our life is hard and our work even harder. But we all must do our duty with vigilance and determination according to the instructions of our beloved President Ho Chi Minh." She looked up at a color picture of the President with a slogan underneath: fight until the Americans go away, until the puppets are toppled.

After a moment she turned to Loc. "I've read your report on the development of the situation in Laos and the C.I.A. activities there. I'd like to ask you for some further details. Please come and see me tomorrow at ten." The meeting was over.

Minh was surprised at its brevity. It wasn't a cold encounter, only serious and businesslike. But Minh had no doubt that Political Commissar Thanh Van was none other than his high-school sweetheart, Phan Thi Thai. The features of her face hadn't changed. She still had that ironic corner to her lips, which reminded him now of Jennifer. Her complexion was much darker, though, deep brown; her hair showed some streaks of gray, and she had certainly developed an air of seriousness and determination that commanded respect.

He assumed that she had read his detailed biography, which Loc and other intelligence organizations had submitted to her; yet she had behaved as if she didn't know him. At the same time, she had shown a great deal of affection for Loc; so she wasn't a harsh person—just businesslike, perhaps. Minh sighed. He would have to take his cue from her, he supposed. There would be no recognition of their bittersweet relationship—not even a resumption of their acquaintance.

X

Common Clothes
and Rites

The North and South make up one universe.
No stream or mountain must divide a home.
For centuries barriers and walls have failed.
Both riverbanks share common clothes and rites.

Linh River
Bui Duong Lich
1757–1827
Translated by Huynh Sanh Thong

Life on the other side wasn't easy. While Minh was in the United States and Hue, he had imagined it as a life of dedication to fighting, with and for the people, full of hardship and privation. He would have to carry a gun, avoid bombs and napalm, withstand attack not only from enemy soldiers but from leeches, poisonous vipers, mosquitoes. He would suffer from agonizing foot sores, hunger, malaria, dysentery. He might even be captured or killed. The last thing he had dreamed of was the environment he found himself immersed in. He hadn't seen an enemy's face, let alone a peasant making booby traps. The climate wasn't even hot—he lived in an earth-conditioned coolness. The only contact he had with open nature was during the very early morning, when the underground inhabitants silently emerged through their secret exit into the nearby jungle to exercise in silence, wash themselves, and swim in the icy water of a deep stream.

Minh had been in the liberated zone for over a month, yet he had no idea from whom the area had been "liberated," nor even exactly who lived there. Except at the daily political courses, which was regularly attended by 56 people, 30 men and 26 women, all in the same green uniform without rank insignia, he never saw the regiment commander. Nor did he meet Thanh Van again after their brief formal introduction. In his own office, besides Loc, his superior, there were two assistants, a man and a woman in their thirties, both fluent in French but only passable in English. They talked little about themselves and Minh's only information about them was that they both came from Da Nang and had studied communication science in Paris. Loc remained his closest physical companion, but he was often absent on outside missions.

Isolated in his bunker, Minh felt totally separated from the real life of his country above ground. He wasn't even sure that he was in Vietnam at all. Yet through radio broadcasts and newspaper accounts he was intimately connected, intellectually and politically, with the world outside Vietnam, especially the U.S.A., ten thousand miles away. He was familiar with the American antiwar leaders: Father Dan Berrigan, pacifist-publisher Dave Dallinger, linguistics professor Noam Chomsky. He followed all the antiwar demonstrations, even recognizing the names of some of his former students at Thomas Paine College—though he looked in vain for Jennifer's. Still, he imagined her among the students who marched and protested by the thousands in front of the Pentagon and the White House. He felt close to her; it seemed he recognized her face, her hair, her dresses among the various fashion ads in the New York Times, the New Yorker, the Boston Globe.

He found the interminable nightly political courses repetitive and boring, although he admired the self-confidence and patience of the two leading and four alternate political cadres who conducted the sessions. He learned from their presentations that they all came from poor peasant and working-class backgrounds, yet through years of struggle "under the light of the Party" they had succeeded in mastering the laws of dialectics, the Marxist-Leninist principles, and the essentials of the political economy of Vietnam.

As for the criticism-self-criticism sessions, which apparently generated genuine enthusiasm among the others, these were, for Minh, truly painful. They consisted of hours of publicly "acting out—acting in," a technique meant to reinforce the participants' acceptance of the revolutionary virtues by endlessly identifying, and rejecting, the evils of the capitalist-neocolonial system and glorifying the rising socialist paradise.

In one session, Minh admitted that he had recently been lacking in concentration in his work because he "had not grasped the full revolutionary importance of it." Actually he had been fantasizing about Jennifer, Political Commissar Thanh Van, and any number of other women he had known. To his confession, the instructor, a man who was proud that his "party age" was thirty but who never told the audience his biological age, advised Minh to read *The Revolutionary Path*, written by "Comrade President Ho Chi Minh in 1929."

Minh suspected that his political isolation and intellectual ostracism came from his class origins. But how, then, did Loc, who was also from an aristocratic Hue family, blend in so naturally and joyfully with the group? Or, perhaps he wasn't viewed as an authentic member of the revolution because he wasn't a soldier, a militant revolutionary who practiced violence with a machine-gun or a Molotov cocktail? But he had never yet seen anyone, even Loc, carrying a weapon, although once, in Loc's company, he had passed through an off limits area designated as an arms and ammunitions depot.

There was no attempt by anyone to "brainwash" him, as the word was defined in American literature. There was only—and always—an invisible pressure to conform, to accept the decisions and pronouncements of an invisible Party.

One evening, hoping to engage Loc in a philosophical discussion, Minh suggested that the place should be called a zone of complete safety, rather than a liberated zone, or still less a military zone. Loc avoided the discussion and in his usual pleasant tone said simply, "You might be right."

Everyone Minh saw and met seemed to exude a quiet, almost serene determination, a noiseless monotonous happiness. They behaved as if they were faithfully married to the Party, as if they were born to fight war and revolution. Minh often wondered what would they become once the war was over and they returned to life above ground.

What united them, and Minh to them, was the ever-present but never-seen enemy of the "people of Vietnam and the progressive peoples everywhere in the world"—visited upon them almost nightly in the form of American planes and bombs. Often at night an alarm would sound and Minh, as instructed, would rush to a deeper tunnel at the next corner, behind a mound of sand bags. More than once he felt the earth-shaking repercussions of bombing in the area. Twice he was thrown from his hammock by a prolonged tremor. Later it was explained that the Americans had begun using their biggest plane, the B52, and the biggest bombs ever made, to escalate their war of destruction. During these fearful moments, Loc comforted him by telling him that there had once been a direct hit against the headquarters, but it had "held strong like the will of the Vietnamese to live and to fight."

Like everybody else in the bunker, Minh kept a diary, but he didn't dare confide his real feelings to it. He believed that his secret bourgeois longings, his carnal desire for Jennifer or for Thanh Van, would pollute the revolutionary morality of the liberated zone and might in some way be detected by the unseen but ever-present Party.

.   .   .

On December 2nd, a Sunday, Loc came back from one of his outside missions just as Minh finished the presentation of his weekly news analysis. He brought with him a letter from Minh's father, transcribed by his stepmother in her usual beautiful and neat handwriting.

November 29, 1967

Dearest Son,

I was given permission to send you news of the family by a person who is going to your liberated zone. The person told me that you are in good health and I am very happy to hear that. You shouldn't worry about me. Rather you should concentrate on your work. I feel stronger knowing that you are fighting for the salvation of the country. Your auntie is well, too. An visits us often, but Phong returned to Hue only once, last month. The night you left, the police came and looked for you. I told them you were in Saigon and I used the opportunity to teach them a lesson in patriotism. Also, one day later, an American man came with another Vietnamese who said he was on the faculty of the University. The American, through the Vietnamese, asked if you were home. They expected you to have dinner with them as you had promised. When told you were not home, the American was apparently disappointed. Four days ago, the American, together with the same Vietnamese and a young American woman, stopped by. This time they said, just for a visit. They asked if I had any news from you. The woman seemed eager to know where you were and she told me that you were her teacher. She asked if she could come and see me from time to time and I advised her not to do so, as I do not speak English, I am old and wish to be left alone. You know well that I do not want to know or to see any foreigners in our country, more so in our home. Take good care of your health and work hard.

Your father

Minh reread the letter. The young American woman could only have been Jennifer. She had arrived in Hue and had actually visited his father! The other American must have been Morgan. He wondered who the Vietnamese was that Morgan had brought along.

Poor Jennifer! How had she taken his father's proud, independent rejection of her friendly American offer to visit him? And when—and how—would he get to see her? The irony of her being so close and at the same time so inaccessible was overwhelming.

Loc had returned from his mission full of excitement over some important news. A special meeting replaced the usual political course that evening—an unprecedented break in routine. Both Regiment Commander Thai Son and Political Commissar Thanh Van attended; it was the first time Minh had seen the commander and only the second he had seen Thanh Van in the two months he had been in the bunker.

The commander introduced a tall, slim, smiling man in his late 50s. With graying sideburns, he looked like a Vietnamese version of Walter Pidgeon. Three stars on his green uniform revealed that he was a general in the Vietnam People's Army, the army of North Vietnam; Thai Son introduced him as Lieutenant General Ngo Quy Trung, commanding officer of Division 240. The general looked serious as he removed a document from his breast pocket and gravely announced.

"Following the orders of the Party and the government, I come here today to effect the merger of Regiment 45 of the People's Armed Forces for the Liberation of the South, with Division 240 of the Vietnam People's Army, so as to form Field Division 325, which the party and the government have given me the honor of commanding. They have also designated Comrade Thanh Van as the division's new political commissar. This merger, which is immediate, is necessitated by the present opportune situation. I call on your patriotism and determination to defeat the enemy and to continue your sacrifices with the same high spirit and vigilance you have always demonstrated. Regiment Commander Thai Son will be my Chief of Staff."

The audience stood up, applauded, and sang The Army Forward March, the national anthem of North Vietnam.

Under General Ngo Quy Trung's command, the quiet and orderly atmosphere of the underground headquarters quickly changed. Now the dining hall was filled constantly to capacity with soldiers from the North Vietnam People's Army in their green uniforms and pith helmets decorated with epaulets and insignia of rank, wearing pistols strapped to their belts and zippered bags hanging from their shoulders. There reigned in the bunkers an organized animation, a disciplined sense of urgency and bureaucratized efficiency, a conventionalized and formalized behavioral code. Cigarette smoking, for instance, was now allowed only in a specially reserved area, from which the smoke was diverted through a complex of holes and smaller tunnels to far-removed places, mostly near Saigon installations. A report circulated that the U.S. Air Force, after tracing the smoke, which they correctly detected as North Vietnamese, often bombed its allies in the Saigon barracks. The Northern accent, soft and drawling, dominated the more vivacious, high-pitched Southern. A subdued tension began to develop between the relaxed Southerners and the disciplined Northerners.

Minh's office was strengthened by two officers from the North whose specific duty was to follow the day-by-day activities of civilian Americans and foreigners in the cities of Hue, Quang Tri, and Da Nang. Loc's position seemed to grow in importance although he remained the same affable, smooth, busy comrade. He was no longer traveling on outside missions, and his presence provided Minh with great support and assurance in the new situation.

The December 23rd evening political course was entirely devoted to discussing President Ho Chi Minh's address to a rally held in Hanoi earlier the same day. He had called for "greater military victories in both the North and South to finally liberate the whole fatherland." On December 30th the audience was asked to participate in discussions concerning the Hanoi government's announcement that "it would begin talks with the United States if bombing and acts of war against the North were stopped." The colonel who conducted the session made it clear that the announcement did not mean that the troops would relax their vigilance. On the contrary "it means that we will have to increase our attacks. The principle by which we negotiate is 'Talk-Fight-Talk-Fight—until the Americans are chased away and the puppets toppled,'" he said, quoting a verse from Ho Chi Minh.

After the long session, which lasted until midnight, Loc walked back to his office with Minh and made some strong green tea.

"I will leave at dawn tomorrow for my longest and most important mission," Loc said. He paused a moment and grinned. "It's possible that we may celebrate Tet of the Year of the Monkey in Hue."

"You must be joking. How can we celebrate Tet in our home town when the Americans aren't yet 'chased away' and the puppets are not yet toppled? Of course this year we'll have the longest ceasefire yet, seven days, but a ceasefire isn't a victory."

"You'll see," Loc said curtly, but with a smile. He leaned closer. "Minh, there's something else on my mind that you can help with. I've noticed an increasing tension between our northern and southern brothers. I hope you'll try to understand the situation and explain the roots of this division to all parties concerned. We're children of the same ancestors, but we've been divided by foreign forces and that's why the reunification of our motherland is so important. As long as foreigners continue to dominate us, we will remain divided."

"Have there been incidents already?"

"Several, but nothing serious. At any rate, I'm counting on you."

"You can, Loc. And, please, have a successful trip."

They shook hands, Loc's gaze averted from the tears brimming in Minh's eyes. Minh felt as keenly as he had when he separated from his mother years ago to go to school in Saigon.

．　　　　．　　　　．

On January 27, 1968, the day when the annual Tet ceasefire began, Minh came out of the bunker to stand outside under the morning rain. He needed to re-establish sensual contact with nature, his nurturer and lover. To his surprise, he saw Loc walking towards him. Minh hugged him, pressing his wet shirt against Loc's parachute cloth raincoat. The two fabrics squeaked as they rubbed together.

"Loc, I'm so happy that you returned during the ceasefire," Minh said gaily. "Maybe we can take a short trip in the jungle tomorrow."

"Minh, there's no ceasefire," Loc said flatly. "Let's go inside and begin our work."

Minh stared at him unbelievingly, but Loc merely turned and entered the bunker.

The underground headquarters became a beehive of activity. Minh was never busier, compiling information for Loc. The next day there was a short evening early Tet celebration and an announcement by Loc himself to a packed dining hall that the general offensive and the general uprising, had been scheduled by the party and the government to start on January 30th, the first day of the Year of the Monkey. These operations were the two spearheads of Operation Quang Trung, named after the Emperor who had chased the Chinese Ming troops from Vietnam in 1789.

The audience cheered. Some were in tears. A group of women soldiers sang a patriotic song. But Minh, without knowing why, felt deeply alienated, though it was for this very day that he had been working and hoping. Perhaps I'm afraid that the major changes ahead might change my situation, he thought. Maybe I'm afraid that with this new phase of the war, I'll lose Loc. Loc would now be called upon to fulfill a higher duty to the Party, the Party that Minh continued to feel foreign from. He had always known that the Party existed, despite its abstract quality, but he had never realized that it was more important than the government, and not being a member now, at this historic moment, practically excluded him from the mainstream of history.

The following day witnessed the total reorganization of the structure of the headquarters, which was now under the direction of Loc himself. He had a new title: Party delegate to Strategic Zone One. He took over the office of Thanh Van, who, Loc said, had been sent on a mission to the front line. New faces, mostly northerners, kept coming, old faces vanishing. It was like a hotel on the last day of a convention. Minh moved his office, along with its radio station, deeper underground, and Loc assigned him an additional duty: the interrogation of American prisoners during the coming days.

D-Day finally came; Minh heard it on the Voice of America. The first attack of Operation Quang Trung took place on January 30th in the beach city of Nha Trang. The Saigon regiment 26 command, located in the former Hotel Beaurivage, was captured. The general offensive itself, however, didn't start until the 31st, with an assault on the American Embassy in Saigon. An hour later Hue was attacked and the National Liberation Flag was hoisted atop the Phu Van Lau Pavilion. The same day, the Voice of Liberation proclaimed the liberation of Hue, the former imperial capital.

Minh was bursting with excitement. He thought of his father, who could die happy now, and of his mother, who would rejoice in her chamber in the Yellow Springs. Loc stopped by, hugged him, and left a pack of Dove tea on his desk.

Radio reception quickly deteriorated. The headquarters was intermittently shaken by bomb concussions, and the heavy bombing disturbed the airwaves, at times cutting them off completely.

The next day, wounded soldiers were brought in. Half of the headquarters was transformed into a field hospital. Even so, Minh still didn't know exactly where the battlefront was, nor did he know even now where he was. The arrival of wounded soldiers brought the reality of war home to him, the face of the real Vietnam, the Vietnam at war with the most advanced technological power on earth. In spite of the suffering of the wounded Minh felt strangely happy, as if the sight of these mutilated bodies united him with the active, brutal part of the war, in the sharing of suffering with his heroic countrymen. Even the news of the U.S. Marines' counter-offensive against Hue didn't trouble him. He rejoiced at the fact that Hue was now in the hands of the liberation armies and administered by a newly formed Alliance of National Democratic and Peace Forces led by two intellectuals, Professor Nguyen Van Hao of Hue University and Madame Nguyen Dinh Chi, former principal of the Dong Khanh girl's school. He had never met Professor Hao, who had left for the liberated zone a few months before Minh's return to Vietnam, but he knew of his integrity and intellectual brilliance. Madame Chi was a distant cousin of his mother's.

.   .   .

Minh was sleeping when he was awakened by a soldier at three in the morning on February 5th.

"Comrade," the soldier said quickly, "we've brought in the first batch of American civilian prisoners of war. Would you like to interrogate them now or in the morning? They're waiting on the east side. I think we should let them rest until morning."

"I think so, too," said Minh.

"Yes, comrade," the soldier murmured and handed Minh the list of prisoners.

Still sleepy, Minh put the list in the drawer without looking at it.

At six o'clock Minh was shaken awake by the most violent concussions so far. They lasted almost an hour. It was like an earthquake. Small pieces of beaten earth fell from the ceiling like a monsoon rain; the bamboo layers shifted and cracked, making a noise that caused Minh's teeth to grind. The alert was sounded. Minh and his staff rushed to the J-shaped shelter on the east side. He spotted Loc in a corner talking with a woman nurse. They smiled silently to each other.

Loc walked toward Minh. "The bombing's getting worse. The Americans are using the heaviest bombs in their arsenal. There were even some hints that a tactical atomic bomb might be used. We'll move northward very soon. Be ready."

"What about the American prisoners?"

"What prisoners?"

"At three this morning, I was handed a list, but I've had no chance to look at it yet. Come to my office and I'll show it to you."

Minh pulled the list from the drawer and read it. Heading the list of six names was that of Jennifer Sloane: age 27; profession, volunteer social worker, Hue. Minh dropped the list, trying to regain his composure. He could sense that his face had turned pale.

"What's wrong Minh? Are you all right?"

"Yes and no. I must talk with you about this," Minh said, holding up the paper.

"About what?"

"About a woman prisoner on the list whom I knew very well in the United States."

"Is she a C.I.A. agent?"

"No, no. She's a woman I loved when I was in America. She came to Hue recently to work as a volunteer social worker with the Quakers. I should have told you about it long ago."

"The Quakers are good Americans, so what's the problem?"

"The problem is that I can't possibly interrogate her in an objective and impartial way."

"The problem is irrelevant. We're moving out of here tonight. We won't have time to interrogate the prisoners. In fact they'll have to move too."

"But ..."

"I can guess what's on your mind," Loc said with a grin. "You want to see her. I'll ask a soldier to bring her to my office and you can have a few minutes alone with her. Will that help?"

"I'm most grateful to you," Minh whispered. "You're very kind and thoughtful."

"It's nothing at all. In a situation like this, feeling should prevail over reason."

· · ·

Minh and Jennifer stared at each other, dumfounded by this unexpected meeting. He mustered his strength. "Jennifer, I'm glad you're here, and safe."

"Oh, Minh, I'm so happy to see you again. Somehow I always expected it." He took her hand in his and pressed it, then quickly released it. He spoke matter-of-factly, but his eyes did not leave her face.

"We're going to move out of here soon. The bombing is getting very bad. You'll be transferred to a safer area, and the liberation army will take good care of you. If possible, I'll see you from time to time."

"I hope so, but if not, I'll understand. I'd like to be as close to you as I can, but I realize that we're in a very difficult situation and an impossible time. Can we keep in touch with each other in some way?"

"I don't know, but I'll find out."

She moved closer to Minh and leaned her head on his shoulder. She sobbed as Minh gently caressed her hair.

Loc came in. "Minh, we've just received an order to evacuate headquarters."

Turning to Jennifer, Loc spoke in French. "Mademoiselle, I'm sorry to meet you in this situation, but I can assure you that you will be treated as a friend by our army and our people." Looking in Minh's direction, he asked, "Please translate it for her."

"No need, she understands French."

Jennifer looked at Loc. "Merci, Monsieur, merci."

She walked out of the office, following the soldier who had brought her in. Minh watched her every step. "Where are we going to move the prisoners?"

"They'll be under the jurisdiction of the Binh Tri Revolutionary Committee."

"Can I contact her?"

"Of course, if circumstances permit. In any case you can certainly write her through me."

"Thank you very much, Loc."

.   .   .

For the first time since the end of Tet, six weeks earlier, the rain had stopped. Through the bamboo periscope in his new H-shaped underground shelter, Minh could see a few stars gleaming in a tiny segment of cloudless sky. There would be a full moon tonight, too, Minh thought. It was the fifteenth day of the second month, the month of fairs and festivals. In the villages, in peaceful times, young men and women gathered in the community house would go outdoors on evenings like this to watch roving theater groups from the North. Minh was tempted to take a walk outside, but he was afraid that the good weather might bring back the deadly bombers. He thought of Jennifer and intuitively felt that she was not too far from him.

The week before, when the Binh Tri Revolutionary Committee had moved its headquarters still further north, Jennifer had made it known to the committee that she would like to go back to America. She wrote Minh that she loved him more deeply than ever and wanted to share all his hardships, but having witnessed the incredible sufferings of the Vietnamese people, having seen the barbarities of war, and still holding the same convictions that she had before about the war, she felt she should not move further north. It would only create more problems for all the Vietnamese around her and especially for Minh, particularly because the committee planned to move yet again to regroup. The first phase of the general offensive and uprising was over, Minh had been told, all its objectives attained. The committee, after lengthy deliberations and consultations with Loc and Minh, had agreed to Jennifer's request and was planning her release.

Minh was eating the last of his daily ration of rice and salted sesame seeds before going to sleep. His eating habits had changed since Tet: he always put something in his stomach before going to bed so that in case of emergency he would have the strength he needed. He was pouring tea into his red plastic cup when the soldier who kept watch on his bunker announced the arrival of the deputy chairman of the Binh Tri Revolutionary Committee, a woman in her late 20s.

"*Dong Chi* Professor, how have you been?"

"I'm well, and you? I think I've seen you once at the old headquarters when we celebrated early Tet together."

"Yes, comrade, I was there. But I've come to tell you that we plan to release Miss Sloane tonight."

"Don't you think it's dangerous to do it tonight, when the rain has stopped and the sky's so clear? The bombers might return."

"No. We've made all the arrangements and taken every precaution. This morning we made contact with the American command and proposed that over the next twenty-four hours we release some American civilians, among them the two women."

"Who's the other woman?" Minh asked.

"She's a medical doctor who worked with the American Friends Service Committee in Quang Tri and volunteered to serve in our medical service. We had to turn down her offer, although we know that she's against the war and has dedicated herself to serving war victims of all sides. We believe it's too risky for her. Her name is Dr. Nancy Johnstone."

"I think I met her once in the U.S., in Philadelphia. Are you going to release her with Miss Sloane? That would be very nice."

"No. They will be released separately."

"I see."

"When we made contact with the Americans, we asked for a 24-hour temporary ceasefire along the Ben Hai River, ten miles deep on each side, to begin at ten o'clock tonight. We've also made the agreement public and made sure that all the wire services and the Voice of America were informed. We were afraid that either the U.S. troops or the Saigon puppets would pretend not to know about it, kill the American prisoners, and blame us. But despite all the precautions, we still have to be very careful. The officer who will escort Miss Sloane will give you more details. They'll be here very soon. The distance from here to the Ben Hai River is about a mile, but we should allow plenty of time to reach Dao Duy Tu Post on this side of the river. From there, a prearranged signal code will be flashed to the U.S. Special Force garrison to send its men to pick up the American prisoners. But now I must go. It's already 10:30. I'll get in touch with you again in a few days."

"Thank you, comrade, for all you've done for Miss Sloane."

"Nothing at all. It's my duty. Besides, she's a good American, a woman. She's not responsible for this war. And she's your friend," she said with a smile.

. . .

Minh sat under a tamarind tree next to the entrance of his shelter. The night was unusually cool, like a November evening in Massachusetts. It was the first night since Tet that the guns had been silent, but it was an uneasy silence, disturbed only by the monotonous song of crickets. In it, he seemed to hear the echo of a familiar folk song, clear and bright as the moonlight.

> " . . . *Stepping into the field, sadness fills my deep heart.*
> *Bundling rice sheaves, tears dart in two streaks.*
> *Who made me miss the ferry's landing,*
> *Who made this shallow creek that parts both sides?"*

Who could be singing at this hour and in a battle zone? Perhaps it was the echo of his own imagination?

Minh noticed an orchid hanging from the branch of the tamarind. It made him think of his father, and whether he was safe, although Loc had reassured him that he would be well protected during the attack on Hue. But why was an orchid growing here? He touched it. Its scent had the same delicious sweet troubling flavor of his first kiss with Jennifer. Curious, he asked Nam, his bodyguard, who stood nearby with his AK47, "Younger brother, where does this flower come from?"

"From general headquarters. The recognition mark for this week in our liberated zone is orchid. Each shelter has one. They were picked by our soldiers in the Truong Son mountains when they marched down here. It's good to see flowers around, don't you think, comrade? I remember when I came south, I saw a few comrades who grew orchids in small wooden boxes that they carried on their shoulders. When they reached the South, they offered them to our compatriots."

He paused to light a cigarette and continued. "Before we unify our country politically, we can unify it with orchids. The Ho Chi Minh Trail will be a trail of fragrant orchids. Perhaps you know that we have some musicians and artists who imitate bird songs while we travel. The American bombing and defoliation have driven the birds and butterflies away."

He looked at Minh as if to seek agreement and added, "Nature develops and preserves our patriotism, which is our collective Vietnamese sensitivity. It strengthens us and our Party steels us."

This was the first time Minh had spoken informally with Nam or studied him closely. He had a baby face set with large dreamy eyes, well-drawn full lips, and jet black hair. His accent told Minh that he was from Hanoi.

"Where did you live in Hanoi?"

"Sinh Tu Street."

"The street of poets and writers," Minh remarked.

Somehow, Nam reminded Minh of Jennifer: the same vulnerable young face, the same touch of idealism, sensitivity, inner toughness.

"Comrade," Nam whispered, "two shadows are approaching. I'll ask them the password." He raised his voice. "Heavenly perfume orchid," he called softly.

"Golden face, another orchid," a tall man in a green uniform answered.

Minh recognized the other figure as Jennifer, but he refrained from going to her. The uniformed escort moved forward.

"Comrade Professor, my name is Captain Hung. I am assigned to provide security for Miss Jennifer Sloane. I'm sure comrade deputy chairman has given you all the essential information about my mission, but if you want to know more, please ask. Right now, for safety's sake, I suggest that you and Miss Sloane get into the shelter. She'll rest inside for a few minutes and then we'll all proceed to Dao Duy Tu Post, the last one on this side of the river."

Once inside, Jennifer threw herself into Minh's arms. "Minh, I've missed you so much. It's been even worse these past two weeks, knowing you were close but not being able to see you."

He pressed her close to him, burying his face in her hair. "Where have you been?"

"About a mile north of here, in a bunker."

Away from Jennifer, Minh had often dreamed of her body. But now that she was here in his arms, it was not desire that he felt; rather, he was overwhelmed with affection for her—for this brave, idealistic girl, so tough and yet so vulnerable. He held her closer. I love her, he thought. They had only a few minutes alone together, he knew. He wanted to memorize every detail of her.

"Minh, you remember one evening in Amherst, you asked for a lock of my hair? I have it here—it smells of the Vietnamese jungle—keep it until we meet again." Moving out of his embrace, she reached down into the front of her shirt and pulled out a tiny package wrapped in green U.S. parachute cloth. Minh put it in his breast pocket and smiled.

"Jennifer, I have to tell you that after we were together one night I gathered a few strands of your pubic hair from the bedsheet and wove them into a keepsake. But I lost it somewhere between Bangkok and Saigon."

"Oh, Minh." She touched his face with her fingertips. "That's beautiful. Crazy, but beautiful. How can I bear to leave you again? It may be years before this war is over."

"I know." He took her in his arms. "I wish you could stay, and that we could be together. But I know why you decided to leave, and I think you're right—and anyway, even if you did stay we'd probably be assigned to opposite ends of the country."

Jennifer put her arms around his neck. "Yes. Wars have a way of disrupting things. I wish we had time enough to make love right now."

"I know," he said again. "So do I." He held her face in his hands and kissed her. This may have to last me a long time, he thought.

.   .   .

The trail to Dao Duy Tu Post passed through a small hill of pine trees, which, under the moonlight, looked like a long honor guard for Jennifer's departure. The group walked silently for a while.

"Comrade Professor," Captain Hung said in a low voice, "We'll arrive in a few minutes. Do you see the three small red lights and the single yellow one under the banyan tree over there?"

"Yes, I do."

"They're the code signals. There'll also be an orchid hung under the tree."

"I see."

"I'll entrust Miss Sloane to the commander of the post and I'm sure he'll see to it that she gets back to Hue and on to America safely. You may be surprised to know that the post's commander is a relative of yours, Major Tran Van Ngoc. He was an officer in the Saigon puppet army, but he joined our resistance in 1966, after the Buddhist uprising in Hue. He's a very good man. We respect him and respect your family's contribution to our revolution."

"Please, don't mention it. We simply do our duty to our homeland," Minh said quickly, thinking of his two half-brothers who were still with the "puppet" army.

Captain Hung took Minh aside. "Comrade Professor, I'm sorry to have to tell you this, but according to our instructions and for your own safety, you and Miss Sloane must separate at the shallow creek over there." He look at Minh apologetically. "I know how you feel. Two years ago, I left my new wife in the North to march South. I said goodbye to her one night by the river. It caused me great pain, but it has passed. We must fight the invaders so people will no longer be separated by rivers, not only our people, but peoples all over the world. Fight we must, and with determination to win." The moonlight illuminated Captain Hung's eyes, bright with hatred. "You can have one minute with Miss Sloane if you wish. I'll be close by."

Minh turned to Jennifer. His hands caressed her hair and neck.

"I have to leave you here. Our escort just told me he'll walk you to the post commander. He's a relative of mine. He'll take good care of you."

"Don't worry, Minh. I'll be safe."

He wanted to kiss her and touch her face but held back. She put his hands loosely around her waist and gently, lovingly, brushed her fingers through his hair.

"Minh, when peace returns, we'll see each other again in the States. No matter where I am, I'll pick you up at San Francisco International. We'll drive through northern California, up to Seattle, and Oregon, and sit under the sequoias you wanted to see with me. Then we'll fly east to Kennedy Airport, rent a car, and drive to New York City. All our friends will come to the Thursday Restaurant for a festival of peace and love, to celebrate your return."

Captain Hung emerged from the bamboo shadows.

"Comrade Professor, stay here. I'll walk Miss Sloane to the post and be back in a short while."

"Thank you, Captain. Goodbye, Jennifer."

XI

The Long Roadway

The long, long roadway never ends.
How many men have traveled on it!
Men of today are plodding on.
But where are they, the men of old?

On The Road
Hoang Duc Luong
15th Century
Translated by Huynh Sanh Thong

The movement of a large cloud over the moon plunged the thick jungle landscape into darkness for a few seconds. Shivering, Minh rolled his handkerchief around his neck as the moon reemerged. Its fullness reminded him of two lines in the *Kieu*:

". . . Who splits the moon disc in two?
One half shines on the lonely pillow of the one behind,
The other brightens the long road of the one departing . . ."

There was no pillow for Minh. Since he'd been living in the liberated underground his pillow had been the flat, cold earth. But the road Jennifer was traveling, the way back to Amherst and America, was indeed long, very long. He imagined her arrival at Dao Duy Tu, her transfer to a fat, crew-cut Green Beret sergeant who would subject her to a grueling debriefing. He heard footsteps coming in his direction. It was Captain Hung.

"She's in good hands now, she'll be safe. She'll be at the Green Beret post in half an hour. By tomorrow she'll be watching U.S. Army TV in Quang Tri City."

He looked at Minh with sympathy, but he said only, "I have another communication for you from the revolutionary committee, actually from your friend, Commissar Loc. You're instructed not to return to your shelter. It's getting more exposed and dangerous, and we expect more bombings and direct attacks to mop up the area. Instead, you'll be moving north with us, and we're leaving right away. We have lots of time, though—the temporary ceasefire will last until morning."

But no sooner had Hung finished his sentence than a distant roar, followed by deafening thunder, threw Minh to the ground. Lifting his head, he saw a rolling sea of orange and white fire engulfing the trees around him. Pulling Minh to his feet and dragging him behind him, Hung rushed into a ravine. Minh threw himself flat, his face pressed to the wet, vibrating earth.

Half opening his eyes, he looked up. The moon had disappeared; it seemed that the sun had risen in the middle of the night. Flashes of orange and blue light flamed through the forests. It reminded him of a hackneyed description from Vietnamese war fiction: frightened heaven and shaken earth. Or was this the terrifying duel come at last between the mythical White Tiger and the Blue Dragon?

More explosions roared through the night. Huge columns of warm smoke hurt his eyes. He tried to open them to look at Hung lying beside him, but at that very moment an avalanche of fire vaporized the grass around him. A bomb tore through the nearby jungle. Minh lapsed into a state of semi-consciousness—a dreamy state in which he was barely aware. He felt warm fluid spreading across his chest. Unable to open his eyes, he could only guess that it was blood. He groped for Hung's face: it was wet and sticky.

"Are you all right?" he muttered.

"Coward imperialists! They don't even honor their own agreements. I'm hit badly. I'm sorry. Keep living for our country, for our revolution, comrade."

Minh mobilized all his strength to reach Hung's face, but he felt a cutting pain and slid into a dream.

He saw his mother and Jennifer cleaning his wounds. Behind them stood Xuan in a nurse's uniform, holding a red flag. Jennifer and his mother seemed to know one another very well. Jennifer held his head as his mother covered his face with kisses. Both spoke to him soothingly: "You'll be all right, beloved, you'll be strong again." Then they disappeared and Minh plunged into total blackness.

When he fully recovered consciousness he was resting in a modern tunnel equipped with electricity and X-ray machines. There were fifty beds in his ward, one third of them occupied by women and two thirds by European-looking men. His left leg was in a sling and his head and shoulders were covered with thick bandages. The doctor who visited him looked Caucasian, except that his complexion was rather dark. He was assisted by a Vietnamese nurse who also served as an interpreter. The nurse, smiling, inquired about Minh's appetite. Minh told her that he wasn't very hungry.

She said, "The doctor is a socialist brother from Cuba. He volunteered to help our revolution. He speaks only Spanish and English."

"I speak English too."

Relieved, she told him to converse directly with the doctor.

"Good morning, doctor," Minh said cheerfully. "I'm very grateful for all your help. The nurse just told me that you're from Cuba and you speak English."

"No need to thank me. I'm fulfilling my duty to our revolution, to our common struggle against our common enemy. Where were you educated?"

"In London, but I've lived in the United States."

"I was trained at the University of Massachusetts School of Medicine. I returned to Cuba in 1965 to serve my people and they honored me by sending me here last year to serve yours."

"I was near you in the States; I taught at Thomas Paine College. I have a friend who studied medicine at the University of Massachusetts."

"Thomas Paine is a new college, an experimental one, as they say, isn't it?"

"Yes, it is." Why did I speak to him of Jennifer, Minh thought. He was glad the doctor didn't ask him more.

"You'll be all right, comrade," the doctor said. "What you need is more rest. We've removed small pellets of fragmented bomb from your head and shoulders. You were lucky, they barely grazed your scalp. There's probably still some in your arms, but they can be removed any time in the next few years. They'll not bother you. As for your left leg, we can remove the splints within the next week. After that, you can return to your—our—struggle."

"Thank you very much, *Dong Chi* Doctor," Minh whispered.

"From tomorrow on, during the late afternoon, that's the safest hours, you can begin to walk a bit with your crutches to accelerate the healing. You don't have any broken bones; you only suffered a few deep cuts in your muscles."

At lunch, to his surprise, Minh was served bread, soup, and boiling tea. The nurse anticipated his reaction.

"It's more convenient and simpler than a Vietnamese lunch. Besides, it demonstrates the international solidarity of our cause. The dehydrated bread comes from the Soviet Union, the tea from the People's Republic of

China, and the soup from America. It's Campbell's chicken rice soup, donated by the U.S. Committee for Peace in Vietnam."

"I'm being served by a conspiracy of superpowers!" The nurse laughed.

"Are you from Hanoi?" Minh asked. "You have a northern accent."

"I was born in Quang Binh in central Vietnam, but I lived in the north for ten years while I studied nursing and foreign languages. My father was in Laos before 1945, then we were evacuated to Thailand, and from there we returned to Vietnam."

"Where's your father now?"

She lowered her head. "He died over a year ago in the first American bombing of Hanoi. He was teaching English at the University. As long as I live, I will always remember that date." Her eyes reddened with suppressed anger.

"I'm sorry," Minh said.

She walked away, quickly.

Immediately after dinner the next day Minh was lifted aboveground by a rope elevator. He exercised on his crutches, closely watched by the nurse. There seemed to be another underground above ground: the forest was so thick that the sunset rays filtered only timidly through the foliage. It was almost as dark as night.

Slowly he took a few steps among the gigantic *Lim* trees, whose solid wood is used for construction, especially for coffins. Far away he heard echoes of elephants braying. He guessed that the underground hospital was somewhere near the border of Vietnam and Laos: the area was well known for elephants and *Lim* forests. He didn't want to ask the nurse directly, so he rephrased his mental question.

"Do you hear elephants trumpeting?"

"Yes, comrade, I do. I even saw a couple of them here once."

"When?"

"Did you notice the two Europeans among our patients?"

"Yes, who are they?"

"They're two cameramen from Sweden. They came to make a film of our struggle, and they were wounded during an American bombing. I don't know where, somewhere beyond our national borders. Three weeks ago, they were transported here on elephants for hospitalization."

"They must have been filming deep in the jungle."

"Yes, the war's indeed in the jungle. But we're safe here. Since I arrived a year ago there's only been one time we detected an American spotter plane overhead. Otherwise, life's strangely normal and peaceful here."

Spotting a leech climbing up Minh's right leg, she took a small branch, scraped the bloodthirsty worm from his skin, and threw it into the jungle.

"It must be six-thirty by now," she mused out loud. "Somehow leeches come out only after six-thirty here, after the sun sets. After the leeches come the fireflies, around nine."

Minh shivered. The weather had turned chilly suddenly. The nurse suggested that they return underground.

"I don't know your name yet," he remarked.

"*Tra Hoa*, Camellias."

"You probably already know my name from the patient list."

"You're comrade Minh."

"Yes, that's correct."

Minh remembered a line from an old poem: "When the camellias bloom, the flower season is over!"

.   .   .

It was a memorable day for Minh when the doctor and nurse removed the stitches from his left leg. They celebrated the occasion. Tra Hoa presented Minh with a bouquet of orchids in a slim earthen vase. The Cuban doctor—Minh never asked his name—congratulated him.

"You're the best patient here, but you won't have to be here much longer. I think you'll soon be getting instructions from the authorities as to what to do next. And I'm sure you'll be able to continue in the struggle with fully restored health."

For the next two weeks, Minh lay in bed most of the time, reading newspapers and magazines published in Hanoi, thinking often of Jennifer and sometimes of Loc. Except for the fact that he was underground, Minh's situation wasn't too much different from that of any patient in any hospital, anytime, anywhere. There was the constant smell of ether and pus, the resigned faces and sad eyes among the patients, the always present cheery smiles from the nurses, and the same encouraging advice from the doctors.

Except for a few short, rather banal, exchanges when she took him above ground each night at six o'clock, Tra Hoa was mostly quiet, reserved, and polite. She seemed to deliberately refrain from being too friendly with Minh. One afternoon, she tiptoed to his bed, thinking he was asleep, and put a letter on his pillow.

Dear Minh,
Within two days at most after you receive this message, I'll be in your area and I'll certainly stop by to see you. Keep well. Until then,

Affectionately,
Loc

Minh jumped from his bed in excitement—and struck his right leg against the wooden bedframe. A sharp pain paralyzed his body and he almost fainted. Tra Hoa called for the doctor, who examined him and found no serious damage.

"This was nervous tension more than physical injury. You have to get back to normal slowly. Perhaps the reaction comes from the few pellets still in your shoulder muscles. By the way, what made you jump out of bed?"

"I just got a note from a dear friend, telling me that he'll be visiting me within two days at the most."

"It's understandable you're excited, but try to rest well until he gets here," the doctor said, patting his leg gently.

When Minh awoke the next morning, Tra Hoa was standing at his feet, all smiles.

"Comrade Minh, we have a treat for you this morning. Instead of having your breakfast in bed, you're invited to share the company of the doctor and his staff in the dining hall. Follow me please."

"Thank you! I didn't know you have a staff dining hall here!"

"Where do you think we have our meals? On the grass above, with elephants, leeches, and fireflies?" she teased. She looked, Minh thought, like a camellia in full bloom.

From a distance Minh could see Loc sitting with the Cuban doctor at a table in the right-hand corner at the end of the bunker. He wanted to run to him, but Tra Hoa held his arm firmly.

"Remember, you hurt yourself yesterday. We can't afford to let you break your leg in the liberated zone, after we saved you from American bombs. Take it easy, comrade."

He slowed down, stretched out his arms, balanced himself for a second and fell into Loc's arms, embracing him. Tra Hoa, watching, said to Loc, "He's yours now. I don't know who you are, but your friend has been waiting for you like a baby waiting for its mother's milk."

The Cuban doctor excused himself to allow Minh and Loc time alone.

"You look very healthy, Minh," Loc commented.

Minh noticed a short scar on Loc's left cheek. "What's happened to you? You look more dew and wind, more experienced."

"What do you mean?"

"The scar on your left cheek. It makes you look tough, decisive."

Loc laughed. "It's nothing, a ricochet from a hand grenade in Hue during the general offensive. Of course, it would have been very serious had it hit my skull. As a good friend once said, 'When a loyal person is in danger, fairies from heaven come down to help!' It was nothing compared to what you've gone through, though. The treacherous Americans! They bombed during a ceasefire and an exchange of prisoners. It was the heaviest bombing in the area so far. All the prisoners they were releasing to us were killed, twenty of them, including a high-ranking senior Party official. You may not know that your escort, Captain Hung, was killed on the spot. It's a miracle that you're alive.

"I learned about your close call two days after the bombing. I immediately arranged to have you transported to this hospital, the best and safest in the whole area. As a matter of fact, there's an American prisoner of war camp not far from here too, which we let the Americans know about through a third country." Loc sighed.

"We sent a protest about the bombing to the Americans through the International Red Cross. Can you imagine what they said?"

"No."

"That it was a misunderstanding of the Saigon Air Force. What a crude lie! The whole world knows that Saigon pilots don't fly B52s. They're not trusted by their masters to use sophisticated planes and weapons. Anyway, we'll fight harder and we'll win."

"I'm sure of it," Minh agreed. "Loc, how long were you in Hue?"

"For the duration of our control of the city. From January thirty-first to February twenty-sixth, when we withdrew strategically above the Seventeenth Parallel. We had attained all our political objectives and it would have been unwise to commit all our forces just to holding the city. It was the most important month of my life, the busiest, too. I had an opportunity to see your father before we retreated. He was happy and in good health. The Citadel was partially destroyed by U.S. Air Force and naval bombardment, but your street was intact."

"There's been incessant propaganda by the U.S. and Western press concerning the so-called Hue massacres and 'mass graves,' you know."

"I know. Even if we'd done nothing but shake hands, kiss babies, drink wine, smoke pot, and make love, we'd still be accused of terrorism. Needless to say, we're not making a revolution for the pleasure of killing people. If that were the case, we'd join the Mafia, though obviously notorious and dangerous traitors should be eliminated." He stopped for a moment.

"And what about their massacre from the air, their B52 carpet bombing, their free-fire zones, and their indiscriminate slaughter of innocent women and children in villages in Quang Ngai during the Tet offensive?" Loc's voice had never been so harsh, and Minh couldn't remember when he'd heard Loc so angry and sarcastic.

"I'm very sorry I mentioned it."

"Minh, we have to deal constantly with realities."

"Is there anything less depressing you can tell me about Hue during the Tet offensive?"

"Well, we recently conducted a campaign of criticism and self-criticism within the Party and realized that our mass organizations weren't as strong and responsive as we had expected. But the most significant thing was my futile attempt to contact your half-brother."

"Which one?" Minh asked.

"Phong. As you may know, he was promoted to major when he was sent to Quang Tri. During our general offensive, he was commanding a combined battalion of special forces and Marines. His unit proved to be the best, his soldiers are unusually disciplined. They fought well and Phong is a brilliant tactician. He nearly annihilated one of our regiments. He kept the road from Cua Thuan to Hue open, buying precious time for the United States to bring in reinforcements and retake Hue's west bank."

"I'm surprised! Phong always seemed timid and soft, sort of romantic to me."

"I never knew him well, so I don't know. I guess he has your father's blood and stubborness. At any rate, on February twentieth, when the battle was at a climax, we wounded his American adviser, a black American and took him prisoner. I can't remember his name. Well, it will come to me later."

"Arthur Bradley's his name. I met him when he was in Hue—in fact he may have saved my life. He's a very good person."

"Yes, he is. We treat him very well, as a friend, not an enemy. We asked him to ask Phong to contact us and talk with me. One of our child couriers took him the note, but Phong rejected it, saying that it was a forgery. Then we tried to get a woman comrade of mine, whom he's been dating since he arrived in Quang Tri, to convince him to come over to our side."

"Was it Xuan?" Minh interrupted.

"Someone else, not your former student. She was one of our top cadres, very attractive. He refused again. It would be a mortal blow to the U.S. and Saigon if he joined us. At one point, late in February, I was thinking of bringing you to talk with him, but by then we had already decided to effect our strategic withdrawal."

"I wish I could have helped you then. Perhaps you should have talked to my father."

"Well, too late, there's nothing we can do about it now. But I didn't come here just to tell you about Hue during the Tet offensive. I wanted to see you, so we can talk about what you'll be doing next."

"I'm anxious to hear about it. I feel well enough to go back to work now."

"Very good. You may not know that after the Tet offensive Washington made contact with us through a friendly third party. They're interested in serious peace talks. At the moment, secret negotiations are being conducted in Paris—it's a sounding-out—but a meaningful exchange could take place in the near future. Both the Embassy of the Democratic Republic of Vietnam and a small delegation of the south's National Liberation Front are there. Anyway, I've proposed your name to the party as an interpreter-press attaché for the N.L.F., and the Party has accepted it."

Minh was speechless. The U.S. had requested peace talks! And he was to be a part of them—at the center of the negotiations that might end this hated war! And what was more, he would be leaving the dull, lonely life of the bunker behind him—perhaps forever. But Loc was still speaking.

"It's important to strengthen the N.L.F. delegation with someone like you, so as to counter U.S. propaganda that the N.L.F. is a mere extension of Hanoi. We insisted that the U.S. should talk to the N.L.F., but most of the time they want to deal directly with us, with Hanoi and the Party, I mean. Your background in English will be of great help. No one else in the N.L.F. delegation in Paris speaks English. Anyway, tomorrow a courier, actually a soldier, will call on you here and make the necessary arrangements for you to get to Hanoi. You'll probably go by convoy at night. It'll take you about a week, and from there you'll go to Paris. You'll have to work hard in Paris, but I'm sure the living conditions will be more favorable to your recovery."

"Thank you very much, Loc," Minh said. "I shall try my best to be worthy of your trust. Can I ask what you're going to do now?"

"I'm returning to my party work around Hue, but you'll see me again."

As Loc said goodbye, Minh shook his hands and held them in his for a minute. He fought back tears. He often wondered what his life would be without Loc. It seemed that whenever a critical moment arose, Loc was there to show him the right direction.

.   .   .

The military convoy took six days and seven nights, following a rigorous schedule, to reach Hanoi. Minh traveled in an army vehicle, starting each evening at sunset and resting at a peasant's home along the road by day. For the first time he saw what the western press called the Ho Chi Minh Trail. In fact it wasn't a trail; it wasn't even a single path, but a maze of roads, both minimal and substantial, zigzagging through high mountains and deep rivers; of diversions and detours; of underpasses and tunnels. It was a heroic testimony to a precise and disciplined mobilization of national labor, to untold sacrifices by the peasantry, and to thousands of volunteer youth, especially young women, who formed the road-repairing teams that appeared everywhere with their primitive tools, every time there was a bombing raid.

Viewed from the Ho Chi Minh Trail Vietnam was like a mutilated, bleeding body. Yet its vital blood continued to flow through hundreds of thousands of arteries: roads and bridges, lanes and shelters, which had to be repaired again and again as soon as they were destroyed by the persistent American bombers. It was a constant struggle between the Vietnamese national intelligence and American computers, between the dream of unity and the "McNamara wall" of electronic barriers. It was Vietnam's daily answer, stubborn and proud, to U.S. Operation Rolling Thunder, which had pounded the Vietnamese landscape since 1964 in an attempt to force Vietnam back "to the stone age."

Despite the bombing, the Ho Chi Minh Trail was never empty. At every hour women and men continued to travel south to the liberated zones hidden in the rubber plantations; political cadres, military commanders, messengers, wounded soldiers were transported northward for conferences, for training, or for rest and recuperation. Watching convoy after convoy of soldiers moving southward was like seeing a re-enactment of the March to the South, when from the tenth to the nineteenth centuries the Vietnamese people left the crowded and poor North to escape the menacing Chinese colossus. Nine hundred miles for nine hundred years—one mile a year—and thousands of miles of sweat, blood and tears a day, as one song proclaimed! It was clear to Minh that the Ho Chi Minh Trail existed not just along its secret length, but in the streets and alleys of Saigon and in the hearts of the Vietnamese peasants and workers.

On the first night, Minh rode with a talkative communications officer who, between cigarettes and strong green tea, told him of his life. He was among the first volunteers of the Quang Trung division of the Truong Son Army, named for the long mountains that separate Vietnam from Laos. He often quoted a line from a poem by To Huu, the poet-laureate of Vietnam and a member of the Political Bureau of the Vietnam Communist Party: "To pierce the Truong Son, to save the nation." In his opinion, the worst enemy of Vietnam was not the U.S. Air Force, but the weather—especially as it had been modified by "vicious American technology."

"You must travel this road often," Minh remarked. "How would you describe it? What does it mean to you?"

The officer thought for a moment, emptied his cup of green tea, and solemnly answered, "The Ho Chi Minh Trail, as they call it in the west, is the collective work not of people endowed with steel skin and copper bones, as we say, but of people with correct ideology, dedication, humanism, comradeship, and the unshakable belief that women and men make history, that the human condition can be changed for the better. In short, it is the accomplishment of revolutionaries and optimists who have grasped the precise meaning of communication in politics and war, and who dream of a world without exploitation of men by other men."

When he left Minh at the next station, he handed over his half pack of cigarettes and gave his final counsel.

"Comrade, if you want to understand the meaning and history of the Ho Chi Minh Trail, you should pay attention to the slogans you'll see along the way. They explain our strategy and tactics, all our determination as well as our sufferings, and our dreams as well as our nightmares."

"Thanks for the gift," Minh said. "It's very kind of you. By the way, what's your name?"

"That's not important. I'm no different from millions of Vietnamese you'll see along the way. I'm sure you wouldn't like to remember all of them. Goodbye, comrade, we'll meet again in peacetime, when the Ho Chi Minh Trail will be known as the Highway of Reunification."

After that, Minh noted down all the slogans he passed along the road. Nearly all were short verses:

Open the road to move forward,
Fight the enemy to march on.

Walk without footprint,
Cook without smoke,
Speak without sound.

Arrive without image,
Leave without silhouette,
Go straight to destination,
Return safely to starting point.

To see the road, Is to perceive the future.

They, the enemy, do their work,
We do ours.

Songs drown thunders of guns.

Let the road wait for vehicles,
Never the vehicles for the road.

Avoid the enemy to march,
Fight the enemy to march,
Deceive the enemy to march.

Above clear, under clean
Arrive in one stretch.

The last slogan was written in big green letters on a large billboard hung under a tree at the crossroad where Highway One merged into a wide street leading into Hanoi. The sky was clear, the earth clean as the weather-beaten Molotova truck brought him in one stretch to the Truong Son Army logistics department on Quang Trung Avenue.

After he presented his papers to a desk officer, he was directed to the office of the representative of the National Liberation Front of South Vietnam, three blocks away. He was eagerly received by a young woman.

"The representative isn't in town today," she explained, "but we were informed about your arrival and mission. You'll depart tomorrow by a regularly scheduled International Control Commission plane." She showed him a small suitcase.

"We assumed that you wouldn't be properly equipped for the occasion, so we took the liberty of making a suit for you. We hope it fits. Once you're in Paris, our delegation will take care of all your basic needs."

"Thank you very much," Minh said. He was suddenly exhausted.

"You can spend the night here. Tomorrow we'll take you to the airport."

She handed him a Democratic Republic of Vietnam diplomatic passport. He noted immediately that his name had been changed once more, this time to Tran Van Thong.

Minh went upstairs to rest. He thought for a few minutes about his voyage to Hanoi, of his companion, the army officer who refused to tell him his name, of the revealing slogans he observed on the road. He dreamed of the day when peace would return, when he would come back to the South on the Ho Chi Minh Trail and compose an "Odyssey on the Highway of Reunification" dedicated to a hero with no name.

XII

Tiger's Jaws, Serpent's Fangs

An angry face speaks out what the heart feels
But deep and dark are those who hate and smile
I must take my own life into my hand
Hers are a tiger's jaws, a serpent's fangs

Nguyen Du
The Tale of Kieu
Translated by Huynh Sanh Thong

The delegation of the National Liberation Front of South Vietnam in France was housed in the Villa des Mimosas, in a suburb five miles north of Paris known as *La Ceinture Rouge*, The Red Belt, because it was populated mostly by industrial workers under the control of the communist-led unions. But the Villa des Mimosas was no worker's home; it was a ten-room, three-storied, elegantly furnished mansion. Once, after the second World War, it had served as headquarters for district five of the French Communist Party. The Party now rented it to the N.L.F. for one franc a year.

Minh found his new colleagues likeable enough. All five of them, two men and three women, lived in the compound. Bui Van Ve, chargé d'affaires of the delegation, pending the appointment of a permanent head, was a pleasant-looking man of about 60. His mouth, full of golden teeth, radiated a constant smile. Minh liked him immediately. Second in charge was Cao Bat Diet.

Minh soon learned that the delegation was a collective, with its members living and working together as brothers and sisters. Among the rules that were quickly made clear to him, one, he found, was inviolable: there could be no communication with outsiders and foreigners without the permission and authorization of the collective's executive committee. Furthermore, members were allowed to correspond by letter only with families at home. Such letters were forwarded to the Embassy of the Democratic Republic of Vietnam for transmission by diplomatic pouch to Hanoi for distribution.

These rules were a disappointment to Minh. He had thought that once in Paris he would be able to communicate freely with Jennifer, and he had looked forward to wider contacts and intellectual stimulation. On the other hand, unlike most Vietnamese Minh had never really liked Paris and the French. He found the city tensely personal, even provincial, and the people impossibly arrogant. He admired the British; they were loyal and didn't talk much. He had often reflected that while friendship with a Frenchman starts with a champagne dinner and ends with a breakfast of cold, bitter coffee, friendship with an Englishman is the other way around; it starts with a breakfast of cold salmon and ends with flaming beefsteak.

Minh wrote twice in his first months to his father—the letters were supposed to be delivered by underground agents—but received no reply.

Minh's first year of work passed quickly, if dully. Only Ve was actually involved in the preliminary work of setting up negotiations; the primary participants, as Loc had predicted, were the members of the Hanoi delegation. His life soon settled into a routine of work: watching French TV, which he found as bad as, if not worse than, its American counterpart; reading newspapers, magazines, and books, and preparing reports. Twice a week he met with the Press Attaché of the Embassy of the Democratic Republic of Vietnam, the D.R.V., at the other end of the city, and on Fridays he called on the head of the Hanoi-government-owned Vietnam Press Agency, Phan Quoc Bao, the only Vietnamese official in Paris who was allowed to live outside of the official residences and drive his own car. Unlike the other members of the Vietnamese mission, Bao was urbane, dressed elegantly, and cracked jokes. He told Minh that his father was a Confucian scholar, a Mandarin. He himself had spent seven years in Peking, which he hated. He described the Chinese cultural revolution as, "neither revolutionary nor cultural. With the cultural revolution, the Chinese people, who were already gloomy, ceased to smile or even to think." He was relieved, he confided, "to leave the Forbidden City for the City of Light," although he had wanted to be sent to Moscow.

"Why?" Minh asked.

"Well, it's the most advanced socialist country. There I could learn something about the practices of socialism. In Peking one learns nothing, except how to abstain from the joys of life. Mao Tse-Tung was right when he said 'the revolution is no dinner party.' The traditional Chinese joy of eating vanished with the Chinese anticultural revolution." He smiled mockingly. "In Moscow, at least people get drunk in the street in the middle of the night. Also, one can go to the ballet."

Bao's opinions were both a surprise and a disappointment to Minh. He had thought that Vietnamese communists—he was sure that Bao was an important member of the party—were as close to the Chinese as "the lips to the teeth," as the official propaganda line claimed. Theoretically and intellectually, Minh had supported the Chinese cultural revolution as a necessary development for the creation of a socialist superstructure. But whenever he tried to talk about China with members of the D.R.V. Embassy he was diverted to other subjects. Once he raised the question with Ve, but Ve barely responded.

"At this moment we're fighting against the American aggressors. Any country that helps us is a friend, and we don't make bad comments about our friends and allies. But when the war's over, the situation might change: our present enemies could be our friends, and vice versa."

During the first week of January, 1969, Minh met daily with other members of his National Liberation Front delegation and with the D.R.V. Embassy personnel to discuss details for the celebration of Tet of the Year of the Chicken, which fell on February 10. All meetings were presided over by the D.R.V. Ambassador, a man with a rough square face who was known for his capacity to work nineteen hours a day and smoke three packs of cigarettes in twenty-four hours. He was a member of the Central Committee of the Communist Party and had spent a total of twenty years as a political prisoner. "We must," he told the group, "counter the enemy's propaganda that the National Liberation Front of South Vietnam is a creation of the communist party in Hanoi. In our initial contacts with the Americans, they insisted on talking only to the North. This is a clever trick meant to bring the situation back to the 1954 Geneva Agreements. We must make our position clear: all Vietnamese wish for the eventual reunification of their fatherland, but this has to be accomplished step by step and with consultations with all the strata of South Vietnamese society. Obviously, this can be done only if the foreign aggressors withdraw. The reunification process might take a decade, if not longer." Therefore, he suggested, the burden of the celebration and reception of the press should fall on the N.L.F. delegation with the logistical support and advice of the D.R.V. Embassy.

Minh noticed that the ambassador called his all-male staff, who all spoke with pronounced Northern accents, *dong chi*, while the N.L.F. delegation, except for Mr. Ve, were referred to simply as *Anh* and *Chi*. It was clear to Minh that all the staff members of the D.R.V. Embassy belonged to the Communist Party and that all the staff members of the N.L.F. delegation, again excluding Mr. Ve, were considered less equal than others. They were "non-party elements." Minh also noticed that Bao, the Vietnamese Press Agency representative, was on intimate terms with the ambassador, who, of course, called him comrade. Bao participated in all major decisions.

.   .   .

Of the 120 select members of the Paris-based press corps invited to the party, 112 accepted: 40 French, 35 from Third World countries, 25 from eastern and other western European nations, and 12 Americans. Two "old-hand American journalists" who had been reporting from Saigon since 1954 and had both won Pulitzer Prizes brought their Vietnamese wives along. Minh knew very few of the guests. But Bao, who called everyone by their first names, was beside him if he needed assistance.

"Minh, I'd like you to meet my friend George, Paris' Washington Post correspondent. Minh is our press attaché, George. He was born in Hue and was there during the Tet offensive last year."

"Glad to meet you."

"It's nice meeting you, too."

Turning to Minh, Bao explained, "George wants to know the truth about the so-called Hue massacres and mass graves during the Tet offensive. His paper is running a series of articles about them next week and he thinks the story might change the minds of some Americans who've been against the war. Why don't you tell him what you saw?"

"Sure," Minh replied unhesitantly. "As you know, the battle for the liberation of Hue was the bloodiest of the war. The U.S. indiscriminately used massive fire power, killing more innocent civilians than soldiers. While the fighting was raging, while the Saigon puppet troops and police vanished or joined the liberation forces, we in the liberation Army had to take care of the dead—dead killed by American fire—and bury them at great risk. And now *we* are accused of killing these people. I must tell you, to be absolutely truthful, that I am aware of several cases when angry people seized a few notorious puppet police officers, looters, and traitors, and attempted to execute them on the spot. We had to intervene, in some cases, to stop the populace from murdering them." Minh paused to sip his champagne.

"You know that we're not engaged in revolution for the sadistic pleasure of killing people. We're not terrorists and neither are the many other third world revolutionaries who are accused of terrorism in the western press. We're fighting for the helpless. If we wasted our time killing innocent people, who would be left to support and feed us, to shoot down planes and repair roads, all of which enable us to deliver devastating blows to the most powerful army on earth? Or are you going to say that your planes were shot down by the Russian Air Force, your tanks destroyed by Chinese artillery, and your Green Berets ambushed by Cuban commandos?"

Minh spoke vehemently, angrily, convinced of the truth of his words—but even as he spoke a part of him realized with some surprise that he was faithfully repeating the official Party line.

"Well, George," Bao asked, "are you satisfied with the account of an eyewitness?"

"Not quite, but let's forget the whole thing. After all, we're at a Tet celebration, the twenty-four hour ceasefire has just begun, and we ought to drink to a year of peace."

"According to an oracle by Nguyen Binh Khiem, a fifteenth century Vietnamese 'Nostradamus,' the Year of the Chicken will see peace restored to Vietnam," Minh remarked.

"To peace!" they toasted, and drained their glasses.

At about 8:30, a commotion at the entrance to the hall turned all eyes towards the door. A tall, dark-haired woman dressed in a black blouse and blue jeans and carrying a load of heavy cameras was trying to explain herself in halting French, but Minh's colleague Diet refused her entrance. Minh moved quickly to her rescue.

As soon as she saw him, she asked eagerly, "Do you speak English?"

"Yes, I do. What can I do for you?"

"I'm Jean Simmons of the New York Clarion Daily, a progressive newspaper. I arrived in town this afternoon and learned about the party here from a friend. I came even though I don't have an invitation. I was reporting from Vietnam over a year ago."

She said all this quickly while flicking her hair from her face at regular intervals. She pulled her press credentials out of her breast pocket, and a marijuana cigarette dropped to the floor. Minh picked it up and handed it to her with a smile. She put it back into her pocket and buttoned it carefully.

"This is the last of my stock from Vietnam. It's without question the best in the world. It smells like honey, tastes like gingseng, and lasts like a good summer dream."

"Thank you for such a poetical appreciation of a product of my land. With such an understanding of Vietnam, you don't need an invitation to join us."

"Fantastic!" she exclaimed.

Her easy gait reminded Minh of Jennifer. He turned to Diet, who didn't understand any of the conversation, and reassured him.

"She's all right. She's a news correspondent from an American newspaper. She's friendly to Vietnam."

Despite her casual appearance, she was poised and self-confident. Without a doubt, she was the most attractive woman at the party.

Minh invited her to the bar. "I'm Tran Van Thong, press officer for the Delegation."

"Thanks for rescuing me," she said. "I really wanted to get in, because I'm trying to track down a human interest story about an American woman who was killed in Vietnam a year or so ago, and I thought someone here might be able to help me."

She fished her joint out of her pocket and lit it, inhaling deeply. Her easy manners, contrasted with her professional air, were intriguing.

"Tell me about it," Minh said.

"Well, I heard about it in New York, from a friend who'd covered Vietnam for five years. It happened last March, during the ceasefire after the Tet offensive. The U.S. Command and the N.L.F. had agreed on a ceasefire to allow an exchange of civilian prisoners of war captured during the Tet offensive. But it was broken by the U.S. Air Force's saturation bombing in the area just north of the seventeenth parallel, and the exchange never took place as planned—in fact the bombing apparently killed prisoners on both sides. Madness! Anyway, an American nurse who worked with a Special Forces unit in Quang Tri told my friend, Tim, that among the Americans killed was a young social worker. I forget her name just now, but I'm sure it will come to me in a minute. She was fatally wounded and was dying by the time she arrived at the unit's surgery room. Elizabeth Howser, that was the nurse, took the woman's clothes off to prepare her for surgery. There was a letter wrapped in plastic in her pocket. Elizabeth removed it after she was sure the woman was dead. She took it and all the other belongings of the deceased to an officer in the military police so that they could be shipped back to her family in the United States." She inhaled the honey-scented smoke of her cigarette, then continued.

"A few days later, a military police captain told Elizabeth that the dead social worker was a Viet Cong spy and that the letter was from her lover, a Viet Cong official working in the underground in Hue." She took out her notebook.

"The Viet Cong official's name is Tran Van Minh, the same family name as yours. The woman's name was Jennifer Sloane. I have a copy of the letter, but let me finish the story first and then I'll show it to you."

But at the mention of his real name and Jennifer's, Minh was overcome with shock and disbelief. Jennifer was dead—had been dead for nearly a year!

"What's the matter? You look pale. Are you all right?"

"Nothing. Just tired. Would you like a drink?"

"Please."

Minh stood up, went behind the bar, and leaned against it for awhile. He needed a moment to recuperate from the shock.

When he returned Jean accepted the drink and went on. "It will take just a few more minutes to finish. Elizabeth told Tim about the story when she saw him in Hue. He tried to confirm it with the military police captain, who finally agreed to see him after avoiding him for days, and showed him a photocopy of the letter."

Jean handed the photocopy to Minh. It was the last letter he had written to Jennifer from Hue. He tried to make Jean believe he was reading it, but his eyes filled with tears.

"Excuse me for a moment."

He walked quickly to the men's room to wipe away the tears and broke down a second time in front of a blurred mirror. When he returned, he offered a feeble explanation.

"I've not been in Paris long and I'm still affected by the differences in time and climate changes."

"That's understandable. I'm almost finished. The captain asked Tim not to publish the letter to avoid what he called 'embarrassment to the deceased's family' who of course were notified by the authorities that she was murdered by the Viet Cong while the U.S. Army was effecting her release through an exchange of civilian prisoners of war. To date, Tim hasn't published the story, not because he wants to comply with the Army's request, but because he believes that there's something suspicious about the whole thing. He's convinced that Miss Sloane was killed by the U.S. bombing. He thinks that the Army faked the letter to justify its crime and that the U.S. deliberately violated the ceasefire in order to eliminate the Viet Cong prisoners. According to Tim, there were fifteen Viet Cong prisoners—one of them was the head of an important sapper unit in Hue—and only two American prisoners, both women. Anyway, I'd like to write a magazine article about the incident in order to expose the Army's duplicity and the madness of this war which has totally corrupted America. But I need to do a lot more digging, and I hoped, perhaps, you could help."

"I don't know," said Minh. His voice was hoarse with pain. "I'm afraid I wouldn't know how to go about it."

"I see." Her voice was startled. "Well, thanks anyway," she said. She shook his hand and left.

.   .   .

Minh ran upstairs to his room. Not since his mother's death had he wept so bitterly. At midnight, when Diet came to knock at his door to invite him to come down for the *Giao Thua* celebration to welcome the new year, he excused himself, saying that he had an unbearable headache because of too many drinks and too much cigarette smoke and that he preferred to stay in bed. He lapsed into an uneasy sleep and woke about three in the morning.

A sense of immense emptiness swept over him. He felt as though he were hanging in an abyss, swinging in a void. For a second, he thought that such a state of nothingness would inevitably lead to the enlightenment a Buddhist heritage led him to expect. Instead, the bottomlessness of it gave way to acute mental torment and a physical ache in his chest. He knelt down and prayed to Buddha the Compassionate, but his prolonged prayers only brought him to more tears. There was no human being around to whom he could confess his grief, no human face he could look into for solace. In his anguish, he wished that Loc were here, standing in front of him as his guide and his master. But Loc was nowhere and everywhere; he was, as always, with his Party.

The next day, the first day of the Year of the Chicken, the whole delegation had a late breakfast together. Mr. Ve was the first to notice that Minh wore dark glasses.

"I've never seen you wear dark glasses before, or any other kind of glasses. What's wrong?"

"The cigarette smoke at the party last night irritated my eyes. They're swollen. It's happened to me before. I'm sure they'll be all right in a day or so."

"I hope so," said Mr. Ve, "because I have a happy announcement for the start of the year. A permanent head for the delegation, has been designated by the Presidium of the National Liberation Front, to meet the demands of the new situation which requires stronger representation of the voices of the heroic people of South Vietnam. I'm exceedingly pleased to announce that our representative will be a woman with remarkable revolutionary achievements, a political commissar in our heroic army, an intellectual who speaks French, English, Russian, and Chinese fluently. She is comrade Phan Thi Thai and she'll arrive the day after tomorrow. All members of the delegation should come to the airport to welcome her."

Only the name Phan Thi Thai broke through Minh's depressed abstraction, but the announcement had no effect on him. He could think only of Jennifer's death. What a cruel irony, he thought: an American bomb paid for by the American people's taxes, made perhaps in some factory not far from Amherst, Massachusetts, killed an American woman—the lover of a "Viet Cong official." And the same bombing raid nearly killed that official after he had sent her away believing that she would be safer with her own people. It would have been less ironic, even logical, if he had been killed with her while they said goodbye in the jungle.

.   .   .

Practically all of Vietnamese officialdom in Paris was present on the snowy, windy afternoon that the new chief of the N.L.F. delegation arrived at De Gaulle Airport. The French Ministry of Foreign Affairs sent only a middle-level protocol officer to greet her, wishing to avoid the implication that France recognized the N.L.F. The French diplomat insisted to Minh that "we still maintain correct diplomatic relations with Saigon for the time being. Our gesture today is to show French goodwill and France's desire to contribute to the coming peace negotiations."

His polite, abstract remarks reminded Minh of the kind of thing he himself used to say in his capacity as a diplomat. Basically, he reflected, there was no difference between that language and the one he was using now to convey the N.L.F.'s official positions. Both were without soul or conviction. They had, however, acquired a meaning through their very meaninglessness.

Phan Thi Thai was received at the ramp of the plane by the D.R.V. Ambassador, Mr. Ve, the French protocol officer, and the chairman of the Association of Vietnamese Residents in France. Minh watched from the window of the terminal's V.I.P. room as a young Vietnamese girl offered her a bouquet of red gladiolas. The remainder of the Vietnamese party was introduced to her inside the terminal. She shook hands casually with Minh without even looking at him. Her touch was less tender, more confident, than it had been years before.

After the introduction, she read a brief statement for the TV and printed press, in perfect French, in which she thanked the French government and the "peace-loving peoples of the world, including the American people, for having supported the just struggle of the people of South Vietnam." Minh stared at the French protocol officer, who lifted his eyebrows when she mentioned the French government's support. She smiled, waved at the airline passengers, and was whisked away, along with Mr. Ve, in the D.R.V. Ambassador's black Mercedes. Minh rode in another car with her secretary, a shy young woman with a pronounced Hanoi accent, as well as three other members of the D.R.V. Embassy.

It was snowing hard. As always, snow had a cleansing effect on Minh and made him daydreamy and sensually aroused. He recalled a popular poem, *Seeing My Lover Off at the Train*, by the Vietnamese poet Cung Tram Tuong:

> *Snow fell all over the train*
> *Inside, you are cold and sad*
> *Why don't you cry?*
> *To warm up our common dream tonight?*

That night Minh dreamt too, but when he awoke he was left only with a sense of desolation. He could not recall his dream.

Phan Thi Thai did not eat breakfast with the other members of the delegation. She got up at 4 a.m.—a habit of years in the liberated zones in Central Vietnam—and ate breakfast with her personal secretary, after several hours of work.

Three days after she took office she held her first formal meeting with her staff. Seated across from her at a rectangular desk, Minh discreetly and attentively followed her every gesture, trying to see how much she had changed since their high school days. In his brief meeting with her in the bunkers, he had recorded few passing impressions of her, and those had faded away quickly in the dim light of the underground. Now, face to face with her, he had all the time in the world to study her.

Her complexion was darker, much darker than it had been when she was young. She had almost completely lost her Hue accent, which was now replaced by an aristocratic Hanoi intonation. Streaks of gray in her black hair gave her smooth, oval face an imposing seriousness. Her hands were bony, callous; her fingernails cut short. But her mouth and lips remained the same—sensual, ironic, provocative.

He noticed the black mole under her lower lip. When they were dating he used to tease her as they sat on the left bank of the River of Perfume watching passing sampans. According to the Vietnamese physiognomy his mother had taught him, a woman who had a mole under her lower lip would have a similar mole on the lower lip of her vulva and would be the future mother to a "hero-savior of the country." But Minh had never had an opportunity to ascertain the truth of his mother's assertion. He could detect no sign that Thai knew his real identity; she called him by his new name, Tran Van Thong, without hesitation.

During her first conference, which lasted the whole morning, she spoke in great detail about the favorable developments at home after the "glorious victory of the Year of the Monkey, the Tet offensive and the general uprising that forced the enemy to sue for peace." She was sure that the peace negotiations would soon officially get under way, in a matter of months, if not weeks. Anticipating this new development, the N.L.F. presidium would soon take two measures of great importance. First, it would convene a national conference in June to form the Provisional Revolutionary Government of South Vietnam; then, in May, it would make public the N.L.F. negotiating positions, the ten-point program for peace.

She circulated a draft of the program for the staff to read. Minh was most interested in point seven: "The reunification of Vietnam will be achieved step by step by peaceful means through discussions and agreement between the two zones, without foreign interference. Pending the peaceful reunification of Vietnam, the two zones will reestablish normal relations in all fields on the basis of mutual respect."

Phan Thi Thai attached particular importance to point four: "The people of South Vietnam must settle their own affairs without foreign interference. They will empower the political regime of South Vietnam through free and democratic general elections. Through free and democratic general elections, a Constituent Assembly will be set up, a Constitution worked out, and a coalition government installed, reflecting national concord and the broad union of all social strata." She reiterated that the duty of the delegation was to educate foreign public opinion about these realities, the most important one being the independence of the N.L.F. "It is vital," she said, "to refute once and for all the enemy's mythical argument that the Communists in the North invented and directed the N.L.F. in the South through the Central Office of South Vietnam. I call on you, the mission's members, to work hard and to accept sacrifices equal to those made by our compatriots at home."

Minh's assignment was to put out a biweekly bulletin, in French and English, on the progress of the struggle in South Vietnam. She suggested a name for the bulletin: "For Independence, Freedom and Democracy in South Vietnam." Minh thought that the name was too long and reminiscent of a similar publication put out by the Communist Cominform years ago: "For A Lasting Peace, For A People's Democracy," but he didn't object. He didn't want to antagonize her at the first working session.

On May 19, the 79th anniversary of the birth of President Ho Chi Minh, she invited her staff to a dinner at a Vietnamese restaurant. Minh had never seen her so relaxed. She emptied a large glass of red wine. Her rosy cheeks reflected the red embroidered *ao dai* dress she wore for the occasion.

After dinner, when they returned to the delegation, she invited them for coffee and liqueurs, although she drank only tea. Later, Minh followed her into the garden. Because she seemed so joyful, he dared to strike up a conversation with her.

"*Chi* Thai, are you from Hanoi?"

"No. I was born near Hue, but have been in the North for many years.

Anyway, we're all fighting for our fatherland now, our personal lives have no importance," she answered curtly. She asked him about his progress on a special issue of the bulletin to announce the N.L.F.'s new program.

·　　　·　　　·

Minh's life sank ever deeper into routine. War and revolution, ever-present at home, seemed far away. Discussions of struggle and sacrifice were somehow unreal held over breakfasts of coffee and croissants. The only reality that mattered to Minh was his loneliness. Isolated from Loc and his family, mourning for Jennifer, he was more and more attracted to the only link he had with his past, but though Thai bore the physical appearance of his high-school sweetheart she was always and only his businesslike superior.

Worst of all, it seemed to him that to attempt to sell the revolution's cause to the international public was close to absurdity. If the Vietnamese peasants had surrendered to U.S. intervention in 1960, would the world still be concerned about Vietnam even though it had existed independently for thousands of years? He was skeptical about the negotiations, which might serve as an excuse for both sides to escalate the war while seeking a military solution. The process seemed to be simple: proposals and counter-proposals, followed by further military attacks, then new proposals, new counter-proposals. Peace and war follow a cyclical life of their own, he thought.

The official position of his delegation was at best ambiguous. The National Liberation Front was now known as the Provisionary Revolutionary Government of South Vietnam, the P.R.G., but neither the United States government nor the international press took it seriously. Only non-governmental organizations, mostly American, were hoping that once peace returned the P.R.G. would form a coalition government composed of Buddhists, Catholics, and other minor religious sects such as the *Cao Dai* and *Hoa Hao*. Personally, Minh didn't see any contradictions or major differences between the P.R.G. and North Vietnam; they were both part of Vietnam. Moreover, the war, which began in the South, was now engulfing the whole country. He wondered why the P.R.G. kept insisting on being independent and separate while in reality the war was being fought by Vietnamese from North to South.

The harder Thai worked, the younger she seemed to grow. Her complexion was lit from within, the gray in her hair less visible. As time passed her Hanoi accent gave way to her original, soft Hue accent. Minh was particularly pleased with this subtle change which, he admitted to himself, could be in his imagination. He had long ago convinced himself that a person born in Hue, especially a woman, always retained that unique combination of the strength of the pine trees of the Imperial Screen Hill, and the sweet elegance of the clear water of the River of Perfume. She had adjusted rapidly to her job and the Parisian atmosphere, wearing a different-colored *ao dai* every day; no longer did she wear the solid-colored dresses she had worn when she first arrived. She began discreetly coloring her lips. Minh fantasized that she had sexual desires too.

Minh daydreamed more in Paris than at any other time of his life. For a long time, the only persons in his dreams were his mother, Jennifer, Loc, and sometimes his father or Xuan. But now Thai appeared as often as Jennifer, always wearing a dress of red brocade embroidered with small phoenix figures. One night, while a cold moon shone into his room, he dreamed he made love to her. When he woke in the cold predawn he found himself fondling his pillow and heard her steps pacing the floor of the room above.

Minh felt more and more frustrated because he was unable to talk with her privately. He felt increasingly jailed. The essence of prison, he thought, wasn't so much being behind bars as being reduced to a state of noncommunication.

Then, in late November, Thai announced to the delegation that she had been named Foreign Minister of the Provisional Revolutionary Government of South Vietnam and that she would be absent from Paris for three or four months. A number of antiwar organizations in Sweden had invited her to Stockholm and the Swedish government had offered her a building to serve as her European headquarters although she would still be head of the P.R.G. delegation. Just before Christmas, she left France with her personal secretary, leaving the delegation in the hands of Mr. Ve as chargé d'affaires.

At first her absence was a relief for Minh. But as the weeks went by, he realized how much he missed her. At the end of the Year of the Chicken, he decided to write her.

Paris, 1st day of Tet

Dear Thai,

As the Year of the Chicken draws to an end, I write you to wish you a happy New Year of the Buffalo.

You may be surprised and even offended that I address you in an informal way. As an official of the P.R.G. delegation, I have no right whatsoever to write anything personal to you, the P.R.G. Foreign Minister. But as a close, former high-school classmate, I have a torrent of feelings to share with you, feelings which have lain deep in my heart for the last thirty years.

You seemed not to have recognized me when we met, deep in the earth of our country. I thought you did it deliberately. Not that I believed that "anyone could forget—for a thousand years—that first moment of love and attachment" as a poet once said, but because I was sure that my friend, your comrade Loc, and the Party knew everything about me, about my past, my present, and were deciding my future. They should have told you about me. You might remember the following incident: a prisoner of war named Jennifer Sloane, whom I knew very well while I was teaching in the U.S., was brought (during the aftermath of the Tet offensive) to my office to be interrogated. I told Loc that I couldn't objectively question her, but that I wanted to meet with her privately. You, yourself, gave me permission, after Loc consulted with you. I was most grateful then for your compassionate gesture. You probably know also that she was later killed by an American bomb which violated the ceasefire that had been arranged for the exchange of civilian prisoners of war. The same bombing raid almost killed me too. I have often thought that because I was wounded during the general offensive and uprising, I was rewarded by the Party and the government with my present post in Paris.

If I remind you of this event in my life, if I mention the name of Jennifer Sloane to you, it's not to gain your sympathy. I'm aware that your sympathies extend to all the suffering Vietnamese people for whom you accept sacrifices and work with dedication. I wish simply to say to you, as a woman, that somehow our lives have been indirectly involved with each other in the recent past, long after we left high school. I don't ask for any special favor. Under the rigors of *Ly*, my reason, I have no right but to serve the government, the people, and you, faithfully. But within the flexibility and the warmth of *Tinh*, my feeling, I can at least implore that we put our relationship on a more humane, that is, personal, basis. Why can't we talk to each other as old friends, even if I'm not your comrade? Why should you deny that thirty years ago, we loved each other? While time might have wiped out all the remnants of these feelings, their essence still exists. At a time when I am experiencing a deep emptiness, they return to reclaim my devotion. In recognizing our common past, you may guide me on the road of comradeship, towards a higher form of love as the Party has proclaimed.

I hope you understand my situation. Forgive me if you think that it is irrelevant to your life and work. Forget me if you think that the past exists only as a past and not as a foundation for the present and the future.

I would be deeply grateful if from now on you would treat me not only as a member of your delegation, but as an old friend. May your stay in Sweden be pleasant. I look forward to your return.

Again, I wish you a happy Tet although it is a Tet among strangers and amidst snow.

> Yours,
> Tran Van Thong
> formerly, Tran Van Minh

Minh found his letter incoherent and wanted to compose a poem for her instead, but he decided to send her the letter as it was.

Minh didn't receive any answer to his letter. He didn't expect it. He stoically awaited her return, which was postponed again and again by her extended visits to other European countries. She was often interviewed by the press. One interview, at the Association of Swedish Women for Peace and Freedom, was particularly interesting to Minh. He reproduced it in its entirety in the delegation's bulletin:

Reporter: Madame, Miss Foreign Minister, we know about your public life as well as your revolutionary activities in Vietnam, but we are totally in the dark about your private life. That is, we don't know if we should address you as Madame or Miss. Are you married? Have you been in love?

Thai: You can just address me as Foreign Minister. Yes, I'm married—to over forty million Vietnamese people to whom I dedicate my life. I've been in love with justice, with freedom, with peace since I was born and that love is everlasting. I'm in love with all the progressive peoples of the world, in particular the people of Sweden, and also with the American people.

Reporter: I don't think that all Vietnamese women are like you. What about the feelings of women in your country, on say, homosexuality, lesbianism? Is that part of the struggle for liberation?

Thai: At the moment all Vietnamese women and men are concentrating their struggle against foreign aggressors and their puppets. They don't have the time or the luxury to talk about homosexuality and other individual emotions, which have no place in our collective efforts to regain our independence and freedom. I myself have never heard of any incidents such as lesbianism now or at any time in the past in Vietnam.

Reporter: Is there any one person, a man or woman, who is particularly dear to you?

Thai: Yes. Oh, yes. The late President Ho Chi Minh. When he died last year, I felt as if I had lost the most precious treasure of my life. I cried for two nights. But afterwards I reread his Testament and works, and I knew he would want me and all Vietnamese to transform our bitterness and sorrow into determination to win the war and to rebuild the country "ten times more beautiful."

Reporter: Is there any particular question you want to ask us, or any message you want us to convey?

Thai: I wish I had the time and courage to ask you the same questions you asked me (*laughter*). I shall do it when you visit my country during peacetime. In the meantime, I would like to convey to the people of Sweden the profound gratitude of the people of South Vietnam for all they have done to support our just struggle. In siding with us at great risk and cost, the government of Sweden proves that it is the keeper of the conscience of humankind.

The interview was illustrated by a picture of Thai holding a blonde baby and a bouquet of red roses; the caption read, "Viet Cong Foreign Minister: a beautiful woman with a heart of steel—a lover of over 40 million

Vietnamese." Minh sent a note to her secretary to ask for a negative of the photograph for "future use in our publication." His note was unanswered.

. . .

On a hot day in late August 1970, Thai returned to Paris. She had been away for almost a year instead of the originally planned three or four months. Radiating energy when she landed at General DeGaulle airport, she looked much younger. Two days later she called an evening meeting of delegation personnel.

Smiling, she opened the meeting by saying how happy she was to return to Paris at the moment when there was definite progress towards serious negotiations for peace. For nearly an hour she told the mission about her successful tour of the Scandinavian countries, her visits to Holland and Belgium, and particularly her activities with the peace organizations in Sweden. Her work, she emphasized, had been made easy by the continuous success of the struggle at home.

Then, in a graver voice, speaking slowly and unemotionally, she looked at Minh and said, "While I was away on this official mission, one member of this delegation, instead of redoubling his work, spent precious time writing me a letter filled with cheap bourgeois nostalgia. The member is Mr. Tran Van Thong."

Minh felt the blood drain from his face. All eyes turned to him; the women at the table looked at him with hostility. Mr. Ve was obviously chagrined.

"His act is serious," she went on, "not just because it shows his feudalistic reactionary attitude towards women, but also because it reveals his disrespect to the Representative of the Provisional Revolutionary Government of South Vietnam and the heroic people of South Vietnam who are struggling under the most difficult conditions while he enjoys a soft life in Paris. He must be severely criticized, but first I'd like to ask him if he can offer some criticism or evidence in his own defense."

Minh could not speak. Humiliated and shaken, he felt at the same time that her criticism—especially of his attitude to women—was unfair. But with an effort, wanting only to end the episode as quickly as possible, he got to his feet.

"I sincerely apologize to the Representative of the Provisional Revolutionary Government of South Vietnam, to the heroic people of South Vietnam, and to all members of this delegation for my criminal act. I have nothing to say except to ask for your forgiveness, or more precisely, for your willingness to re-educate me and show me the correct direction." He didn't know where the words came from; he felt he was parroting phrases he had heard in criticism-self-criticism sessions over the years. Blindly he sat down.

Thai was speaking, a smile on her face. "As you all know, the policy of our government has been and continues to be based on tolerance, generosity, and faith in the power of education and re-education of an individual by the collective. *Anh* Thong, having publicly admitted his mistake, will benefit from that policy. I therefore suggest that he be put under the guidance of Comrade Ve, who will re-educate him until he is purged of all his decadent, romantic, feudalistic, bourgeois mentality."

Mr. Ve's response was eager. "Comrade Foreign Minister, I shall make it my sacred duty to re-educate *Anh* Thong and show him the way to be a worthy revolutionary Vietnamese. I shall arrange the details of our instruction and report all progress to you and to the members of this mission."

The session over, the hostility and disdain toward Minh disappeared, though for a week no one except Mr. Ve talked to him. His instructions began the next day immediately after dinner. Three times a week, Mr. Ve lectured him about revolutionary virtues, about the new socialist man and woman. Minh, his confidence shaken, made a real effort to show an interest; he had a sincere respect for Mr. Ve's integrity and conviction. But alone in his room, the pain was intolerable. He felt alternately humiliated and depressed, not only because he had been rejected and reprimanded by a woman who was once his sweetheart, not only because he, a Ph.D. in political science, was being taught by a man whose only education was Party work among the peasantry, but because he realized how ignorant he was of the realities of Vietnam, how insensitive he was to the transformation of Vietnamese women by revolution and war. It seemed to be true that though he was fighting for a new society, he was still chained to the old values.

Minh had always conceived of life as an unbroken chain of events. Now that chain had been broken by his own foolish act. A profound emptiness seized him each night, much deeper and more penetrating than the loneliness that followed his discovery of Jennifer's death. In the past, in situations such as this, he would find refuge in Buddha. But Buddha was now a stranger to him. Buddha could not possibly understand that in the twentieth century there was such a thing as "the Party," which had transformed people and arbitrated new values. Minh was in theory and in practice "a blown-out candle." He had reached Nirvana, but he was not enlightened at all. He had experienced Nirvana, because of his humiliating confession, but he had to reject Nirvana because it was only perpetuating his suffering. Instead of an aureole of truth and deliverance, it was a cloud obscuring the path to enlightenment.

·   ·   ·

On a cold, autumnal moonlit night several months later, Minh walked home from an official dinner party. The quiet River Seine reflected the distorted contours of old buildings along shady boulevards. It was midnight. He stopped in the middle of a bridge and watched his face trembling in the wavy water. For a second he had the idea, for the first time in his life, that he might throw himself into the Seine and rid the revolution of his unworthy self. But the idea had hardly formed before a prostitute, her painted face half hidden under a black fur hat, approached him and invited him to get into her car.

"It's midnight, it's cold, and you're all by yourself," she whispered. He hesitated, then approached her car, but as he did so a policeman suddenly appeared. Hastily Minh gave her 500 francs, the monthly allowance he had just received only the day before.

"Merci, merci, Monsieur," she shouted and sped away, a second before the policeman arrived.

This brief unexpected encounter with a woman brought him some comfort. Minh had always been attracted by female company, not necessarily for sexual reasons, but mainly because of intellectual curiosity and the artistic creativity women generated in him. But this attitude was often misunderstood by both men and women; he had never been able to explain it, either verbally or in his books and poems. Perhaps it came from his exceptional affection for his mother; perhaps it originated in his fascination with Taoism and its proclaimed respect for the strength of water, woman and the child; or perhaps it came from the knowledge all men have, deep in their subconscious, that they owe their existence and their hope for continuity to women.

It was late when Minh returned to the Villa des Mimosas. Thai was still in her office, but he didn't pay attention to her presence. Something had radically changed in him. His experience on the bridge had forced a simple truth into his mind: he must preserve his sense of awe, he must nurture his detachment, and above all he must exist. In order to exist, he must resist. Life was not a chain of unbroken events as he had thought. It was a continuous cycle of existence and resistance, resistance against what is destructive. And how does one resist? By nonresistance, by nonactive action. From now on, he would exist, he would resist, and he would live naturally.

Yes, live naturally. The picture of a smiling Lao Tsu riding a blue buffalo north, which he had first seen as a child on the cover of the Imperial Calendar, appeared to him with more integrity, beauty, authenticity, and poetry than ever before. Indeed, the founder of Taoism had shown him both the Way, the Tao, and the power of water, of the feminine, and of the child in a state of nature. He recited a favorite verse from the *Tao Te Ching*:

> *Creating, yet not possessing,*
> *Working, yet not taking credit.*
> *Work is done, then forgotten.*
> *Therefore it lasts forever.*

Minh was neither excited nor happy when, with Phan Thi Thai and the P.R.G. Delegation, he attended the ceremony on January 27, 1973 for the signing of the "Agreement on Ending the War and Restoring Peace in Vietnam."

Yes, the "just cause," as it was called in his press releases, had triumphed, but Minh still couldn't return to Hue, and Vietnam was still divided. Yet Minh didn't want to stay one day longer in Paris and he was sure in any case that Thai didn't want to keep him in her delegation. He was anxious to go home, to live for a long time in a normal Vietnam, a Vietnam that defined for him his duties and responsibilities, a Vietnam whose city streets were filled with students and workers, its ricefields crowded with brave peasants, its markets overflowing with women chewing betel nuts. But when?

Like a first rain after a long drought, Loc's letter waited for him when he returned from the ceremony. The only one he had received from Loc in the four years he'd lived in France, it was short, even formal, but not lacking in tenderness. Loc told him that he "should return to Hanoi at the first opportunity" to work as an expert in the Ministry of Foreign Affairs' American Department. He added a P.S.: "The head of the department is an old friend of mine and I'm sure you'll like him too."

His long exile was over.

XIII

Red Cloth, Mirror Frame

Sad, idle, I think of my dead mother,
Her mouth chewing rice, her tongue removing fish bones.
The Red Cloth drapes the mirror frame:
Men of one country must love one another.

Vietnamese Folk Song
Translated by John Balaban

After four years in the City of Lights, Minh returned to Vietnam with nothing of value except a manuscript and a hand-written collection of twenty-seven poems entitled *Niet Ban May Phu, Nirvana Under a Cloud*. The poem he liked best was *Farewell*, dedicated to Jennifer. Often he recited it softly to himself to improve what he called "the soul of the musical undertones":

The orange fire in an illuminated
Heaven spilled your crimson on
the dark soil of the land of

the Blue Dragon,
The palpitating thirsty earth
accepted your monthly stream of
creation in a single quaff,
Your generous bequest melted into
the wandering streams
of the Truong Son mountains
and blended with the River of Perfume,
to nurture the orchids
now turned into gold
like your glowing hair
now turned pink
like your hesitant lips.

Yes, Jennifer, we are separated—
But you are united with my mother,
with my motherland.

One starry night,
contemplating Nirvana Under a Cloud
in a heaven no longer burned up by fire
In the earth no longer made bald
and darkened by defoliants,
I reverently offer my blood to
the running water
and join you and my, our, mother
in the Yellow Springs.

Together, we bid farewell
to the world of nothingness
the world of absolute reason
of packaged ideologies and
amateurish mad dictators
of existence without life and
resistance
of resistance with existence and life.

It will be then
our real Farewell
also
our everlasting Reunion.

Minh landed at Hanoi's Gia Lam Airport on Restoration of Spring Day, February 27. But there was no spring in the air. Although it had been snowing when he left Paris, he felt colder at the Vietnamese airport than he had there. An opaque drizzle carried threads of icy northern wind through his bones. The terminal was almost deserted except for the military personnel who managed it.

"Are you Professor Tran Van Minh?" a lieutenant at the immigration desk asked him.

"Yes, but my passport gives my name as Tran Van Thong."

"We're aware of that. You can reclaim your old name now that your overseas mission is over," the lieutenant said with confidence.

"I will be happy to."

The officer asked Minh to surrender his passport to another officer standing nearby and handed him an envelope. In it there was an order of assignment advising him to present himself to the Ministry of Foreign Affairs of the Democratic Republic of Vietnam the next day.

At the ministry Minh was greeted by the head of the American Department, Trieu Quoc Dan. He welcomed Minh with a broad smile.

"Comrade Loc has recommended you highly to our ministry and we're pleased to have you working with us as an expert. Your job will be to provide us with regular, objective surveys and analyses of the political situation in the United States, in particular the debates in, and the mood of, the U.S. Congress. As you know, thanks to the heroic struggle of our people, the farsighted leadership of the Party, and the inspiration of our beloved Ho Chi Minh, we have won the most glorious victory in our history. But despite the fact that the United States has been forced to sign an agreement to end the war, we suspect, based on our experiences since 1954, that the American ruling class will continue the war in some way. Our campaign to maintain and defend peace will be as hard, if not harder, than our struggle to drive the foreign aggressors out of our land. From now on, unless the U.S. dares to unleash another assault, our war is political and diplomatic. To win this new war, we of course first have to consolidate our national strength and unity. We also have to read their intentions precisely. The Congressional appropriations will provide us with the clearest guide to these intentions. Our American friends tell us that the mood in Congress as a whole is unfavorable to any increased assistance to Thieu and his administration, but we can't be sure, and we must be sure if we're to correctly decide policy and strategy. We're counting on your patriotism and your abilities to help us answer these questions. Comrade Loc has told us of your excellent credentials and your deep knowledge of U.S. politics. You'll start tomorrow. Your office is to the right of mine."

Dan stopped. "I'm sorry, I've talked too long. Do you have any questions?"

"No. Not at the moment. I shall try my best not to disappoint you and our friend Loc. Can I ask you where he is now and how I can see him?"

"I know you're eager to see him. He was here, a month ago, in this office, sitting in the chair you're in now. But he's returned to his duties in the temporarily controlled enemy areas. He's much esteemed by all of us. A model Party member. Did he tell you that last year he was awarded the Order of Hero of Labor by the Party and the government? I hope you can see him sometime in the near future, but I can't tell you when. I don't even know where he is exactly."

"I hope you understand and will forgive my indiscretion. We're very close friends."

"You've committed no indiscretion of any kind, no need to apologize," Dan said. "Your curiosity simply shows the depth of your feelings toward him. As Comrade First Secretary of the Party once said: 'We are not made of copper bones and steel skin. We're people with compassion, reason, and feeling.' Now, I'll take you to the director of personnel who'll give you all the details about your life here. We're still in a state of war, we're poor, but we share our poverty with the rest of the population. We shall rebuild our country ten times more beautiful, as Uncle Ho has commanded us to do."

The director of personnel, Truong Trung Nghia, was a man in his 60s who wore a large brown woolen scarf around his neck. He took off his glasses, put his pipe down on an ashtray made of aluminum from a B52, shook hands with Minh, coughed, and murmured, "Welcome to our ministry. We'll do our best to provide you with good working conditions."

"Thank you very much."

He pulled a thin notebook from his desk drawer. "Here's a ration card for all the necessities. They can be purchased at any state store: salt, pepper, fish sauce, rice, eggs, vegetables, pork in limited quantity, one chicken per month, cigarettes, tea, and one bottle of beer per day. If you have more money, you can buy other commodities for any amount in the open market. Of course it will cost you much more." He lit his pipe. "About your accommodations. I understand that you're unmarried and have no dependents. You'll be assigned an apartment in Block M of Minh Khai Flat in Hue Street."

"It was thoughtful of you to have found a place for me in a street named after my home town. I don't know Hanoi very well. I only visited the city briefly once in the 40s. Where is Hue Street? Is it near our ministry?"

"It's not very far, only three streets away. You're not far from the Museum of History, the Art Museum and the Museum of the Army. As for your apartment, you're lucky. The woman who lived there just left two days ago for further studies in the Soviet Union. She won't be back for five years. We're suffering from a housing shortage made more acute by the barbaric American bombing."

Nghia filled his pipe with a blackish tobacco. "This is very good tobacco," he commented. "A comrade who just returned from Bulgaria brought some for me. It burns slowly and leaves no bitter taste in your mouth." He sucked on the pipe, sighed, and continued, "As director of personnel, I'm also secretary to the Union of Intellectual Workers in this ministry. You'll find you'll have a number of obligations besides your work here."

"You see, *Anh* Minh, although the peace agreement is signed, the country is still in a state of war preparedness. We can never trust the

American capitalist ruling class; therefore vigilance is still the order of the day. You will be a member of the ministry anti-aircraft defense unit, you'll have military training three times a week after work, and you'll participate in the activities of the union, which meets at least once a week. For those who are party members, and I think you're not, not yet that is, the obligations are much heavier and there are more meetings to attend. Any questions?"

Minh shook his head.

"We'll let you have half of your monthly salary right away, the rest you'll get at the end of the month, of course. I hope this arrangement, an exception we made for you at the insistence of your friend, *Dong Chi* Loc, is satisfactory to you?"

"Yes, it is. I shall do my best to fulfill my obligations. Should I report to work tomorrow?"

"Yes. You know the office hours, I presume. They're the normal ones, eight to noon, with a break of two hours for siesta and lunch, and back again from two until six. If the bombing starts again, we'll have a different schedule." He stood up, went to a filing cabinet and pulled out a file.

"Here's a map to help you find Hue Street and learn the city. Show your assignment order to the secretary of your block and he'll give you the key to the apartment." He stretched out his hand. "Goodbye, and I'll see you tomorrow."

Minh left the Ministry of Foreign Affairs relieved and happy. For the first time in many years, there was order in his life. He knew what he would be doing. He felt freer, but it was a different kind of freedom: freedom from uncertainty, from personal worries, from the need to plan for survival. The first shock of his new life in the North was actually an absence of shock.

After walking for an hour along shadowy and badly maintained asphalt roads lined with bomb craters like holes on the face of the moon, he realized how quiet Hanoi was. The absence of noise at first was as annoying as the cacophony he had had to live with elsewhere: the monotonous noise of London, the vibrant noise of American cities, the hysterical noise of Saigon, the multi-pitched noise of Paris, the ghostly noise of the underground headquarters. He counted no more than a dozen cars and heavy machines on the streets. Thousands of bicycles silently cruised all over. He passed many young men and women in army uniform, but they looked unaggressive, like students on the eve of a tough examination. No one in the United States would have believed that these were the soldiers who had downed the U.S. planes listed on huge billboards along the boulevards: 3,891 since April 17, 1966, when Hanoi was first bombed, until the odious B52 bombing of Christmas 1972.

In Hue, Minh had had a nostalgic sense of history. In Hanoi, he witnessed history in the making. Hue had become the national capital only as the Vietnamese nation declined, and it had retained that status for fewer than one hundred years before the French conquered the country and left

Hue to bear a burden of shame and humiliation. But Hanoi had become *Thang Long*, the Ascending Dragon, ten centuries ago when the country triumphantly emerged as an independent state after one thousand years of Chinese domination. It grew as an optimistic nation prepared to move South and face the northern colossus. To move South and to resist the North were indeed the two prongs in the destiny of turbulent Vietnam.

.   .   .

Three months after his return to Hanoi, the latest-model Peugeot bicycle he had ordered in Paris with four years' savings finally arrived. It quickly became the envy of the block, where many owned less advanced bicycles, made either locally or in the People's Republic of China. His French model was cream-colored, four-speed, with white tires and an elegant shape. He could now organize his life around this new means of transportation. Hanoi wasn't a very big city, but public transportation wasn't adequate: old, tired trolleys left over from colonial times, a few buses on main thoroughfares. The real private-public transportation facility was the bicycle. As he had seen when he had come North along the Ho Chi Minh Trail, all available mechanized transportation was reserved entirely for the military.

On Sundays, the only day he was really free from all official and community duties, he visited each of the historical monuments in and around the city. When he exhausted these, within a year, he figured he would visit the areas at the border between China and Vietnam where the major ethnic minorities lived. But that had to wait.

He began his historical "self-education" by pedaling to the Restored Sword Lake. He sat on a bench and looked in the direction of the Jade Hill Temple, located on an islet in the lake. The temple was linked to the shore by the Sunshine Bridge. The lake was so named because, according to legend, the national hero, Le Loi, restored his sword to the Tortoise God after his victorious ten-year war against the Minh Chinese forces in the fifteenth century.

Minh spent a whole Sunday visiting the *Co Loa* Citadel, where there were the remains of a fortified construction with spiral-shaped walls built in the third century B.C. to serve as a capital for King An Duong Vuong, founder of one of the first Vietnamese dynasties. Of the nine spiral coils that had covered an area of more than five square kilometers, only three were left; in some places they were only about two meters high and fifteen meters wide.

At the center of the Citadel, among a number of valuable structures and sculptures, stood a temple dedicated to the King and his daughter, Princess My Chau. Her story had fascinated Minh since he was very young. Married to the handsome prince Trong Thuy, son of General Trieu Da of the Chinese Ch'in dynasty, she had betrayed her country: she revealed to her beloved husband, and therefore to the enemy, the Vietnamese secret for making a sacred brass arrow. Various versions of the story flourished; hundreds if not thousands of plays, poems, and folk songs had been written about her.

Minh remembered a heated discussion between his father and mother on the subject. His mother argued that the story of the princess' betrayal wasn't true and was circulated by cowardly men who lost an empire in 179 B.C. and blamed it all on a woman. His father beat a strategic retreat behind the smoke of a vague statement: "Truth is relative; life itself is relative and thus history is relative and betrayal is as relative as loyalty." At this his mother looked away, smiled gently, and asked his father if he wished to have tea. Minh secretly sided with his mother but he didn't dare offend his father by offering his opinion. He just asked if he could prepare the tea.

Never before had Minh felt so much a part of the Vietnam he was slowly discovering. The new sense of belonging revived his long-dormant creative urges. He devoted a great deal of time at night to writing, and he attended several meetings organized by the Association of Writers, where he recognized a number of famous literary figures of the late 1930s and 40s.

The most successful of these was Huy Can, who had become vice-minister of culture. But though Minh found them interesting, they were no longer exciting to him. They all lived under the shadow of the most formidable talent of the country, the poet laureate To Huu, an alternate member of the Politburo of the Vietnamese Communist Party. Minh knew by heart some of To Huu's early poems. As a high-school student in Hue during the late 1930s, To Huu, whose name then was Nguyen Kim Thanh, had written revolutionary verses that influenced a whole generation of Vietnamese. The French arrested him and sent him to a prison in the highlands. He later escaped, to emerge in 1945 as a prominent communist leader.

At one of these meetings, where most discussions concerned the role of writers and artists in the new period of reconstruction, Minh was impressed by the woman writer Nga Mien, author of a best-selling book that had sold 100,000 copies in its first three months, according to the government-owned National Distribution House. It was called *A Thousand Miles Across the Country*. The title was taken from the first line of a nationally famous song in the Sad South style, which told the story of a Vietnamese princess, Huyen Tran, who was forced by her father to marry the king of neighboring Champa in exchange for a large piece of territory that later became Hue and Quang Tri.

Minh had just finished reading Nga Mien's novel. It was full of fascinating details, with a definitely romantic touch. Yet they were all blurred and submerged by the omnipresent Party references, the "only valid source of strength, justice and comradeship," its hero believed. The

Party emerged in the book as the sole arbiter and dispenser of *Tình* and *Lý* to all characters, the bad as well as good.

At the end of the meeting Minh approached the author and introduced himself. He congratulated her on her book and invited her to a teahouse near the One Pillar Pagoda. He discovered that she had been with the Vietnam People's Army during the Tet offensive as a member of their cultural entertainment group. She told him that she was in the process of writing another story about the liberation of Hue, tentatively titled *The Perfume River Was Red*. She knew Minh was from Hue because of his accent; she herself had visited that city only briefly. She asked if he would read her book as soon as the first draft was finished and "add realism to my description of the former imperial capital." Minh agreed to help her.

During the conversation he asked her opinion about writers and artists in the temporarily controlled enemy areas.

"In general," she said, "most of them are idealistic, romantic and try to imitate the French existentialists. Some are outright reactionary and antisocialist. Practically all of them are pessimistic and squander words lamenting unhappy love affairs and unfulfilled dreams. Even so, they are dissatisfied with the Saigon government and dislike Americans. Probably their major weakness is a lack of historical and economic analysis in their philosophies. Like most bourgeois writers, they confuse cause with effect, executioner with victim." She finished her tea and continued. "To be fair, I must add that there are one or two good writers with progressive ideas such as Co Tung. I've read all his novels. They're very penetrating and poetical. But of course they're banned in Saigon. Some of these writers are in prison, some have gone to the liberated zones."

Minh was flattered that she had read his works but didn't reveal his identity. He walked her back to her apartment in Sinh Tu Street and said good night, hoping to see her again. He felt as if he were picking up the threads of his life—or at least of his creative life. But it was a new life. He had no ties now with the past. Jennifer was gone, he was separated from his family, and he had no idea of Loc's whereabouts. Paris was like a bad dream. Though he was home he was still alone, and still without purpose.

.   .   .

But as the months passed, Minh did get to know Nga Mien, and her family as well. She became like a younger sister, and the family treated him more and more like a relative. He even spent the three-day Tet holiday in 1974 with them.

Nga let him read several chapters of *The Perfume River Was Red*, and he was impressed. The title came from the conclusion of a poem about Hue by the Argentinian poet Enrique Molina, which had been translated from the Spanish in Literature Magazine, and which she often quoted:

> *Hue of stars that boil like a new constellation in the sky of hell*
> *Hue inviolate where the Perfume River turns slowly around the moon.*

Minh found Nga's work sensitive and perceptive but felt that her constant references, direct and indirect, to the inspirational power of the Party actually weakened both her writing and the image of the Party she wished to project. She strongly disagreed with him.

"Are you a Party member?" she asked.

"No, I'm not."

"It's difficult, if not impossible, for a nonparty member to understand the life and creativity the Party can bestow."

Minh never brought the subject up again.

．　　　．　　　．

Minh's office was increasingly active after the Tet holiday. A sense of urgency was developing, and Minh found himself attending more meetings. All the discussions and analysis revolved around the "21st Conference Party Central Resolution of October, 1973," and the "March, 1974, Central Military Commission Resolution," whose guiding slogans were, "Coordinate the political and military struggle with diplomacy," and, "If the enemy does not implement the Paris agreement and continues its Vietnamization—essentially a neocolonial war aimed at capturing the South—we have no choice but revolutionary destruction of the enemy and liberation of the South." Newspapers like the People's Daily, and the People's Army, printed accounts of daily violations of the peace agreement by the United States and Saigon. War preparations were evident everywhere. Younger officials in the ministry were recalled for active duty in various branches of the armed forces. New recruits, uneasy in their uniforms, walked in large numbers in the streets before they were transported at night in silent camouflaged trucks.

Minh worked into the night, reading the United States Congressional Record, analyzing news from American magazines and newspapers, charting the increase or decrease in the amount of United States economic and military aid to Saigon, measuring the dynamism of the antiwar movement in American colleges and universities, and following the development of the Watergate affair and its effect on the American public.

An already austere standard of living became more so. His rations had sharply decreased, but Minh felt content, accepting new sacrifices as part of the legitimate duty of a Vietnamese in his country's struggle for life and death.

One evening, two weeks before the Tet of the Year of the Cat in 1975, just as Minh was about to leave for home, he was urgently summoned to the office of his department chief. He opened the door—and stood stunned as Loc sprang out of his chair to embrace him.

"I'm glad to see you again, Minh!"

Minh could hardly speak. "Loc! It's been so long!"

Loc laughed. "Five years. And a lot has happened since then."

"But where have you been? No, I'm sorry, I shouldn't ask you that."

"It's all right, Minh. I've just been talking with comrade Trieu Quoc Dan here and he tells me that you've been doing a very good job, which is fully appreciated by the highest echelons of the Party and government. Your studies and analyses will have a most decisive effect on their decisions. In fact we believe that your conclusion that the United States will not re-enter the war if we attack Saigon is objective and correct."

"Indeed," nodded Dan. "But Loc, there'll be plenty of time to talk business. Now, may I invite both of you to dinner with me at a new restaurant on West Lake? It serves authentic Southern food."

"We'd be delighted, thank you," Loc and Minh said at the same time.

They walked quickly through the Reunification Park, an area reclaimed from swamps in 1955. It was still cold and the north wind gusted, but several couples nestled on park benches. When they crossed the park to a small street, Minh immediately noticed the restaurant's name: *Nam Tien*, March to the South.

"It's an appropriate name," Minh observed.

"It could happen very soon," Loc replied.

They were lucky. It was the day of the week when beef was available. They ordered a typical Southern dish of *Thit Bo Bay Mon*, beef in seven different styles. In less than an hour Loc and Dan, with immense appreciation, consumed what they called "mountains of fresh vegetables and hills of tender meat," and finished four big bottles of beer. Minh felt a little dizzy after only one glass of beer, but Loc and Dan remained perfectly sober and suggested that they return to the ministry.

Dan prepared tea in the deserted ministry's cafeteria. They sat at a round table near the kitchen.

"*Anh* Minh," Dan began the conversation, "I'm both happy and sad to let you know that tonight's dinner will be your last one in Hanoi for years."

"That's right, Minh," Loc chimed in. "In a few hours, you'll be marching South. Not really marching, you'll be riding in a not-too-uncomfortable car as part of the advance staff of the People's Army. The Party and the government have given us the honor of liberating the South and reunifying our country, an operation bearing the honorable name of Ho Chi Minh."

"I'm very happy to hear that," Minh said. "I hope my assessment of the U.S. intentions was correct and we won't need to spill too much blood in this operation." His voice rose in excitement. "Without American support, the demoralized Saigon army should collapse under the weight of its own corruption and disorganization like rotten fruit."

But even as he spoke Minh regretted his words. He remembered Loc's telling him how his half-brother Phong had fought so valiantly during the Tet offensive. The Saigon army is Vietnamese, too, he thought. Why did he repeat these thoughtless slogans so blindly?

"Are you marching South with me?" he asked Loc.

"I'd love to, but probably not."

Minh turned to Dan. "Can I go to my apartment to pick up my clothes?"

"I'm sorry, but you can't. You're leaving within a few hours, and secretly. We'll send someone to pick up what you need. What do you need most besides your clothes?"

"The books on the shelf and a folder of my writings on top of my bed."

"I'll be staying at your apartment for a few days before I return to my job," Loc told him. "That way I can contribute to the secrecy of the operation. Your neighbors won't be suspicious of your leaving town suddenly. When I leave, I'll let the executive secretary of your block know that you've been sent to study abroad for an indefinite period."

"I wish you were coming with me," Minh complained.

"We'll meet again when the South is liberated and we'll have a better, bigger southern dinner with Dan! But I have something to tell you. I had an opportunity to visit your father and stepmother secretly in Hue a few weeks ago."

"How are they? I've had no word from them in all these years."

"They're doing fine, and hope that they'll get to see you in the not-too-distant future. Your father is very proud of you. As for your brother, Phong's been promoted to lieutenant-colonel in command of a regiment in Quang Tri, and An is now a major general in charge of planning and operations for the general staff. As far as I know, they're both in good health. An's still the same incurable woman-chaser, but Phong's becoming more and more dedicated to his military duties. He's very ambitious and tells his friends that he wants to be the youngest general in the army, not because of his influence with his superiors or the Americans, but as the result of his own accomplishments on the battlefield."

Minh shuddered. What would this liberation of the South bring he wondered? Would the Saigon army resist? He pushed the thought of his half-brothers out of his mind.

He wanted to tell Loc of Jennifer's death. Loc couldn't have known about it, or he would by now have referred to it. But Minh hesitated. He didn't want to discuss something so emotional in front of Dan.

A driver in military uniform appeared at the office door.

"Comrade, we have an order to pick up a passenger from your department."

"He's right here," Dan said.

Both Loc and Dan shook hands with Minh, who followed the driver down to the quiet street.

There were other passengers in the car, all military officers. They greeted Minh with a nod of their heads as he got in. He sat in the front seat of the car, an old French Citroen that was still running well. The car followed a convoy of camouflaged covered trucks speeding out of the city in the dim light. Minh fell asleep quickly.

In the morning his fellow passengers invited him to follow them to the headquarters of division 968, located in a series of thatched houses along Highway One. He guessed he was somewhere in Ha Tinh Province, about 200 kilometers south of Hanoi. They were received by a general, a short, fat man with crew-cut gray hair. The general greeted Minh first.

"Professor Minh, we're pleased to have you with us. You'll be attached as a civilian expert to communications regiment 67 of division 968 of the Vietnam People's Army. At this moment, all you do is rest—our division won't move south until tonight, right after dinner. Your duty, when we reach our destination in the South, will be to monitor all broadcasts in foreign languages, English and French, and prepare a daily bulletin in Vietnamese for us. We know of your experience and we're counting on your patriotism to help us reach a quick victory."

The general turned to the three other officers, a colonel and two majors. "As for you, comrades, you can report to the logistics department in the next house to your left."

The general walked Minh to a hut about 100 meters from command headquarters. "You'll be a guest of this peasant family. You'll eat lunch and dinner with them. I'm sure they'll treat you well and feed you well. I suggest you take a nap for now. We'll probably travel a very rough road tonight."

.   .   .

Minh celebrated Tet somewhere in the jungles, under the forest pines of Dalat Hill in the western highlands of South Vietnam, with his communications group. About three thousand feet above sea level, the area was known for its moderate climate: sunny, dry days and cool nights. It was a welcome change after Hanoi's cold, humid weather. The sight and flavor of the pine trees elated him.

Minh fit into the rigorous military routine without much difficulty. When not monitoring news and writing bulletins, he daydreamed about the Ho Chi Minh Operation. It began on March 10th with a massive attack on

Banmethuot, the western highlands' major city. In less than 24 hours the city was liberated and so was the nearby town of Dalat, where his unit moved to set up an emergency listening post. On March 26th, Minh learned through an army news flash that his home town, Hue, was "completely liberated" and that "Saigon's puppet troops disintegrated without a fight after having looted a number of residences in the Citadel."

On April 30th the liberation armies marched into Saigon, their tanks smashing the front gate of Independence Palace, the South Vietnamese presidential residence. The skill of Hanoi's experienced divisions was like an unstoppable torrent that engulfed the enemy. By following the radio announcements, Minh could feel the powerful pulse of that historic torrent.

On the day that Saigon was liberated, Minh was drafting a summary of U.S. public opinion on the Ho Chi Minh campaign. The major in charge of Minh's unit told him excitedly, "Forget about it. We don't need to know what the Americans think about us anymore. We're the victors, they're the vanquished, and the vanquished have no voice." The major then informed him that all military personnel of his unit would move quickly to rejoin their division in Saigon, now Ho Chi Minh City. As for Minh, who wasn't a soldier, he would remain in Dalat and wait for further instructions.

After ten days of idleness and rest at the hotel Lake of Sighs, surrounded by a park of weeping willows, Minh was notified by the Dalat military management committee that he was to report to the Ho Chi Minh City military management committee for new duties no later than May 31st.

He arrived in Saigon on a crowded commercial bus that stopped often on the road to be checked by security personnel, most of them young women. When his bus entered Ben Thanh Central Market, Minh realized that he had no place to go. He didn't want to report to the management committee too soon. He bought a copy of the newspaper Liberation, at a newstand and discovered quickly that he didn't have any Saigon piasters, which were still in circulation, but only Democratic Republic of Vietnam currency. The vendor, an old woman, refused to accept the North Vietnamese money.

"I don't know what kind of money this is. You better get some real money, pre-liberation money."

Minh left without his newspaper. He didn't want to argue with her, knowing that revolution and reunification had not yet affected the former regime's financial institutions.

Ho Chi Minh City still had Saigon's chaotic and stinking traffic jams: cars of all sizes, Honda motorcycles, three-wheel cycles, buses, and military trucks, not only American ones but Russian and Chinese as well. The jumble was further aggravated by the disappearance of the regular traffic police. At various intersections, students with red armbands, holding cardboard disks reading STOP, directed the tumultuous flow of smoking machines in a most unprofessional manner. Minh wondered where all these cars got gasoline. He had learned a few days before that all gas stations had been closed by government order.

The only difference from pre-liberation days was the presence among the crowds of North Vietnamese soldiers in wrinkled green uniforms, baggy trousers, and colonial pith helmets. Women in groups of two and three, wearing black trousers and white or brown shirts, walked nonchalantly on the pavement, with AK47 rifles slung on their shoulders, their soft wide-brimmed hats fluttering in the breeze. They were the P.R.G. armed forces.

Minh followed Freedom Street, which had already been renamed *Dong Khoi*, General Uprising. It was crowded with improvised sidewalk cafes, many more of them than at any time in the past. He ordered a filtered coffee and reached for a pile of newspapers on a small table near the cashier. On the front page of a back issue of Liberation dated May 8, 1975, was a large picture of the members of the Ho Chi Minh City military management committee under the leadership of General Tran Van Tra. Minh hoped to see Loc's name listed under the picture, but it wasn't there. He looked more closely: Loc's smiling face was partly hidden behind the general, who was dressed in a Russian-style uniform with three stars on his collar tabs.

Minh paid with North Vietnamese money. The cashier looked at him for a minute and said, "You must not be aware of the government's recent decree making the old piaster the only legal currency. All the *Bo Doi* were ordered to change their currency into piasters. Did you sell something to the *Bo Doi*?"

"No, I didn't. I just got here this afternoon from the North."

"But you don't look like a cadre and your accent's not northern."

"I've only been in the North for the last few months."

"All right," the cashier conceded. "I know it's not legal, but I'll accept it. It's such a small amount."

It was amusing, Minh thought, that the people were calling the soldiers of the Vietnam People's Army of the North *Bo Doi*, which literally meant "military unit," and still used the words "Viet Cong," bestowed on all the communist fighters by the U.S. press, to designate the armed men and women of the South.

Most of the shops along Dong Khoi Street were closed or half empty. The long-famous Givral coffeehouse, the gossip mill of Saigon, was still in business but practically deserted. Revolutionary banners brightened the streets while portraits of the late President Ho Chi Minh were framed by the omnipresent inscription:

Nothing is more precious than independence and freedom.

The park between the Cathedral and Independence Palace, now the seat of the Ho Chi Minh City military management committee, looked like a huge open arsenal: anti-aircraft batteries, cannons covered with palm branches, Soviet tanks, Chinese trucks, American armored vehicles. Small circles of children and even adults formed around youthful *Bo Doi*, who politely answered all kinds of questions with ready-made phrases.

Minh approached a soldier standing guard in front of a Russian tank that blocked the front gate of Independence Palace. He pulled out his temporary identification card, which noted he was an "expert at the Hanoi Ministry of Foreign Affairs" and handed it to the soldier.

"I'm afraid, comrade, this can't be used here. It's valid only in the capital, I mean in Hanoi only."

Minh brought out another paper, a certificate stating that he was an "expert attached to unit A, communications regiment 67, division 968." This time the *Bo Doi* was visibly impressed. "Please, comrade, wait here for a minute," he said, and ran to a tent pitched in the middle of the palace front lawn.

In a moment a captain politely approached Minh. "Good evening, comrade. I was with division 968, too, and our division was the first to liberate Saigon. Where have you been for the last ten days?"

"I was waiting in Dalat until I got my orders to report to the Ho Chi Minh military management committee." Minh showed his papers to the captain.

"I don't think you need to present yourself today to the committee. You have until the end of the month to do so. But do you wish to see anyone in particular?"

"Yes, I'd like to see a good friend of mine. Brother, I mean comrade Loc, comrade Le Duc Loc," Minh stammered.

"Please wait, I'll check inside."

In a few moments he returned. "Professor Minh, I've checked with the security officer of the committee. I'm sorry to tell you that your friend left yesterday on an overseas mission to Paris. But he left a letter for you. Here it is."

Minh put the letter in his pocket. It looked thick and personal.

The captain continued, "We've made arrangements for you to stay temporarily at the Old Majestic Hotel, now called Reunification Hotel, with the other cadres and experts until comrade Loc's return. Take this note to the secretary of the hotel's management committee and everything will be fine. You know how to get there, I'm sure. It's just six blocks away. The hotel's on General Uprising Street."

"Thank you, captain. I know where it is."

·   ·   ·

The Majestic Hotel, favored by foreign visitors in pre-liberation days because of its central location and proximity to the Saigon River, was now government-owned and managed. The new management had taken away all the air-conditioners and replaced them with ceiling fans. Many cadres coming from the North were unaccustomed to air-conditioned rooms. They lost sleep and were stricken with severe colds. When Minh checked in, he was told that he would share the room "with comrade Loc who's now on a mission overseas."

"So much the better," Minh said cheerfully to the secretary.

Even with the ceiling fan at maximum speed, the room was hot and humid. He decided not to join the others in the collective dining room where dinner was being served, as the secretary had suggested. He went instead to his room, took a shower, and read Loc's letter.

Ho Chi Minh City, May 10, 1975

My dear Minh,

First, I'd like to apologize for the inefficiency of the Dalat military management committee, which should have sent you to Ho Chi Minh City immediately after the liberation of Saigon. I also regret that I've had to go on an unexpected mission and won't be in the city when you arrive. I'll be away no more than a month, I hope. In the meantime, please see, as soon as you can, (although officially you still have until the end of the month to do so), comrade Ha Sinh Chau in the foreign affairs section of the committee. His office is at the old Ministry of Foreign Affairs at Alexandre de Rhodes Street. I'm sure you know the place. I'm the head of the section, but in my absence comrade Chau will be in charge. He'll give you your assignment.

Now, concerning some private matters that will be painful for you. After the liberation of Hue (March 26), I rushed to our city from Quang Tri to assist in setting up the Hue military management committee. Although I was very busy, one of my first acts was to visit your parents. As the city was then still not quite secure (some mad soldiers, saboteurs, gangsters and hooligans were still roaming the roads), I asked an officer in our army security to escort me. When I mentioned your family's address, the expression on his face changed. He told me that just a few hours before, he had gone there to investigate a hideous crime committed the day before by a group of retreating soldiers. They had looted a number of houses in the Citadel, including your parents' home. When our officer got there, your father and stepmother were both lying dead on the floor. All their belongings had disappeared. The library was ransacked, nothing valuable was left. I cried when I saw the devastation. As it was impossible for me to contact you, I didn't know exactly where you were at the time, I immediately arranged a dignified burial for your parents. Members of Hue's military management committee and I attended, and followed their coffins to their final resting place in a field near Imperial Hill. I know how painful this news will be to you and I sincerely wish that I were by your side to offer you my condolences.

Your half-brother Phong, according to the reports I got when I was in Quang Tri before leaving for Hue, was killed by his own soldiers and thrown into the Ben Hai River. He had forced his demoralized troops into the mountains to continue resisting the liberation armies. They refused.

An presented himself to the Ho Chi Minh City military management committee and is now being sent to a re-education camp in the North. It will be good for him, I think. Your uncle, the Rector, and his family left town a week before liberation. He chartered a plane which flew him, his wife, daughters, and two servants to France.

Obviously, this is not happy news for you, but I'm sure you have the courage to overcome your sufferings, submerge them under the joy of national liberation. If you wish to visit your parents' tombs in Hue, please wait until I return and I shall help you. Before I left I made arrangements for you to stay in my room temporarily at the Majestic. Just now, I think you need some time to yourself. Until my return,

Affectionately,
Loc

XIV

Ten Times More Beautiful

Our mountains, our rivers, our people will always be;
the American invaders defeated,
we will rebuild our land ten times more beautiful.

Ho Chi Minh
1890–1969
Testament

Lying in bed, desolate, his eyes following the slow murmuring revolution of the ceiling fan, Minh could not cry. His throat and eyes were dry. Perhaps there were no tears left after Paris; his relationship with his father, always correct, always conforming to reason, perhaps had been lacking in deep feeling. His relations with Phong and An had been superficial and he had hardly known his stepmother, although he admired and liked her. Maybe there was no "water quality" in his relationships with males, with the exception of Loc. He thought of the Buddhist precept that nothing is permanent, that life, birth, old age, sickness, and death are successive and continuing stages in the eternal moving wheel of existence. But he rejected the Buddhist easy way out. He wanted very much to exist, and witness the rebirth of his Vietnam.

Thinking of his father, Minh mused, "Mother now has a companion in the Yellow Springs, but she has never been lacking in companions, she created them, and besides, she has had Jennifer with her."

He dressed and went down to the lobby. He wanted to walk in the garden in front of the hotel, but the security guard reminded him that curfew time, until the next week, was still eight o'clock. He returned to his room, re-read Loc's letter, and put it in the file containing his collection of poems.

Minh was awakened at six by stirring revolutionary music broadcast over a loudspeaker attached to a tree behind the hotel. He had noticed earlier the day before that loudspeakers were set up in most of the squares and street crossings. The hotel's guests went out to the front garden for their morning calisthenics. Minh followed them. The physical exercises tired him a bit, but he felt invigorated after taking a cool shower.

He ate breakfast in the collective dining hall where everyone was smiling at everybody else. Minh had noticed in Hanoi, and now here, that everyone wore a ready but silent smile. In America most people just grinned and said "hi."

After breakfast he walked to the Ministry of Foreign Affairs. Some *Bo Doi* in their white undershirts were still running through the streets. He passed the former National Assembly which, during the French occupation, had been the Opera House. In front of the National Assembly the Monument of the Unknown Soldier, the landmark of the last Saigon military regime, had been demolished. The concrete head of the soldier still lay at the foot of the pedestal, unnoticed by passersby. It was the first visible sign that the old regime had been guillotined and was definitely dead.

The ministry hadn't changed much, except for the new flag of the Provisional Revolutionary Government of South Vietnam, a big picture of Ho Chi Minh in the reception room, and the casual way people dressed for work. Before liberation, everyone from the Foreign Minister down to the janitor had worn a suit and tie, usually black. Today, everyone wore khaki pants and white shirts.

Ha Sinh Chau's office was in what Minh recognized as the former bureau of the Secretary General of Foreign Affairs, the number three man in the ministry after the minister and his chef de cabinet. Chau took off his plastic-rimmed reading glasses and shook Minh's hand with both of his.

"I didn't expect you to arrive so soon. I understood that your assignment order wouldn't take effect until the first of June. But you're welcome and I'm glad to see you. I've read your books and poems, so I feel as if I know you already, and of course comrade Loc talks highly of you."

"I'm very grateful for your kind words about me," Minh said, admiring Chau's smooth face, alert eyes, and well-drawn mouth.

"We'll have time to talk more about what we have in common, but as long as you're here let me give you a few details about our duties. To start with, this isn't, in the regular sense, the P.R.G. Ministry of Foreign Affairs, although a lot of people call it that. Officially, it's Section K-Four of the Ho Chi Minh City military management committee, headed by comrade General Tran Van Tra. Our section is in charge of relations between the committee and foreigners, that is, anyone not of Vietnamese nationality. The head of our section is, as you know, comrade Loc, and I'm his assistant. Before he left on his mission overseas, he and I had some preliminary discussions about your responsibilities. He suggested that you should continue your study and analysis of American affairs. I was told you were correct in your assessment of America's probable position before the Party decided on the launching of the victorious Ho Chi Minh campaign. We need the same kind of assessment again. We want to forget about the past and have good relations with the United States. Anyway, we can wait for comrade Loc's return for a definite decision. In the meantime, until the end of the month, you can come here as often as you wish. Your office will be next to mine. You might want to look at the Ministry's library and see if there's any valuable material we should preserve."

"I shall come regularly to work starting tomorrow. Remember, we should eat half as much and work twice as much, to carry Uncle Ho's mission to completion. This morning I had a good breakfast but I've not done twice as much work. As a matter of fact, I've done nothing," Minh said half seriously, recalling the slogan he had seen on the young soldier's helmet in front of Independence Palace.

"You're right," Chau replied with a smile, "we have a lot of work to do. I went to Ca Mau last Sunday and I was impressed by the vast land and the limitless resources we have, but we've suffered, and continue to suffer, extensive devastation from the American style of warfare. While I was there, two farmers were killed when a supposedly dead bomb exploded as they tilled their abandoned land." He took a pot and cup from a stool in a corner of his room and poured tea for Minh.

"I was in prison from 1966 until just recently, you know, and that's where I learned of your work."

"How was that?" Minh asked.

"Well, when I was arrested I was chairman of the Committee of Academics for Peace and the Withdrawal of U.S. Troops. I had met comrade Loc five years before that when I taught mathematics at Saigon University right after my return from Paris. After my arrest, the committee was disbanded but a few of my friends, including Loc, reorganized it into the Association of Intellectual Workers for Liberation. Although I was still in prison, I was informed regularly of the activities going on outside. Then during Tet of this year, I was transferred to another prison in Bien Hoa, where I met a writer, the novelist Pham Toan, who told me that he knew of you and admired your work."

"How?" Minh interrupted.

"According to him, one day in 1967, while he was in prison, he met the writer Long Van. He told Pham Toan that he had met you before he was arrested."

"Yes, I met Long Van. We spent some time together, but after his arrest I couldn't locate him. I was told rather cynically that he had become what they called a 'lost file.'"

"It was true. A good source informed me that they shot him one week after his arrest."

Minh bowed his head, silent for a moment. "What a good writer, what a harmless person he was, and what a crime they committed by killing him. I had an intuition that he would be eliminated. Fascist governments like the Thieu administration are afraid of ideas."

Chau poured more tea. "To be worthy of the sacrifices of men like Long Van, we should try our best to rebuild a Vietnam 'ten times more beautiful,' as Uncle Ho urged us. A Vietnam not only economically prosperous but culturally progressive."

"Yes, we must," Minh said in a determined voice. "Were you released after liberation?"

"No. Pham Toan and I escaped from Bien Hoa prison in February, a few days after Tet. He bribed the guard. During Tet, his wife visited him and secretly brought three hundred dollars in U.S. money with her, which he gave to the guard to close his eyes during our escape."

"Where is Pham Toan now? I don't know him personally, but I've read his fiction, especially *The Bald-Headed Mountain*. Also, as you might know, we were linked together by reputation in the 1960s."

"He died two days before the liberation of Saigon in a stupid accident."

"What happened?"

"His bicycle was overrun by a U.S. army truck carrying a full load of whiskey. The truck tried to avoid him but overturned, and Toan died with two American soldiers, under a pile of broken whiskey bottles. It was ironic. When he was alive he always said that he hated only two things, American soldiers and whiskey. He drank only Vietnamese beer. I felt guilty about his death."

"Why?"

"Like me, he was a liaison-cadre for the Party's underground, working on the approaching campaign for liberation. He replaced me on that day's mission. I had been called at the last minute to an urgent cell meeting.

A comrade had prematurely killed a policeman and exposed the existence of the cell."

"So much wasted life in our country," Minh sighed.

"Indeed. Perhaps you're interested in knowing what happened to those in the association of intellectuals?"

"Of course. I was going to ask you."

"Now, let me see. Pham Ngoc Lam was arrested in 1970 and released after liberation. So were Ngo Duc Hoa and Le Minh Thuy."

"I'm glad to hear that. They're good friends of mine. I knew Dr. Hoa in the States."

"I didn't know that. He's very much respected because of his dedication, particularly his work with the poor."

"I remember once at Lam's house meeting the Dean of Saigon's Law School, a violent anticommunist. What's his name?"

"Cung Dinh Chuong. He became Minister of Justice under the puppet government. He was a bad man, a traitor in fact; he'd been working for the C.I.A. since his student days in America. He left the country. It was best, I suppose, though I would have liked to have seen him spend a few years in a re-education center."

Chau stopped talking and poured some tea for himself. He continued. "Before I forget, there's a meeting this Sunday of the Committee for the Eradication of American Decadent Imperialist Culture, at the former Cercle Sportif, now the Workers Club. I'm vice-chairman. You're welcome to attend. It's a limited, preliminary meeting, our first. The chairwoman is Madame Ngo Ba Thanh, a lawyer, a professor who was active in the open antiwar movement in Saigon. You probably know her."

"I know of her. She's well known internationally, but I've never met her. Anyway, I'm pleased to see a woman leading such a committee: victims of decadent cultures, imperialist or not, American or Asian, are usually women. We have a perfect example in our literary heroine, Thuy Kieu."

"I agree."

"How many will be at the meeting?"

"Ten. As I said, it's preliminary. What we plan is to clearly outline our objectives. We'd like to define exactly what we mean when we say to the masses, 'decadent,' 'American imperialism,' and 'culture.' Also, we need to decide how far we should go in eradicating that culture without generating a 'hate America' campaign. Also, how deep has that culture penetrated the masses or did it only touch the privileged in the cities? We'd like to assess the difference between the traditional and the emerging socialist cultures of Vietnam, what we should reject and what we should retain from our cultural past, which contains both the progressive elements of popular culture and the reactionary aspects of feudalistic culture. A very complicated task indeed! After the preliminary session, if we can come to some conclusions, we'll arrange a discussion of these topics by a few members of the committee for a special television program."

"I'm surprised we kept the television," Minh interrupted.

"Why not? TV is a powerful, efficient means of communication."

"I don't think so," Minh replied curtly. "I don't think we need it. I also don't believe anybody in the *world* needs it. TV's neither a means of communication nor an efficient one. It's a powerful method of conveying fragmented facts and dissipating illusions."

"It's that way," Chau retorted vehemently, "because it's in the hands of capitalist corporations who use it for making money, advertising, and mindless entertainment. Our TV will be different. It's government-owned. The content of our programs will be historical and progressively Vietnamese."

"Well, even in European countries where TV is government-owned, the disastrous effect of it on the population, especially on children and old people, is not much different from that in the U.S. Besides, to eradicate a decadent capitalist-imperialist culture by using the heart and pillar of that culture's communications medium is, to me, a blatant contradiction. There's a small group of communications researchers in the States who actually propose the elimination of TV altogether."

"And you agree with them?" Chau asked sharply. He sounded a little annoyed.

"Yes, I tend to."

"I don't. That's a form of extreme leftism. TV exists in socialist nations such as the Soviet Union and Cuba and it doesn't hamper the development of socialism in those countries."

Unwilling to antagonize Chau during their first meeting, Minh softened his words.

"I may be wrong. I need to study the subject more."

"You should. And if you come to some scientific conclusions, instead of idealistic opinions, please write a study for us. But remember, we're for progress, for the advancement of science and technology to be used by the masses, for the masses."

"I shall remember that," Minh said. He stood and shook hands with Chau.

"By the way," Chau said, "there are a few events coming up that I'd like you to make a note of, as they're central to our national activities. This weekend there'll be victory celebrations followed by the eighty-fifth birthday anniversary of Uncle Ho on May nineteenth. June sixth is the anniversary of the formation of the P.R.G. During the next twelve months we'll all be busy with the campaign for the country's reunification and the election of a National Assembly for the reunified homeland."

Minh was startled. For years he had repeated to the international public, and believed, that the reunification would take place over a period of years, step by step. When had the decision been reached to accomplish it within a year?

He shook hands with Chau. "Goodbye, *Anh* Chau. I'll see you tomorrow. I don't think I'll be able to make your committee meeting Sunday, but please let me know of any conclusions you reach."

"I will. See you soon."

Minh spent the rest of the day walking all over the city to familiarize himself with the deceptively disorderly transformation of Saigon into Ho Chi Minh City. On Le Thanh Ton Street, in front of the old city hall, an old French building with a baroque style stucco facade, he still saw shoeshine boys waiting in vain for clients; many people now wore sandals. Beggars still pursued everyone. Nearby, a unit of volunteer youth were sweeping the streets. Revolutionary and socialist governments in all countries had one thing in common, Minh thought: clean streets. A symbolic gesture, perhaps. In early 1958, while he was in Rangoon, a group of senior army officers had seized power from the government of Buddhist Prime Minister, U Nu. The first act of the regime, which declared itself socialist, was to mobilize young people to sweep streets. "Bourgeois democracy means having dirty streets," one officer was quoted as saying at the time.

At a square off Hong Bang, the wide boulevard leading to Cho Lon, Saigon's Chinatown, Minh stopped next to a huge thieves market, an "open sky market," the Vietnamese called it. It was a kind of U.S. people's drug-store, without walls or roof. *Bo Doi* in long lines were eagerly buying luxury goods made in the U.S.A. and Japan: watches, TVs, stereos, fans, air-conditioners, airline plastic bags, scattered back copies of Playboy and Penthouse magazines. He had seen similar, but much smaller markets in other parts of the city, and he wondered if these heroic, innocent-looking, clumsy North Vietnamese soldiers wouldn't soon be corrupted by these luxury goods.

On his way back to the hotel, he passed Maxim's, once the rendez-vous of the rich and powerful, of diplomats and spies. It was now a police station. Noticing a commotion, he stopped and asked a woman holding a rifle, "What happened, sister?"

"We just arrested a team of hooligans. They're part of a roving band of bandits who assassinate *Boi Doi* to get their uniforms and use them to terrorize people, destroying the good name of the revolution. Some of them are rapists and carry out their crimes in broad daylight."

"What are you going to do with them?"

"The people will decide their fate. There will be a public trial in the next day or so. If the crimes they confess are serious, they'll be shot on the spot. If not, the perpetrators will be sent for re-education. The revolutionary government is always generous and magnanimous, but it has to deal with bad elements like rapists, hooligans, and obstinate elements, in a drastic way. Three days ago, the people in Khanh Hoi passed the death sentence on a young man who raped a sixty-year-old woman. He dared to wear a shirt bearing a picture of Uncle Ho. Can you believe it?"

"It's terrible, hard to believe. By the way, who are these obstinate elements?"

"Those among the puppets who refuse to present themselves for registration, who evade the population census and circulate harmful rumors."

"Have any of them been shot?"

"No. We don't shoot them. We only shoot criminals. We send them for long periods of re-education. To the North."

"Why not send them to prison?"

"Prisons are colonial and imperialist institutions. We don't have them. We have re-education centers."

.   .   .

Turning uptown, Minh headed for the Huong Giang Hermitage coffeehouse. But when he reached it the front door was closed. He rang the bell and an old man showed his wrinkled face.

"I'm looking for Madame Luu, the owner," Minh politely inquired.

"She's out of town for some time. She went to Hue," the old man answered in a voice broken by a persistent cough.

"Thank you very much, uncle."

The nearby Kim Phuong restaurant was also closed. A handwritten sign on the front door read: "Property of the people. Owner fleeing the country without the government's permission." Minh chuckled at the terrible logic used in the sign. How could a person flee the country and ask the government's permission?

A voice called to him from the next block. Turning, he saw a figure running toward him.

"Have you forgotten me, *Anh* Minh?" he shouted. "It's Pham Ngoc Lam!"

"Lam! I was talking about you only this morning at the Ministry of Foreign Affairs. Ha Sinh Chau told me you were arrested and released after the liberation."

"Yes. I was arrested in 1970 with the others. But that's the past, and it's over. When did you arrive? I haven't heard about you at all since 1967. I was told you joined the liberated areas."

"That too, is the past," Minh joked.

"Are you doing anything tonight? I'd like to invite you home to have dinner with us. Your old classmate Dr. Hoa will be there. And did you know I'm married again? I married Le Minh Thuy. You met her, I think, when you were last in Saigon."

"Congratulations! Of course I remember her! When did this happen?"

"In May 1969, exactly one year before both of us were arrested."

"Didn't you have children from your first marriage? Where are they now?"

"They're with us."

"Where do you live?"

"The same place, behind Gia Long College for Women on Duy Tan Street. Let's get in my car. It's parked over there. We may be a little late. At the last minute I decided to buy a bottle of French wine on the black market."

"I'm surprised to see so many cars still on the streets since the government closed all the gas stations."

"This is one thing that neither the revolution nor the liberation has changed yet in Saigon. There's a black market for everything, from French wines to Japanese stereos. As they say: 'In Saigon, if you have money, you can even buy fairies from heaven.'"

Lam stopped to look for his keys in his pocket. "I'd say that as long as Cho Lon exists, the black market will exist, and corruption prevail. But I don't buy gasoline on the black market. These are the last three liters left in my car. Wait until the end of the month. Private cars, unless they're needed by people with some important responsibility, like doctors or cadres, will be surrendered to the government. I intend to do so. We don't need a car. I'll buy bicycles for my wife and me."

"How is Minh Thuy? Is she still a painter?"

"She's well. Very busy now, but not as an artist. She's one of the founders and the secretary of the Association of Former Political Prisoners. At the moment she's organizing an exhibit at the Cercle Hippique, which is now the Old Workers Recuperation Club."

"I can't wait to see her. Let's go." For the first time in years Minh would find himself in the company of old friends.

.   .   .

"Who's with you in the car?" Le Minh Thuy shouted from the porch.

"A bourgeois puppet I just captured in the street and brought home for re-education!"

"Don't joke. You're late. *Anh* Hoa's already here."

Minh and Lam walked into the living room. Hoa recognized Minh immediately.

"What a happy surprise! How come a hero like yourself is returning so quietly without a welcoming parade from the citizens?" Hoa exclaimed, hugging Minh.

"I'm no hero. I didn't even have the honor of being arrested, as you were."

Le Minh Thuy rushed from the kitchen. "Professor Minh!" she cried. "After all these years!"

"Congratulations," Minh said, kissing her on both cheeks.

"For what?"

"For being Madame Pham Ngoc Lam."

"But where have you been, Minh?" Hoa asked. "How is your family?"

"My family—I just heard yesterday that my father and my stepmother were killed in the liberation of Hue, one of my brothers is dead . . ." He stopped. "Let's not talk about the past. Everyone has tragedies and losses to tell of. Let's talk about the future, about what we can do for the reconstruction of our country."

"Yes," Le Minh Thuy agreed. "Revolution means anger at the oppressive past and hope for a liberated happy future. Tonight we have a happy reunion, so let's forget our anger and loss and talk about our dreams for a better life for all Vietnamese."

"What about this exhibit you're organizing?" Minh asked.

"It's exclusively for the artists who lived and worked in the liberated zones and who followed the liberation armies as cultural cadres, not for reactionary bourgeois abstract painters like myself."

"But you're not reactionary, you're not even bourgeois," Minh protested.

"Just a joke," she answered. "Some paintings are being flown in from Hanoi. I met an artist this morning who's also a major in the Vietnam People's Army. I wanted to sound out his reaction to abstract painting."

"What did he say?" Hoa inquired.

"He said bluntly, that 'it's a bourgeois, reactionary concept.' He believes that art must serve the people, and that people and their needs are not abstractions, but realities. I asked him what he thought of Picasso and he said he didn't care much for him."

"I'm not a Picasso fan either," Minh interceded, trying to change the subject from abstract art, which might upset her. "What about your work with the Organization of Former Political Prisoners?"

"That's the most important and difficult work I'm engaged in now. I've decided to give it my full attention. Art can wait, ex-political prisoners cannot."

"You're right," Hoa said. "It's an urgent problem and Minh will be pleased to know that I'm helping *Chi* Thuy in the organization. Our major task is to re-establish not only the physical health but mainly the *mental* health of those who've spent their lives in the most inhumane prisons. Many of them are broken, psychologically mutilated people, especially those who were incarcerated in the notorious 'tiger cages' on Con Son Island. Not that their physical treatment was worse than it might have been in the other penitentiaries, but their sense of isolation was more acute and that really destroyed them."

Minh smiled in agreement, remembering his sense of isolation in Paris when he had been driven to try to communicate with Thai.

"What are you smiling about?" Lam asked.

"Nothing. I'm just dreaming a little bit because of the good wine and fried fish. I saw myself riding a blue buffalo across the golden ricefields of Can Tho, your home province."

They all laughed, but Minh doubted if anyone had recognized his allusion to Lao Tsu riding his buffalo.

Hoa continued, "It's interesting to note that those political prisoners who were members of the party before being detained and those who were secretly organized by the party while in jail came out mentally stronger than the others, though they were physically weaker. They have a clearer vision of the future and a deeper sense of commitment and attachment to society. Our work will take a long time, but we'll succeed." He paused to light a cigarette.

"Prostitutes are another example of the value of commitment," he continued, "I just talked with a colleague who's working in the Committee for the Reform of Prostitutes, five hundred thousand of them mind you. He was very optimistic. Believes the problem will be resolved within a year."

"I don't understand," Lam said. "What's the connection?"

"He's convinced that women have a much stronger sense of commitment and attachment than men, and a greater capacity for daydreaming. And daydreaming, if not excessive, like Minh's," he smiled at Minh, "is healthy. He also argues that prostitution is exploitation and degradation by society, not isolation from it."

"Very interesting," Minh Thuy commented. "We must invite your colleague to come and meet with us."

"I already have," Hoa responded quickly.

Minh turned to Lam, "You seem to have been well fed in prison. You must have gained a few kilos since I saw you eight years ago. What are you going to do with this new weight?"

"I gained one kilo a day after I was released. I lost one a day while I was incarcerated. Anyway, I'm going to use my extra weight to serve on various committees and organize our scientific and technological curricula. Next week, Professor Tran Dai Nghia of the State Committee for Science and Technology in Hanoi will be visiting us. As you might know, the general policy of the Party and the government is to carry out a triple revolution: in productivity to develop a socialist economic structure, in culture and ideology to create a new socialist man and woman, and in technology and science to catch up with modern advances. This last one has the highest priority, because if it fails, the other two will collapse. I hope to be able to continue my contacts with M.I.T., receive some scientific publications and carry out scientific exchanges, but of course that depends on our future relations with the United States."

"Your field is nuclear physics, right?" Hoa asked.

"Yes. We're looking at all sources of energy, including nuclear."

Minh Thuy looked at Minh. "And you, *Anh* Minh, what are you doing now?"

"I'm temporarily with section four of the Ho Chi Minh City military management committee."

"What's section four's responsibility?"

"External relations."

"Interesting. You should be able to help my husband develop good relations with M.I.T. and other American universities."

"I don't know yet. I begin working tomorrow," Minh said, looking at his watch. "Oh, this is terrible. It's ten o'clock already. The curfew began at eight, right?"

"Yes," Lam answered. "Where do you live? I forgot to ask you when we met on the street."

"At the former Majestic Hotel."

"You must be a very important cadre," Thuy remarked. "That's a collective for the highest cadres from Hanoi. The middle-level cadres stay at the old Continental."

"No, no," Minh refuted. "I was put there temporarily in a room occupied by an old friend who's head of section four away on an overseas mission."

"Who is he?" Lam asked.

"Le Duc Loc. Have you ever met him?"

"I remember meeting him once in the late '60s. I saw him from a distance recently when the military management committee introduced itself to the public on May seventh. He stood behind General Tran Van Tra. Both were smiling constantly like two lotus in bloom."

Hoa, laughing at the comparison, said, "Minh, don't worry. I can take you back. I have a special pass for my car because I'm a medical doctor. But we should be going. Tomorrow we have more work, more meetings and more committees."

"*Anh* Minh," Minh Thuy inquired, "did you say that you're temporarily at the Majestic?"

"Yes. Why do you ask, sister?"

"I think you should move in with us." She turned to her husband. "Right, Lam?"

"I was thinking of that too," Lam said, putting his hand on Minh's shoulder. "You're most welcome here. Our house isn't very big, but we have an extra room looking into the garden. You can move in any time."

Minh was speechless.

"We and our children will be happy to have you," Lam reiterated. "It's better than a hotel, even a collective one."

"I would love to come," Minh said at last. "You don't know what this means to me—I've been alone for more than six years."

"Good," Lam said, "it's settled. Come as soon as you can."

"I'll move in sometime in the next couple of days. Thank you, Lam, Minh Thuy."

XV

Wind and Dust

If you don't wander, can you taste of life?
Beneath the dust lies hidden your proud face.
How mean and wayward, He who made the world!
You want high deeds, yet He holds you down.

Wind and Dust
Cao Ba Quat
1809–1853
Translated by Huynh Sanh Thong

Loc returned at the end of June on a muggy Sunday afternoon. He sent word that he would like to meet Minh at a new restaurant called Unity, for dinner that evening. The restaurant served uniformly priced meals and was owned and managed by the Workers Club. The large brick house had once been the property of a wealthy Chinese importer of American movies, who left the country for Hong Kong in April, 1975.

Loc was late. "I'm very sorry, Minh," he apologized. "As soon as I returned, I went to report to Chairman General Tran Van Tra, and he was delayed. I felt bad about not being in town when you came down from Dalat and also that I had to tell you the sad news about your family in a letter."

"I understand, Loc. I'm very happy to see you, and better late than never. All the bad news belongs to the past. We must talk about the present now and work together for the future. The whole population is ready to make new sacrifices for the reconstruction of our homeland."

"You have a correct attitude, which reassures me. How's your work at section four?"

"It's all right. Chau is a very good man, but I don't seem to have enough work to fully occupy myself. The U.S. has said that after April it will leave Vietnam behind and let the dust settle in Indochina, and there's little interest in Vietnam among the tired and fragmented American antiwar activists of the '60s. But I keep busy with other things. I moved in with Pham Ngoc Lam and his wife Le Minh Thuy, and two days ago I volunteered to teach evening courses for the anti-illiteracy campaign."

"I'm glad. It was wise of you to move out of the hotel. I know you need a lot of human affection and our comrades at the hotel are too busy for such things."

As they talked, a waiter put a tray in front of each of them, set with one large bowl of rice, a small cup of water, beef soup, and half a fried fish. Loc paid the waiter and thanked him. They finished their dinner quickly and walked outside in the direction of the Saigon River for some fresh air.

"Minh," Loc said in a serious voice, "I'd like you to know that I've recently been made a member of the central committee of the Party and assigned to the central committee's Foreign Affairs Commission. Its secretary is comrade Xuan Thuy, whom I'm sure you met during the Paris peace talks. This is a great honor for me and a much heavier responsibility."

"Congratulations," Minh said, shaking Loc's hand. "Yes, I know of Mr. Xuan Thuy, but as a poet, not a negotiator. I was with the N.L.F. and P.R.G. delegation you remember. We had little to do with the real negotiations."

Minh's voice was bitter. Loc changed the subject.

"Thanks for your congratulations, but the reason I mention it is to bring up something else more important. I've been thinking for some time now, especially since that time I saw you at the underground hospital years ago, that some day you should apply for membership in the Party. In my new position, I could introduce you with much greater authority. According to the new statutes, the probation period will be four years instead of three, after which you become a full-fledged member. But given your contributions to the revolution in the past, I can petition to have your probation shortened to two years. You don't need to answer me right away, but think about it. It will be the most important decision of your life."

"I'll think about it, but can I ask you now why you think I should join?"

"You know we're very good and close friends," Loc began.

"I've no doubt about that. I'll always be grateful for all you've done for me. Now that my parents are dead, you're the closest human being on earth to me."

"But we're not comrades," Loc continued, "and that's a very real and important difference. Friendship is a legitimate, beautiful feeling, but it's personal and limited. When you join the Party, or to put it more correctly, when the Party accepts you, we will become comrades. Essentially, it means we'll be friends in both a personal and a collective way, on national and international levels. Looking at it another way, and realizing full well your dedication to the country and our people, you can really serve the masses only through the Party. The Party is the mother of our feelings, *Tinh*, the father of our reason, *Ly*, and it's the family that serves all our needs, material and political. Outside of the Party, you don't really belong to our struggle. Within it, you're a part of the great social and political, as well as moral and intellectual, movement that is changing the world, bringing humanity to a higher stage of civilization. As a communist, you'll be a soldier in the heroic army which is defeating all the forces of injustice, inequality, exploitation, and degradation. Of course, as a soldier, you'll have to respect discipline and obey orders, but you'll find that you'll have a sense of commitment and belonging you've never had before. And from a practical angle, once you're in the Party you're free of all your personal worries. There'll be only one concern left: how to be worthy of the confidence of the masses, the Vietnamese masses as well as the oppressed masses of the world."

"If all Party members were like you, Loc, then I'd have no hesitation, but . . ." Minh paused. He was thinking of Thai.

Loc anticipated his reservation. "You shouldn't judge the Party by its individual members. Some members haven't grasped fully the meaning of *Tinh* and *Ly* in a dialectical way. Some deviate to the right and some to the left. A very small group are being corrupted by the newly discovered capitalist wealth in Saigon, some are even influenced by the remnants of the American decadent culture. But collectively the Party represents our clarified past, the progressing present, and ever-brightening future. Thanks to its leadership since its creation by our beloved Uncle Ho in 1930, our masses, the workers, and the peasants have accomplished wonders. We defeated the French colonialists and the American aggressors. Our people will accomplish greater wonders in peacetime and socialist reconstruction."

"Loc, have you ever for a moment been critical of the Party or doubted the correctness of its policies?"

"Never. I've been critical of the attitude of some individual members and my criticisms were expressed openly in our meetings. More often I've been critical of myself, and that again was expressed within the Party, which then re-educated me. As for the correctness of its policies, I've no doubt they're correct. Why? Because they were arrived at as the result of debates and scientific studies."

He looked affectionately at Minh. "I know you're a good poet, so I can say this to you. The Party is like a river, our River of Perfume, if you wish.

It follows its course from the mountains and merges into the high seas. It carries with it beautiful fishes, but also bad microbes. But the water itself is always perfumed, always pure. Every year in September and October it cleanses itself with floods and torrential rains."

"You know, Loc, whenever water is mentioned, my resistance disappears," Minh said and laughed.

He took leave of Loc at the gate of the Majestic. The curfew had recently been advanced until eleven, so he walked home slowly, pondering Loc's words and his comparison of the Party to the River of Perfume.

.   .   .

By the middle of 1976, less than a year later, public order had been restored to Ho Chi Minh City. Private motorcars disappeared from the streets, which became clean and quiet, mostly because of the absence of Honda motorcycles. Bicycles were everywhere. Open-sky thieves markets transformed themselves into a tolerated secret network of black markets. State-owned department stores exhibited on their half-empty shelves goods from Russia and the socialist countries of Europe as well as handicrafts made in the North. The population census was completed. All the residents were organized at their workplaces and on the streets where they lived. Revolutionary committees were formed everywhere, from hamlets to city blocks. Lines of communication between the invisible central committe of the Vietnam Communist Party in Hanoi, now the nation's capital, and the village cells were strengthened.

Elections of the First National Assembly for a Reunified Vietnam were held in April. On July 2nd, 1976, Vietnam officially became the Socialist Republic of Vietnam, ruled by the same party and government that had ruled the North since 1954. The flag of the new Republic was the old flag of the Democratic Republic of North Vietnam: a five-pointed star on a red background. The "step-by-step reunification" program proclaimed to the world in the 1960s by the Provisional Revolutionary Government of South Vietnam and by the National Liberation Front of South Vietnam was realized in one giant leap within twelve months after liberation.

After December the party was known once again by its original name: the Vietnam Communist Party. Since its creation by Ho Chi Minh forty-six years before, it had taken different names to suit the zigzags of international and national politics. Born as the Vietnam Communist Party in 1930, it became the Indochina Communist Party that same year. It restricted itself to a Marxist Study Group in 1946, to emerge in 1951 as the Vietnam Workers Party. A cycle of forty-six years of clandestine and official activities was closed and a new one begun with the resumption of the old name and the adoption at the Party's fourth congress of the second quinquennial plan.

Why a five-year plan? Minh wondered when he heard of it. Why not three or ten? According to Vietnamese belief, the number five brought bad luck.

Tet of the Year of the Dragon, 1976, was celebrated with austerity and restrained joy amidst the generalized poverty of the country, especially the South, which no longer benefited from billions of dollars of American aid. On the second day of the New Year, Minh accompanied Loc to Hue for an official conference. He used the opportunity to pay a visit to his parents' tombs, which were cared for by a seventy-year-old servant of the family who was now a member of the village's revolutionary committee. The old man, affectionately called *Bac U*, Uncle Bump, because he had a prominent bump in the center of his forehead, drew Minh aside and spoke in a whisper.

"At a recent district party committee meeting, it was disclosed that within the next three years all the tombs in the Ngu Binh district will be removed to a collective cemetery to gain more land for cultivation," Bac U whispered with visible concern. Like most old Vietnamese, Bac U believed in *Dia Ly*, the logic of the earth, which governs the "life of the dead" and influences the living according to the propitious influences of the Blue Dragon and the evil forces of the White Tiger.

With the back of his hand, Uncle Bump wiped away a few drops of sweat from his face and continued, "An old scholar in the village told me that the place where your parents are buried is auspicious, well protected from the bad elements of the cosmos by the Imperial Hill. Generations coming after you will surely reap prosperity and longevity. But if they're transferred to a communal cemetery, all these good things will be lost forever. What can we do?"

Minh stared at the worried old man whose missing teeth made his face look even thinner and longer. He took all the money he had in his pocket and gave it to Bac U.

"Take this money to buy yourself some perfumed soft rice. And please, don't worry. We're living in a socialist country now, where everybody's equal, even those who've already died. If and when the Party and the government decide that my parents' remains should be removed, please do so. Cremate them and send me the ashes."

"Would your parents consent to that?"

"I think they would. When I return to Ho Chi Minh City, I shall organize a simple ceremony to tell them all about it and ask for their permission."

"Why don't you do it here, at the Linh Mu pagoda? The Patriarch is an old friend of the family."

"I know, but I'm afraid I won't have time. I have to go back right away."

"Too bad," the old man murmured. A tear rolled down his hollow cheek.

On the plane returning to the city, Minh asked Loc about the Party's plan.

"Is it true that the tombs around Hue will be regrouped in a communal burial ground to provide more space for cultivation?"

"Yes, it's true, but the plan, which was carried out successfully in the North in the late fifties, will be implemented step by step in consultation with the families concerned."

Minh was thinking of the 1968 N.L.F. plan for "step-by-step" reunification of the country, "with consultation with the people of the South," when Loc added, "The plan is part of the general policy of 'everything for production.'"

"Yes, it's logical, reasonable," Minh commented. He stopped before adding, "but where's the sensitivity?" He changed the subject.

"Loc, have you been at Linh Mu pagoda since the liberation of Hue?"

"No, although I was invited to participate in a meeting there a few days after liberation. The meeting was called to organize the Association of Patriotic Buddhists." He paused for awhile and said, "The role of Buddhism is still important for the promotion of patriotism."

Minh kept silent. Buddhism, even the respected Patriarch of Linh Mu, had become unimportant, almost irrelevant, to him over the years.

At Ho Chi Minh City airport a large banner hung between two electric poles in front of the terminal. It bore two slogans in large red characters,

TO PRODUCE IS TO LIVE!
GO BACK TO THE LAND TO PRODUCE!

The campaign to encourage millions of unemployed among the city's population was in full swing.

With the restoration of public order, a kind of secret, invisible disorder emerged. Rumors circulated in restaurants and coffeehouses that an "army for the restoration of the country," formed by "obstinate elements" and the remnants of Saigon troops aided by modern arms, had been parachuted in at night by U.S. planes based in Thailand and had occupied parts of the western highlands. Ho Chi Minh City was still Saigon: a rumor mill.

A few days after Tet of the Year of the Dragon, a strange story circulated in the city like a spreading fire: a U.S. submarine, built like a dragon, was seen off Da Nang port. It re-emerged in Cam Ranh and a regiment of U.S. marines and Vietnamese refugees trained in the U.S. since 1975 had landed and taken over the naval base for several hours.

Even the official newspaper, Liberation, printed a full front-page story about a counterrevolutionary plot organized by a group of antipatriotic Catholic priests. According to the account, agents of the city's public security had seized a radio transmitter and a huge cache of ultramodern weapons in a church in Cho Lon. All persons implicated in the plot were arrested, the story said.

Meanwhile food rations were getting smaller. Ironically enough, those who could afford to buy beef and chicken at expensive prices in the legal or black markets were the relatives of the puppet government who had fled the country in 1975. They were sending back U.S. dollars which could be exchanged at a favorable rate and with appreciation by the government into Vietnamese currency. Most of the goods received, from blue jeans to toothpaste, eventually found their way to the black market.

.   .   .

Although Minh lived with Lam's family, he hardly saw them. Everyone was busy from dawn to midnight, not only at work, but at endless meetings. Interesting at first, these daily meetings tired and drugged Minh into depression. It was, as a Vietnamese saying affirmed, "like eating glutinous rice all the time." The meetings were hard to digest, and even harder to comprehend. They were all the same, whether block meetings or professional ones. The audience knew in advance what the ultimate decision would be and where it came from: the Party's cadre. Meetings turned into ceremonials, but without the splendor, the music, the magic or colors of feudalistic ceremonies. Gradually Minh came to the conclusion that the communists of present Vietnam were the orthodox Confucians of earlier centuries. They were obsessed by the same concepts of law and order, hierarchy and propriety. Only the text was different.

Before he was to leave for three months of training and research in Hanoi at the end of July, Pham Ngoc Lam took a two-day leave. He and Le Minh Thuy decided to go to Can Tho Province to visit their relatives and to witness the development of the new economic zones. Minh was invited to join them.

Their bus arrived at Can Tho on a rainy and hot afternoon. Lam dropped his children at his uncle's, a teacher at the local high school, while the three adults went to see a cousin who had moved North in 1954 after the temporary partition of the country. The cousin, Comrade Phan Ngoc Truc, secretary of the Revolutionary Committee of Can Tho Province, was busy talking with a group of farmers when they dropped in at his office.

When he had finished his discussions with the peasants, Truc invited them to a teahouse.

"I regret I won't be able to spend much time with cousin Lam and be properly introduced to Mrs. Lam," Truc said, "but I've more work to do since the revolution succeeded than during the difficult days of resistance against the Americans."

"We understand," Thuy answered.

"You must be busy these days with the development of the new economic zones," Minh commented.

"Yes, and a lot of headaches. Not so much with the undisciplined elements who came from the city, but with the peasants."

"What's wrong with the peasants?" Thuy inquired.

"They now want to have titles to their personal land so they can leave it behind for their children when they die."

"Is that wrong?" Minh asked.

"It's not in accordance with the goals of the Party. You see, during the first Indochina War against the French, in the areas controlled by the Viet Minh, land was distributed to the peasants. That's why they supported the Party and fought the French and their Vietnamese puppets. From 1954 on, various pro-American governments in Saigon carried out some form of so-called land reform, at least in theory. In fact, what they did was to return land to absentee landowners that had been given to the peasants by the Viet Minh. The peasants again resisted, and supported the Party and the national liberation movement. Now, with the victory, they demand their land back and want a title to be sure." He became thoughtful and added, "But we can't do that."

"Why not?" Lam asked.

"We can give them back the land to cultivate and produce, but we can't give them the titles."

"Why?"

"Because, you know, once a peasant is a legal owner of a piece of land, no matter how small it is, he'll not give it up to anyone, even the government."

"Naturally," Minh commented.

Truc seemed surprised, even annoyed, by Minh's remark. He explained, "Our country is now building socialism, and socialist productivity requires collectivization of the land and the establishment of large-scale agricultural development. We can't have socialist production, nor solve the old problem of starvation, without collectivization. We did it successfully in the North. Without land collectivization, the North couldn't have resisted the American war of destruction, and without the existence of the socialist North, there would be no liberation of the South. Period."

Truc's face, hardened and tanned by work in the open air, relaxed. He lowered his voice. "Of course, this can't be done immediately. It will be done, step by step, with discussions and consultations with the peasants. But what's left to discuss if we grant them a title which makes them legal owners of the land? Once the government officially confirms the peasants' ownership, it can withdraw its decision only at great risk and danger. In the past, revolutions were instigated by land-hungry peasants. Modern socialist revolutions are led by an alliance of peasants and workers under the leadership of the workers."

Step by step again, Minh thought. And consultation.

Feeling the tense reactions of his guests, Truc proposed they walk to his home, half a mile from his office, for a rest. Talking animatedly with Lam, Truc walked very fast. Minh and Thuy, visibly upset by Truc's ideas, trailed behind.

"I think it's unfair to the peasants, to say the least," Thuy said, looking at Minh. "For the past thirty years, millions of our peasants carried the guns to fight and die for the revolution. They accepted all kinds of sacrifices: bombs, gas, napalm, defoliants, to serve a revolution which promised them land. Now that the revolution is victorious, they're still denied the legal ownership of their land. I think the revolution has betrayed them."

Minh was somewhat surprised by such a strong statement from Minh Thuy.

"I think I agree with you," he said. "It's a lack of both reason *and* feeling."

The next morning, one of Lam's children was taken ill. They returned to the city sooner than they had planned without visiting any of the new economic zones.

.   .   .

With Lam in Hanoi, the atmosphere of the family changed little: even when he was home, he was hardly around except in the early morning. Minh Thuy was equally busy with daily meetings. One evening she returned late, and upset.

"What happened?" Minh asked.

"I was unduly and severely criticized by a cadre."

"Maybe he's a male chauvinist?"

"No, it was a woman. Incidentally, you may not have noticed, but the majority of leaders in committees are now women. We must grant that much credit to the Party and government."

"What did she say?"

"I proposed to conduct a series of lectures on art and social development, but she insisted that there had been no art before the revolution, only fantasies concocted by sick minds to please and serve the even sicker ruling class. Knowing that I painted abstractly—I had explained my work earlier to the meeting—she launched into a vicious attack on abstract art as 'unrealistic, a product of bourgeois art at its lowest decadence.'"

She prepared some strong tea for them. "*Anh* Minh, you know that Lam and I both trust you as our own blood brother."

"I know that and I appreciate it very much."

"So I can tell you that I've lost practically all my hope and fervor only one year after our revolutionary victory. There's too much dogmatism among the cadres, too obvious a domination by the cadres from the North where conditions, even before the revolution, were different from those in the South. For example, one doesn't need to collectivize the peasants' land in the South for the development of agriculture and industries. The South has never starved, even under the French. There's plenty of land left without clearing more."

"I must confess," Minh said, "that I am surprised by the dogmatism too. The North is the prevailing model among the leadership at all levels. At the same time, the conditions of the people in general are getting worse. Look at the present ration. The workers may have more rights now, but they've little to eat."

"I'm not much concerned about economic hardship, which I'm willing to bear for the sake of our nation. But I can barely stand the narrow-mindedness and monopoly of reason by the Party."

"Buddha condemned dogmatism," Minh said, but immediately regretted his words. Both Lam and Minh Thuy were Catholics.

"Because you mentioned Buddhism, I can tell you that a close friend of mine, a Buddhist nun, was very angry when the government ordered the Buddhist hierarchy to reorganize into an Association of Buddhist Patriots. It's the same with the Catholics. Why is it so necessary to take measures like these that antagonize the people who contributed significantly to the resistance against American aggression? What threats do such people pose? The Party's supreme, why does it feel so insecure?"

"I really don't know, but I've often had the impression that the Party and the government act like programmed machines, according to a set of tested plans."

"What tested plans? The South's not the North, at least now. Look at our workers. They work hard, but in the evening they want to have a beer, go to the Cai Luong Theater. But they can't. They have to attend all these meetings and participate in endless study sessions on proletarian internationalism. I don't see why a Vietnamese worker in Ho Chi Minh City has to love a Chinese worker in Peking when he or she doesn't even like his or her brother and sister worker in Hanoi. Of course the workers status is much higher now than in the past, they all have guarantees, but what do they amount to when they have no work or money? These guarantees can provide social security but they can't automatically provide joy and happiness."

Minh listened attentively to every word Minh Thuy said. She was putting into words his own half-formulated thoughts, thoughts that had existed beneath the surface of his mind for—years, he realized. He thought of Loc. What would *he* say? Perhaps the same things as Pham Ngoc Truc had said in Can Tho, but with a smile?

The next day Thuy came home late again. Minh was reading Nga Mien's recently published *The River of Perfume was Red,* when she entered the house by the back door. She asked Minh to come into the backyard for some fresh air.

"I've made some lemonade for you. I saw fresh lemons in the street and bought some," Minh said.

"Thank you. I'm not thirsty right now."

"Is something wrong?"

"I'm scared."

"What's happened?"

"After work and the meeting, I went to visit an aunt of mine. She told me that she and her family, her husband and five children, are leaving tonight."

"Leaving where?"

"They're crossing the national borders by boat to Thailand and from there to America."

"Why are they doing that? It's very dangerous."

"They know that, but they say they're being asphyxiated in Vietnam and they want to get out to breathe easier. Her husband used to be a driver for a businessman who's left the country. Although he wasn't forced to go to a re-education center, he's considered a puppet, so he can't find a job. A few months ago, they volunteered to go to a new economic zone, but later they left—secretly, of course."

"How did they plan their escape?"

"I don't recall exactly what she said. She contacted a friend through a Chinese in Cho Lon, they bribed the corrupted cadres, something like that. Oh, maybe the government knows all about it but closes its eyes to rid the country of 'useless elements.' "

"This is a serious matter, and very risky," Minh commented. "They could be shot by the security agents, they could be lost on the high seas and drowned, they could be killed by pirates . . ."

"Yes, I know, but they seem as determined as they are desperate."

"Why did she tell you all this? Why did she trust you so much?"

"She was very close to me after my mother died. I was two then. She raised me as her own daughter," Thuy said. She began to cry. "She even suggested that I go with her, but I told her I couldn't possibly do that, especially when my husband's in Hanoi. She gave me the name of a man and his address to contact in case I change my mind."

"Did you try to dissuade her from doing this?"

"I should have, but deep in my heart I know she's not wrong. Oh, it's terrible for me to say that, even to you! When I said goodbye to her, she hugged me and we both cried."

"I understand you perfectly."

"Thank you." She paused for awhile. "On my return home, there was a security check on Hong Bang Boulevard, but the security agent didn't ask anything when I showed him my identity card."

"You should go to bed and rest. Have a lemonade if you want. It's on the dinner table."

"Thank you, Minh."

.　　.　　.

Minh couldn't sleep all night. For the first time, the idea of leaving the country came to him. He wasn't really against the Party, or the government, or even their basic programs for the socialist reconstruction of the country. He thought that all these were logical steps to build an orderly socialist society such as he had seen and liked in the North, although he lived there only briefly. Besides, how could a bad Party hold such a good man as Loc? How could a bad Party lead the people to such glorious victories against two of the most powerful nations on earth?

Perhaps he would feel differently if he'd joined the Party as Loc had asked. As a nonparty member, he'd been asked to participate in everything but belonged to nothing. And yet he could not bring himself to join. To join the Party was to refuse to exist, because once he was in it he wouldn't be able to resist it. How could one resist the source of one's own life, one's "family," as Loc called it? The Party to him was a logical development of Vietnamese history, but it wasn't a natural one.

To Minh, that night, the problem was to choose between two impossible alternatives, to accept reform or to undergo transformation. To reform was to give up one's reason; to transform was to deny one's feeling. He reached no conclusion, but he realized that he desperately wanted to break the chain of monotonous meetings he was caught in, the cycle of orderly and ordered ideas. Should he confide in Loc? Definitely not, he thought.

When he got to his office the next morning, Loc called.

"In the next few days, most probably Monday, I'll change jobs. I'll be in charge of a study under the direct supervision of the Party's Commission on Internal Security, on the nationalization of Chinese businesses in Vietnam, especially Cho Lon, and its effects on the international sphere. This will be a crucial decision made by the Party at the very moment when our relations with the People's Republic of China are at the lowest and when China's definitely supporting the reactionary Cambodian Pol Pot regime against us. If the situation's not handled well, we'll face an unprecedented crisis. We may have to fight a war against our neighbors. I'd like you to be my expert because I believe that the role of the United States is fundamental in these future developments. What do you think?"

"I'll follow you wherever you go because you're my closest friend."

"We shall remain so, until we become comrades."

Minh glanced at the picture of the late President Ho Chi Minh hanging over Loc's desk. Under the picture was the slogan, in bright red characters:

Khong con gi quy hon doc lap va tu do,
Nothing is more precious than independence and freedom.

As he walked back to his office Minh said to himself, "I shall remain independent and free, according to your advice, respected Uncle Ho."

XVI

Exiled Souls

Those boats keep rushing out to restless sea
with wind-puffed sails and souls stressed taut and tense.
In quest of hope they will go courting death,
dreaming that one day freedom shall be theirs . . .

The Sea, The World, and The Boat People
Ha-Huyen-Chi
1935–
The Vietnam Forum
Winter–Spring 1983

It was two weeks before Tet of the Year of the Horse, 1978. Minh seated himself in the Dai Nam movie theater and stared at the screen as a Cuban film, *Memories of Underdevelopment*, unfolded. It was the story of an intellectual who, after the Cuban revolution, continued to live as a tolerated, parasitic, bourgeois in the socialist paradise. A few minutes after the show began, a man came in and sat to Minh's right. Under cover of a crescendo in the background music, he whispered in Minh's ear, "My name's Hoang."

"I'm Chuong," Minh replied quickly. The code signal was taken from the name of Vu Hoang Chuong, a well-known Vietnamese poet rumored to have died in a re-education camp after the liberation.

In the darkened theater, the man shook Minh's hand firmly and murmured, *"Tao Quan."* Minh nodded, never taking his eyes from the screen, seeing nothing. The man sat for a few minutes, then left.

Well, that's it, Minh thought. In just one week, on the twenty-third day of the twelfth month, the day the legendary *Tao Quan*, the God of the Kitchen would go to the Kingdom of Heaven for his annual report on the state of the earth to the Emperor of Jade, Minh would leave Ho Chi Minh City—and Vietnam—forever.

He sat on in the darkened theater, thinking about what he would do with the last week of his life in Ho Chi Minh City. He would visit all his favorite places, fix all the familiar scenery in his mind. He would fill his stomach with all the spiced delicacies typical of Vietnamese cuisine. It would not be possible to say goodbye to his friends—it would be too dangerous both for himself and for them. He wanted to make a quick trip to his native Hue, but that was out of the question. He would have to ask permission, and that could take months, even if it were allowed.

Departure day seemed to approach rapidly and yet slowly, like a terminal cancer eating up his body and soul. On the 21st, he vacillated, wanting to call the whole border crossing off. Living in poverty in one's own native village, he thought, would be better than eating Tet in opulence year after year under cold, strange skies. More than once the idea had come to him of confessing the plan to Loc, whom he hadn't seen for months even though they worked in the same building. Finally he left a note on Loc's desk inviting him to dinner the next evening. At noon, Minh received a formal response asking him to come to Loc's office after office hours that afternoon. The note was typewritten, with no mention of dinner.

Loc was alone in his office, a large room so dimly lit that it looked like the anteroom of a movie theater. Politely but coldly he invited Minh to take a chair by the desk, on which lay a pile of several files marked "top secret." The top file had an additional note: "for comrade Loc only."

"What brings you here?" Loc asked. His voice was grave, almost brutally unfriendly, Minh thought with a shiver. He fought to compose himself.

"I didn't bring myself here. I invited you to dinner and you responded by ordering me to come to your office."

"That's correct," Loc said briskly, his eyes automatically glancing down at the closed file. "Still, I'd like to know what was on your mind when you invited me for dinner. What can I do for you?"

"I'd like to have a week off—for personal reasons."

Loc smiled and stared at the ceiling. "That isn't necessary," he said abruptly. "We know every detail of your border-crossing plan, code-named *Tan Xuan*, New Spring. We know that you're leaving by bus for Vung Tau Beach tomorrow, and that you're going from there, by boat, to find 'your freedom.'" The last two words were spoken sarcastically but without harshness.

As Loc spoke, his eyes glued to the file, Minh began to sweat. He was sure that from this office he would be taken straight to the Chi Hoa prison or to one of the re-education camps for hard-core reactionaries located somewhere in the northern jungles at the Chinese border. Yet as this thought became a certainty he grew calm.

When Loc finally looked into his eyes, Minh saw in his face a glow of sympathy, even tenderness. It was as if the old Loc of the days of underground work in the Association of Intellectuals for Liberation had come back.

But the harshness returned to his voice as he spoke. "Minh, I'm sure you realize the extent of your crime."

"Yes, I do, and I'm in your hands. If you plan to have me arrested, I ask only one favor. Let me go to my apartment and take a few books with me. That's all." He sat back calmly, even arrogantly, awaiting Loc's decision.

"It's not necessary. You're not under arrest. You probably won't be arrested. I've had a talk with the executive chairman of this office's committee and we've agreed, in principle for now, to let you leave the country as planned, together with the other nineteen co-conspirators." He paused and leaned back in his chair. "And now that the official matter's practically settled, we can talk for the last time as friends."

Minh was unable to speak. He felt totally confused. Was this a trap? Was Loc playing with him? But Loc returned his gaze now with apparent friendliness. "Thank you," he murmured at last.

"You've nothing to thank me for. It's the temporary policy of the party and the government to selectively let people like you go. But still, I wonder why you make a decision which puts an end to your future." There was a note of urgency, frustration in Loc's voice. "From the minute you leave our shores, you have no future as a Vietnamese. It's too bad. I was always aware of your weaknesses, but I'd hoped you could transform yourself, align yourself with the socialist transformation of the country."

Loc offered him a cigarette. Minh took it and laid it on the desk.

"Loc, because you allow me to speak to you as a friend for the last time, I'll take this opportunity to express to you what I think has driven me to make this decision to leave a land which my ancestors built and defended for centuries. You just talked about my future. I know you believe in and sacrifice for the future, but I can live, work, believe in, and sacrifice for the present only, and to do so I need all the personal freedoms that make me creative as a writer and an individual. You're part of a country, a Party; I'm all by myself."

"Free and lonely? And for whom will you create in your freedom and loneliness? Who gave you your existence as a creative writer in the first place, Comrade Individual? It was the Vietnamese people, the country of which you so brazenly announce you are no longer a part. Freedom! Freedom! You sound like a silly bird that has learned something by rote. The type of individual freedom you seek for yourself requires the enslavement of the very people you presume to represent in your creative writings. You talk about our ancestors centuries of struggle to build and defend our land, and just when it's finally rid of foreign invaders, you begin to whine and whimper because temporary sacrifices interfere with your individual freedoms. The really sad part of it all, Minh, is that while you'll certainly be lonely, you'll never be a free man. Freedom isn't some abstract gift to be handed out by this or that government or regime. All our past experience shows us . . ."

"But that's just it!" Minh broke in. "You analyze the past to justify your present and the future. I want to forget the past because it clouds my present. I ignore the future because it hampers the present. Perhaps after ten successful five-year plans our country will be rich, strong, and communist, 'ten times more beautiful,' but neither you nor I will be around to enjoy it.

"You say that leaving will end my future as a Vietnamese. But I'm convinced that only with freedom can I be a Vietnamese, can I appreciate the Vietnamese culture, wherever I may be. You agree with me, I'm sure, that our history is the history of a free people. Only in freedom can I understand the Vietnamese language, the poetry, the literature, the romantic stories, the sentimental, heroic women and their flowery *ao dai*. Only in freedom can I taste the subtle Vietnamese food, and fully savor the joy and imagery of Tet."

"But the Vietnamese culture," Loc intervened with renewed animation, "has always been rooted in struggle and perserverance—its language, its literature, everything you claim to believe in. And the sentimental women, as you put it, are indeed, heroic. So much so that *you*, with your romantic dribble, will never be able to understand them."

Minh sat back, once again fighting for composure. He took the cigarette from the table, lit it and deeply inhaled the bitter smoke.

"Loc," he said tensely, "You have often said that *Tinh*, feeling, and *Ly*, reason, are the two components of our intellectual and moral life. I agree. But since your Party took power, it has claimed to have the monopoly on all the *Ly*. The *Ly* of the past, the *Ly* of the present, and the *Ly* of the future. What's left for people like me is only *Tinh*, and my *Tinh* tells me that unless I leave, I'll lose it as well. I'll become a dead tree."

"A pine tree?" Loc interrupted with a smile. "A 'Lone Pine Tree?' But as you know, Minh, a pine tree never dies."

"Yes, it does, a little bit during the winter. But it rejuvenates in the spring, it sings in the summer with the warm breeze, and dreams in the fall in its multicolored forest."

"How pretty," Loc laughed, "and how boring! How gracious of you to take with you only the *Tinh* and leave the *Ly* with me and 'my Party.' So, then, you're an incurable romantic dilettante and I'm an unrepenting optimist and that's perhaps one of our differences? How easily you attempt to justify your desertion of our people, your failure as a Vietnamese, by parroting the old 'communists have no feelings' slogan of the defeated would-be rulers. Do you remember how incessantly they sang that tune all the while they napalmed our people and devastated our villages?" He stopped and shook his head as if in disbelief.

"It's true, Minh. I'm a materialist and you're an idealist, and simply speaking, the history of politics and civilization consists of a battle at the national and individual levels between materialism and idealism, or between what our ancestors believed to be the White Tiger and the Blue Dragon. Sometimes the White Tiger disguises itself under the cloak of the Blue Dragon, though. Obscurantism and tyranny have always followed the rise and triumph of idealism, and human liberation has always been the result of struggles for the concrete, the real and the essential." Loc stared at a picture of President Ho Chi Minh surrounded by children.

"There's no contradiction here between *Tinh* and *Ly*," he went on, "except the one you've manufactured in your desperation to justify the feeling you have only for yourself. And speaking of *Tinh*, consider this: when you die, you'll be buried with a bunch of plastic flowers in a snow-covered cemetery, your frozen soul wandering in the cold wilderness of New England, a crippled, aging white paper tiger. When I die, I'll be returned to the warm golden earth of Vietnam, enriched and nurtured by the sweat, blood, and bones of our patriotic intellectuals, our workers, our peasants, and protected by the tender Blue Dragon holding high a red banner proclaiming peace, justice, and love for all on this planet. But I'm sure," he quickly added, "that both you and I will continue to live for many more years to come."

"How can you be a communist," Minh asked him, "a man like you . . ?"

"Why not? I'm a Vietnamese who was born in tradition and lives in revolution. Tradition clarifies for me the historical necessity of revolution and revolution cleanses tradition of its foreign and suffocating substances. Tradition gives me time, and revolution lends me space.

"Minh, there's little left for us to talk about. I have a meeting to attend. Remember, I said that we've agreed to let you go in principle. The final decision will be made tonight at the meeting. You don't have to come to the office tomorrow. If the security cadres haven't come to your place by midnight, you can rest assured that you're permitted to proceed with your plan."

Before Minh could respond, Loc picked up his files and walked to the elevator. A moment later, from the window of the third floor, Minh saw

Loc's Peugeot 405, its curtains down, speeding along the almost deserted Nguyen Hue Boulevard.

Minh deliberately avoided the boulevard and the large avenues. He felt naked and scared with so much space around him. He wandered through the side streets and alleys, coming at last to the Huong Giang Coffee Hermitage. Since the liberation he'd come here several times looking for Madame Luu, but he had never found her, though he knew she still owned the place. Now, on his last night in Vietnam, he was driven to seek her again, this woman he had known since childhood, the sister of Thai.

.   .   .

Only two tables were occupied. Four serious-looking middle-aged men sat absorbed in the evening newspaper, Liberation, under the eye of a big picture of Ho Chi Minh. Minh had always liked his intelligent face, bright eyes, and the sparse beard, which seemed to add a note of clarity and irony to his well-drawn lips. The President appeared to be reading a colored poster urging people to "compete for the building of the new economic zones," and to "denounce corruption, bureaucratism, and commandism." Minh remembered when the Diem government started its campaign to set up "agrovilles" and denounced corruption. Perhaps agriculture and corruption were the permanent problems of all Vietnamese regimes, anticommunist or not, he thought.

Minh sat down in a corner and glanced over the three-line menu glued to the table. "Coffee: 10 cents, first cup; 25 cents all others. Cakes: 2 cents, first piece; 5 cents all others."

Suddenly feeling that someone was standing in front of him, Minh raised his lead to look straight at Madame Luu.

"*Chi* Luu, I'm so glad you're here!" Minh exclaimed.

An upward movement of her eyebrows cautioned him to lower his voice in the quiet room. She asked him, in a voice strained to appear normal, "Would you like some coffee?"

"Yes. Coffee and five cakes."

"I'll be back in a minute."

Minh's eyes followed her to the kitchen. Beneath her fading brown pajama-like costume, he could detect a shapely body, and small waist with well-developed hips. Her face had grown harder over the years, and she looked much more like her sister, Thai. Still, she retained something vulnerable, something devastatingly sentimental.

By the time Madame Luu emerged from the kitchen all four customers had gone, leaving money on the tables. As she set his coffee and cakes on the table, he noticed that she had rearranged her hair, washed her face, and put a little rouge on her cheeks. She was the picture of freshness.

"Are you closing now?" Minh asked.

"In a few minutes, but I'd like to invite you to stay on."

"Thank you very much. I would love to," he answered, his voice warm with gratitude.

"Relax and enjoy your coffee. I'll be back soon. Take your time, please."

She went to the front door, closed it, and hurried back to the kitchen. She returned about ten minutes later wearing a brand-new flowered *ao dai*, lipstick, high-heeled shoes, and a familiar-smelling perfume.

"You're beautiful," Minh smiled.

"Thank you. Let's go to the back room and talk." She took his hand.

The back room, which used to serve as an annex coffee corner for special guests, was now a combination living room and bedroom. A wooden bed with a thin mattress and a rectangular yellow pillow was in a corner, and a round table with four chairs stood in the middle. In the center of the table was a vase of red gladiolas.

She invited Minh to an easy chair near the bed, upon which she seated herself cross-legged. "*Anh* Minh, you don't know how happy I am to see you tonight. It's like an unexpected gift from heaven."

"I never believed I'd see you again. Ten years passed so quickly. I've been looking for you since I came back here in '75, but I was told you were out of town."

"Let's talk about that later. That's the past. We must live with the present and not worry about the past."

Minh smiled, remembering his own words to Loc.

"Now," she continued, "let me explain to you what you may consider as rather strange behavior on my part, dressing up this way."

"Not strange," Minh said, still smiling, "refreshing."

"Whatever it is, here's the situation," she said, blushing. "Today's my birthday. I'm fifty years old, with no husband, no children, no family." The self-mockery in her voice was clear.

"Don't you ever hear from Thai?" Minh asked.

"Since the liberation, when she became vice-minister of education, I haven't seen her at all. I see her picture in the newspaper from time to time. Strange as it may seem, I see no one, since our country was liberated and unified, except those who live in my neighborhood. I've never seen our leaders, except their speeding cars and well-guarded residences. But I'm now the deputy secretary of our neighborhood committee, so that makes me one of our leaders too, doesn't it? I'm supposed to attend a meeting tonight and every other night of the week at eight o'clock, but I asked the committee secretary's permission to stay home tonight. I told him that today is the first day of my menstruation and that, at my age, it's painful and smells bad. The secretary's an old taxi driver, a prude. He quickly agreed that I shouldn't attend. Of course, I lied to him. I reached menopause several years ago. So now I can celebrate my fiftieth birthday, not all by myself as I thought, but with you. So much the better!"

She roared with laughter, proudly, as if she'd won a significant victory.

"Actually," Minh said softly, "you smell very good. The perfume is familiar to me."

"It should be. It's Caron's *Pour Un Homme*," she answered quickly, pronouncing the name in a perfect Parisian accent. "It's the only perfume I can buy on the black market. But that makes no difference. We're in a socialist country where women and men are equal so there shouldn't be any difference in the perfumes we use. The difference was a capitalist invention." Raising her right arm, she proclaimed in a louder voice, "*Vive la différence!*"

Giggling, she pulled Minh's arm around her waist, then, as if suddenly remembering something, she jumped up and opened a trunk partly hidden under her bed.

"For my lone birthday celebration, I bought two bottles of Coca-Cola, one pound of Kraft cheese, one dozen hot dogs and a bottle of Moet-Chandon champagne in the black market. The whole thing cost me one of my gold earrings. But one cannot eat gold."

She spread a white napkin on the table and asked Minh to open the champagne. Like two children who have stolen food from a supermarket, they ate and drank heartily. From time to time she hugged him, laughing. Slowly he relaxed and entered into the spirit of her celebration.

"I never thought I could eat hot dogs; they taste so good," Minh commented.

Suddenly she became serious. Taking his hand, she asked, "*Anh* Minh, are you happy?"

"Why do you ask?"

"Because I want you to be happy."

"At this moment, I'm happy because I'm with you on your birthday. But I don't know whether I'll be happy when I leave you."

"Then don't leave. Stay."

"No. I'm sorry but I have to. I have an appointment."

"With a woman?"

"No. With the security police, at midnight."

"Please, don't joke like that."

"All right. I have to do some work that has to be finished by six o'clock tomorrow morning. I must start it no later than midnight."

"As you wish. What time is it now?"

"Nine," Minh guessed.

"We still have three hours together, and three hours is," she paused, counting with closed eyes, "one hundred and eighty minutes. And one hundred eighty is, let me see, ten thousand, eight hundred seconds. A lot of time." She emptied her glass and lay back on the bed.

To the monotonous music of a slow-moving ceiling fan, they made love passionately, tenderly, consciously. Both knew, without discussion, that the union of their flesh provided a temporary diversion for their fears and frustrations. Suddenly, she laughed and her body shook in spasms.

"What happened?" Minh laughed.

"I saw two small lizards making love. The male just lost his tail. It dropped to the ground."

"You laughed, the lizard lost his tail, and I exploded!"

They lay in bed talking long afterwards.

"*Anh* Minh," Luu said, caressing his hair, "I haven't made love to anyone since the liberation. Successful revolution isn't known as an aphrodisiac. I guess liberation isn't as liberating as it's supposed to be. It seems to create sexual impotence."

He laughed. "It's the same with me. That's why I wasn't able to 'make the yellow river flow backward' just now. The Taoists believe, you know, that by refraining from ejaculation, your sperm will return to the brain to nourish it and help you reach immortality."

"Forget about immortality and technique. Massage my neck."

"Luu, how long do you plan to be in the coffeehouse business?"

"I don't know. There's really nothing else I can do. After the liberation, I went back to Hue hoping to find something meaningful to do, but no luck. Besides, since Thai's gone to Hanoi, I've no relatives left in Hue. My two brothers and my aunt were killed during the Tet offensive in the Year of the Monkey, some say by the liberation forces, some say by the Marines. I never really wanted to find out the truth. A dead person is a dead person, and there's no angel in any war on any side.

"More than once, I've felt so lonely that I wanted . . ."

"To leave the country?"

"Never, never!" she answered defensively. "As a matter of fact, two months ago a Chinese friend offered me a place on her boat sailing for America, but I told her that even if the lampposts and the trees in the city were to depart, I would stay. To leave the country would be worse than committing suicide, a slow, gradual, by installments sort of self-destruction. Besides, what do you do when Tet comes?"

"I really don't know. But what will you do here when you are desperately lonely?"

"I once had the idea of stripping myself naked and running through the city singing the 'March of the Revolution.'" She paused. "Of course it's a mad idea, but sometimes even a mad idea can provide relief, if it's not violent."

Why couldn't Luu, this desperately lonely woman who lay beside him, see that only one alternative lay before her? He had to fight down anger and frustration before he spoke again. "But Luu, isn't that also a form of suicide? What have we become, then, if we can only find relief in madness?"

She lay quietly, her right hand caressing the earlobe now robbed forever of its golden ring. "We are surely dying, Minh. Not everyone, but we are, people like us. I guess that's why we're so lonely."

"People like us," he repeated, a note of irony in his voice. "People like you," Loc had said. What would Luu say now if she knew he was leaving Vietnam in a matter of hours?

Suddenly, there was a knock at the door. Minh was terrified at the thought of his imminent arrest, but the voice only cried out, "Comrade Luu, are you home? Are you asleep?"

"Yes, comrade, I'm home and about to go to bed," she shouted. Turning to Minh, she said, "You looked scared."

"Yes, I was, to be honest."

"Nothing to be afraid of. The Tu Ve patrolman checks on every house in the neighborhood every night between ten and eleven."

"I think I must go," Minh said. "Thank you for a memorable evening."

He rose and dressed in silence. She followed him to the door, opened it, and peered into the deserted street.

"Please keep well, and promise to return here on Tet's eve."

"You take care too."

Both had tears in their eyes.

.   .   .

The sky was filled with stars, as the evening drizzle permeated his skin. He shivered and repressed a strong desire to return to the warmth of Luu's arms. But he kept going, accelerating his steps. As he entered his street, a Tu Ve guard holding a U.S.-made M16 recognized him.

"*Dong Chi* Minh, you're very late. Too much work during the last week of the year, but you'll have three days to rest during the Tet holiday."

"I hope so," Minh answered curtly and kept walking. He had often met the guard, a worker at factory fifteen in the neighborhood, but tonight was the only time the man had ever addressed him as "comrade." Minh found it ironic that only a day before he was to sever all his indirect connections with the Party and his direct service with the government, he was considered a comrade by a man who before the revolution would never even have had the chance or the self-confidence to address an educated fellow Vietnamese as an equal, let alone as a comrade. Minh stopped, and returning to the guard, took a pack of Salem cigarettes he'd bought on the black market out of his vest pocket. Slipping it into the guard's hand, he insisted, "Take it. The night will be long and cold. You'll need it."

"Thank you, *Dong Chi*," the guard said and put the pack into his pocket without looking at it.

"It's nothing. . . . *Dong Chi*," Minh whispered. The word came naturally from his lips for the first time.

The Tu Ve's friendliness reassured him. If the public security were about to arrest him, he reasoned, they would have replaced the Tu Ve with a regular policeman, or the Tu Ve would have been warned and not have been so friendly with him. Or was this friendliness just a trick?

The alarm clock on his bedside table stood exactly at midnight when Minh turned on the light in his one-room studio. As he boiled water on a portable stove to make tea, a song he had heard and liked at least fifteen years before, "*The Last Night*," came back to him. He sang the last lines:

> *Tonight is the last night I'm close to you . . . Please do not weep over our separation: the flowing tears will wash away the springtime of our lives . . .*"

And yet, he thought, that song was a love song, a farewell to a loved one. Except for Lam and Minh Thuy there was no one he was close to. They had become to him, it was true, like a beloved brother and sister in the weeks he had lived with them, but they were not his family; indeed, he could not even say goodbye to them lest their knowledge of his departure endanger them.

Overwhelmed, Minh lay down on the floor. He wanted to be as close as possible to the beloved earth he was about to leave.

After a few minutes, he rose and began to throw on his bed the few things he would be packing in his knapsack, a few clothes and 300 pages of an unfinished manuscript. He decided to take with him only seven books from among the few hundred that lay scattered over the floor: *Kim Van Kieu* the Vietnamese "literary Bible" with its French and English translations; a translation of the *Tao Te Ching*, the major Taoist work; a Vietnamese version of the *Buddhist Lotus Sutras*; Dag Hammarskjöld's *Markings*; and a copy of his family geneaological tree handwritten by his father in both Chinese and Vietnamese.

He checked his wallet to be sure that his mother's picture and a small gold Buddha statue were there. He counted his money: 110 *dong*, more than enough for his bus ticket and meals. Hidden between his mother's picture and his identity card was a one-hundred-dollar bill for emergencies abroad. He set the alarm for six and tried to catch a few hours sleep.

He woke at five, tears rolling down his cheeks. In a frightening dream, he had seen his father in shining red armor sitting on the back of a whirling blue dragon, accompanied by his mother in a golden gown riding an emerald phoenix. They were leading an army of angry lions and white tigers that invaded his apartment, calling out his name. Blood flowed from his mother's mouth and eyes, and fire roared out of his father's ears and nose. They insulted him, accused him of treason, of having sold his soul to the barbarians, of denying his Vietnamese blood and cultural heritage. One tiger, its head marked by a huge black star, pounced on him and, with long pointed claws, pulled his eyes out. It was then that he woke, crying out in pain and imploring, "Please, father, mother, please forgive me. I've betrayed you. I have betrayed the country, my people, but I cannot live under the present regime. I'm finished, I know, so please forgive me. Don't pursue me anymore."

He burned a few joss sticks and knelt to pray to Buddha the Compassionate. He was afraid to go back to sleep. He waited anxiously for dawn, for the sunlight to disperse all the horrors of his nightmare. He reached for the *Kim Van Kieu* and sought a clue to his future. Holding the book over his head, he closed his eyes, opened them and ran his forefinger over the pages, coming to rest on the two bottom lines of page 85:

> *Take good care of yourself, more so than of gold or jade, so that those who remain at the feet of the clouds and at the end of the sky need not worry.*

It was the advice given to Thuy Kieu by her lover Kim Trong before he departed on a long journey. Minh saw it as an omen and was pleased, thinking it appropriate for the occasion, an indication that no misfortune would befall him.

The alarm clock rang. He opened the window and looked down the street. The Tu Ve was gone. A middle-aged man with long messy hair was gesticulating wildly and talking with an older man with a wispy goatee. At one point, they seemed to be very angry at each other, but they parted company without incident. Minh shaved but decided not to shower. "I'd like to remember *Chi* Luu for awhile, and all the Vietnamese smells. Besides, once I'm on the high seas I'll have all the water I need to clean myself."

He ran down the stairs and hurried to a nearby restaurant for a large bowl of steaming beef *pho*, only to find that under the new restrictions, beef was available only on Sundays. He had to satisfy himself with chicken. He was tempted to go to the hermitage for coffee but decided against it. It would only would make his departure more difficult. He stopped at his usual coffeehouse two blocks away. The coffee wasn't very good, but he left a very generous tip for the waitress. From there, he ran to a newsstand and bought the morning paper. Returning to his apartment, he took the knapsack, left the door unlocked, and dropped the key on the threshold. Once in the street, he looked around and felt that a man in khaki shorts was paying unusual attention to him. He hailed a taxi for his trip to the bus station.

·   ·   ·

The crowded and overweighted bus left promptly at eight, a punctuality he had seen only in America and Japan but never before in Vietnam. It rolled slowly through green ricefields and isolated huts along Highway 3, stopping to disgorge passengers and take new ones about every half hour. There were checkpoints almost hourly. At each one the driver jumped out, produced his paper for the inspection of nonchalant policemen, and was allowed to continue his route. At the last checkpoint all passengers were ordered by three tough-looking soldiers armed with AK47 machine guns to get off while the bus was thoroughly searched. One soldier, who spoke with a distinctively Hue accent, asked for Minh's I.D. He glanced at it and returned it to him quickly.

"Comrade," he asked, "are you on official business in Vung Tau?"

"Yes," Minh answered firmly.

"You may go back onto the bus, comrade. No need to open your luggage," the soldier said.

Minh was a little unnerved by the very polite and exceptional treatment reserved for him. Had security been warned by Loc to treat him decently until the moment of his arrest at the very last stage of the New Spring plan?

At Vung Tau, Minh was to go to a restaurant called Sea Sky, for dinner. At about the time he'd be finishing his meal, an elderly woman dressed in black peasant pajamas, with a checkered scarf on her head, would enter carrying a pile of books and newspapers for sale. He would signal her to his table and ask for the latest collection of *To Huu* poems. He would buy the collection and then follow her out of the restaurant.

Everything went according to plan. He followed the woman up the street and into an alley. They climbed to the second floor of an abandoned house.

"Everything's all right," the old woman announced calmly. "We'll leave in a few minutes. Just leave your knapsack here and someone will pick it up later. Now, we will walk north together. Let's go."

They walked silently along the beach. Here and there a few men and women in uniform passed, totally unconcerned about them. They passed a rocky corner flanked on the right by a huge, white marble Buddha statue. Under the starlight, they saw a few fishing boats cruising on the black water. She asked Minh to stop and wait as a sampan approached the beach. The old woman wished him good luck and disappeared behind the rock.

Minh stepped into the sampan, which was rowed by a woman whose face was hidden under a conical hat. About half an hour later, the sampan stopped alongside a big junk that resembled a dead buffalo floating on a river after a flood. A silent man helped Minh climb onto the deck and guided him down under the cabin's roof. There he squatted in the dark with other persons, all silent. The sampan discharged another silent passenger nearly every hour until about 2 a.m., when the junk finally began to move away. With the first motion of the ship Minh felt as if he had been lifted into space, and the combined sighs of relief from all the passengers seemed like a gentle breeze pushing them onto the high seas.

XVII

Truce in Heaven, Peace on Earth

When Heaven in its yearly changing mood
Brings back golden leaves and crispy Autumn air
The tired Blue Dragon-refilling its dwindling Yin,
The exhausted White Tiger-recharging
its shrinking Yang,
Will declare a temporary truce
To let people live and work in peace on Earth
And birds fly and sing in pairs in sky.

Tran Van Dinh
Heaven's Changing Mood
Unpublished Poem
Translated by Author

The passengers were falling asleep with their heads buried on their
knees when a bell rang furiously, piercing the silence of the boat. Minh
opened his eyes quickly, thinking a fire had broken out on board. The sea
outside the cabin was engulfed in sunlight. A commanding voice announced

in a clear, southern accent, "Uncles and aunties, brothers and sisters, nephews and nieces, please wake up and welcome your newly found freedom. We are safe now."

The announcer clapped his hands and everyone joined in the applause as he continued, "My name is Vu Tan Don, and I'm your skipper. You can have confidence in me. Before the communist takeover, I was a lieutenant commander in the Navy and I'm familiar with the coastline in the Gulf of Thailand. But the organizer and leader of Operation *Tan Xuan* is my co-skipper, a man I have learned to respect and admire, Professor Trang."

As he spoke, Professor Trang stood up to the applause of the passengers. Minh could hardly believe his eyes. It was his colleague from Hue University, Chau Minh Trang. As Minh was about to approach him, Trang, with a gesture of his right arm, invited everyone to sit down. He spoke in a grave, sonorous voice.

"I'm very, very happy to see all of you here. Although I've known all about you, your backgrounds and especially your determination to flee the communist tyranny, I've never met any of you personally, except, of course, my former colleague from Hue University, Professor Tran Van Minh. Professor Minh, who until a few days ago was still working in the Ho Chi Minh City management committee, is also a well-known writer and poet. He has in the past lived several years both in the United States and Thailand, and his presence here is a particular piece of luck for us: he is a personal friend of the new Prime Minister of Thailand, Chamras Panyakupta. I'd like to ask Professor Minh to stand up so we can welcome him properly."

Minh stood, murmuring, "thank you," his voice muted by deep emotion.

Trang continued, "As all of you know through your underground contact, the organization of this operation began during the Tet of the Year of the Dragon, exactly a year ago, about a month after I learned of the death in a so-called 're-education camp,' of our great poet, Vu Hoang Chuong. I'm sure his spirit will animate this operation. I'm circulating a copy of his poem *"Distant Horizon,"* which I think is appropriate for the occasion."

He turned to the square-shouldered skipper Don, who began to distribute the poem. Trang waited a few minutes for everyone to read it.

> *The Anchor is lifted, O boat!*
> *Let the waves push you to the east or*
> *drift you to the west.*
> *Away from the earth, amidst the*
> *immensity of height and space,*
> *My lonely, bitter heart could perhaps*
> *gradually empty itself.*
>
> *We five, seven of us, lost and bewildered,*
> *Determined to leave Ho Chi Minh City*
> *On the unlimited sea, why bother about direction?*

O boat! O dear boat! let yourself
wander with the wind.

The spirit of wine has penetrated us
we wait for sundown
To hoist the high mast and sing our rowing song.
The wind has blown with the rising
melancholy evening moon
O boat! dear boat! please gently
follow the wind.

Minh knew the poem, which was composed in the late 1940s. Trang had changed a line, he noticed: "determined to leave Ho Chi Minh City," had originally read, "rejected by our native village, despised by our nation."

Trang continued, "Not only do we have the poet's spirit with us, but his family as well. Let us salute his sister, Mrs. Thao, and her three children. Her husband, the writer Le Quoc Thao, died of exhaustion over a year ago in a so-called new economic zone."

A middle-aged woman wearing a white turban, a sign of mourning, stood with her three teen-aged children. They bowed silently to the audience. After the applause, Trang picked up his unfinished speech.

"I shall now call the roll. Please stand when your name is called so that we can properly welcome you to our boat family. Mr. and Mrs. Nhat and their four children. Mr. Nhat was, until last month, a mathematics teacher at the Le Loi high school in Nha Trang. Mr. and Mrs. Tuyen. Until two days ago, Mr. Tuyen was working in the import-export section of the State Commercial Enterprise. Also with us are their cousins, Mr. and Mrs. Bat. Mr. Bat was, for the last nineteen months, an engineer in state factory number fifteen. Major Thap, who escaped from a re-education camp and hid for six months in various places in the city, and Miss Lai who, until the day before yesterday, was a technician in the education section of the Ho Chi Minh City management committee. She speaks excellent English. And, last but not least, Mr. Hoa, a Chinese merchant in Cho Lon, owner of the boat."

Everyone stood in a final round of applause. Minh glanced at Lai. She looked familiar. Except for her hair being longer and a darker complexion she looked very much like Xuan, the student he had known in Hue in 1967. He dismissed the thought. Probably the presence of Trang had put those years in his mind.

Trang lit a cigarette. "Our boat family, as you can see, is made up of twenty members who according to the communists, belong to the reactionary bourgeoisie. But at this moment, we are truly a classless and propertyless clan." A few people chuckled. "I suggest that you wash up and prepare for your first breakfast in freedom. For this memorable beginning of our 'New Spring,' we'll have a breakfast of cooked glutinous rice and pork sausage. After breakfast we'll get together for a longer meeting to discuss every detail of our operation and assign daily tasks for each of us. With Heaven and Buddha on our side, and with the skill and experience of our skipper, Don, we'll be in Thailand in less than one week, and eat Tet with the Vietnamese community in Chantaburi.

"I'd like all of you to bear in mind that our situation is rather exceptional. Our group is small and homogeneous, our preparations, meticulous. It's almost like a pleasure cruise, except of course, for our intellectual and moral agony. But we should never for a second forget that before us there were, and in the future there will be, thousands upon thousands like us, compatriots who suffered greatly in their desperate attempts to leave the communist hell. A number of them perished in the depth of unknown oceans. We should remember them and pray for them. They, and now we, are the most eloquent denunciation to the world of the bankruptcy of communism, which has always used nationalism, only to devour it later. They and we, the 'boat people of Vietnam,' are carrying the banner of the will to live free, just as our ancestors did through their persistent heroic resistance against all foreigners. Our message to humankind is that we, children of motherland Vietnam, will never learn to surrender our souls nor our bodies to foreign or domestic oppressors. We're leaving Vietnam not because of economic difficulties, as the communists have loudly proclaimed, but because we were born free and want to remain free. Someday, we shall return to live on the soil of our ancestors and join hands with our existing underground national restoration resistance in cleaning our mountains and rivers of communist inhumanity."

Trang broke into tears, which he wiped away with the back of his hand. But he quickly regained his calm and said with a smile, "I shall have the honor of serving your breakfast, and I shall ask Minh to prepare the coffee and tea."

Minh followed Trang to the front cabin.

"Minh, I'm so happy you're with us. I've looked forward to this meeting with you for months!"

"For me it's a happy surprise," Minh replied. "I thought of you often, wondering how with your strong feelings against communism you were surviving."

Serving the coffee and tea, Minh had an opportunity to take a closer look at the boat. It was about thirty feet in length and ten feet in beam, a converted commercial junk of a type he'd seen before while passing through Hong Kong. It was divided into two cabins—a long one that served as a bedroom-living room for all the passengers except Don and Trang, and a small studio in the front cabin that they shared and that housed a kitchen and toilet. Minh couldn't help but be impressed with Trang's attention to detail. From pencil and paper and medicine to a set of chess for recreation, everything had been thought out in advance.

Trang asked Minh to keep a diary and dutifully he complied, starting
with the twenty-fourth day of the twelfth month of the Year of the Dragon. In
his romantic excitement, he called each day a "Bloom of New Spring."

First Bloom. Have seen sunrise from the beach before but never on the
high seas. Quite a discovery. It's like being immersed in lava of melting
gold and silver. The sun is so red and the sea, black—not blue. The contrast is mind-blowing. First meeting for introduction and assignment of
duties went well. Trang's leadership and eloquence quite remarkable. Was
tempted to tell him that Loc and the Party knew all about the operation,
but thought it would be cruel, even dangerous, to do so. Am being
assigned to listen to foreign broadcasts and brief our boat family before
bedtime daily. Suggested help from another passenger, Miss Lai, who looks
so much like my former student, Xuan, it's remarkable! Shall try to find out
who she really is. Everybody except Trang and Don seem to be dazzled by
the new-found freedom. Hard to say if they're happy or sad. It's like the
feeling I had while driving around the country roads of Massachusetts in
the fall; a blend of joy and sadness. Had Jennifer lived, what would she
think of my "escape?"

Second Bloom. Skipper Don seems to be very familiar with the route.
He looks like a sea pirate with his horizontal, bushy eyebrows and his
large chest. Could he be a member of that smuggling ring of top Saigon
officers in the 60s? He's a real expert and manages the boat so smoothly,
steering only in the calmest waters. A noisy visit by a band of seagulls,
some white, some light gray. Their company lifted everybody's spirits. The
sea was rough for about two hours. Five got seasick, but not seriously.
Voice of America from Manila announced the refusal by the Singapore government to let four hundred boat people ashore. Twenty drowned. News
distressed all members of our family.

Third Bloom. Had a long talk with skipper Don, a very simple man who
misses the sea, as he puts it, "the way one misses a lover on Tet." He hates
the communists because "they are joyless, humorless, and heartless." He
confided having joined a group of officers at the end of 1975 to form a
battalion against the new government, but gave up and returned to Ho Chi
Minh City to live clandestinely with his girlfriend who died of an abortion
nine months ago. After her death he decided to leave the country. News of
boat people elsewhere continues to be bad. Why do the U.S. and the free
world shirk their moral responsibility to the Vietnamese people? Hope
someday to tell the American people the whole story of the "boat people."

Fourth Bloom. Had a massive, but friendly, invasion by seagulls. I gave
them some dry fish yesterday. Had short conversation with Lai. Am now
convinced she's really Xuan, but she avoided talking about her days at Hue
University except to say simply, "I studied there once." I shall persist. Must
confess, she's very attractive and I feel a strong desire for her. Mr. Nhat's
family is apparently very unhappy. The mother and children weep, but I
think I had better leave them alone. Talked with Major Thap who said that
the "re-education centers were nothing but productive concentration

camps." He remarked, "After ten daily lectures by a communist cadre, one develops a kind of biological revulsion and mental rejection. Hard labor is much preferable to communist lectures. I wonder why there are still people who believe in communism?" Engineer That joined the conversation. He's not ideologically anticommunist but believes that there's no future or happiness in his work. Communist management, in his words, is "no management, because there's no initiative and no flexibility." He wishes to go to the U.S. to study business administration and asks lots of questions about America. Am going now to an evening session on Vu Hoang Chuong and his poetry. Wish I had known him better when he was alive. Is he really dead?

Later.

After the session, while most of our "passengers to freedom" slept, I decided to have a serious talk with Lai. I have no doubt in my mind that she's Xuan, by her smile and the tone of her voice. I invited her outside to sit and talk. "Xuan," I addressed her by the name I was convinced was really hers, "I knew from the first day on the boat that your real name wasn't Lai. Perhaps in your too literary and sophisticated way of changing your name, you've betrayed your secret. I'm sure you know the saying, 'Xuan Bat Tai Lai, spring never comes twice in the same year.' I don't understand why you denied knowing me. I knew that you were close to my brother Phong back in 1967. He was killed at Quang Tri, by the way, and his body thrown into the Ben Hai River. I also knew then that you were suspected by the police as a Viet Cong agent. What have you really been doing since 1968? Why are you leaving Vietnam?"

She answered, surprisingly without any hesitation or emotion. "Your suspicion is correct, as was the police suspicion back in '67," she said. "I am Xuan, but that's not important. I'm a member of the Party and I'm not leaving Vietnam. I've been assigned to follow your operation and integrate myself into the Vietnamese community in the United States. My life is wholly dedicated to the Party, and this fact alone determines who I am and what I do. I don't hate people like you, I just know you're wrong. You're swimming against the tide of history, Vietnamese history as well as human history. But someday you'll repent. Then like a good mother, the Party will forgive you. As far as my relationship with your brother ten years ago, it was only a part of my duty. I was attempting to get military information. He might have loved me, but I had only affection for him, even admiration, but no love."

I felt hurt and interrupted her. "Then he was completely deceived. He certainly believed you loved him."

"Love, as you conceive it, is a decadent, bourgeois concept. Comradeship is a higher, deeper, more lasting bond between men and women who die and live for the Party." In the milky light of the starry night, I detected a sarcastic smile spreading across her sensual lips. Her determination impressed and intrigued me. I asked her, "How can you be so supremely self-confident, so sure that you're right, that you have all the reason on your side, so you can easily categorize all the feeling of others?"

"It's because I know that the Party is our history, it's our nation in distress, in humiliation, in triumph and revolution." But suddenly her attitude changed. She began to stammer. "Also, there are personal circumstances," she told me. "In 1964, when I was a young girl in Hue, I was raped right in my living room by two army officers, one American and one Vietnamese. Perhaps because of your class background, or because you're a man, you don't realize what it means to be raped. For a woman, it's the deepest fall, one from which she usually doesn't recover. Yet I didn't fall, I recovered, thanks to the care of the Party. The Party was the only place where I could regain and maintain my self-esteem. It was the warm womb from which I was reborn." It was interesting to notice how her voice got stronger as she spoke of the Party. Then she said, "When we reach Thailand, you can expose me as a communist to the Thai authorities. I could be put in prison, but the Embassy of the Socialist Republic of Vietnam will simply exchange me for a number of Thai officers we still have in our prison, and I shall be free again to serve the Party." Her self-assurance and arrogance disarmed me. I couldn't reply, I just said goodnight. As I did so I touched her hand. It was cold.

I am disturbed by her confession and I'm sorry I know the truth. I hate her, I admire her, I desire her. I'm at a loss to know how a woman like her could surrender all her *Ly* and *Tinh* to an abstraction called "the Party." But maybe Loc was right. Maybe it is the Party that gives her time and space, which she never had before, as a woman.

Anyway, she went back to her sleeping corner and I watched her. In the dim light, her curvaceous body rested elegantly among the other boat people who had to leave everything behind because her party monopolizes all the reason and selectively interprets all the feeling. Unable to sort out my conflicting thoughts and passions, which pulled me in all directions, unable to forget them just by closing my eyes, I went to Trang's cabin. Don, the skipper, was there too. I told them the whole story about Lai/Xuan. They listened with angry surprise. After advising me to catch some sleep, Trang said, "Thank you so much for having revealed to us something I should have discovered myself before we implemented Operation Tan Xuan. But we'll solve the problem soon. I shall kill her the night before we reach Thailand." His voice was broken. He tried to suppress his anger and whispered, "Goodnight." Now I am devoured by guilt.

Fifth Bloom. I don't know when I fell asleep. When I awoke, the sun was high in the sky and breakfast was ready. Skipper Don announced the good news. Thanks to Buddha's blessings, "the sails are in line and the winds are in tune." We will reach Chantaburi, south of Bangkok, tomorrow afternoon.

Minh closed his diary. Nothing more of importance, he believed, was going to happen and he didn't want to record the details of how Trang would kill Xuan during the night. He felt as if he had already committed a crime and he didn't want to think about it.

At breakfast he avoided Xuan's eyes. When she asked about the following twelve-hour schedule, he answered briskly without looking at her, "We don't need to know where the world's going because soon we'll be part of that world." He added quickly, "Tonight, we'll have a sound sleep to wait for a brighter tomorrow." But the word "we" reminded him that Xuan was to be eliminated from that world.

Wanting to give her a subtle, indirect signal, he added, "I need a rest more than anything else. I'll have to put up a hard painful struggle to re-enter that world." But Xuan didn't hear what he said, and wouldn't have understood his hint if she had, he realized. He took out the *Tale of Kieu* and read the book's concluding sentences:

All things are fixed by Heaven, first and last.
Heaven appoints each creature to a place.
If we are marked for grief, we'll come to grief.
We'll sit on high when destined for high seats.
And Heaven with an even hand will give talent to some,
*   to others happiness.*
In talent take no overweening pride—
Great talent and misfortune make a pair.

He repeated the last sentence to himself several times—admiring the ingenious way the author linked "talent" and "fortune" by playing upon the different sounds of the Vietnamese words. In Vietnamese, talent is *Tai* and misfortune is *Tai*. They rhymed with each other almost naturally. He wondered if Xuan had to suffer *Tai* because she had a great deal of *Tai*, political *Tai*.

He felt at peace with himself. He noticed that on the eve of the success of their operation all the passengers on the boat, even the children, were strangely quiet. Perhaps, deep in their hearts, they all realized that soon they would be separated forever from the romantic land of the Dragon and the Fairy, whom Vietnamese accepted not as mythical figures but as their real founding parents. Tomorrow they would be in a land where neither their ancestors' bones nor their mothers' placentas lay buried in the bosom of the earth as they were in Vietnam. There, when a child is born and the umbilical cord cut, the placenta is buried, often under the same bed where the baby has been delivered. A native village is called "a place where your placenta is buried and your umbilical cord cut."

.   .   .

Minh looked at the sea beyond. It was bluer than it had been on any other day of the whole journey. He imagined that a majestic Blue Dragon surged from the depths of the blue sea and with his ivory claws took all of them to the Isle of the Eastern Ocean where there would be no frontiers to cross or politics to tear people down.

The sky wasn't as clear as the day before. Isolated mountain-shaped white clouds began to appear. They brought to his memory a line by the famed Chinese Tang poet, Tu Fu:

In the sky, a cloud appeared as a white cloth
Suddenly, it turned into a bluish dog.

Minh didn't see any bluish dog. The white clouds now converged to take the form of a huge attacking tiger. A cold wind blew. Minh smelt the odor of dead fish. He heard Thai voices but could not understand what they were saying. A motorboat appeared suddenly alongside the junk, with three bronze-skinned men on board.

The tallest among them pointed a machine gun at Minh and asked loudly, "Vietnamese fleeing Communists?"

"Yes," Minh said, his teeth clenched. Before he could ask them if they were Thai Navy patrolmen, the man with the machine gun ordered his two revolver-carrying followers to jump over to Minh's boat. One fired a shot in the air. "Thai bandits!" Minh shouted.

But it was too late. The bandits lined everyone up on the deck. While the machinegunner stood guard over the victims, his two aides searched all corners of the boat. They took one submachine gun that Don had had neither time nor the chance to use. Then all three searched the Vietnamese, who lowered their heads more in shame and anger than in fear. From the Chinese merchant they took gold ingots that were hung on his shoulders under his T-shirt. They stripped Trang of the brand new hundred-dollar bills that had been sewn so carefully under his coat, as well as removing his watch. Then the tall bandit took Xuan aside and led her down into the cabin.

Minh could hear Xuan's metallic voice screaming at the Thai bandit in Vietnamese as she struggled furiously. The attacker shouted in Thai, "Devil, stubborn woman, submit to me! You dare to try to kill me by biting my testicles? Submit or you'll soon see your ancestors in the depth of the sea!"

A deadly silence followed. About five minutes later the bandit emerged, his hands stained with blood, his face scratched, carrying Xuan's broken body. Laughing, he threw it into the blue water. He jumped back into his motorboat with his two accomplices and in a few seconds they had all disappeared into the white cloud-covered horizon.

Minh looked at the sky with imploring eyes. Indeed, the White Tiger cloud had now been transformed into an advancing bluish dog.

The sky darkened. The wind blew stronger and colder. Winter seemed to descend on the New Spring operation. Everybody wept and sobbed. For the next twelve hours, they all lay on the deck, numb with the misfortune that had befallen them. No one ate anything, no one said anything.

.   .   .

Late the next afternoon Trang called the passengers together.

"My friends," he said, "despite our misfortune we have reached our goal. We'll be in Chantaburi no later than five o'clock. I have told you that the Prime Minister of Thailand is an old friend of our dear friend and brother, Doctor Minh. With your approval, I shall ask him to be our representative to the Thai authorities. We can celebrate the Tet's eve in Chantaburi, but I think it would be proper that we do so on our boat which is, according to international law, Vietnamese territory."

With the end of their journey in sight, the passengers seemed to have forgotten the nightmarish incident that had engulfed them in sorrow and despair the day before. They applauded Trang's announcement, and Minh was asked to speak.

"I shall never forget, as long as I live, our boat family. I shall do everything I can to help all of you settle in the new lands of freedom, either in Thailand or America. Obviously, the situation here is very favorable to us because of my connection with the Prime Minister, but one always has to be careful about politics in Thailand. The Prime Minister reached power through a *coup d'état*, and there could be a counter-coup at any time. When we arrive there, I'll contact the Prime Minister and see what his attitude to us will be." His short speech ended with several rounds of applause.

Early in the evening the junk lowered its anchor off Chantaburi. Operation New Spring had come to an end. A police motorboat met the refugees. In Thai Minh asked the police officer to take him to the local army commander. Within half an hour, Minh and the police lieutenant were at the office of Colonel Amneuy Luksanand, commanding officer of the 25th Royal Thai Infantry Regiment. Minh explained the situation, reported the bandits attack, and requested that he be allowed to contact the Prime Minister, his old friend Chamni. The colonel politely invited Minh to wait while he phoned Bangkok.

Minh was admiring a pot of blooming orchids when the colonel entered the living room.

"Professor, the Prime Minister is on the line. You can use the phone in my office."

Minh picked up the receiver. "Hello, Mr. Prime Minister. Congratulations."

"Stop it, Minh, I'm still Chamni, your old friend."

"But I'm now a boat person without a country, a wandering soul, as we say in Vietnamese."

"Forget about your boat and your wandering soul. You can stay in Thailand as long as you wish, as my government's guest. Thailand is now your country. Buddha will protect you. I'll have the colonel bring you to Bangkok tonight so you can have a good rest and we can meet for breakfast tomorrow. As for your compatriot boat people, how many of them are there?"

"Nineteen, including me."

"They'll be given special consideration by the Ministry of Interior, but in the meantime they'll have to stay in a refugees camp. I'm sorry about that, but I can't change all the laws even as a Prime Minister. I have to leave for a meeting now. I'll see you tomorrow. Sleep well, my dear friend."

"Thank you and goodnight, Mr. Prime Minister."

The colonel invited Minh to have dinner with him before his trip to Bangkok by helicopter. Minh explained that because it was Tet's eve, he preferred to eat with his compatriots. The colonel quickly proposed that the whole group be invited along to a Chinese restaurant. They accepted the invitation but they had no appetite: Minh had warned them before dinner that they would be temporarily sent to a refugee camp.

.   .   .

Minh slept soundly in his spacious room at the Royal Thai Army guest house, the same one he'd slept in before when he'd passed through Bangkok on his return to Vietnam from the States. He woke refreshed and relaxed. A hot shower, a luxury he'd almost forgotten, in a large marble bathroom in a foreign residence in a foreign land, brought back to him memories of the night he'd spent with Jennifer at the Statler Hilton in New York ten years before. He vividly recalled the passage from *Markings* that had come to him so suddenly that morning as he'd watched her sleeping beside him:

> As she lies stretched out on the riverbank—beyond all human nakedness in the inaccessible solitude of death, her firm breasts are lifted to the sunlight—a heroic torso of marble-blond stone in the soft grass.

Minh had feared then that she would die. And now she was dead, killed by a bomb. But her actual death didn't frighten him as he had imagined it would. He was almost grateful that she had passed away. With her, his innocence, their innocence, was gone. He now had to face life in all its brutal realities, without illusion, without the benevolent protection of the Blue Dragon, by himself and for himself; and only as a lonely individual, outside the communist discipline of collectivism, could he fully develop and maintain his integrity as a writer. Will the White Tiger leave me alone, he wondered?

He sank into a blue velvet sofa and lit his pipe, following the spiralling smoke with his dreamy eyes. Pulling the *Tao Te Ching* from his knapsack, he read Chapter 42: "One gains by losing and loses by gaining."

He smiled at these wise words of Lao Tsu. "Indeed," he said to himself, "I've lost everything, but at the same time, I'm gaining everything back. I'm reclaiming myself. Thank you, Jennifer, and you too, Xuan and Loc. Thank you, Vietnam, thank you, Vietnam Communist Party. Thank you all. I've lost all of you in different ways and in different circumstances, but I've gained everything. I've regained myself."

There was a knock on the door. A soldier stood at attention and announced, "Sir, the Prime Minister is in the living room."

Minh hurried downstairs.

"*Swasdi*, my good friend Minh. Welcome to Thailand. Make yourself at home." Prime Minister Chamras Panyakupta, in a dark blue civilian suit, greeted him, his arms opened wide in a welcoming gesture.

"Thank you, Mr. Prime Minister. Thank you for everything you've done for me," Minh said, his eyes wet with gratitude.

"As I've always said, we were friends, we are friends, and we'll always be friends, regardless of our personal situations."

"Yes, I know, and again, congratulations on your new position."

"Well, it makes little difference. I had to stage a *coup d'état* to protect the monarchy and to cleanse the country of corrupt and opportunistic elements. Now, I simply have to work harder and longer hours at the office and be a little more careful about my private life."

They laughed and went into the dining room for breakfast.

"Mr. Prime Minister."

"You can still call me Chamni in private."

"Chamni, you don't know how grateful I am for your inviting me to stay in Thailand as your government's guest for an indefinite period. But I've thought it over, and no matter how much I'd like to accept your kind offer, I still feel I must decline it, at least at this particular moment in my life. I plan to return to America as soon as possible. Really, I don't know exactly why I want to. I hope you understand. Perhaps when I settle in America, I'll write and explain everything."

"You don't need to explain anything to me. But to be honest, I don't quite understand why you want to go to the United States. There, you'll always be a stranger. Here, you're among people of the same color skin, the same religion. Still, it's your decision. But you can rest assured that if and when you change your mind you can always count on me. I'm sorry we don't have much time to talk the way we did in the good old days, but I deeply sympathize with what has happened to you."

"Someday, Chamni, you'll know why, perhaps when I write a book about my own experiences. But for the time being I'm numb with gratitude and affection for you, and I can't say much about anything."

Chamni pulled an envelope from his breast pocket and handed it to Minh. "Take this. It's just a little something for your needs while you're in Bangkok. If you need more, don't hesitate to contact my aide-de-camp and tell him what you want. He's the same officer who greeted you at Dong Muang Airport when you passed through here ten years ago."

"Thank you so much, Chamni. You're very kind and thoughtful."

"And now that I know of your plan to leave for the U.S., I'll ask my office to get a first-class open ticket for you on the Royal Thai Airways. There's a direct flight now once a week from Bangkok to New York City, with a stopover in Paris. Minh, I'm sorry I have so little time to spend with you. I must go now."

At the door Chamni stopped and put his arm on Minh's shoulder. "Goodbye, my friend. Be happy. Life is for living, and not to be worried about or even understood. Remember our Buddhist doctrine of the impermanence of all things." He paused. "By the way, I've asked my secretary to pack some of my new clothes for you, we wear about the same size, and other things you might need. It's up in your room now, I'm sure."

"Thank you, Chamni, thank you, Mr. Prime Minister," Minh murmured to himself as Chamni's black Mercedes sped away flanked by an escort of police motorbikes.

·   ·   ·

Minh tried each of the three brand-new suits and found that they all fit him perfectly. He thought mockingly to himself, "The communists haven't treated me badly after all. I still keep my shape and my mind in order."

Dressed in a light brown Manchester cotton suit and a striped dark blue Thai silk tie, Minh walked slowly to the American Embassy on Wireless Road, six blocks away. The morning was still cool. The noise, the dirt, the smell, the chaotic traffic on the crowded narrow streets didn't bother or annoy him as they had the last time he was here. He even liked them now. They were, he believed, part of the necessary, insignificant price one had to pay for individual liberty. And after all, he thought, smiling, "I can always go back to the clean, air-conditioned suite at the Royal Thai Army guest house."

Minh asked a Thai woman clerk in the consular section of the American Embassy for an application form for an immigrant visa to the United States of America. He glanced at it and discovered that he didn't have all the necessary information to fill it out properly. He had no passport to prove his citizenship, he'd forgotten the number of his green card, (the permanent resident identification issued to him fourteen years ago by the U.S. authorities), he didn't have five passport-sized pictures, he didn't have a job. He decided to fill in only his name, place and date of birth, skipping other items, with the exception of two: respondent in Thailand—the Royal Thai Army guest house; and actual and former professions—one of the boat people, formerly professor of political science, Thomas Paine College, Amherst Massachusetts, U.S.A.

He gave the form back to the clerk who couldn't hide her surprise at so many unanswered items. She politely asked him, "Sir, are you sure that the address of your respondent in Thailand is given correctly?"

"Yes, Madam," he answered softly and added, "May I see the vice-consul?"

"Yes sir. I think so. I'll give him the form. Please wait."

To Minh's amazement the interview with the vice-consul went without a hitch. He was questioned about his credentials and his past, a quick phone call was made to Chamni's office to confirm his identity, and he was issued a temporary entrance permit. When he arrived in the States, he was told, he must go to an immigration office, where his status as a permanent resident would be promptly restored.

Minh decided to leave Thailand on the seventh day of the lunar New Year. Officially, it would be the last day of the Tet holiday, the day when the Vietnamese took down the traditional *Cay Neu*, the bamboo tree they planted in front of their homes before Tet to ward off bad spirits. On that day, on the wings of a Royal Thai plane, he would fly to New York. He would kneel at the foot of the Statue of Liberty. He would leave behind all the Tets of the past with their thousand-year old ceremonials and traditions. From then on, he would spend his Tets in the cold and snow of the United States, deprived of all the perfumes and tastes of his native Vietnam. He would surely miss them. But, he hoped, he would have gained something new, something he had never quite understood before: the real meaning and essence of Tet, the spirit of Tet, the moment of truce between the Blue Dragon and the White Tiger, the harmonization of *Tinh*, feeling, and *Ly*, reason, among his fellow men and women, among the living and dead, between tradition and revolution, among the past, the present, and the future. But it would be henceforward the spirit of the historic Vietnam that he held in his heart, not the political one—the mystic Vietnam, not the vulgar and brutal one.

He would live and work in New York City. Jennifer would have liked him to do so. For the first time in many days, he thought of Loc, no longer in admiration and gratitude, only with compassion. He felt liberated.

Suddenly, vivid details of the last night he spent on the soil of Vietnam and in the bed of Madame Luu surged back into his memory. He burst into a prolonged and tearful laughter. He *knew* he was laughing at his own laughter.

ABOUT THE AUTHOR

Professor Tran Van Dinh, a native of Hue, the former imperial capital of Vietnam, is a teacher of international politics and communication in the Department of Pan African Studies, College of Arts and Sciences, Temple University. He is author of numerous articles and books including the forthcoming publications: Independence, Liberation, Revolution: An approach to the Understanding of the Third World, and, Diplomacy and Communication, to be released respectively in 1983 and 1984 by Ablex.

Calling the Wandering Souls, translation by Le Hieu, Vietnamese Studies, No. 4, Hanoi 1965

John Balaban translation can be found in *Ca Dao Vietnam: A Bilingual Anthology of Vietnamese Poetry*, Unicorn Press, 1980

Huynh Sanh Thong translations can be found in *The Heritage of Vietnam Poetry*, Yale University Press, 1979